Finding Joy

Voice of Joy series volume 1

by Sarah Floyd

DEDICATION

To my encouragers

I Thessalonians 5:11

ACKNOWLEDGMENTS

I would like to thank my husband, Jason, for motivating me (within an inch of my life) to finish the process of creating this book. Your faith in me gives me faith in myself.

I would also like to thank my first readers, of this book and of others I've written, for persuading me that my stories are worth telling.

Finally, I would like to thank Lynne Becker and Lucy Harris, two of my high school teachers, for giving me the courage to share my writing with the world.

CHAPTER 1

"And don't think I'm going to trek up there and dry your tears either when you change your mind!" Cal hissed. Sophia tried to protest, but a click and a dial tone interrupted her. She sniffed and wiped her eyes. Just like that, a three years' relationship was terminated.

After she had indulged in a few minutes of sobbing, Sophia took a deep breath and crossed her trendy bedroom to her streamlined desk. She sat down in her ergonomic swivel chair and removed an application packet from a manila folder at her desk. She chewed on the end of her fountain pen as she pondered what she should write on her application essay. She could hardly write what was on her mind: "My name is Sophia Joy Carnegie, and I want to attend Coburn College because I am twenty-four years old, and I don't know what I want to do with my life!"

Sophia finally began putting words to paper. She wrote, "I wish to attend Coburn College because writing has always soothed me like no other pastime. I spent the past two years as a successful realtor in Pittsburgh, but I found no fulfillment in my job. I am considering a career change to writing."

Sophia saw no need to mention in her essay that her commission had totaled more than $500,000 last year, or that she had only acquired her real estate position after her father had "anonymously" informed Coldwell Banker that Sophia was a direct descendent of Pittsburgh steel tycoon Andrew Carnegie. She also failed to mention that her boyfriend, Calvin Barrett, had just dumped her for her decision to quit her lucrative position and winter in Woodfield, Vermont, at an "obscure" college for authors, or that her mother would be en route from Philadelphia to scream at her as soon as she learned of Sophia's actions.

Although it was after five p.m. when Sophia finally finished writing a final draft of her essay she could live with, and the local post office had closed at four, she went ahead and addressed and stamped the envelope so it would be ready to go first thing in the morning. She hesitated as she wrote the return address. On the application, she'd been compelled to write her entire name...a name she had despised for years. On the envelope, however, Sophia wrote "Joy Carnegie" in her typical bold script. Somehow just seeing the middle name her family scorned scrawled across the manila surface made her feel better already.

Sophia ran her fingers through her frosted, layered hair and climbed down the silver staircase to her tiny kitchen. She hadn't felt like lunch – again – due to the stress of her anticipated conversation with Cal, so she supposed she should get some dinner. Unfortunately, none of the low calorie, low sugar, low fat, and low taste options in her well-stocked refrigerator looked appealing, so she ordered a pizza from the bistro down the street. A pepperoni *and* sausage pizza. Stuffed crust. Surely she deserved a treat after being dumped on the stupid telephone.

When the delivery man arrived, she paid him twenty-two dollars for the medium pie, thanked him in Spanish since he was unable to tell her the price in English, and shut and locked her door. Sophia didn't think she could handle being civil to anyone who might drop by tonight; nor did she want any former or current clients to see their chic realtor slurping down pools of grease and cheese.

Sophia ate four slices of the pizza before her strange appetite was satisfied and then polished off four Ghirardelli chocolates a client had given her months previously. She didn't wash her glass and plate. She didn't shower or remove her makeup. She didn't moisturize. She unplugged her land line phone, silenced her cell phone, closed her laptop, and fell into bed. It was 7:30 p.m., and the sky in Pittsburgh hadn't been dark for long. She wished she could stay in bed until she heard back from Coburn...they promised online to fill this unexpected vacancy within one week.

By the end of the week, Sophia could no longer bear to go through her usual motions of perfection. Every aspect of her job – the sleek, modern office she inhabited in a skyscraper downtown, the six other realtors who thought bar-hopping was an Olympic sport, and the wealthy clients who came to her prattling about "ambiance" and "upgrades" and "revitalized neighborhoods" - disgusted her. Friday afternoon, Sophia left the office holding back rare tears. She'd quit – quit before even hearing from Vermont, but she had to get away regardless.

Sophia didn't go straight home. First, she went to the park near the river and sat on a bench for an hour, trying to make plans. She prayed, something she'd not done enough of since her baptism during her senior year of college. She cried a little again about Calvin, although she was still too numb to mourn him completely. And at the end of the hour, Sophia knew just three things. She was moving to Vermont for a while, no matter what. She was going to find her aunt Joann. And she was never going to answer to the name Sophia again.

Joy spent a few seconds considering whether she would look more ridiculous shopping at Wal-Mart and Goodwill in her current outfit – power suit and heels – or in her designer jeans and tops at home. She couldn't decide and wriggled out of her jacket, tossed it in her Mercedes, and drove straight to the downtown Goodwill. She wandered the clothes racks in delight, relishing her sudden freedom. No more pinstripes or trendy geometric shapes. No more dazzling gold jewelry. No more stilettos. Positively no more stilettos.

Joy tried to remember what Vermont women had worn a decade ago, when she had spent the best summer of her life on her Uncle John and Aunt Joann's farm. She couldn't recall. Probably they just hadn't bothered much with what they wore, except maybe to church. Oh, well. She could come back. She wasn't leaving yet, so maybe she'd pick up a couple of outfits for the moment. Plus...she'd hopefully be in Vermont as a writer, so she'd probably be excused from all fashion conventions anyway.

A peasant blouse and skirt, two flannel shirts, a pair of faded Faded Glory jeans, and a denim bag with a long strap later, Joy was finished, for scarcely more than the cost of Monday night's pizza. She wished she could change clothes in the bathroom, but she didn't have that option since she still wore her heels and wouldn't purchase used shoes.

The checkout clerk eyed Joy suspiciously. "You okay, ma'am?" she said. "Your mascara be runnin' *all* down your face!"

Joy wiped her cheeks. "Oh, yes, thank you." And also...no

more mascara. Ever again. It made her eyes itch anyway.

Joy's next step was Wal-Mart, where she purchased two pairs of flip flops, easing her feet into the red ones immediately. "Ahhh..." she breathed aloud. The teenagers nearby stared at her unashamedly. Neiman Marcus silk blouse, purple pinstriped pants, diamond stud earrings, red flip flops. Runny makeup. Joy stuck the earrings, a college graduation gift from her parents, into her pocket. Nothing left she could decently remove now.

Before Joy left Wal-Mart, she stepped into the salon. "I don't have an appointment," she said to the nearest employee. "But are there any openings soon?"

"Whatcha want done?" the woman asked.

"Umm...coloring, cut, and um...reverse manicure?"

"What in the world you talkin' about?"

"Can you remove my acrylic nails?" Joy asked with a sigh.

"Yeah, we can work you in – 'bout fifteen minutes, okay?" The woman hurried away, mumbling under her breath.

An hour later, Joy gasped as she looked at herself in the stylist's mirror. Her fifteen-year-old self – no, make that her twelve-year-old self, stared back at her. She took in her "natural" face, sporting – oh, horrors! A pimple! The shoulder-length hair in something near her original color (plain nut brown), and the uneven, slightly-sticky nails. In her present state of mind, she felt as though she'd never looked better...other than the pimple, that is.

"You on the run from the law, hon?" the stylist asked her curiously as Joy paid with a fifty dollar bill.

"Yeah, actually, I'm wanted for kidnapping in fifteen states," she snapped as she took her change and exited the salon. She could hear the stylist's gasp even above the thwacking of her flip flops as she strode from the store.

Joy allowed herself the uncommon luxury of daydreaming as she navigated after-school traffic back to her house. She imagined hiking into the woods behind her Uncle John's farmhouse near Windsor, notepad and pencil in hand, and dashing off an ethereal ode to the falling snowflakes. She pictured herself sipping milk and eating pumpkin bread at her aunt's kitchen table as she read aloud from her latest story to the only two relatives who'd ever listened to her. She switched gears mentally and envisioned herself sitting in a classroom of authors of all ages and backgrounds, sharing writing tips and bits of latest masterpieces.

The sight of her mother's cobalt Porsche parked at her curb brought her back to reality with a thud. Uncle John was dead – had been for seven years, and Joy had no idea where Aunt Joann was. Joy was unemployed. She hadn't heard from Coburn. And Amelia Claire Montgomery Carnegie had arrived to make herself heard.

Joy parked haphazardly behind her mother, gathered up her purchases, and barged through her front door. Her mother sat coiled attractively on Joy's black couch, surveying her daughter coolly.

"Just when were you planning to tell me you're deserting Cal?" Amelia said, her icicles dangerous.

"Hello to you too, Mother," Joy answered. "This is a pleasant non-surprise. How was your time in Monaco?"

"Don't attempt to distract me, Sophia. I demand to know what's going on."

"It's a long story, Mother. Let me change clothes and I'll try to explain."

"Please do. You look ghastly."

Joy raced up the stairs with her bags and pulled on the faded jeans. She also scavenged in her huge closet until she found an old T-shirt from her years at Brown. It hung on her size four frame. She brushed her new ordinary-person hair into an ordinary-person ponytail, washed off the remaining traces of cosmetics, and descended to face the music...make that screamo music.

Amelia was on her iPhone when Joy re-entered the living room with a bottle of New Zealand spring water for her mother.

"Yes, thank you for working her in. Seven p.m. Saturday. Au revoir, Monique." Amelia ended her call, accepted the water, and stared once more at her only daughter.

"I don't know *what* you have done to your hair, or *how* you could have created so much damage since I last saw you on Labor Day, but fortunately I was able to schedule you an appointment with Monique for tomorrow evening. She will repair the havoc, and-"

11

"Mother, wait. Who is Monique?"

"My stylist. If we leave immediately, you can enjoy a soothing weekend with me in Philadelphia and get over this strange aberration of yours. You can cancel your weekend appointments, surely."

Joy rubbed her eyes. Might as well get everything over with at once. "Mother, please hear me out without interruption."

"Of course. I'm dying to understand why you've let yourself go and abandoned your precious boyfriend. He called me in tears last night, Sophia."

"First of all, my name is Joy from now on. The only reason Father named me Sophia at all was because the obstetrician said she'd list her home in the Hamptons with him if he gave me her name. No, don't looked shocked. We both know it's true. Secondly, *I'm* not abandoning Cal; he ended our relationship because he refused to support my decisions to quit my job and enroll in a writing program at Coburn College this winter. Oh, and by the way, I did this to my hair and nails on purpose. I'm sick of being frosted, layered, and glazed. I might as well be a cake."

"You can't be serious!" Amelia shrieked after a full ten seconds had passed.

"Oh, but I am. I'm leaving for Vermont in three or four weeks. I intend to look up Aunt Joann while I'm there."

"Sophia Carnegie! You are destroying your life. I'm going right back to Philadelphia to tell your father!"

"Please do, Mother. And cancel my appointment with Monique. I believe I'll just braid my hair tomorrow."

Amelia surged out of Joy's house with more energy than she would typically exert in a week. Joy grinned. It had been almost a decade since she'd heard her mother slam a door.

The postman came jogging past with Joy's mail around eleven the next morning. She tied her cashmere and silk robe around her and stepped outside to get it, her heartbeat accelerating. She tossed the bills in her small stack on the counter and ripped into the long-awaited envelope from Coburn.

"We regret to inform you..." Joy read, then dropped into her aluminum dining chair and buried her head in her arms. Couldn't she have this one little success on her own terms? Was it too much to ask God to bless her with something she wanted? Joy slowly raised her head to scan the rest of the letter.

"We regret to inform you that the opening for our winter semester has been filled. If you are interested, however, we still have several openings in our December Fiction Workshop, which lasts one week. Your deposit of $500 toward the winter semester may be placed toward the $850 price of the workshop. Please call our admissions office immediately if you wish to attend the workshop; otherwise, Coburn College will refund your deposit."

One week. One measly week. Joy tried to justify it in her mind – four months in a snow-covered country village with no job or other income, all on the strength of a week-long workshop. She'd have to rent a house, probably, unless Woodfield (population twelve or something), had some sort of residence inn. Every money management tip Joy had heard in her business courses at Brown rose up to haunt her. She drowned them in cappuccino as she started up her laptop.

First, Joy studied her August and September bank statements. The great majority of her expenses – rent, food, clothing, entertainment, public transportation – would be reduced significantly in a Vermont village, but she'd have a storage fee for her furniture, as well as her car payment and insurance and some kind of independent health insurance premium. Unless, of course, she sold her furniture and traded her car for, say, a jeep with four-wheel drive to combat icy roads. Never mind she'd never driven a jeep.

Financial matters bored Joy, but from what she could estimate, she wouldn't be hurting monetarily even if she stayed unemployed for a year. She exited her bank account window and sat still for a moment, staring at her default homepage. Slowly, she typed her uncle's name into Google.

It only took a moment to locate John Eliot Carnegie's obituary from 2005. Joy quickly read the brief tribute from the Windsor newspaper. She blinked back sudden tears as she realized two things she'd never known about his death. One, it had been from a farming accident, not a disease, and two, a neighbor had died at the same time.

13

Joy scrolled down to the end of the article where the survivors were listed. Sure enough, there was her own name, as well as the names of her parents, despite the fact her father had not spoken to her uncle John since long before his death. And her aunt's name – including her maiden name! Joy gasped. She had searched for her aunt's whereabouts once before on Google but had found no hits for "Joann Carnegie." But she'd never tried "Joanna Hudson."

Thirty seconds later, Joy had her aunt's address, phone number, and place of employment, Montpelier Public Library. It had really been this easy to locate her all these years. Joy was ashamed she hadn't tried harder...but why had her aunt gone back to her maiden name?

On a sudden hunch, Joy typed her aunt's name into the search engine on Facebook. A profile registered immediately, with a photo of a covered bridge and no information, implying the user's privacy settings were set at the highest possible level. Joann was not making it simple to reconnect with her niece – Joy would have to do it the awkward way with a call or a visit.

Suddenly, Joy's cell phone sounded to a classical version of Pachelbel's 'Canon in D.' She groaned. It was her father. She answered calmly but braced herself for a tirade. George Carnegie did not disappoint.

The torrent of angry words rained on Joy's ears for five full minutes without pause, and although Joy attempted not to listen, her father's threats of disownment and blacklisting with all the real estate agencies in Pennsylvania reached her consciousness anyway.

George changed tactics next, realizing his daughter would not be concerned about such mercenary aspects of the situation. "Sophia, dear, you must be reasonable," he said, softening his voice to what he fancied was a tender whisper. "Joann has avoided all contact with us for more than seven years now. She clearly cares nothing about you, as a relative by marriage alone. You can't go running to the backwoods and expect to relive your childhood."

Joy bit her lip. How did her father do it? How did he manage to put his thumbs directly onto her most vulnerable points...and press down as hard as possible?

14

"Father," she said. "I'm an adult now, and I'm not going to live my life according to anyone else's specifications any longer. And please, call me Joy now. I've hated my first name for years."

When George began to splutter anew, Joy very gently tapped the "end" icon on her phone and turned it off to prevent further verbal abuse. That garbage could go the way of the stilettos as far as she was concerned!

CHAPTER 2

Thursday, September 27th. Joy noticed the date in her planner as she drew lines through the last items of her packing list. She could hardly believe it had been nearly two weeks since she'd quit her job, and now, at six a.m., she was ready to walk away from her Pittsburgh home forever.

She loaded her new 2004 Jeep Cherokee with three suitcases, four boxes, and her coffeepot, rice cooker, and blender. Everything else had gone to a tiny storage unit or had been sold days ago on Ebay. Joy was determined to rid herself of every item she did not truly want or need, and she'd been shocked to discover that desire had led to the banishment of all her furniture and art and the vast majority of her wardrobe.

As Joy zipped through the city's light traffic, an overwhelming sense of freedom hid every fear or insecurity for several minutes. She had never been so free. The only time she'd even felt close to free was in Vermont that summer after eighth grade.

Joy reviewed her plan as she headed east. Tonight – crash at whatever motel appeared safe for a woman traveling alone, preferably in Montpelier. Tomorrow – sleep late and recover from the hours of driving, until three p.m., that is. Then, she'd face her past and her fears, show up at the library as it was closing, and see if she could persuade her aunt to speak with her, and maybe, just maybe, have dinner or something, if Joann was particularly forgiving. Saturday – find a house, preferably furnished. Sunday – go to church, something that had happened far too rarely during Joy's realty career.

By two p.m., the enormity of Joy's decisions began to haunt her. She was leaving all the familiar things in her life, not many personal relationships, no, but all her routines and just – well, life, to winter in a place she'd visited once as a child. She was infuriating her parents, guaranteeing she'd never re-unite with her boyfriend, and basically discarding her entire identity, on the strength of a chance to write and say a few words to her estranged aunt. She felt completely

16

discouraged until she finally stopped for a grilled chicken sandwich. Amazing how food could improve your mood!

Joy drove until after ten, stopping only once more for food and fuel, and, as she pulled up to an Econolodge on the edge of Montpelier, she no longer felt emotion. Joy unloaded her suitcase of casual clothes and toiletries, grabbed her purse, and entered the musty ground-floor room at top speed. She had showered and was sound asleep in less than half an hour.

The first sensation that assailed Joy at ten the following morning was extreme cold. She pried open her eyelids and gasped at the chilly air inside the motel room. Her thin pajamas, bed sheet, and comforter were not enough to keep her warm in this place. Evidently, she'd forgotten even to consider switching on the heating unit last night.

She scrounged in her suitcase without opening her eyes and dug out a pair of her Goodwill jeans, a big purple sweater, and some wool socks. She watched the Weather Channel as she dressed as quickly as possible. Joy saw through her haze of drowsiness that it was 30 degrees in nearby Burlington this morning, but no one on the TV seemed the least bit concerned about the temperature although it was still September.

There was a can of Starbucks cappuccino in Joy's purse, so she chugged it eagerly as she continued to prepare herself for the morning. When her mind cleared almost instantly, she reflected it might be a good idea...at some point...to reduce her dependence on caffeine...but not today.

After deeming herself presentable, Joy threw open the door and secured the "Do not disturb" sign on the handle. She was outside and headed to her jeep to explore the town before she thought to look up...and there were the mountains, glowing with the autumn colors just beginning in Pittsburgh. Joy felt goosebumps move across her body. Whatever happened, she was home, in the only area that had ever felt much like a safe haven to her. She'd have to trust God would protect her – and maybe even allow her a little happiness.

Joy drove slowly around the small city of Montpelier and the nearby town of Barre for most of the morning and early afternoon.

17

She stopped for a bowl of soup at a cafe in downtown Barre around 1:30, not hungry, but hoping the broth and vegetables would settle her nervous stomach. She choked down most of the bowl, paid her bill with cash, and didn't leave. If she went directly to the Montpelier Library, she'd be there forty minutes early. No sense in being a total stalker. If she missed her aunt today, there was always Monday – and as many more weekdays as Joy chose to spend in such a fashion.

Joy sat back and studied her surroundings. The cafe was tiny, decorated in turn-of-the-20th-century vintage, and screamed "New England." A place like this should make her simply ache to put words down on paper, for her personal writing urges had always been strongly connected to location. The thought barely appealed to her, though; all she could focus on was the opportunity to see her aunt again. It occurred abruptly to Joy that perhaps coming to Vermont to become an author was actually a secondary motive.

Joy sipped some more of her coffee and allowed her mind to drift back to her summer in Vermont, a series of memories she had blocked out until the last month.

She had never been supposed to come. The summer after eighth grade was scheduled to be a magical time – a trip to the Bahamas with her parents. Snorkeling. Deep-sea fishing. Sand castles. A new purple bikini – Joy cringed at that memory. And best of all, her parents' almost undivided attention for three whole months. She'd actually counted the days – 94 days of time with her career-driven parents. The only condition – she had to make an A in every class on her final report card.

Joy hadn't been worried. She loved school – at least – she loved learning, and every class except math was easy for her. She'd studied hard in math and had a solid A until March, when the teacher had made a sudden decision to introduce algebra. Despite her best efforts, she'd ended the year with a D.

At that point, Joy had realized her parents were determined to enjoy their vacation with or without her. They refused to listen to her protests about why her grade had dropped, refused to take her with them to Nassau, and also refused to alter any of their plans.

"After all, Sophia," her mother had told her. "We already have to cancel reservations for you. It would be terribly expensive if we had to cancel *everything*. You understand, don't you? And your father is too exhausted. He simply *must* have a vacation."

And so Joy, who knew her father was worth a cool 17 million, was shipped off to Vermont in disgrace. As she boarded the plane in Pittsburgh, her father had handed her a large flat package. "Open this after you take off," he'd said. Inside had been an algebra textbook, much more advanced than the one she'd used at school. He had attached a sticky note that read, "Learn algebra while you're in Vermont, and you'll get $200 added to your allowance in September." There was no mention of what she'd get if she could not succeed, nor were there any suggestions as to how she should master a college textbook while visiting family she'd never met on a farm miles from any tutors.

Joy shook her head to come back to the present. She was on her own now – accountable only to herself, well, and God, if the preacher in the huge Pittsburgh church she attended once in a while could be believed. She didn't have to remain captive to her father's disapproval anymore. She glanced at her watch. Finally. She could head to the library and only wait five or ten minutes.

It was 2:58 when Joy slid into a parking place near the front door of Montpelier's library. She sighed in relief, cut the engine, and prepared to wait for the staff to close the place down and begin exiting. She hardly noticed when another jeep pulled up near hers, nor when a woman got out and strode up the stairs.

Suddenly, Joy focused on the woman's retreating back. There was something familiar about that long braid, and the way she carried herself...but why would Joann be entering her place of employment at closing time? Perhaps the Internet listing of the library's hours was incorrect...or perhaps she was seeing things. People generally changed a good deal in over ten years.

Before Joy looked away, the woman was headed back down the stairs toward the parking lot. Joy gasped, untangled herself frantically from her seat belt, and flung open her door. She tripped as she missed the curb up to the sidewalk and almost mowed down a toddler who was leaving the library with his mother.

19

"Oh, sorry! Um...excuse me!" she called out, staggering toward her aunt's jeep.

Joann looked up and let out a cry. "Sophia Joy?"

"Yes, it's really me," Joy exclaimed. She stopped three feet short of her aunt, not knowing what to say next. Suddenly, it seemed presumptuous for her to be forcing herself back into Joann's life like this.

"You don't know how long I've prayed to see you again," Joann whispered. She opened her arms, and Joy forgot everything else and went into them.

When they finally ended their embrace, they stepped back to study each other as if by mutual consent. Joy stared at her aunt as if she were memorizing a spelling list. Same blue, blue eyes, same kind smile, same dark hair pulled back into a single braid, although there were more lines on her face and gray streaks in her braid. And she was deathly pale under her tan.

"Do you need to sit down?" Joy asked quickly. "I know I've given you quite a shock."

"Yes, maybe so," Joann said, slipping into the driver's seat of her car and motioning for Joy to sit beside her. She took several deep breaths, coughed, and drank from the water bottle in her cup holder.

"All right. Much better," she said. "I'm sorry. I've just been a bit under the weather." She smiled, looking more like herself as her color returned. "To what do I owe this special treat?"

"I-I had to see you," Joy whispered. "I've never felt any peace about losing touch with you, and I wanted to tell you in person how sorry I am about Uncle John – and that I didn't come to the funeral." He eyes filled with tears and overflowed before she could stop them.

"Thank you," Joann said. "I wish you could have come. John loved you very much."

"I know. I loved him – and you – too. Really. I-I should have come back sooner, but I didn't know...I mean, I don't understand..." Joy's voice trailed off. How did she wade through all the pieces of speculation and hurt to express herself?

"The summer I spent with you and Uncle John was the best of my life," Joy started again, still crying. "I know...many things have...changed...since then – but I just wanted you to know that."

Joann handed her a tissue. "We were very happy to have you, even if it was only for one visit. You were a delightful guest."

Joy blew her nose. "I-I wanted – to-to come back," she sobbed. "I actually never – wanted to – leave, but I wasn't allowed. And then..."

"Then you weren't sure if you'd be welcome?" Her aunt's tone was completely non-accusatory.

"Yes!" Joy cried harder, burying her face in her hands. "My father said you – you had moved on with your life...and...and..."

"He was wrong, kiddo. Dead wrong."

Joy looked up in surprise at the anger in Joann's voice. She wondered abruptly if she even knew the entire story of her parents' relationship, or lack thereof, with John and Joann, but she could not bring herself to question her aunt. Joann was here...and *wanted* to be with her...and for the moment, that was enough.

CHAPTER 3

After a few more minutes, Joann invited Joy to ride with her to her house, which was only a few blocks away. Joy grabbed her purse and climbed back into the passenger seat.

"We'll come back for your car later," Joann promised. "It will be perfectly safe here. We have hardly any crime. In fact, I typically walk nearly everywhere, even at night."

Joy glanced over at her again. She suspected her aunt had been ill; she was too thin, and she'd never been one to drive when she could walk. "Are you okay?" she said. Distressing scenarios flitted through her mind in the two seconds it took Joann to answer...she wasn't old, so did she have cancer? A heart attack?

"Yes, Joy...or rather, I will be. I've been in the hospital, so I'm just a little shaky right now."

"What's wrong?"

"I had pneumonia, and the coughing caused my heart to lose its proper rhythm. I've had a slight problem with that for years, but I've always controlled it with medication. My cardiologist sees no reason to believe I can't continue to do so now I'm recovering."

"I'm glad," Joy murmured. Imagine...all these weeks she'd been obsessing about finding her aunt, Joann had been fighting for her health. The thought sent shivers up her spine.

Joann's home – a small cottage with a steeply-gabled roof and an abundant fall garden of 'mums and asters – was not at all the kind of place Joy would have pictured her living, but then neither had she been able to envision her aunt living anywhere except the farm near Windsor. The inside was simple, old-fashioned, and spotless, and smelled of lemon and a gingery spicy scent Joy remembered but couldn't put her finger on. Few of the furnishings looked familiar, but Joy's eyes immediately caught a large framed photo displayed prominently over the old piano – a fourteen-year-old Joy in overalls, hanging upside-down from an apple tree, her eyes closed and mouth wide open in happy abandon. Joy knew her aunt was speaking to her, telling her to make herself at home, but she could not respond. She moved to the photograph and touched the frame as if she were in a trance. Surely Joann would not have displayed such a photo in her living room if she had sought freedom from John's relatives.

Joy whirled as one of her aunt's strong hands landed on her shoulder. "I didn't mean to startle you. That's a lovely picture, isn't it?"

"You – you...you missed me?" Joy asked, her throat nearly closed.

Joann bit her lip. "Of course I did." She sighed and wiped her palms on her jeans. "Joy, dear, please, sit down. We need to talk some more, I think. Would you like something to drink?"

"Ummm..." Joy cleared her throat. "Do you have any – uh – coffee?"

"Not a drop, I'm afraid. How about some green tea?"

"Sure. Thank you."

As Joann returned to the kitchen, Joy struggled to regain control of herself. What had reduced her, the once-powerful ice queen, sophisticated woman of the city life, to a blubbering mass who wanted to be cuddled like a child? She had cried more in the past month than in the past five years. At least. Her aunt probably thought she was some sort of damaged wimp. Whatever Joann would to reveal to her, Joy determined to absorb with composure and dignity.

Joann brought two mugs of tea and a plate of spice cookies into the living room and laid them on the coffee table. She lifted her own mug and blew the scented steam before speaking again.

"I need to tell you some things I don't think you want to hear, Joy," she said. "I hope you'll hear me out, and that you won't leave when I say them." Joann coughed deeply before continuing. "I would have never told you these things if you hadn't come looking for me like this, but I can't allow you to go on in such confusion."

"Please tell me. I won't leave."

"First of all, did you know John and I contacted your father several times while you were in high school, inviting you back to visit again?"

"No..."

"And did you receive the letters and cards we sent you the first two years after you left us?"

"You *wrote* to me?"

"Oh, yes, frequently, but after two years or so, George called John one night and told him to stop the contact – to stop trying to convince you our 'primitive lifestyle' was best. Let's just say George implied somehow that if we didn't stop 'annoying you,' we would face serious consequences."

"But...but Aunt Joann! I never read a word of any of those letters! He – he kept them from me!"

"I suspected he had. Anyway, John's death happened a year or so later, but before he died, we had agreed to begin trying to contact you again once you were eighteen."

"And he died just five months before that...oh, Aunt Joann!" Joy's eyes filled once more.

"After his death, I wanted so much to find you myself, but my life was in such upheaval. I had to sell the farm...one middle-aged lady cannot keep up a working farm, complete with orchards, no matter how tough she flatters herself she is. I had to get a job, which wasn't easy since I didn't even finish high school...yes, gasp in horror, Joy...my terrible secret is out!" Joann smiled wryly.

"Once I had barely begun to establish my life again, your father paid me a visit, at my little house I was renting in Windsor. He had just learned I'd promised to sell the farm...his ancestors' farm...to my best friend. George has some...misdeeds...in his past that cause him to dislike this particular person very much. He demanded I sell the farm to him instead, and when I refused...and removed him from my home...he became...resentful...and called me often...and well, bothered me...so I returned to my maiden name and moved up here. It was a drastic step; I know I had the law on my side, and I assumed he'd calm down eventually, but I couldn't handle the stress. I was afraid if I contacted you George would locate me and get...irate...once more." Joann dropped her eyes. "I'm sorry."

"Let me get this straight. My father withheld mail from me, lied to me, and threatened you so badly you moved and changed your name?"

"Yes."

"Wow. That's just *great*." Joy's tone was at its harshest. "And what about this – this 'misdeed' you mentioned?"

"I can't tell you that, Joy. Your father should have been the one to tell you all of this, in reality, but..." Joann's voice broke, and Joy looked at her in alarm until she realized her aunt was about to cry too. "But I couldn't hug you and eat and chat with you and let you continue believing I just didn't care enough to stay in touch." She pulled a tissue from her pocket and wiped her eyes.

Joy jumped up from her seat facing her aunt and scrambled to sit beside her instead. She put her arms around Joann's wide shoulders and held on tightly. "George Carnegie has no say-so in our relationship anymore," she said.

"Never again."

As soon as the proverbial elephant in the room had been identified and stampeded out the door, conversation flowed much more easily between Joy and Joann. Joann was ecstatic Joy had actually moved to the area for a short time, and she offered her spare bedroom until Joy located a rental property. She also asked cautiously if Joy would be interested in attending services with her with the East Montpelier church of Christ.

"Yes, please, I'd be glad to go," Joy said, realizing her aunt had never even heard of her baptism. "I – um – tried to go in Pittsburgh, but, as a new realtor, I usually had appointments all day on Sundays. I intend to go as often as possible in Vermont." She blushed, ashamed she had skipped so many services.

"Have you ever become a Christian, Joy? I remember how interested you were so long ago."

"Yes, about three years ago," Joy replied. "My roommate at Brown was a Christian, and I finally got baptized my senior year...but I haven't really – learned much – since then, you know."

"Now that is some wonderful news! I've been praying to hear that for many years too, Joy," Joann said, beaming.

"Well, please keep praying. I'm pretty sure you're more religious in your pinky finger than I am in my entire body."

Joann chuckled. "It's not a contest. And we'll talk and study while you're here, if you'd like."

"Very much."

Suddenly, Joy's stomach growled. She ignored it, but the noise persisted, causing Joann to smile. "Excuse me. I've been sort of – sporadic – in my meals lately," she admitted.

"We can remedy that. I'll whip something up for supper," Joann said, rising quickly. "It's – oh, my – it's already after six! You're probably starving."

"No, no, I don't want you to go to any trouble," Joy said, standing also. "You've only been out of the hospital – how long?"

"Five days, but I'm going back to work on Monday. That's why I was at the library this afternoon. I'm quite capable of cooking us a meal!"

"Let me take you out to dinner," Joy said. "Then, if you're sure you don't mind, I'll get my stuff from the motel and stay at your house for the weekend."

"Dinner out does sound nice," Joann said. "And of course I'd love for you to stay with me, if you can tolerate hanging out with an elderly lady for that long."

Joy did some quick mental math and burst out laughing. "You aren't even fifty yet!"

"No, but I'm so close I can spit on it. I'll just get a coat and my purse and we can go appease your lion right away." Joann collected their mugs and disappeared from the room.

Late that night, Joy sat on the antique double bed in her aunt's guest bedroom, trying to read the Agatha Christie she'd picked up at Goodwill last week. She couldn't sleep, thanks to the numerous cups of coffee she'd consumed with her dinner, and she couldn't write because she couldn't figure out how to connect to Joann's wireless Internet to access the research she needed for the short story she'd begun. She read twenty pages, turned to the twenty-first, and couldn't even remember how the characters were connected to each other. "Who's the real elderly lady?" she muttered, easing off the bed springs. She padded over to the wall opposite the dormer, where several large frames full of small photos were hanging.

She smiled at a wedding photo of John and Joann, who were

so happy and self-conscious at the same time that they looked like adolescents. And there...a picture of John and Joann in early middle age, most likely around the time Joy had visited them. Joy examined the next photo – of her father and her uncle together as young adults. Even at that age, they'd been so different – in dress, appearance, and facial expression. The last photo in that frame was of two young children who resembled George and John. Even her father had been adorable as a six-year-old! What had happened?

The next frame held photos of Joann, as a toothless school child, a slender teen, and a young woman holding an American flag. Joy stared more closely at the first photo, the only one of professional quality. The studio's name and location were printed in one corner – Fabre's in Coaticook, Quebec? Her aunt had grown up in Quebec? Was she Canadian? And was the flag picture significant – like when she got citizenship in America or something? She hated she had so many unanswered questions about her family.

The next morning, Joy awoke to the aroma of bacon and...could it be? Coffee! She dressed and dashed downstairs barefoot in five minutes flat. Joann was standing at the stove turning pancakes when Joy entered the sunlit kitchen.

"You shouldn't have done all this!" Joy said, staring at the stacks of fluffy pancakes, the plate of crisp bacon, and the coffee perking on the counter.

"Are you kidding? This is a very special day. And how long has it been since you've tasted real maple syrup?"

"Oh, about a decade," Joy said, examining the brand new can of coffee. "But I ate so much of it when I visited before, I actually gained twelve pounds in one summer! That was yet another reason my parents were so mad at me when I got home." She cocked her head. She seriously thought she'd just seen her aunt rolling her eyes. No.. couldn't be.

The meal was as delicious as it appeared, including the coffee, despite the fact Joy usually preferred South American blends. "Did you drive to the store just for me this morning?" she asked.

"No, I just walked down to Main Street. There's a little grocery shop there."

27

"But...did you buy a coffee pot too? I can pay you back if you'd like!"

"No, this one was a wedding present," Joann assured her. "It's never been out of the box before. I'd forgotten I even had one."

"You're certainly going to too much trouble on my account," Joy said. "You should...rest...or something...and let me do things for you."

Joann just looked at her.

"Seriously, is there anything I can do to help you? I know you weren't expecting company," Joy said.

Joann smiled at her niece's persistence. "First of all, no, because I'm feeling quite healthy enough to take care of myself. And secondly, no, because you aren't company, you're family. I want us to have a wonderful time together but I have no intentions of trying to impress you." Joy grinned uncertainly. "If you're determined to do something for me, though, I wish you'd just go on a drive with me. I know some roads where we can escape most of the tourists but still catch some good color."

"Oh, of course! I noticed the trees were changing on the mountains, but I've been so preoccupied with finding you, I've hardly appreciated them."

"I'll pack us a few sandwiches," Joann said. "The areas we're going don't have many restaurants. You should probably wear hiking boots too, in case you want to see a waterfall or two."

Joy stopped short. Hiking boots. Had she ever owned any? During her last visit, she hadn't worn shoes, except in town, and they'd been far too busy on the farm to traipse around the state hiking to waterfalls. "Um...I don't have any..." she began. "Would – just – normal tennis shoes work?"

"Oh, probably for today. I guess we won't go anywhere too treacherous today, but before the snow comes you've got to buy good boots."

Joy nodded and headed upstairs. What had she gotten herself into?

CHAPTER 4

The old-fashioned bed complained as Joy flopped on her side to turn off her iPhone alarm. She groaned as she attempted to drag her aching muscles from under the covers to dress for worship services. Obviously, she and her aunt had quite different ideas of the definition of "treacherous"...and "strenuous" too. The waterfall they'd visited was so deep down in a ravine in the Green Mountain National Forest, Joy had become sore just driving there – over tens of miles of gravel roads in her jeep, which apparently lacked effective shocks. Not to mention her wrists and hands hurt from grabbing the steering wheel in sheer terror as she navigated some of the curves. And then, of course, the trail...a mile in either direction and about a 25% grade. Joy's muscles had muscles that were tight and burning.

Joann was already eating oatmeal when Joy reached the kitchen. "I don't think you have time for a bowl," she said in concern.

"That's fine. I'll just have coffee," Joy said. "I'm not a breakfast person normally."

"I'll spare you the lecture about how bad it is for your health to skip meals," Joann said.

"I know, I know. And the caffeine is terrible too. I'll reform soon."

"Joy, will you sit down for a minute while you have your coffee?" Joann said. She seemed to lose interest in her own breakfast.

Joy sat quickly, not sure how to interpret the strained expression on Joann's face.

"Joy, I – I need to tell you something before you meet my church family this morning. There is a man named Alex Martin who attends services in East Montpelier...and he and I...well, we are seeing each other...I guess you'd say. We have been for a few months now." Joy's eyebrows shot up and her mouth dropped open. Joann coughed, tried to take a deep breath, and continued. "I – I know it must seem strange – or – maybe – sad to you to think of me with any man other than your uncle...so I wanted to warn you that you will most likely

29

meet Alex today."

To Joy's dismay, her eyes filled with tears. Somehow this scenario had never occurred to her, but she kept them under control as she answered. "Well, I...I can't say it won't take some getting used to...but most of all I want you to be happy...so I – um – I *will* get used to the idea." She blinked rapidly. "Thank you – for – for telling me."

Joann leaned across the table and patted Joy's arm. "Thank *you* for trying to understand. It's been a surprise to me too, but I think you'll like Alex. He's a good man."

Joy smiled slightly, nodded, and carried her mug to the sink. "I'll be back as soon as I grab my shoes and purse and stuff."

Joann fell back against her chair in relief as soon as Joy had left the kitchen.

Joy drove them to worship services in her jeep. "Tell me about your church," she said, steering through the narrow downtown streets.

"We are very small, about thirty-five members, mostly people my age or older. We meet in a house instead of a typical church building so we can afford to pay a preacher a small salary. And...we support a missionary in northern Maine. The church has been meeting in this city for many years, but there've never been very many of us."

"Wow, I've never gone to church in a house. Do you baptize in the bathtub?"

"I believe a teenager was before I came, but most people are too large to go under completely, so the baptisms I've seen have been in the Winooski River or a swimming pool. Once, we baptized someone in the Holiday Inn's indoor pool because the rivers were frozen. The church had to pay for the price of a night's stay in the hotel before they'd allow it!"

"Amazing," Joy said, making the final turn into the driveway of a small brick house with the church sign displayed prominently in the front yard. She turned off the engine but hesitated to move. "Do I look okay?"

"You look beautiful," Joann said, smoothing her own denim skirt and cardigan.

"Thank you, but I mean, am I dressed appropriately?" Joy tugged at a wrinkle in the only pair of dress slacks she had brought from Pennsylvania.

"You're decent and clean. That's enough," Joann assured her. "And no one would turn you away even if you weren't."

Joy grinned, but her stomach was suddenly coiled like a spring. Church services made her so nervous – that is, except the church she'd attended in college. Her parents' church, for example, met in a massive historical cathedral, where a two-story organ dominated both the room and the choir's singing; Joy could not feel she was personally praising God there. The church she'd visited infrequently in Pittsburgh called itself by a Biblical name, but Joy also felt quite uncomfortable there because the members practiced patterns of worship she could not find sanctioned in the Bible. Joy strained to remember the services she'd attended with John and Joann in Windsor so many years ago, but she just recalled she'd been a bit bored and appalled by the off-key singing.

Joy proceeded quickly up the sidewalk, following Joann as closely as possible. Suddenly, Joann turned and hissed, "Relax!" before continuing through the front door.

Inside, an elderly man and a husky younger man were setting up metal folding chairs in neat rows in a large, well-lit living room area. The room also contained a well-worn blue couch, a recliner, and a maple podium, as well as a small wooden table. The table held two oak trays and a basket. Joann placed her purse and Bible on a chair in the middle of the room and motioned for Joy to do the same.

"Good morning, Miss Joann!" the older man called out, stopping his work to come and hug her. "I am surely happy to see you out and about again!"

"Thanks. It's great to be back."

"And who is this lovely lady?" the man added.

"This is my niece, Joy Carnegie," Joann said. "She's planning to spend a few months in our area."

"Proud to meet ya, Joy! I'm Wilson Roberts...but I answer to Robert Wilson too 'cause most people can't remember which is my first and which is my last!"

Joy murmured a polite greeting and shook his hand. Apparently, this entertaining character was not her aunt's boyfriend!

The younger man finished his row and headed their direction as well. He hugged Joann too and introduced himself to Joy. "I'm Paul Graham," he said. "Welcome to Vermont!"

Joy found herself wondering about Paul's age as she exchanged greetings with him. She'd thought at first he was about her own age, but he had such prominent dimples when he smiled and freckles across his cheekbones that she suddenly decided he was still in college. She also noticed he spoke correctly and carefully despite his Vermont accent, much as her aunt did.

Joann left Joy for the kitchen so she could retrieve the grape juice to fill the communion cups, so Joy sat and watched as about twenty-five more people trickled in, including one family with small children. However, most of the members did seem to be gray-haired, and some of them actually looked as old as Methuselah. Joy kept her eyes peeled for a likely candidate for Alex Martin, but by the time the service began, she'd seen no one promising.

The announcements were finished and the first song was in progress when a slender man with graying blond hair slipped in the door and slid into the empty seat beside Joann. "Sorry," he whispered. She merely smiled and continued singing "When We All Get to Heaven."

It was a full hour until the service concluded, but Joy was shocked when she realized so much time had passed. Her nervousness had faded without her having noticed, for something about this congregation felt – right – from the hearty acapella singing to the simple gospel sermon to the chorus of enthusiastic amens that had followed the preacher's "welcome back" to Joann. Oh, and, incidentally – the curious Wilson Roberts had turned out to be the preacher, and a very capable one at that...and the freckly Paul had led the songs with a surprisingly mature and tuneful voice...and Joann's slight friend was in possession of a positively booming tenor voice! Joy felt a twinge of guilt as she realized just how few times she'd attended services since her college graduation. Maybe this comfortable little church would be her way of jump-starting her spiritual life again.

Joy was introduced to Alex at last as soon as the final prayer was finished. "Ah, you must be Joy," he said. His eyes were brown and kind. "Joann has told me so much about her time with you when you were a teenager!"

Joy shook his hand, liking him rather well in spite of herself. "I'm glad to meet you," she said, unable to claim any such degree of knowledge of him.

"I'm usually off work on Sundays," he explained. "But today, I'm afraid I'm going to have to be rude and rush off in about five minutes instead of getting acquainted."

"Oh, no problem. I understand."

"Alex is a pediatrician," Joann said.

"Do you make rounds at the hospital or something?" Joy said.

"No, not typically. I have a little patient there right now who hasn't been listening very well to the hospital physicians. That's why I was late this morning, and I've got to skip Bible study and go back now."

"Oh, I forgot about Bible study," Joy muttered. She might as well have super-glued "heathen" in neon lights across her forehead!

"Yes, most churches have it before worship, but we've set the later time for it so more children from the community will come. But now – I really must run..." Alex said, kissing Joann's cheek and patting Joy's shoulder. "I'll call you if I can't come to worship tonight, Jo Jo!" He had left the building before Joy found her voice.

"*Jo Jo?*" she squeaked. "He calls you '*Jo Jo*'?"

Joann laughed. "Yes, but not normally in public. Don't you think it suits me?"

Joy rolled her eyes. "I guess he can call you whatever he wants...but seriously...Jo Jo? Sounds like a baseball player or a character on the Flintstones."

"Perhaps I will start calling him Pebbles," Joann said, sitting once again and demurely crossing her ankles.

Unfortunately, Wilson Roberts chose that moment to begin Bible study – unfortunately for Joy and Joann, that is. Joy had started giggling at her aunt's remark and had just pointed out Pebbles was a *girl* when Wilson started leading the opening prayer. Joann made a mortified face and bowed her head immediately.

33

Joann's expression was too much for Joy, who was over-tired and not in control of her emotions...she snorted. The frantic coughing noises she commenced instantly afterward were no less disruptive – or convincing – to Joann, who began shaking with silent laughter.

At least the prayer was short, because by the end of it, Joy was so exhausted from laughing without a sound that she was in pain, and Joann was coughing in earnest. The elderly woman behind them slipped them *two* cough drops, which almost set Joy off once more. Her ears burned. She could honestly say that in all her years of sporadic church attendance, she had never created such a disruption! She cautiously tore the wrapper off the cough drop and popped it into her mouth, wanting to be polite in one way at least...and nearly gagged. The potent menthol flavor kept her quite solemn – and wide awake – for the next ten minutes!

Joy's embarrassment increased after Bible study, when several people, including Paul Graham and Menthol Lady, asked her if she was all right. "Yes," she said, staring at the floor. "I – um – think I just need to rest. I've had a long week."

"Yes, you should, dearie. And so should that aunt of yours! Go home and take a nap!" the woman said, emanating enough menthol fumes to make Joy's eyes water slightly.

As soon as she could tear herself away from the talkative woman, Joy jingled her keys at her aunt and fled to the jeep. Joann followed at a more leisurely pace, but within five minutes, they were en route back downtown. "All of a sudden, my church attendance tolerance level was just gone," Joy said ruefully. "That must sound terrible to you."

"We all can get a little tired of being around our brethren sometimes, and you have every reason to be exhausted," Joann said. "Do you want to take a nap this afternoon?"

"I don't know – I'm not sleepy, just sorta strung out. Sometimes it hits me that within three weeks I've totally tossed my old life out the window...job...boyfriend, although that wasn't my choice...home...parents..."

"Just let me know what you need me to do to make things easier when those times hit you."

"Well, for starters, not make me laugh when Bible class is about to begin!"

Joann started chuckling again. "My, we were disruptive, weren't we? But I doubt too many people noticed. They probably just thought I was coughing and hacking like I've been for the last three weeks."

"What! Practically the whole church noticed! Even Paul, that song leader guy, came up afterward to check on my general well-being!"

"Or maybe he was hoping for an opportunity to speak to you again. After all, there aren't exactly herds of single women his age running around in our congregation."

"Oh, don't be ridiculous! And is he my age? He looks very young."

"I think he's even a bit older than you, actually. It sounds familiar that he was twenty-five when he moved there last year."

"You mean, moved here, to Montpelier?"

"No, I mean, moved into the house where the church meets. He's serving as a caretaker for us until he finds another job."

"He lives there?"

"Um-hmm."

"But...wow...and he's been unemployed since last year. That's not a good situation. I wonder what happened..." Joy swung into the driveway of her aunt's house.

"I could tell you the whole story, but then you'd have nothing to talk over with him this winter," Joann said, mischief sparking in her eyes.

"And who says I want to talk to him?"

"Oh, you only want to talk about him – all the way home?"

Joy sighed with gusto as she headed for the front door, even though she knew she'd have to stand and wait for Joann to unlock it.

The two women ended up spending most of the afternoon with Joann's photo albums. The first one they paged through was from the summer Joy had stayed at the farm. She stared at the photos in awe, a bittersweet sensation filling her heart. How special to be reminiscing here with her aunt, but how tragic that her uncle was gone forever, and they'd lost so many years of time together.

Then, Joann opened up an album only half full. "Here are some pictures of John and me after that summer. After his accident, I stopped taking any, so I never finished the album, but at least you can see what he looked like right before his death."

Joy turned the thick pages cautiously, smiling at the images of a couple who'd still loved each other like newlyweds. The final shot was of John on a ladder in one of the farm's ancient apple trees. He looked healthy and happy and exactly as she remembered.

"What happened?" she said. "I never even knew what happened, Aunt Joann."

"John was on Pierre and Angelique's land – you remember them? The French Canadian couple?" Joy nodded slowly.

"Well, their horses had broken loose during a storm and John was helping Pierre catch them. Pierre had been feeling ill the past few days, so he called John when the lightning spooked the horses into breaking through a weak place in the barn.

"John found Pierre in their pond – about three feet deep, I think it was – trying to restrain the panicked horses. But before John could reach Pierre, the man dropped like a shot into the water, holding his chest. When John tried to pull him to safety, the horses kicked him in the head, and he blacked out and went underwater."

"How – how do you know what happened?" Joy said, her eyes streaming.

"Because Pierre had managed to pull himself into a sitting position by the time Angelique found him ten minutes later, and he managed to get out the story before he also died. He'd been unable to lift John above the water to breathe. The coroner said neither man would have died if they hadn't been so determined to save each other."

"I can't believe it!" Joy sobbed.

"Yes. In ten minutes' time, my best friend and I were both widowed, and her three sons were fatherless."

"I wish I could have been there to stay with you afterward," Joy said. "But at least you had your best friend."

"Not really. Angelique blamed herself for the accident because she'd insisted Pierre call John for help. She didn't speak to me for several months afterward, and then I moved shortly after that."

"Sometimes, I get so angry at my parents, I want to – to punch someone!" Joy said. "If they hadn't alienated themselves from you and Uncle John, you wouldn't have been so alone!"

Joann half-smiled. "I know, dear heart. But we've found each other now...and although I just promised you earlier I'd do anything I could to help you, I must say, being your punching bag is going a bit too far...sorry!"

"You're way down on my list of candidates, I promise!"

"Let's look at a less painful album." Joann rummaged through the stacks on her coffee table and pulled an old one with a peeling green cover into her lap. "Beware – vintage photos ahead!" she laughed. "This one is from my childhood and teenage years."

Joy made appropriate cooing noises at several pages of strangely-colored 1960's photos from Joann's babyhood and toddler years. She stared at a photo of Joann and her mother in front of a small brick church building.

Joann peered at it as well. "Ah, yes. My Catholic days." She caught a glimpse of Joy's huge eyes and laughed. "You didn't know I became a member of the church of Christ after I married your uncle? My mother was a devout Catholic."

"I thought you were born in the church of Christ...well, I mean...that your parents took you from birth."

"No, I wasn't baptized until I was twenty-two," Joann replied. "I didn't even go to Mass regularly as a teen, either."

"Wow...but hey, the name of this Catholic church...that's not in English, is it? It's French!"

"Yes, of course. Especially in the 1970's, very few signs in Quebec were in English because of the language conflicts going on at the time."

"Are *you* Canadian?"

Joann laughed so hard at Joy's expression, she started to cough and had to dash into the kitchen for some water. When she came back, she explained.

"I'm American now. I've been a citizen longer than you've

been alive. But yes, my ethnicity is Canadian."

"You speak French?"

"Yes, I grew up bilingual. My father – he's still alive – is from Prince Edward Island, and my mother was Quebeçois. I haven't spoken it much in years, though – just occasionally over the phone with Angelique back in Windsor."

"How did I not know this?" Joy exclaimed.

"It's ancient history...something that probably didn't interest you at fourteen."

"And how did you meet Uncle John?"

Joann leaned back on the couch and crossed her legs. "I met him my junior year of high school. My mother died when I was fifteen, and my father couldn't stand to live in Quebec any longer. There wasn't any work in P.E.I., so we moved down to Island Pond, Vermont. That's up in the northeast, less than an hour from Coaticook, where I'd grown up. John was the janitor at Island Pond School, saving up money to buy a farm. He was much kinder to me than most of my classmates, who laughed at my clothes, my big glasses, and my accent."

"Wait – I'm confused. You said the farm in Windsor was the family farm? But isn't that a long distance from Island Pond?"

"Yes, about two hours or so by interstate now. But John's plans changed after we fell in love. He married me and took me home to his family instead of waiting for a farm of his own."

"How old were you?" Joy asked gently.

"Seventeen."

"Wow."

"Yes. Your uncle helped me in so many ways. He took me out of poverty – for my father and I had been living in a cheap motel in Island Pond. He coached me on my English pronunciation so I wouldn't receive so many stares. And most importantly, he taught me the Gospel."

"Okay...so...you're telling me my middle class, American, well-educated aunt from a Christian background is actually a Canadian high school dropout who grew up Catholic and in poverty?"

"Yes. Strange, isn't it?"

38

"Yeah...I mean...it's not that I'm being...critical...but you're not much...like the rest of my family, you know?"

Joann nodded. "Believe me, I know."

"Next thing I know, you'll tell me I'm descended from Pocahontas and have 27 siblings in a cave in the mountains."

Joann smiled but said nothing, although Joy could sense her aunt was still a fount of untold family stories. The two women parted ways soon afterward to rest a few minutes before evening service at five.

Joy set her phone alarm in case she fell asleep, but she needed not to have bothered. Joann's stories swirled in her head and prevented her eyes from even growing heavy.

CHAPTER 5

"I forgot to mention you will only have to control yourself for short periods of time tonight," Joann said as Joy reached the small gravel lot of the church building that evening. "It's singing night, so you can snort and giggle all you wish during most of the service, and no one will notice."

Joy parked the car and stared at her aunt. "I do believe you're making fun of me," she said. "And I'm not sure quite what to think of it."

"I make fun of Alex all the time," Joann confessed. "It's very entertaining."

Joy was still laughing when they entered the building and almost plowed into Paul near the door.

"Sorry!" she gasped.

"No problem," Paul said, looking at her a little too closely. "I'm glad you and Joann are enjoying each others' company so thoroughly."

"Apparently Paul just found out again what a nutcase I am," Joann said. "I do usually attempt to be a little more dignified in public."

"You amaze me," Joy said.

The service passed rapidly for Joy, who reveled in song after song of beautiful old music, despite the fact she only knew a few of them well enough to sing herself. Paul, Alex, and another middle-aged man alternated in leading the songs. Joy felt Paul's eyes on her as he led, so she tried to at least mouth the words as often as possible. Fortunately, his final song was "Faithful Love," a newer song in a supplementary paper hymnal she had learned at her college congregation, so she could actually allow words to leave her mouth without feeling too embarrassed. Not many other worshipers sang, although Joann and a few other seemed to be sight-reading the notes, so Joy wondered if Paul had guessed she'd know the more modern songs and had chosen it for her benefit.

40

As soon as the closing prayer was finished, Alex appeared at Joann's side. "May I have the pleasure of taking the loveliest ladies in Vermont to dinner tonight?" he said. Joy hid a grin and let her aunt respond.

"I don't know. Maybe you should ask them," Joann said.

Alex blinked, then smiled. "Jo-Jo, don't tease me. It's been a long day."

"I'm sorry. Joy – you up to dinner out?"

"Of course. Thank you, Dr. Martin."

"Please, call me Alex. If you say 'Dr. Martin,' I'm going to start looking around for a baby to weigh or a grubby little boy to vaccinate!"

"Will you follow us to my house first, and then we can all drive together? I'd like to grab a heavier coat before we go eat," Joann said.

"Sure. You can be thinking on your way home about what sounds good."

"Aunt Joann, why don't you ride with Dr. - uh – Alex," Joy said quickly. "I've been absorbing all your time lately. I can find my way back if our cars get separated."

"Are you sure?" Joann said, noticing the grateful look Alex had given her niece.

"Positive. See you there!" Joy abandoned them immediately and practically jogged to her jeep. She grinned to herself. Alex might be fifty or so years old, but he'd been as excited to be alone with her aunt as if he were sixteen. It was hard to stay upset at the idea of Joann with a different man when they were clearly so happy together.

The restaurant on which they all agreed was a small "Mom and Pop" place downtown, so they walked there instead of driving. The dining room was bustling with local families, obvious tourists, and older couples, but they managed to snag one of the last available tables.

Joy surveyed the menu with a slight sense of alarm. The only available options were the very type of "comfort food" she had avoided since college so she could maintain her size four figure. She had been eating all sorts of appetizing meals in the past month, telling herself she "deserved" to be able to relax a little, but she'd also noticed a difference in the waistbands of her tighter clothing. She resigned herself to ordering New England clam chowder and a salad without dressing...and coffee...always coffee.

Despite Joy's dietary concerns, she enjoyed the meal. The chowder was excellent, the salad was fresh, and Alex and Joann were incredible company. They complemented each other perfectly, and their banter kept Joy in stitches throughout much of the dinner.

Joy had taken her last spoonful of chowder when her phone vibrated. She glanced at the caller ID, gasped, and rose. "I'm sorry. I have to take this," she said, dashing out the door. She should have changed her phone number. And her name. And her fingerprints.

"Why are you calling, Cal?" Joy spat into the phone without preamble. She had made it abundantly clear to Cal the day he'd dumped her that she never wanted to speak to him again if he couldn't support her in her decisions.

"This is not Cal, Sophia. This is your mother."

"Don't call me Sophia. And why are you using his phone?"

"Dear Cal has come by our house today to confess he still wants to be with you."

Joy grabbed a handful of hair and pulled on it, stepping to the side of the building so Joann and Alex could no longer observe her movements. "That's his problem, and it seems he's an awful wimp if he's coming to cry to you about it."

"Cal is a fine, upstanding man with an excellent background!" Amelia Carnegie said, her voice trembling. "You'll never find anyone else like him, especially up there in the wilderness!"

"Mother, I refuse to take your bait. I am not suffering from my lack of a wealthy husband at the moment."

"Cal also came to inform me that it's time for him to select his date for the Barrett Christmas Party. He would like you to accompany him, provided your appearance can be repaired, but if you don't hurry and accept, he'll be forced to invite someone else...Christine Swanson, perhaps."

Joy could hardly believe her ears. Cal thought her so desperate he imagined the threat of him dating her old high school rival would be enough to send her racing back to him? What a pathetic melted marshmallow of a person she must have been back in Pittsburgh! The comment about her appearance hardly rankled in contrast to the insults to her intelligence and perception.

"Mother, this conversation is finished. I will not accompany Cal to the Christmas party or anywhere else, and I will no longer accept calls from his number even if he's continuing to be too chicken to speak to me personally."

"But he's such a stunning young man, and so alone since you left..."

"Then you should adopt him or something. I have to go – my aunt is waiting on me. Good night, Mother," Joy ended the call amid her mother's indignant splutters. She marched back into the restaurant with the stance of a conquering general but stopped short at the roaring silence of the patrons, including Joann and Alex, as they watched her.

"Sorry," she said to the room as a whole as she slipped, subdued, into her seat at the table. She sat, trembling, the adrenaline rush of anger dissipating almost immediately, and humiliation taking its place.

"That was my mother," Joy said. "Calling on my ex's phone. I'm sorry for the commotion I caused."

"It doesn't take much commotion to fascinate people in this town," Alex said kindly. Joann patted Joy's arm, but Joy could tell from the lines around her mouth that her aunt was angry. She hoped it wasn't directed toward her.

Alex walked with Joann and Joy back to Joann's house shortly after that, the tension Joy could not hide breaking the happy mood of the evening. Joann hugged Alex as soon as they arrived, murmured something in his ear, and disappeared immediately into the house, slamming the door behind her. Joy stood awkwardly beside Alex on the driveway, wondering what had come over her unflappable aunt. Surely she wasn't really mad because their pleasant meal had been interrupted!

"Joy, let's sit down and enjoy this nice – frigid – air for a few minutes while your aunt has some time to herself," Alex said, heading over to the porch stairs. He lowered himself easily to the top step and motioned for Joy to join him. She followed uncertainly.

"Joann asked me just now if I would explain some things to you," Alex began. "She wants you to know she is not angry with you at all."

"Well, that's a relief," Joy said, her tone cautiously casual. "I didn't mean to ruin the evening with my personal issues."

"Your personal issues are very important to her. That's not the situation. She is angry at your parents, specifically your mother."

"She doesn't even know my mother!"

"Actually, she knew her before you were born, but that's not my story to tell. Joann is mainly angry at her because of how she treats you."

"I appreciate her concern, but it's nothing new."

"She knows that," Alex said. "But it's a little more complicated than that. Joann has confessed to me in the past that she resents your mother for her treatment of the precious gift God allowed her." Alex looked at her intently.

Joy searched his face as her mind scrambled to make the connection he sought. "What are you saying?"

"Are you aware of your aunt's struggle to have children?" Alex finally asked.

"No – I mean, I can see she doesn't have any – but, well, I've never questioned her about it."

"Joann comes from a family with a medical history of problems with conception and childbirth. She was an only child, as was her mother. Her mother died in childbirth when Joann was a teenager. Joann herself had two miscarriages, one quite late term. That was before you visited, of course. Anyway, her second miscarriage nearly killed her, and the complications from it made her unable to become pregnant again. She and your uncle considered adoption but were unable to afford it, so Joann has never had a child of her own."

"Oh, my," Joy said, goosebumps rising on her arms.

"Joann sometimes becomes very angry when she encounters cruel mothers," Alex continued. "She still struggles to understand

44

why women who are incapable or mean have children but she cannot. She is especially angry at your mother because she cares so much about you. Joann told me to explain these things to you because she can't stand to do so herself."

"Thank you," said Joy. "I had no idea."

"Almost no one does because Joann is always so encouraging and positive," Alex said. "But she has allowed me the privilege of sharing her difficulties – and confiding in her niece."

"I'm glad she has you," Joy said with total sincerity.

Alex actually blushed, which further endeared him to Joy. "I am a blessed man," he said. He paused, removed his glasses, polished the lenses, and peered at Joy. "Please understand, though, I am not trying to take your uncle's place. I know he was a good man, and the two of you were close. I appreciate your willingness to get to know me."

Joy chose her words carefully. "I want my aunt to be happy, and you're doing that. Thank you for making her happy again, and for taking care of her. I hate I missed so many years with her, but I'm relieved she has you now no matter what I do."

Alex smiled, hugged her, and rose with the grace of a much younger man. "I think it's safe to go inside now," he said. "And I'm going to catch some sleep. My patients expect me at seven tomorrow morning."

Joy let herself in quietly, unsure of her aunt's location or state of mind. She scanned the empty living room and dropped into the couch with a book of Vermont photos from the coffee table. Alex had given her too much to process. Well, more accurately, Vermont had given her too much to process, and she'd only been there three days!

A few minutes later, Joy heard her aunt's footsteps on the stairs, and she glanced up nervously.

Joann had changed into jeans and a sweater, and her eyes were red-rimmed.

"Hi," Joy said tentatively.

"Hi," Joann said, sitting beside Joy on the couch. "Did Alex talk to you?"

"Yes, and I only want to say I'm so very sorry," Joy said.

Joann nodded. "*I'm* sorry," she said. "I should have told you myself, but I'm a bit of a coward. I hope you can forgive me for my terrible attitude."

Joy shook her head in slightly-frustrated awe. "Forgive you? I ought to thank you! You've shown me more – more – care than my own parents even though I obviously hardly know you. Why would I need to forgive you?"

"It's wrong for me to be jealous and ungrateful," Joann said. "And conceited – everyone makes mistakes, and it's conceited for me to compare myself so arrogantly to other m – to others when they behave in ways they shouldn't."

Joy could grasp with her brain what Joann was saying, but emotionally, she felt her aunt to be completely justified. "Okay, fine then. I forgive you for – whatever way you've acted you shouldn't have." She rubbed her eyes. "So...Alex is sure a nice man."

"Yes, he is."

"And he loves you," Joy added. "It's obvious."

"Yes. He's been such a help too, especially the last few weeks. He actually took a few days off – closed his office and everything – while I was in the hospital. And then of course his willingness to do my duty for me tonight."

"He must have been really worried about you. Do you know how you got sick?"

"Oh, I suspect from work. There are always plenty of sick people in town this time of year, as the weather's changing, and I handle books, movies, and computers after practically the entire town has sneezed and coughed on them. I get sick more frequently here than I did on the farm."

"Do you really think you should be going back so soon?"

"So soon! I've been out three weeks. If I don't go back, they'll replace me. Besides, I'm fine. Since you came, I've even stopped taking my cough medicine." She lowered her eyebrows. "To tell you the truth, I think I wish you'd found me a week or two later. It hurts my pride for you to see me for the first time in so long when I'm looking old and haggard and barking like a – like a seal with emphysema. I promise I'm quite all right. You needn't worry."

46

Joy hid a smile. "It's just that when I was a kid, you were like...well, like Super Woman to me or something. I never saw you sick or crying or afraid or losing your temper. I didn't know about your difficult times with – with things. You were so tough and funny and you always had it together. I wanted to be like you. And now – well, it's all still true, but I'm seeing who you really are inside, too, and it makes me feel – protective or something."

"I'm not sure whether to be embarrassed or flattered," Joann said. "But let me tell you this, kiddo. I feel protective of you too. Let's just watch out for each other!"

"On that note," Joy said, feeling the air had been cleared thoroughly. "I'm going to call a realtor tomorrow first thing and look at some rental properties."

"I hope you don't feel I'm rushing you to leave," Joann said. "I'm really glad you've been visiting me, and my spare room is yours as long as you want it."

"Oh, no. I just want my own place again as soon as I can. I'll still be in your hair, though. You'll probably be sick of me by the end of the winter."

"Not likely! But I will warn you there aren't many good rental sites around here unless you choose to sign a long lease. And you may have a bit of trouble finding landlords willing to rent to a non-Vermonter without a job."

"But – I have plenty of money. I mean, not to be obnoxious, but I've had a very well-paying job the last two years."

"We tend to be a little closed-minded about some things up here, dear. Try calling Bonnie Johnston at Prudential Realty. She's the only prominent realtor I know who even handles short-term rentals in this area. She's a nice, honest person; I work with her mother. And of course, you can use Alex and me as references if necessary."

Joy shook her head in disgust.

CHAPTER 6

Joy got up the next morning early enough to drink coffee as her aunt ate breakfast. Joann was running a bit behind, so Joy persuaded her to leave her dishes. Before Joy called Prudential, she washed their cups, spoons, and bowl. By hand. No dishwasher in this old-fashioned kitchen, although at least Joann had a microwave!

At nine, Joy placed her call. Fortunately, Bonnie answered the phone herself and was quite friendly, especially when Joy explained her relation to Joann. "I'm available all day tomorrow, as well as tonight after five," she said. "But I only have four rentals right now, and none of them are – exactly – luxurious."

"I'm just looking for something basic," Joy said. "And I'd be glad to start tonight."

"We can begin right at five as long as you don't mind viewing the houses after dark."

"Let's see one or two, then, because my aunt might want to come along, and she will have worked for several hours. We can go to the others tomorrow."

"Oh, has your aunt recovered? I heard she had an awfully close call a couple of weeks ago."

Joy had not heard anyone put her aunt's illness in such a grave light and sincerely hoped the realtor was exaggerating. "I – I think she's doing very well," she choked out.

Sure enough, when Joann came home at four, she accepted Joy's house-hunting invitation with enthusiasm. "So Bonnie says the rentals aren't 'exactly luxurious,' eh? Well, that means this trip may be an adventure, because her mom's just an old country girl like me."

Joy giggled. "Bring it on! This is a nice, clean, safe, small city. How bad could they be?" Joann said nothing, having searched for a rental herself several years previously.

The two women sat on the porch swing, savoring the fading sunshine, until time for their appointment. "It felt good to be back at the library," Joann said, stretching. "I'm tired, but I'm so ready to have

48

a routine again."

"I'm sure. Oh, by the way, beware of Bonnie. She's almost got you dead and buried."

"Maybe she wants to list my house!"

"Hey, I thought you said she was nice and honest!"

Joann stopped swinging. "Joy I *did* almost die, all right? And Bonnie's husband is an EMT. I think he heard about it firsthand."

"Oh." Joy was dismayed to notice her eyes filling.

"Come on. Let's walk down to the realty office," Joann said, suddenly rising. "You're going to sit there and fret yourself to death."

"But should you.."

"Hush, dear, or I'll *run* to Prudential, eh?"

Bonnie Johnston proved to be an energetic woman in her mid-thirties. She was dressed in brilliantly-colored, tight-fitting clothing, and she wore heavy makeup and heavier jewelry. And hiking boots. She also drove a minivan, but she drove it, to Joy's alarm, like she was being chased by the Mafia or something.

Joy had never been troubled much by motion sickness, but she was grateful for her light lunch, and that she had not eaten since lunch, as Bonnie tore around mountain curves and barreled down gravel grades. Apparently, the first house was a "little out of the way" - as in eight miles from downtown, four on heavily-rutted gravel roads. Joy noticed upon their arrival that Bonnie had made the trip in ten minutes. Joy had aged at least ten months from the trip.

"Does everyone drive like this around here?" she whispered to Joann, who was calmly unbuckling her seat belt. "It occurs to me I haven't even seen you drive, except downtown."

"I try not to scare anyone too badly."

Bonnie had told them that this house, with a monthly rent of $1100, was the nicest of the four, and sure enough, the Cape Cod-style structure appeared well-kept, with a wooded yard and a beautiful mountain view, visible even through the darkening forest. Joy sighed with relief. It was no Pittsburgh penthouse, but she could deal with a house like this. Then Bonnie opened the door.

Smoke actually came billowing out of it in a small plume, causing all three women to step back involuntarily.

49

"Is there a fire?" Joy gasped, covering her mouth.

"I don't know...I'm going to check," Bonnie said. "It's not like the whole house is on fire yet, but maybe one just started."

"We'll go with you," Joann said.

The three women tiptoed through the living room, which was neatly furnished, quite tidy, and murky with smoke. Joann paused and deliberately inhaled. "Bonnie, I don't think you'll find a fire," she said, coughing. "This is cigarette smoke."

"It couldn't be *all* cigarette smoke!" protested Bonnie. "I was just here three months ago, and the place smelled fine. I've got to check the whole house. If the owners know it caught fire, and I didn't check, they'll have my head on a platter."

Joy and Joann followed her through the rest of the rooms downstairs, still locating nothing, and up the carpeted staircase. Joy thought the smoke was even thicker up there, if that was possible. She wondered if it could have risen from downstairs.

Joann had only been upstairs a few seconds when she began to cough uncontrollably. She leaned against a wall and took a long drink from her ever-present water bottle, but she couldn't stop the spasms of coughing, horrible, hacking coughs Joy had never heard come from a person in real life. "Bonnie, we have to go outside *now*," Joy said, taking her aunt by the arm. Joann made no protest and allowed Joy to lead her downstairs and out the front door. There was a porch swing nearby, and the two women collapsed into it.

"What do you need?" Joy demanded. "Should I call 911?"

Joann held up a hand for Joy to wait and shook her head. She rummaged in her denim purse and found a bag of cough drops, which Joy grabbed. She unwrapped one immediately and gave it to Joann. Joann continued sipping her water as much as possible, and Joy held onto her shoulders to brace her as she coughed. It seemed like an eternity, but the coughing finally subsided, and Joann fell back against the bench, exhausted, with streaming eyes and nose.

Bonnie stepped out on the porch at that moment. "Oh, my, do we need to go to the hospital?" she asked.

"No!" Joann gasped. She wiped her face and coughed again, but regained control quickly.

"Well, if you're sure...anyway, there doesn't seem to be a fire, and I did see several cartons of Marlboros in the master bedroom..." Bonnie said, closing the door.

"It was all cigarette smoke," Joann whispered. "I lived with a chain smoker the first seventeen years of my life. I – I guess I can't tolerate it as well since my pneumonia this time."

"I'm sorry, Joann. I didn't think about how bad that smoke would be for you. I should have insisted you stay in the car or outside once we discovered how bad it was," Bonnie said, locking the door. "Are you sure you'll be okay?"

Joann tried to reply, but began coughing again. Finally, she was able to speak. "Yes, of course. I guess I know what to stay away from now!"

"Let's get back to your home," Joy said. "You need some cough medicine right away, and to get out of this cold air."

"Actually, I was thinking we could take Joann home on our way to see this other rental I have the key for tonight," Bonnie said. "It's on the other side of town, so it would be on our way."

"Thank you, Bonnie," said Joann.

"Are you sure, Aunt Joann?" Joy said as they moved slowly toward the van. "I can stay with you -"

Joann placed her hand on Joy's shoulder. "Yes." Her voice was still quite scratchy but very firm.

More than an hour later, Joy entered her aunt's house very quietly, although it was only seven p.m. She had no idea how Joann might be feeling or if she would even be awake, despite the fact Joann had already begun to feel better by the time they had reached her house. She tiptoed down the entry hall in her socks but had only gone ten feet when she had another sneezing fit. Rats. Or, rather, guinea pigs. So much for being quiet.

"Joy? Are you all right?" Joann called from in the living room. Joy could still hear her coughing, but she sounded much better.

"Yes," Joy said, sounding congested even to herself. She crossed the room to the couch, where Joann reclined with a book. "I think I'm having an – an – aaahchoo! - allergy attack!"

"To the smoke?"

"No, to the – the – rodents in that last house!" Joy said, sniffing. "The house wasn't bad, but they had, like, eleven guinea pigs. Achoo! I guess I'm – allergic." She looked down at Joann. "Are you using all those Kleenexes?"

"No, dear," Joann said, handing her the box and sliding into a sitting position so Joy could join her.

Joy sat and blew her nose gratefully. "This is ridiculous," she said. "I've never sneezed this many times in my – AACHOOO! - life!"

"That's how I am around cats," Joann said. "We couldn't even have barn cats on the farm."

"So – how are you?" said Joy, scrubbing her nose, which was already becoming raw.

"Oh, a bit tired and sore from so much coughing again, but much better. I'm thankful I still have some prescription cough medicine left."

"Has the coughing affected your heartbeat?" said Joy.

"No, no, not in such a short time period. Please don't worry. I'll be fine by morning."

Joy tried to respond, but began sneezing uncontrollably instead.

"Eleven," Joann said when Joy finally stopped.

"Huh?"

"Eleven. You sneezed eleven times...one for each guinea pig," Joann said, mischief sparkling in her eyes. Joy glared at her before giving in to a chuckle – and another sneeze.

"Seriously, Joy, you'd better go shower and change clothes," Joann said, coughing. "The allergy attack will continue until you do. Not to mention, you still reek of cigarettes."

"Oh, yeah, right," Joy said, rising. "I'll go now."

"When you come back, we can eat some chicken soup and watch a chick flick," Joann said. "It beats sitting around cuddling our tissue boxes!"

"Okay...sounds good...and do you have any – Achoo! - allergy medicine?"

"In the medicine cabinet in my bathroom."

Joy hurried directly into her aunt's bathroom, which she'd not yet seen, and began rummaging shamelessly. The cabinet was quite full of homeopathic remedies in addition to a few ominous-looking prescription bottles, so Joy had to stop twice to blow her nose before she finished her search. At last, she located some Zyrtec, hiding behind the contact solution – what? Joann wore contacts? - and she read the label and gulped one down with water from a disposable cup. Then, she plodded back to the other bathroom, sneezing, a bit disillusioned with the state of Vermont in general.

The evening ended up being sort of fun after all. After the chicken soup, which had been frozen from Joann's famous "sick soup" recipe Joy remembered from her summer cold years ago, they'd huddled under an afghan (with the tissues and lemon and honey tea) and watched the latest *Pride and Prejudice*. The romantic ending made Joy cry, and then laugh at herself for crying, and Joann laugh at her. The Zyrtec knocked Joy out by ten, so she went on to bed at the same time as her aunt. She wanted a good night's rest before risking life, limb, lungs, and nasal cavities at the last two rentals in the morning.

Both women were awake and downstairs by eight the next morning. "Good morning, how do you feel?" they said in unison, completely by accident.

"Stopped up, but not sneezing," Joy answered first.

"Hoarse, but not coughing much," said Joann. "I guess we're going to survive."

"Maybe, although I have two more places to see. Honestly, I don't know what I'm going to do. It's no wonder the college has residence halls even for their creative writing master's program students!"

"I'm certainly not sad to be missing this morning's house hunt," Joann confessed. "There's no telling what you'll encounter today."

"I'm bringing my backpack with your allergy medicine, Tylenol, my camera, a change of clothes and shoes, snacks, and three bottles of water, and a flashlight," Joy said. "And I'm braiding my hair. Tight. And putting it into a bun."

"Are you serious?"

"As an allergy attack!"

Bonnie seemed relieved to see Joy at their 9:30 appointment. "I was beginning to worry I'd killed off you and your aunt," she said, only half joking. "Looking for rental properties in this area can be a bit – epic – as my fourteen-year-old says."

"No, we're all right. I'm sure today will be better."

Bonnie dropped her eyes. "I showed you the newer, cleaner homes last night," she said. "I had hoped one of them would actually be acceptable for you. I'm not real hopeful about these."

"Why is the rental market so bad here?"

"It's not too bad if you're looking for a one or two year lease, or an apartment, but the owners have gotten sick of tourists renting single-family houses on the cheap, trashing them all summer and for a week or two in the fall, and dumping them before the first snowfall. Not many people want to stick around to deal with winter maintenance, repairs, and heating bills."

"But I'm doing the opposite!"

"Not many Vermonters are willing to go out on a limb with that much money..."

Joy sighed and wished for the days when she could trust others, even if they were frequently the household staff, to take care of her.

The first home of the morning was a cottage resembling Joann's on the exterior, minus several coats of paint. The resemblance ended there. The yard was full of weeds, doggie deposits, and rusted lawn ornaments. The interior was occupied by one very old woman with blue hair, a senile poodle with lavender ears, and enough knickknacks to sink a medium-sized ship. The décor might have been stylish when Joann was a child. Maybe. If avocado and burnt orange carpet had ever been stylish. A stiff odor of nail polish – gold glitter, for the poodle – clung to the rooms.

The woman, who introduced herself as Maude, talked nonstop to Joy from the time she set foot on the porch until after Bonnie had begun to drive away. By the time they left, Joy had learned that Maude was only moving four doors down to live with her sister

Clorinne, poor dear, who'd suffered a cardiac, that the house was *only* to be rented furnished, and that Maude would be by often to see it was kept clean...and to count her porcelain teapots so's she could be sure none got stoled by the renter...not that *Joy* would do such a terrible thing because she looked like a pure angel – 'cept angels didn't have brown hair. Joy had also been bathed by the poodle's slimy pink tongue, doused in hand sanitizer after she discreetly blew her nose so she wouldn't "infect" the poodle, and regaled with the virtues of all the single men at three different denominations in town.

"Tell me," Joy said, gasping with laughter as Bonnie sped away. "Was that for real?"

"One hundred percent."

"Are there any blue ladies or purple dogs at the next house?" Joy said. "If so, we can just skip it."

"No, the renters just moved out last week. I've heard from another agent that they left it pretty bad."

"Blue ladies and purple dogs are scarier than dirt and dust," Joy said.

The final house was actually near Barre. It looked harmless enough on the outside, but as Joy neared the front door, she actually thought she might be able to smell it – through the door.

Nothing in Joy's relatively-short and quite pampered existence had prepared her for the sights and smells that greeted her in this house. The previous tenants had literally left the house in the middle of their grubby lives...empty beer cans in mounds on the living room floor, rancid food in the kitchen, roaches swarming the kitchen sink, and a random, eighteen-inch hole in the dining room ceiling. Joy stared up through it and saw a cloud that resembled a monkey.

"Let's just leave," Bonnie exclaimed in utter disgust after Joy pointed out the hole. "This place is beyond – well, beyond words."

Joy turned to follow Bonnie out the door and stepped on something more substantial than the dried pizza crusts she'd found before. Bending down, she cried out in alarm. She'd crushed the blunt end of a hypodermic – and it wasn't empty.

"Bonnie, I think I know why they left," Joy said calmly, but inside she was horrified...and grateful for her heavy athletic shoes.

Bonnie glanced at the needle, let out some extremely unprofessional language, and dragged Joy out the door. She slammed it, locked it, double-checked it, and made a beeline for her van.

Bonnie did not speak until they were two miles down the road, and then she pulled over to the shoulder and covered her face and groaned. "What a disaster!" she said. "We're going to have to get a professional cleaning crew in there and pay them triple the norm."

"I just hope it's not a drug house," Joy said, shuddering. "That wouldn't be safe for future tenants!"

"Surely they wouldn't sell drugs in a rental!" Bonnie groaned. "At any rate, I haven't helped you at all. In fact, I may have shaved a decade off your aunt's life. If my mom hears about this, she's going to slaughter me. She thinks Joann Hudson is a saint."

"Don't worry. She won't go tattling. Besides, none of this fiasco was your fault. If I were you, I'd refuse to show short-term rentals anymore. It seems downright dangerous."

"After the last twenty-four hours, I may!"

CHAPTER 7

Joy pounced on her aunt as soon as she arrived home from work that afternoon and shared her harrowing tale. Joann alternated between peals of laughter and utter horror.

"Oh, my, what a day you've had," she said at last. "But what are you going to do about a place to live?"

"I have no idea. I guess I could buy a house and then rent it out after I leave, but I hate to spend that kind of money while I'm unemployed."

"I wish I could help."

"You are helping me! If it weren't for you, I'd be stuck in that dreary motel!"

As if rehearsed, the house phone and Joy's cell rang simultaneously. Joy groaned as she saw her father on the caller ID. As Joann dashed to pick up the kitchen phone, Joy stepped out onto the porch to take the call.

"Sophia, you are to pack your bags and leave immediately. I've located you another real estate position, here in Philadelphia. You begin work on Monday. I've also made a deposit on an apartment for you. It's not quite as nice as yours in Pittsburgh, but it will do for a short time..."

"Wait! Stop!" Joy's voice was finally functioning once more. "I don't want that job or apartment! And I'm not leaving Vermont!"

"You must. Your mother has informed me you are specifically defying me by associating with your uncle's wife. That is simply unacceptable."

"Why did you threaten Aunt Joann?" Joy said, hoping to shock her father from his icy resolve. "Why did you hate her friends so badly?"

"I have no idea what you're talking about. Joann has been filling your mind with trash. She always has been an ignorant, common person."

"Father, if you don't tell me what's going on, I'll find out myself. And don't ever insult her again. She has done you the courtesy of giving you the opportunity to explain yourself."

"Come back to Philadelphia at once, Sophia, or don't come back at all."

Joy sighed. "I'm not coming."

George Carnegie affected a heartfelt sigh. "I suppose I can't keep you from ruining your life – and your aunt's."

"What -"

"Your mother and I want to protect you. What makes you think a woman you hardly know wants you in her life?"

All of Joy's insecurities came rushing back to the surface. "I – I don't need *anyone* to take care of me," she faltered.

"You have no job, no house, no possessions, no husband or boyfriend, no close friends, and no sense. If you stay in Vermont, you'll also have no backup income. I'll see to that."

"Are you disowning me?"

"You'll receive no support from me in the future if you don't return. Tonight!"

"Man, Dad, I'll really miss all that *support*. Especially the *emotional* support!" Joy hung up on her father for the second time in her life. She drew a ragged breath. She was alone...totally alone. Suddenly, a noise behind her caught her attention, and she whirled.

Joann was standing at the screen door, still as the proverbial statue, her hand over her mouth. Crying. For her.

"Did you hear that?" Joy asked. Joann nodded. "All of it?"

"Almost."

"I hate you had to hear it. We were being pretty ugly with each other."

"I'm sorry I listened. I heard your angry voice, and I – I became nosy." Joann sniffed. "Thank you for defending me. I hate I've caused more problems between you and George."

"None of this is your fault, and it's okay you listened to our conversation. I wasn't exactly hiding it – I may have destroyed your reputation with your neighbors."

"Nonsense." Joann rubbed her forehead. "But...I think it is time to clear up the rest of the secrets about my past with your parents."

"You'll tell me what my father did that was so awful and has caused you so many problems?"

"No. That's still not my place. Your father should be the one to tell you, but since he won't, I can take you to someone else who was directly involved."

"Who?"

"Angelique DuPont. How would you feel about visiting the farm this weekend?"

"Oh, Aunt Joann! Really?"

"Yes, as long as Angelique doesn't mind. I've only been back once myself, not long after I moved to Montpelier."

"Won't it be awful for you – to go back?"

"Not so awful. I have moved on. And it's a necessary trip for you. I'll call Angelique now."

Joann disappeared inside, and when she didn't return after ten minutes, Joy ducked inside and went back to the porch with the couch afghan. It was growing frigid again out there, but she was afraid if she stayed inside, she would be too tempted to eavesdrop as well.

Alex found her there thirty minutes later when he drove up quickly in his SUV. "Hello, Joy," he called out, climbing down from the vehicle. "Is your aunt on the phone?"

"Yes, she has been for at least forty minutes."

"Ah, okay. I couldn't get through, and apparently she's let her cell phone die again, so I wanted to check on her."

"She has a cell phone?"

"Yes, I bought her one when she was in the hospital, but she doesn't take it with her very often." Alex sighed. "Sometimes your aunt worries me to death!"

Joy grinned. "I understand."

Alex then inquired about Joy's house-hunting, and his polite questions brought back all the emotions of the past hour back to Joy with a painful rush. "Rotten. It's been rotten," she said, sharing the details rapidly and without humor.

Alex dropped to the porch stairs. "What are you looking for in a rental, Joy?" he said.

"After this week? Not much!" she said. "Hmmm...well, seriously? I'd like something small and clean with some sort of...character or...or...'scope for imagination'..."

"Like Anne of Green Gables, huh?"

Joy's jaw dropped at least two inches.

"Wait, wait. Don't get any idea I'm some kind of super-sensitive male who reads *Anne of Green Gables*. The truth is Jo-Jo forced me on threat of decapitation to watch the movies right after she got home from the hospital. They're fresh in my memory."

"Still – you just got a lot of brownie points with me."

"Anyway, I'm asking because I have an extra house in Woodfield, about ten miles from here. It was my parents' house until they passed away last year. I've been planning to sell it, but there's no point in me even listing it until spring. You're welcome to rent it from me if you'd like, at least until April."

"Oh! Really?! And it's not full of...guinea pigs or purple dogs or – worse?"

"No," Alex chuckled. "Just some plain, old-fashioned furniture I didn't want to put in a storage building. It's not in perfect condition, but it's safe and will keep you warm."

"You'd do that...for me?"

"Joy, I don't know you well personally yet, but your aunt loves you dearly, and I see no reason why not to learn to do the same."

Joy's mind was spinning. She didn't trust her father – hadn't for more than a decade, but logic seemed to correspond with what he'd said – why would a woman like Joann, to whom she could claim no blood relationship, want Joy around? On the other hand, if her father were right, why would not only Joann, but also the people who cared for her, insist that Joy was indeed welcome?

"I'll give it a try," Joy said finally. After all, what did she have to lose? "How much will you charge?"

"I can't say I've considered it, but I wouldn't feel right charging much for such an old place so far from the city. What do you think about - $650 a month with no deposit? If you feel cheated after you move in, we can always lower it."

Joy was appalled by the low figure until she recalled that even the largest house she'd viewed was renting for a mere $1100. She envisioned a tiny country cottage with a claw foot bathtub and peeling wallpaper...maybe that number wasn't abnormally low after all...and a deposit would be a bit unreasonable between friends. She nodded. "I'm sure $650 will be fine."

"Well, I came over tonight to ask you both to dinner again, but maybe you'd rather grab fast food after we look at the house."

"That sounds good to me, but you'd better ask Aunt Joann. She was still on the phone a minute ago. I heard her laugh."

Joy and Alex stepped inside, and Joy went to sit in the living room as Alex headed to the kitchen. Joy realized she needn't have worried about eavesdropping. Her aunt was not speaking English anymore.

Joann and Alex joined Joy in the living room shortly afterward. "Angelique is anxious for us to come," Joann said as she dropped beside Joy on the couch. "She's asked us for Sunday supper, but we can attend services in Windsor if you don't mind getting up so early."

"Oh, wow! That will be so weird," Joy said. "I'll feel fourteen again!"

"Do you want me to come?" Alex asked. "I'm available."

"Thank you, Alex," Joann responded. "But I think we need to make this trip alone. Joy and I have some memories to face."

"If you're sure," he said, putting his arm around her shoulders. The simple gesture made Joy feel a bit lonely – had she ever had anyone to protect her like that?

Suddenly, Joy remembered her own wonderful news. "Oh, I need to tell you!" she said. "My housing problem is solved..." She proceeded to relay the exciting information Alex had given her. Joann was nearly as enthusiastic as Joy.

"Of course!" Joann said. "I never even thought of that. Alex, dear, you're so smart!" He beamed at her self-consciously.

By six, Alex, Joann, and Joy were on their way to Woodfield. Although the sun had already set behind the mountains, Joy could tell the winding country road would be a pleasant drive in full daylight. After a fifteen-minute drive, Alex turned onto a gravel road that paralleled a rushing creek. Tall spruces on either side of the road created a sheltered, safe sensation.

The house was located about a mile from the highway at the junction of the road they'd taken and another gravel road. Joy gasped as Alex pulled into the driveway.

"This is a huge house!" she said, staring at the full-scale farmhouse, complete with wraparound porch, barn, and massive garden plot.

"It's large, but you can close off the part you don't use. It's heated by fireplaces, so that's not difficult to do. My parents always did."

"Alex, I – I can't pay you such a small -" Joy began, but he stopped her.

"Wait until you see the inside," he protested.

The porch creaked as they all walked across it, but it appeared quite stable. Alex handed the key to Joy, who unlocked the heavy wooden door, shoved it open with difficulty, and crept inside. "I'm afraid I only have one flashlight," Alex said, clicking it on. "I'll call to have the utilities turned on again tomorrow, if you'd like." Joy nodded.

She wandered through the large, musty, bitter-cold rooms in a daze, unable to believe this ancient monster would actually be her home in a day or two. It was certainly an interesting place, and an answer to the timid prayers she'd managed to send up, but she kept expecting to run into John Boy Walton or Laura Ingalls Wilder. She sniffed and sighed. Her still-abused nose had begun to run.

"How old is this house?" Joann said as they climbed the solid maple stairs.

"Let's see. My parents said it was 104 years old when they bought it...and that was when I was...twenty...so...1979...so...it was built in 1875. It's one hundred thirty-seven years old."

"Whoa!" Joy said. She opened the door to the upstairs bathroom. Claw foot tub...awkward shower.

By the end of the tour, Joy had definitely decided she could deal with the house, which was in good condition and quite clean considering its months of vacancy. Over hamburgers at McDonald's, something Joy hadn't touched in years, she made plans to go clean the house the next day before Bible study, move her few things in on Thursday, and buy the supplies and groceries she needed on Thursday afternoon. She hoped to begin living there by Thursday night.

"Are you sure you don't want to wait to clean until Saturday, or even Thursday evening, when I can help you?" Joann said. "That's an enormous place to clean by yourself, especially with a year's worth of dust."

"I'm sure. I'm just so ready to get settled! I mean, one of the reasons I came to Vermont was to write, and I haven't been able to write a sentence!"

"You'll need help getting some of the furniture down from the attic," Alex pointed out. "The beds, for example, are still up there from when I had the floors refinished this summer. I didn't want the mattresses to absorb the odors of polyurethane and such."

"I'm sure Joy and I could manage," Joann said. "Each piece of a bed is not so heavy by itself."

Alex stared at her as if she'd grown horns. "Are you kidding? You got out of the hospital a week ago, Jo-Jo, and you plan to move beds? Not to mention that's not all that's up there!"

Joann sighed. "It was more than a week ago, and I wasn't in the hospital for my arms."

"I am going to find a man to help Joy," Alex said. "If she can't wait for me to get off work Thursday night, we'll find someone else."

"Hey, what about Paul, that unemployed guy at church?" Joy said suddenly, recognizing Alex would not concede to letting the women lift the furniture on their own. "He might not be busy since he has no job."

"Paul is always busy," Joann said. "He may not get a regular paycheck, but he's rarely idle. At any rate, I'm sure he'll be happy to help if he can. Good idea, Joy."

Joy was at her new place with a jeep full of cleaning supplies by eight the next morning. Although her deep cleaning experience was fairly minimal, her determination to do the job herself kept her busy despite her ignorance – and a very stuffy nose. By the time Joann drove up at four-thirty to give her a hand for a few minutes, Joy had cleaned all the rooms she planned to use regularly except the bathroom, which she was scrubbing, and the kitchen. She also had a raging headache.

"Thanks for coming to help me," Joy said, hugging her aunt. "You certainly didn't have to."

"Of course I did," Joann said. "I couldn't let you have all the fun."

"Fun? Huh..." mumbled Joy, blowing her nose once more.

Joann eyed her. "I'll finish up in here and then scrub the kitchen up a bit. You take some Tylenol and sit down and rest."

"I didn't bring any medicine," Joy said, rubbing her eyebrows, which ached also.

"There's aspirin in my purse. Come on. Take a rest." Joann took the filthy sponge from Joy's hand and turned her toward the door of the bathroom.

Joy tried to resist but finally realized she felt too badly to do anything but obey. Five minutes later, she had doped herself up on aspirin and a cough drop – because her throat hurt too – and was reclined in the big comfortable chair in the living room, watching from a distance as Joann began to tackle the kitchen. She had already finished the bathroom.

Joy's headache and sore throat improved as the aspirin took effect, but her humiliation increased. She decided few things were as embarrassing as observing an efficient woman clean a kitchen when you were hopelessly inexperienced yourself. In Pittsburgh, "cooking" had meant assembling her own sandwich or salad, which Joy had avoided as often as possible. "Cleaning the kitchen" had meant loading the dishwasher with spoons and mugs and wiping drops of coffee from the counter.

By the time Joann had finished thirty minutes later, Joy was ready to leave and had gathered her purse, backpack, and the supplies she'd borrowed from her aunt. She was also ready to slurp down a few cups of strong, hot coffee. The yogurt and bottle of water from noon had long since disappeared from her system, although she didn't feel hungry.

Joy did manage to eat a healthy portion of the grilled chicken and avocado salad Joann prepared for supper, and felt better enough to take a quick shower and go to Bible study. In her former life, Joy would have seen her hard day, discouragement, and runny nose as perfectly good excuses to skip Bible study. Tonight, she opened her mouth to attempt to justify them to Joann...and could not...

Paul was definitely present at the Bible study – along with a scant fifteen others – and cheerfully led the two songs that accompanied the brief message before class time started. Joy found herself nervous about asking him to move her furniture when she barely knew him – such presumption! Maybe she could pay him, she thought as she tried to force a few notes from her throat.

But Joy needn't have worried. As soon as the Bible study concluded, Alex made a beeline for Paul. "Hi, Paul," Joy heard him say. "Do you think you'd have time to do a favor for my girls tomorrow?"

Joy did not hear Paul's answer. She was still reacting to Alex's words. Yes, she'd been someone's "girl," her father's daughter and Calvin's girlfriend, but never had anyone offered such selfless kindness when they claimed her. Joy sniffed. Must not cry. Must not cry! She tuned in to Alex's voice again.

"Joy can't get it down on her own, and I prefer my Joann healthy and in one piece, but I'm scheduled to see patients until eight p.m."

"No problem," Paul said. "I'm driving Miss Louella to an appointment at four, but I don't have any commitments before that. I'll go see what time Joy needs me."

Joy straightened, wiped her eyes, and started flipping through her aunt's Bible. It was suddenly very important to her that Paul not think her too shy or helpless to carry on her own conversations.

"Hi," Paul said as he approached her. "Hope I'm not interrupting your studies."

Joy looked up very fast. "Uh, no...no...um...hi!" she spluttered. Man, his eyes were *blue* behind his glasses.

"I heard you needed a hand with your furniture," Paul said. "What time would it be convenient for me to come?

"Oh, maybe about two o'clock, if you can," Joy said, hoping

she wasn't blushing. "I think there are only a few pieces to move down one flight of stairs."

"I'm all yours until 3:30," Paul promised, smiling.

"Do you know how to get there? It's Alex's parents' old house in Woodfield."

"Oh, yes. I've been there several times. See you about two then!" Before Joy could even thank him, Paul was gone, winding his way through the folding chairs to Menthol Lady, who he escorted cautiously out the door. Joy wrinkled her forehead in confusion, then sneezed, the pressure in her nose driving all further thoughts of freckly young men from her consciousness.

CHAPTER 8

The next morning, Joy could hardly stand to drag herself out of bed before Joann left for work. Her throat was raw, her congestion had settled into her sinuses, and she suspected she was running a low-grade fever.

"What if I'm contagious?" Joy wondered for the first time. She shuddered at the thought of all the people she'd exposed if she was and decided to keep blaming Monday's allergy attack. She swallowed two Tylenol and another Zyrtec, making a mental note to buy some allergy medicine of her own tonight when she went shopping.

Joy made it downstairs right before Joann left, just in time to confirm her aunt would come over to the farmhouse as soon as her work was finished. She avoided breathing on Joann just in case, and congratulated herself on an acting job well-done. She'd certainly faked good health before; last winter she'd shown seven homes and signed a contract while sick with the flu.

Next, Joy loaded her jeep with the few belongings she'd unpacked while staying in Joann's house. An abrupt rush of dizziness as she bent to pick up the box she'd set on the ground nearly knocked her off her feet. Maybe she should go find a thermometer...

Joy searched Joann's bathroom for several minutes, locating every health and beauty aid her aunt had purchased in the past decade, but she could not find a thermometer. She was ready to give up when she noticed a promising pile of objects on the bedside table as she passed through the bedroom. Feeling like an intruder, she investigated, and sure enough, under a pair of glasses, Joy found the thermometer.

It registered exactly 100 degrees, so Joy carefully washed and dried it, replaced it on the table, and pronounced herself sick. She considered calling off her day's activities and going back to bed...but she couldn't tolerate the idea of such a delay. Better to just fake it a few more hours until she was on her own, and then recover at her own pace.

Joy had finished unloading her vehicle – ever so slowly – when Paul arrived.

"Oh, hi, is it two o'clock already?" she said, smoothing her hair.

"Just one-thirty, but I realized you might have a few more things you needed help with," he said.

"Well, thank you, but I'm not sure..." Joy's voice broke and she began coughing – where had that come from?

"Hey, you don't sound like you feel so well!" Paul said. "Are you sick?"

"I had an allergy attack on Monday," Joy said, staring at the ground. "It sort of hasn't gone away."

"Well, I'm no doctor, but you sound like you've progressed beyond that. Why aren't you resting at your aunt's house? I'm sure she's not kicking you out!"

"First of all, if I'm contagious, I need to stay away from her of all people. She insists she's fine but she must still be weak from her pneumonia. And also, it's just time for me to be on my own again. I'm very independent."

Paul grinned. "Whatever you say. Why don't you sit down and boss me around, then? I don't know where your furniture goes."

Joy agreed to do just that, and within five minutes, she had settled herself in a straight chair at the base of the attic stairs. It bothered her to sit and watch Paul work as if she were some sort of princess, but he had been persistent, and she felt too sick to argue. Her cough was getting worse, deep and productive. Also, if Joy was perfectly honest with herself, it wasn't too terrible to have a young man taking care of her, even if he was rather ordinary-looking...and unemployed.

Joy sneaked another glance at him as he wrestled the second full-size mattress down the narrow staircase. He was certainly strong, but as far removed from "her type" as east was from west. Calvin Barrett had been her type for sure...tall, slender, and sophisticated, with a sleek, tan complexion, a goatee, and meticulously-groomed blond hair. And Paul, while not unattractive, was, well, shorter, thicker, and much paler, except those childish freckles! His hair was dark and tousled and in desperate need of a trim. Cal had taken pains to be sure no aspect of his physical appearance was ever in desperate need of anything.

Suddenly, Joy realized with a start that Paul was speaking to her. "I think that's all the furniture," he was saying. "What else can I do for you? Bring you some medicine, maybe?"

"No, I have some," she said. "But wouldn't you like to sit down and rest a few minutes? You've worked very hard, and I really appreciate it."

Paul hid a smile. It had been many years since moving a few pieces of furniture had seemed like a big job for him, but he wasn't about to turn down the invitation – an opportunity to chat with a beautiful Christian woman near his age. He pulled two highly-weathered rocking chairs out onto the front porch, then asked, "Oh – is it too cold for you out here?"

"No, I'll be fine with a coat," Joy said. "Besides, you've probably worked up a sweat. You might like to cool off."

"Yeah, that's me...Mr. Sweaty," Paul laughed. "I'm so warm-natured. I hate hot weather."

"Are you from this area?" Joy said.

"I grew up in Stowe, so yes, pretty close by. Have you been there?"

"No, I've never been anywhere except...let's see...the airport in Burlington, White River Junction, Windsor, Barre, and Montpelier. None of the tourist places for sure, except a couple of covered bridges near Windsor."

"Maybe you can do some traveling with your aunt," Paul said.

"Oh, yes, I forgot, we did go on a drive into the edge of the National Forest," Joy said. She coughed. "We went to a waterfall down in a *pit*." She sighed. "I can't even keep track of my life these days."

Paul patted her arm, instinctively comforting her, and brushed her bare wrist. He frowned, and placed his hand on her again. "Joy, you have a fever!"

"Oh, just a little," she said.

"Does Alex know you're sick? He's a pediatrician, I know, but he could probably prescribe you something."

"No," Joy admitted. "But I don't need to see a doctor. I'll be fine soon."

Paul lowered his eyebrows but did not press the issue any further.

"I can't offer you anything cold – or hot – to drink," Joy said. "I haven't gone shopping yet. I think I'll put that off until tomorrow."

"Thanks, but I'm not thirsty," Paul said. He held back a sigh. So much for getting to know each other...robots had probably had more successful conversations!

After a few more minutes of small talk, Paul left for his driving appointment. Although Joy had been extremely grateful for his assistance, she was relieved to see him leave. She simply had no energy to make friends or be entertaining. Joy removed her tennis shoes, padded to the ancient but surprisingly comfortable couch, and stretched out on it. She dozed off almost immediately.

Joann called just after four, jolting Joy from her feverish sleep. "Hi, Joy," she said. "Enjoying your new home?"

"Uh...I guess," Joy said, beginning to cough.

"Awww...you're sick!" Joann said. "Why don't you just come on back until you feel like unpacking?"

"No, I'll be fine," Joy said with as much enthusiasm as she could muster.

"What are your symptoms, kiddo?"

"Well, my throat is raw, I have a productive cough, my noise is so stopped up I can hardly blow it, my face hurts, I have a fever, and I'm sort of – weak, I think. And cranky."

Joann laughed. "I'll take your word on that last one, but it sounds like you might have a sinus infection. I used to get those after allergy attacks before I knew I was allergic to cats."

"Maybe. I don't remember the last time I had a sinus infection...but, then, I've never had an allergy attack before."

"Well, I have some good natural remedies you're welcome to try. I always use them before I try antibiotics or anything like that."

"Okay, why not," Joy said. "It's better than being totally zonked out on Zyrtec."

"I'll bring by some echinacea and Ziacam...and some other one I can't recall the name of...in just a few minutes, dear. In the meantime, you should drink some juice. The vitamins will help even if you just have a head cold."

"I haven't gone shopping yet," Joy said, wincing.

"Joy Carnegie! Have you eaten today?"

"Uh...no, I guess not. I haven't been hungry, and I'm too dizzy to drive."

"Have you drunk anything?"

"I had some water this morning when I took Zyrtec and Tylenol."

Joann exhaled loudly. "Okay – I'll be by in about forty-five minutes with your supper and tomorrow's breakfast, as well as the remedies. But Joy? You really need to take care of yourself. You're too thin as it is."

"You'll be exposed to my germs," Joy protested, annoyed at receiving a lecture from someone who regularly risked her own health.

"I doubt you're contagious. Besides, you can't just lie there and starve and dehydrate."

Joy groaned in defeat and fell back against the couch cushions. She basked in her frustration for several minutes...how dare Joann scold Joy about being thin when she herself had probably lost twenty pounds since Joy had last seen her? How dare she admonish Joy about taking chances with her health when she herself was risking a serious relapse by exposing herself to Joy's germs? And – how dare Joann challenge Joy's ability to care for herself – her independence – when she clung to her own independence so ferociously?

Joann was late. After an hour, Joy dialed her aunt's home phone number, but no one answered. Next, she tried her cell, doubting Joann was carrying it, but she received no answer either. Joy tried to assure herself that Joann was surely on her way, and had lost track of time cooking or couldn't find something, but she did begin to feel nervous.

As darkness fell, she also grew quite cold – and cold with fear as she realized this house was heated by a wood stove and wood

71

fireplaces, and she had no wood...nor did she have any tool with which to chop wood...nor did she have the knowledge or strength to chop it. Joy shivered, and wrapped her only blanket closer around herself. The temperature would likely fall below freezing tonight, and she had no heavy coat, no gloves, no heat, and only one blanket...and a fever...and no hot food...or food of any sort.

Joy's anger toward her aunt quickly dissipated; it was true – she'd done a poor job of taking care of herself. Soon, sheer panic set in. Joy realized with a nauseating thud that she was alone in a huge, old house, who knew how far from any neighbors, too sick to leave safely, with no provisions...and no common sense. Only three people knew she was there, and two of them she'd just met. The third was missing. She had no job, no friends, no Vermont bank account, and no blood relatives to support her in her life choices. Joy sneezed so violently her ears stopped up, and she began to sob. What had she done?

After a few minutes, it occurred to Joy that she did have God. He was her heavenly Father and promised to hear her prayers...but would he listen when she'd given Him only occasional attention since college? And Joy knew God was supposed to be perfect, and without sin, but would He really help a dumb, snotty-faced girl like herself when she had been so lackadaisical toward Him? Her earthly father had received many more years of obedience and open love from her, but he certainly didn't listen to her. Joy took a chance and prayed for herself and her aunt anyway.

She felt a little better afterward and decided to go find her Bible. She had to pause twice on the stairs to keep from passing out, but she managed to locate her box of books, open it, and retrieve the small, pink, lightly-used volume she'd been given shortly after her birth. It was a King James Version, full of the Shakespearean lingo she had so despised in high school and college, but she had investigated a couple of modern paraphrases and thought they seemed irreverent somehow, so she'd stuck to the tiny-print KJV.

Joy had collapsed on the couch again and was reading Psalm 23 when she heard a car crunching down the short driveway. She jumped to her feet, nearly fell down, and staggered out onto the porch, the cold night air triggering a coughing fit.

"Joy!" Joann exclaimed, hurrying to the porch, her arms full of bags and packages. "Get back inside! You'll freeze!"

"What happened?" croaked Joy, staring at her aunt, whose braid had come undone and whose face bore streaks of mud.

"What – oh, yes, I am a mess, aren't I?" Joann said matter-of-factly, dumping her armload onto the kitchen counter. "I had a flat tire about five miles back, and my spare was flat too. Sorry I'm late. Let's get some food and liquid in you, dear."

"What – did you do?" stammered Joy, sinking into a chair at the kitchen table.

Joann glanced at her in surprise, then returned to her work, unloading and organizing. "I pumped up the spare and then changed the tire. It took me a few minutes longer than usual because I lost two of the lug nuts and had to hunt them in the bushes."

Joy wondered tiredly if a lug nut could possibly be related to a macadamia nut, and what it had to do with changing a tire. "*You* changed the tire?"

"Yes – have you never learned how?" Joann said, placing three small bottles in front of Joy. "Take one of each and let them dissolve under your tongue," she instructed in an undertone.

Joy obeyed mechanically before answering. "No, I have no idea how to change one."

Joann sighed. "I can't believe your father let you go off to live in another city without teaching you how to change a tire!" Fortunately, Joann did not seem to expect a response.

In less than ten minutes, Joann had set the table for two and placed a steaming bowl of chicken soup and a cup of tea at each of the places. "If you aren't used to cooking much, you might want a microwave," Joann said. "This stove isn't the easiest character to operate." Suddenly, she rubbed her hands together and shivered.

"Aren't you cold, Joy?"

"Yes, there's no heat," Joy said. "It's wood heat, and I forgot about that until a few minutes ago."

"Well, the kitchen stove can warm us until we're done eating," Joann said, shaking her head. "I wish I'd thought of this before I left.

Oh, well. We'll come up with something."

Perhaps the sinus remedies were already taking effect, or perhaps the chicken soup and tea were calming Joy's body, but her panic continued to subside as she ate slowly. Perhaps it was also comforting, despite her desire for independence, to be nursed by someone caring and capable. By the end of her second bowl of soup, Joy no longer felt so alone in the world or as afraid of her immediate future. She even found herself confiding in Joann about her problems with praying.

"It's only understandable that it's hard for you to trust God when you've suffered from your earthly parents," Joann said.

"Yes, I guess." Joy coughed. "But that's not an excuse, is it? Lots of people have bad relationships with their fathers – or no fathers at all."

"No, it's not. You're exactly right. But you shouldn't criticize yourself for struggling – only for being unwilling to struggle."

"So you're saying if I do my best, God will see that?"

"Something like that."

"But I haven't been doing my best for a long time. I don't deserve love and protection and blessings!"

"None of us deserve those things," Joann said. "But God gives them to us anyway. Don't you think His gift is worth an awful lot of effort on our part?"

"Yeah...it is. Look, Aunt Joann, can you show me a few Bible verses to help with panicking – or, not panicking? I'm feeling so overwhelmed right now."

"Of course. Let me see your Bible." Joy retrieved the Book she'd put aside when Joann arrived. Joann opened it and carefully flipped some pages.

"My, what small print!" she said. "How can you stand to read this?"

Joy smiled slightly. "I have perfect vision."

"Well, I don't, and neither will you by the time you reach your next birthday if you keep reading this." Joann squinted. "I'll give you one of my extra Bibles tomorrow. I hope you don't mind a different version."

"That would be amazing...as long as it's not one of those versions that says, like, and Jesus said, 'Yo! Dude! What's up?'"

Joann rolled her eyes. "Certainly not," she said. "I think I have an extra New American Standard. It's more modern than the KJV, but still an exact translation. And the print is not so tiny you'll blind yourself."

"Oh, thank you," said Joy, her fears lifting further. She'd never felt excited about a Bible before...

Joann had written down several verses and was washing the dishes she'd brought over as Joy read the verses when they heard a car drive up.

"Is that Alex?" Joy said.

"No, he's still working. I'll go check."

Joy felt a bit alarmed at the prospect of a mysterious night visitor, although it was only 7:00, and a bit of dread at the thought of spending her nights alone in such an isolated place. She heard Joann talking normally outside, as well as a male voice that somehow seemed familiar. She opened the kitchen door and heard Joann say,

"Thank you for rescuing us. I was about ready to go out and start breaking branches off the bushes."

"Who is it?" called Joy hoarsely.

"It's Paul, and he's brought a load of wood. He's going to split it for you so you'll have heat."

Joy padded across the cold wooden floor in her sock feet so she could see him. Sure enough, there he stood, in a plaid flannel shirt, his breath making puffs of steam in the air.

"How did you know?" Joy said.

"I didn't see any wood this afternoon, and I didn't figure you'd be well enough to find any. There's also some peanut butter and jelly sandwiches in the pickup if you're hungry – afraid I don't have a lot at home right now."

Joy stared at him so long he grew uncomfortable. "I should probably start chopping so you can get back inside," he began.

"Why?" Joy said. "Why did you do this for me? I'm nobody to you."

Paul raised his eyebrows. "You're my sister in Christ, and

75

you're a lady, and you needed wood. Those are plenty of reasons. And it's not much – you'll need more in a week."

"Thank you," Joy whispered. She found herself wanting to throw her arms around him in gratitude, so she stayed completely still instead. Finally, Paul smiled awkwardly and turned to unload his pickup, and Joann gently steered Joy toward the door.

To Joy's relief, Paul left as soon as he had split and stacked her wood. She felt very humiliated by her response to his kind gesture and she dreaded the idea of having to sit in forced polite conversation with him so quickly afterward.

It took almost two hours for Joy to get the hang of operating the stove and fireplaces. Joann showed her patiently again and again until she felt confident Joy would do well on her own. Throughout the process, visions of fireplace mishaps in *Little House on the Prairie* danced in Joy's head, but Joann assured her Alex had had the chimneys inspected and cleaned recently (as well as the wiring and plumbing) and everything was in order and perfectly safe.

"Now," Joann said as they descended the stairs to the living room again. "How are you feeling?"

"Better," Joy said. "I'm still very congested, but I don't have as much pressure and I'm not so weak."

"Good! If you do really have a sinus infection, those remedies will continue working. Your congestion won't dry up immediately like it might with an antibiotic, but you'll feel much better by tomorrow, I'd imagine."

"Thank you so much!"

"You're very welcome. Also, there are two cinnamon rolls in the fridge for your breakfast, as well as some milk, and I think Paul has taken care of your lunch. Would you like to go grocery shopping after I get off tomorrow...if you're up to it, of course?"

"Yes, that sounds great. I'm sure I could take myself, though, if you have better things to do."

"No, I'm free. Besides, you might want my top secret advice on where to buy groceries!"

Joy smiled. "You bet!"

"Can you think of anything else you need before I leave?"

"No...just keep your cell phone on you, please. This house is so isolated."

"I guess you haven't had a chance to explore the area," Joann commented. "If you continue on Hummingbird Lane, there are three or four houses over the hill from here. And if you turn onto Wagon Creek Road, the town of Woodfield is located maybe a half mile or less away, across the covered bridge."

"Well, that still sounds pretty isolated to me, as a city woman, but it's better than I thought." Joy began coughing and could not say any more.

"Oh, I almost forgot. I also brought you tea, lemon, and honey for that cough," Joann added. "Anyway, do you need me to stay with you tonight? I could run home and grab my toothbrush and my medicine and be back in half an hour."

Joy glanced around the old-fashioned home. The aroma of chicken soup hung in the warming air, and the place seemed much less frightening than it had earlier. "No, I'll be all right," she said. "Thanks entirely to you and Paul."

Joann hugged her before Joy could protest on the grounds of germs. "I'll see you tomorrow before five. And *eat*, dear, or you'll feel completely nasty again, okay?"

Joy promised to eat and stood by the door and watched as Joann reversed expertly down the driveway and drove away. Then, she banked the stove and living room fireplace, grabbed her Bible, and plodded slowly upstairs. She sighed in relief when she saw her bed – Joann had somehow found the time to slip up here and make it up for her with Joy's single set of sheets. Joy bypassed the bathtub and, for the first time in her adult life, climbed into bed without undressing and went to sleep. It was ten p.m.

CHAPTER 9

It was almost eight when Joy finally woke for the first time. She blinked at the brilliant sunlight streaming into the curtain-less upstairs window and began moving slowly. She'd grown stiff from nearly ten hours in one position without moving. Her face was stiff too – from dried drool. Revolting.

Joy lifted her head – which didn't hurt – and coughed experimentally. Whoa – still plenty of congestion, but everything felt much better, and she was sure her fever was gone. She'd never doubt the power of homeopathy again. Now for a long, hot bath, and maybe she'd actually feel human once more.

By the time 4:30 rolled around, Joy felt a sense of accomplishment. She'd managed to unpack her meager belongings, make a grocery list for that evening, and eat breakfast *and* lunch...her first cinnamon roll since college and her first peanut butter sandwich since childhood. She'd also taken another dose of the sinus remedies followed by a short nap, and her coughing was growing far less frequent. When Joann arrived shortly before five, Joy was dressed and ready for adventure.

"You look healthier this evening!" Joann called out as she climbed from her jeep.

"No kidding! I don't feel like a zombie anymore," Joy said. "I'm ready for some serious shopping!"

"Great! Let me just put these recipes on your counter before I forget. I wrote down a few of my favorites during lunch today."

Joy took the small cards and scanned the smooth cursive. "Oooh...Asian chicken salad! That sounds good – and healthy. I want to make that soon."

"May I?" Joann said, a pen posed over the list she'd noticed on the counter.

"Oh, yeah, sure. I'm glad you saw that. I would have walked right out without it."

Joann added the ingredients for the salad to Joy's list, glanced at the rest of it, and started to laugh.

"What?"

"Your list just – makes me laugh!"

"Why?"

Joann regained control of herself and read aloud from the list, "Some sort of protein, vegetables, fruit, something for breakfast, cleaning stuff, and Aromatica Coffee, Colombian or Venezuelan Blend or Java Town African Blend."

"I'm a coffee snob. What can I say?"

"Did you ever cook in Pittsburgh?"

"Um...well, I cooked rice. And toast. And once in a while I made a salad, if I didn't have time to buy one from a restaurant."

Joann bit her lip. "Joy, this grocery shopping trip is going to be dreadful, isn't it?"

Joy nodded sheepishly. "Yeah, probably. I really haven't spent more than ten minutes on a single trip to a grocery store since, well, since my last trip to Vermont, probably. Are there any restaurants in Woodfield?"

"I think you can buy pizza and pretzels from the gas station," she said. "But that's all. And I imagine the pizza is oilier than the fuel."

Joy sighed and scooped up her list. "Let's go. I'm sure you'd like to be done shopping before midnight."

As Joann navigated the winding roads back to Montpelier, Joy realized she had never even ridden with her aunt other than their three-minute ride from the library the first day she'd seen her...could it have only been a week ago? Fortunately, although Joann wasted no time, her driving lacked the utter terror of the realtor's. Joy leaned back and relaxed.

The largest grocery store in the Montpelier area, Price Chopper, seemed comparable to Pittsburgh's, although Joy did not recognize the name. She realized the inadequacy of her list as soon as she had selected her coffee, the ingredients for the Asian salad...and nothing else. "Aunt Joann," Joy admitted. "I don't even know if I like this stuff or not." She indicated the rows of canned vegetables. "My mother has a cook, but I never went shopping with her. And I have no clue about things like spices."

"Well, you might want to start out with basic raw ingredients, like fresh produce and plain meats," Joann said. "You can experiment with flavors, but it's hard to ruin fresh food if you just add a little salt or pepper and eat simply. It's also very easy to stick to a budget that way."

Joy stared at her. "Oh, right, a budget. I – I guess I should make one of those...soon."

"Also," Joann continued. "I would be glad to give you a few cooking lessons if you'd like."

"Yes, please!" Joy said. "I mean, I literally might starve living way out there with no restaurants. I didn't consider that angle of living in the middle of nowhere!"

Joann, who had been fourteen before she remembered eating in a restaurant, just grinned.

The two women bought Joy enough fresh groceries for a week as well as some basic staples. They also bought cleaning supplies, although Joy secretly expected to have to buy more soon. Surely she couldn't really clean nearly everything with vinegar and baking soda!

As they left the store for the jeep, a blast of cold wind hit them, causing Joy to have her first coughing fit in an hour. "Oh!" she shivered, zipping up her denim jacket. "The temperature just plummeted!"

"Yeah, the higher elevations may get some snow," Joann said. She studied Joy's jacket, shoes, and thin socks. "Do you want to go clothes shopping tomorrow in Burlington? I'm afraid you'll get sick again if you go much longer without a proper coat and boots."

"Oh, I'm a pain to shop with," Joy protested. "Especially now I'm choosing clothes based on need and preference instead of Pittsburgh fashion rules. And you've spent so much time helping me already!"

Joann placed the last bag of groceries in the back of the jeep and closed the hatch. "Well – maybe you should research coats and boots on the internet – or maybe you already have. But unless you're extremely warm-natured, you'll want to buy good quality items, and the clothing stores in Montpelier are overpriced."

Joy sighed. "On second thought, I – I guess we should go together. I have the feeling my life here will generally be easier if I listen to you."

"I've never lived in any other climate, so I do know how to stay comfortable in the winter," Joann said. "But I certainly don't have to go with you. You're an intelligent and capable adult. I just thought it might be fun to do something other than my routine. I'm afraid my life must seem boring to you."

"Then we'll make a girl's day of it – and have fun," Joy decided. "But let's sleep in first. I'm exhausted from this shopping trip!"

It was late the following night when Joann dropped off Joy at the farmhouse. The house was frigid when she entered, so she pulled on her new coat as she struggled to feed the stove and fireplaces with wood. After several attempts, she succeeded and flopped down onto the couch to survey her purchases – an expensive but simply-styled blue coat fit for an Eskimo; lined boots with heavy tread; two more pairs of used jeans; warmer pajamas; old-fashioned long johns; and five pairs of low-temperature resistant socks. She'd grab a few more thick sweaters from a Walmart and be set in her wardrobe for the winter.

Joy turned her thoughts to the next day. Throughout the flurry of house-hunting, moving, a sinus infection, and two days of shopping, she'd had scant opportunity to ponder their upcoming trip to Windsor. She felt herself growing nervous. The memories of her summer on the farm marched unchecked across her mind...and she knew actually going back would trigger even more of them. She could hardly imagine visiting the farm without the gentle presence of her uncle John. And if it would be so difficult for her, how much more painful would the memories be for Joann? Watching her suffer would be the worst feeling of all.

She dreaded the information Angelique would give her, but she felt a sense of upcoming relief as well. By tomorrow afternoon, she might finally understand what had happened to make her father despise Joann.

CHAPTER 10

Joy was still half asleep when Joann arrived the next morning at eight. "Thanks for picking me up," she said between yawns. "We could have used my car instead."

"No offense, Joy, but I don't care to bump out to the farm in your jeep. My old backside hurt for three days after our trip to the waterfall last weekend!" Joann said.

Joy giggled. "Mine too. I'll get the shocks replaced soon. I promise!"

"In your backside?" asked Joann.

Joy rolled her eyes, and they left Woodfield laughing.

They drove into the parking lot of the tiny church building in Windsor eighty minutes later. "It – it looks exactly the same!" Joy said. "Like I've gone back in time over a decade!"

"It *does* look about the same, and last I heard, the people are about the same too. Do you remember many of them?

"No – I have very few memories of anyone except you and Uncle John. I can't even recall Angelique very well."

"You know she doesn't attend here, right?"

"No – I thought she went to church with you..." Joy wrinkled her forehead in confusion.

"She's never come, despite the fact we were as close as sisters, but she knows we'll be here until the fellowship meal is done. Then, we'll go to her house on the farm."

"Which is your old house, right?"

"Right. Now – I know it's still very early, but there are already several people here. Are you ready to go in?"

"I – I think so."

The Bible study and services, while following the same basic pattern as those in Montpelier, lacked visible enthusiasm. The singing was almost dismal, even when the fifty members were singing about hope and heaven, and Joy found herself wishing for Paul's spirited song-leading. Joann tried to sing alto, as no one else seemed to be straying from some rendition of the melody, but after two verses of the first song, she gave up, winked discreetly at Joy, and fell back into her typical quiet soprano. The sermon was far from uplifting either – a rigid outline of information about eating meat sacrificed to idols in biblical times. Joy realized with a sudden jolt of astonishment that Joann had probably been baptized into this very congregation – but maybe they'd had a little more energy back then. It was hard to imagine the tired little group of people attracting new members.

After the service was finally over, everyone trooped down to the basement/fellowship hall for a hearty meal. Joy eyed the tables of calorie-laden, home-style cooking and winced. The waistband on her dress pants was definitely growing uncomfortable, but she had no intentions of going up a size until she was at least...forty or something. She surveyed the vegetable choices but didn't find anything worth giving up honey glazed ham and cheesy potatoes and homemade macaroni and cheese. She didn't realize she'd sighed aloud until Joann whispered, "You can't diet at a fellowship meal, dear heart." Joy sighed again and filled her plate. Yet another reason to learn how to cook for herself...fat by fellowship meal!

In Joy's mind, she looked very much like the awkward, long-legged teenager who had visited Vermont a decade ago, especially with her natural hair color and face devoid of makeup. Either she was wrong or the church members had short memories; none of them recognized her.

Almost every five minutes, a smiling older person or two would walk up to Joy and Joann and say one of three first sentences - "Joann! Where have you been keeping yourself?" or "Joann! You're looking so young still!" or "Joann! You've hardly changed a bit – and look at me!" Then, the members would ask, "And who is this little lady with you?" and express shock that she was little Joy, all grown up. And their third and fourth sentences were inevitably, "Ohhh...we sure do miss you and John. This church isn't the same without you."

By round five or six of this routine, Joy would have gladly stood on the table and made a public announcement that yes, Joann was here and looking young and missing her deceased husband and yes, Joy was back after more than ten years and an adult now, but she smiled and nodded and chewed as Joann fielded conversation after conversation. Eventually, it occurred to Joy that her uncle had been loved beyond measure in this congregation of chatty people, and also that they still cared very much for her aunt. And, Joy reflected, love was a lot more important than carrying a tune or speaking eloquently.

It was 2:00 by the time Joann and Joy could break away from their old friends and leave for the farm. Joy stared anxiously out the window as Joann navigated Highway 44 west of Windsor and then turned left onto Back Mountain Road, on the west side of Ascutney Peak. Frost heaves had almost destroyed the narrow paved road, and although Joann drove slowly, the bumps jarred the jeep quite violently.

After two miles, they turned onto Singing Star Lane, the private drive leading to the farm as well as the DuPont's old farm. This road dropped steeply for a quarter of a mile through the dense woods and past the DuPont's old house and ended abruptly at Joann's old farm. Joy, who had been growing steadily more excited as they neared the end of their trip, stared as she climbed stiffly from the vehicle. The house hadn't really changed either, but it looked so small and weather-beaten! The screen door slammed as three tall boys in overalls dashed outside and stopped short at the sight of Joy. Their petite mother stepped out after them.

"Joann!" she called out in a musical voice. "You are here at last!"

Joy watched in amusement as Angelique and Joann ran into each other's arms, talking in French and laughing and crying all at once. Suddenly, Joy felt so – plain and boring and unemotional and – American – next to the frantic greetings of Angelique and her aunt. She glanced at the boys – all adolescents – and grinned. They were staring at the two women with a mixture of amazement and utter humiliation.

Suddenly, Joann wiped her eyes and became herself again and calmly re-introduced Joy once to Angelique and her three sons, Pierre, Jr., Hugo, and Jean Marie, ages seventeen, fifteen, and fourteen. Joy shook hands with them solemnly, but they hardly looked at her as they mumbled polite statements in voices free from their mother's French accent.

"They were not expecting Joy to be a beautiful young woman," Angelique said, rubbing her knuckles on Pierre, Jr.'s black head. "And now, they are shy."

Joy felt embarrassed, but Joann just hugged each of the teenagers as if they were five years old, and they seemed a bit more at ease after that.

"And now, we must talk, before I lose the nerve," Angelique said. "Boys, please feed the animals and allow us to speak alone." The boys disappeared immediately. She took Joy gently by the hand and led her quickly into the living room. "Would you both like tea? It is hot and sweet."

Joann accepted, but Joy was too overwhelmed to be sure she could choke down the nasty stuff without spilling or gagging. She'd counted on at least having a tour first, to reconcile the memories splatting across her mind, before she had to face The Story. Joy looked carefully around the room, grateful at least most of the furnishings and décor had been changed, although her uncle's favorite rocking chair did still sit in the same corner. Joann followed Joy's gaze to the chair and patted her hand.

"Couldn't stand to look at that piece for the rest of my life," she whispered. Joy nodded, hoping she wasn't going to cry already.

Angelique came bustling back in less than two minutes with tea for herself and Joann. She sat delicately in the recliner across from Joy and Joann's couch seats. "I am sorry to hurry this conversation," she began. "But Joy, you must understand some information, and I cannot make small conversations with you until I have told this." Joy nodded, not even noticing the expression "small talk" had temporarily escaped Angelique.

"Joy, your father, George Carnegie, hates your aunt and her lifestyle because of me..."

"That's ridiculous! He never-" Joy broke in.

"No, wait. Please listen. I am sure he never speaks of me. That is because he wants no one to know I exist." Angelique took a deep breath. "Joy, I was once married to George Carnegie."

Joy fell back against the couch cushions. "*What?*" Joann put her arm around Joy.

"It is true. He married me in 1981, when I was just fifteen years old."

"But – but – how...I mean – why..." Joy said, wringing her hands.

"He divorced me to marry your mother in 1985. But he never told her about me."

"So...so...your sons are – are-"

"Your stepbrothers, but they do not know that. I married Pierre in 1990, so our three sons have his blood, not your father's."

"He *left* you?" Joy screeched.

"Yes. I was very young and a terrible housewife. He became tired with me quite soon. I also have no chic style or experience of city living, and George hated to live in the country. We never should have married, but I was impressed of his rich life – I thought – and American ways. I only arrived in the United States from Canada that year."

Joy shook her head to clear the shocked haze from her mind. "So – why does my father despise Joann?"

"He did not like her ever. When John brought her to the farm to live in 1981, I was there with George two months. I was so happy to have a friend. We spoke French all the time, and George was angry because he spoke English only. And Joann was a wonderful friend to me. She listened to my problems and told me not to allow George to be a bully to me. She could not speak English perfectly herself, but she taught me everything she knew. She was older by two years only, but I admired her, and George became jealous.

"When George gave me the divorce, Joann did not make a secret from him of how horrible he was. She said he was as stinking as rotten fish guts and she hoped he would be miserable with Amelia."

Joy covered her mouth and stared at Joann, who was looking ill.

"George moved to Pennsylvania to be with Amelia, and Joann became a church of Christ member one year later. Then she sent George a letter of repentance for her words. But George thought she also repented of taking my side.

"When you visited Vermont, you returned to Pennsylvania speaking of Angelique – your aunt's best friend. At this time, Amelia learned of George's first marriage – I do not know how exactly. But since that time, George has been quite afraid that you, Joy, his daughter, and also his business associates, will learn of his adultery."

"But he couldn't take the farm from Uncle John because he owned it, right?"

"Yes. When John died...and your aunt sold me, the enemy, the *Carnegie* family farm, your father flew to Vermont and threatened Joann so terribly she went to Montpelier. She tells me of his threats to disown you also. That is because you are with us, perhaps learning his dangerous secrets."

Joy buried her face in her hands. She could not believe so much pain and unhappiness had come from her father's sins. She could not believe she had lost so many years with her aunt and uncle because her father so resented their continued friendship with Angelique. Waves of humiliation and anger washed across her mind.

How awful to have been Angelique – a nineteen-year-old divorceé in a foreign country, cast aside because she was too inexperienced and "French." How awful to have been Joann, a widow with her ties completely severed from her husband's family, and no children to help her? Joy shuddered. She would discuss the situation in full detail later with her aunt. Now, she had to decide what to say to Angelique.

"Does my father pay alimony or anything?"

"George sent me a check for three hundred dollars each month, addressed to 'Angel of Mercy,' until he heard I married Pierre. I think that was after the last visit from Joy. Perhaps I should not use them, but I was too angry, and I placed them in a fund for the boys' education."

Joy was outraged. "My father is a very wealthy man," she said. "He could have certainly paid you more than *that*."

"It is not important, and I did not need George Carnegie any longer after his divorce. I would not speak of this, but Joann says it is necessary for you."

"Yes, thank you," Joy said more quietly. "May I ask you one more question?"

"Of course."

"How did my mother enter the story?"

"She was vacationing in Burlington with her grandparents who raised her, and George met her at a business dinner. Two months later, he brought me the papers of divorce." Angelique caught sight of Joy's horrified face. "No, little one, I do not know if his true adultery began at that time. But he told me at the time of the papers that he *was* leaving even if I refused to sign. And you must remember your mother knew nothing of me."

"But how did Joann know her? Alex said she did."

"He was mistaken," Joann said, her first words in several minutes. "I've only met her a few times. I know *of* her."

"Oh. Well. Angelique, on behalf of my father, who was a first-class jerk, I apologize," Joy said. "I know the past can't be changed, but I am totally ashamed to be his daughter."

"Please, don't apologize. That is his duty alone, and you are not much like George. Somehow, you are a kind and decent woman."

"I have John and Joann to thank for any decency in my character," Joy said. "And, well, God, I guess."

"Ah, yes, enough difficult talking!" said Angelique quickly. "We are together, eh? We must celebrate. But first – Joy, would you like a tour? Yes? And Joann? Are you recovered enough to walk about the farm? I can still hear the coughing in your voice from the pneumonia."

Joann assured Angelique she had almost regained her strength, and the three women set out to stroll the property. Joy tried to push her devastating news from her mind and to focus instead on the mostly unchanged farm and lilting voice of their tour guide. At first, understanding Angelique's accent and occasionally haphazard prepositions consumed most of Joy's attention, but soon, she began to ignore Angelique and to reminisce, not about her father's betrayal, but about her summer on the farm.

The memories were crouching everywhere – in the barn where Joy had cried as she groomed the horses and missed home...in the apple orchard where she had climbed trees and made up stories in her head...in the cellar where she had hidden when Aunt Joann had told her she could *not* swim in her new bikini, even in the farm pond...on the back porch, where Uncle John had told her tale after tale about growing up with her father and the grandparents she had never known...and in the huge garden, where Joann, who had never finished high school, had drawn algebra problems in the dirt until Joy understood. Joy discovered she had, in reality, forgotten very little about life on the farm, and more than once she half-expected to see her six-foot uncle rounding the corner of the barn, whistling "This Is My Father's World."

"How can you stand to come back like this?" Joy whispered to Joann as Angelique paused the tour to herd a chicken back into her pen.

Joann smiled slightly and took Joy's hand. "This isn't my life anymore," she said. Your uncle and I had twenty-four years here together, twenty of them alone. It was a precious time...but I've had seven years to accept that it's over."

"You do have Alex now," Joy ventured timidly. "And a nice, safe house...and a good church...and, well, and me..."

Joann squeezed her hand and released it. "Yes, I have so much to be thankful for."

The rest of the visit passed smoothly. After the walk around the farm, the six of them sat at the large, scarred oak table and played dominoes until the vegetable beef stew was done. They then enjoyed a pleasant meal. Joy could not help but feel a sense of nervousness around the boys, but she also felt very welcome. The boys eventually relaxed and tucked away gallons of stew and enormous slabs of cornbread, until Joy, an only child, thought she would be sick just watching them.

Dessert was fresh apple pie with Jonagolds from the trees on the farm. Pierre, Jr. ate so many slices Joy couldn't help but wonder how often the family had dessert. She tried a small slice herself, knowing today was not the time to start shunning carbs again, and was impressed with the rich flavor.

By the time dinner was eaten, with no leftovers remaining, and

Angelique and Joann had washed the dishes, it was 8:00, and Joann suggested they make their way back to Montpelier.

"After all, morning comes early when you have animals," Joann said.

"Oh, it is no bother, but you should go home now so you can sleep before work tomorrow," Angelique said. "My dear friend, you need more rest so you don't sicken again."

Joy hid a smile as Joann winced behind Angelique's back. "Angelique, you know I'm fine," Joann said, hugging her.

"Yes, yes, you say this, but the heart problems, they are tricky, and you are too thin. Joy, please watch your aunt, and bring her down here bound like a chicken if she overworks!"

Joy promised with a smile she could not hide, and both women promised to visit again soon, possibly at Canadian Thanksgiving, if the weather allowed.

As soon as Joann pulled out onto the road again, she sighed loudly.

"Difficult to leave?" Joy said.

"It's not that. I miss Angelique, but since Pierre's heart attack, she has treated my small health problems like major issues. I have used heart medication for years – since before you met me – and this year was the only time I've even been hospitalized with the rhythm problem. I don't know why everyone worries about me so much!"

"I suspect it's because you don't seem to worry much about yourself," Joy said slowly, keeping her face to the window so Joann wouldn't see her grinning. "We feel like we need to worry for you."

"Hmmm…I think I'll set Angelique straight the next time we visit. This is becoming ridiculous."

Joy continued grinning at the window.

"And stop smirking, young woman, or I will ask after the condition of your sinuses seven times a day until Christmas!" Joy snorted, which caused them both to begin giggling.

The trip back to Montpelier seemed long and incredibly dark, with endless black forests and no billboards. Joy finally asked a question that had been plaguing her for hours.

"What does Angelique believe about – you know, religion –

and church and stuff?"

Joann hesitated. "She believes in God, but she does not trust churches. I don't think she'd mind me telling you why. As a child in Quebec, she was rejected by the Catholic church because her mother was, shall we say, promiscuous, and had no husband. Then, the Catholics here have rejected her because she's divorced and remarried."

"But her husband – my – ugh – father," Joy choked out. "My father deserted her for someone else."

"I don't think anyone in the Catholic church knows that. I have studied with her, pleaded with her, and, I regret to say, shouted at her, in the past, to convince her to give my home congregation a chance to love her, but she has always refused."

"At least you're a good example for her."

"Not always. Angelique and I were heathens together during her first marriage. I know I gave her bad advice and said things I shouldn't have. You heard what I said to your father back in the day."

Joy snickered suddenly. "Yeah, that was pretty awful, but at the moment, it sounds about right."

Joann half-smiled. "Well, just because something might be true does not mean I have the right to say it, and God, not I, will judge George Carnegie."

Joy was silent for a full minute. "You are a good woman, Aunt Joann," she said at last.

"I am a forgiven woman, dear heart."

"Yes, but you are also a good one. You've lived seven years with my father's sins directly affecting your life, and you still waited to allow me to find out this information from Angelique so you wouldn't spread gossip. And you've welcomed me like a long-lost loved one even though I'm the daughter of your worst enemy."

"Joy, I am thankful to – to have your respect, but my decision to welcome you hasn't been difficult. I am so grateful for this time with you, because I love you as if you were my own."

"I wish I were," Joy said, so softly she wasn't certain Joann had heard her. A sniff from the driver's seat soon confirmed her words had been understood.

CHAPTER 11

Joy's phone buzzed at nine the next morning, waking her abruptly. She groaned when she saw the time – why had she slept *nine* hours? She stretched and took a deep breath – and another – and smiled. No congestion. At last! Joy sat up and read her text message with an improved attitude.

"Hi, it's Paul. Alex gave me your number. Snow is coming, and you need wood, etc. Call me when you can!" she read.

"At least the man can punctuate," Joy muttered as she touched the "call" icon.

Paul's voice was far too perky when he answered, indicating he had been up a long time already and was an annoying morning person. "Joy, I'm so glad you called," he said. "We're going to have some nasty weather in a couple of days, rain and maybe ice and snow too. You'll need to winterize your house and jeep before it hits or you'll have a rough time of it."

"Do you usually call people first thing in the morning to ask them about winterizing?" said Joy.

"Ummm...yes, when they are unaccustomed to wood heat and have bald tires and probably no chains," Paul said, sounding slightly offended.

Joy sighed. She had to learn to stop being so abrupt in the mornings...and to stop relying on coffee to make her brain function. "I'm sorry," she said. "I'm a grouch in the mornings. Thank you for warning me."

"No problem. Are you well from your cough and fever yet?"

"Yes, I feel all better. Thank you." Joy sighed once more. This conversation was beginning to feel like an etiquette lesson in a foreign language class.

"Would you like me to stop by and give you some wood-chopping lessons?"

"Lessons?"

"Yes, if you learn to chop your own from cords of wood that

you can have delivered, it's much cheaper than buying those little bundles outside stores. I deliver wood for a logger sometimes, and for a very reasonable price, I can put you on my list."

"Um...okay...sure," Joy said. "I'll – uh – need to get a – a chopper, though."

"You can use my maw today. If you go to get new tires later, you can buy a maw too. It's good to have around."

"Oh, right. Well, what about two o' clock?"

"Fine with me! See you then!"

Joy spent part of the morning assembling the ingredients for her aunt's Asian salad – including chicken breast pieces (from a can this time), soy sauce, mandarin oranges, cashews, snap peas, and mixed greens. It was after one when she finally sat down to eat it and to drink some of the tea Joann had brought her while she was sick. She still didn't care for tea, but she couldn't imagine coffee or juice tasting right with her flavorful meal.

The salad was quite good, and Joy felt pleased with herself for preparing such a complex and balanced meal without any in-person assistance from anyone. Best of all, there was enough left for a second meal!

Joy was finishing the last of her tea when she heard wheels crunching on her driveway. 1:50...must be Paul, she thought. A sudden impulse of gratitude caused her to call out as he walked up, carrying a maw, "Hey, have you eaten lunch?"

"Hi...uh, yes, I had some yogurt around eleven..."

"Would you like some salad? I have some left from my lunch."

"I'm fine, thank you," Paul said, but Joy could tell he thought the salad looked appetizing.

"Come on, it's the least I can do to repay you for all the help you've given me," Joy said. "And I'm sure it tastes better fresh."

"Well...all right...if you insist," Paul said, sitting down and placing the maw on the floor out of the way. "I *am* hungry."

Joy gave him a generous portion of the remaining salad and sat down awkwardly across from him. Suddenly, this situation seemed just a bit too – domestic – or something.

"This is excellent," Paul said.

"Thanks. It's my aunt's recipe, and my first time to try to make it. I – I don't have much experience in cooking."

"Well, it's a great salad," Paul said. "I really appreciate the bonus meal."

Joy recalled his statement about eating yogurt and was puzzled. She did not know many men who ate yogurt at all, and far fewer who'd consider it a full meal. "Do – do you have enough food?" she said. "I've heard you're out of work – and it's hard to have enough energy to chop wood on a cup of yogurt!"

Paul chuckled. "Yes, my odd jobs keep me from starving. And don't feel too sorry for me. I was eating my homemade yogurt, which is full of fruit, granola, and nuts, and I ate a lot more than a few spoonfuls too."

"Mmm...sounds good. Not sure I've ever met a man who made his own yogurt before."

"I had to learn to cook after college," Paul explained. "Being a bachelor with a desk job was murder on my body, and although I get plenty of physical activity these days, I still feel better if I mostly eat my own healthy cooking."

"I'm going to have the same problem if I keep eating all this heavy country cooking," Joy sighed. "I'm gaining weight already." She blushed, suddenly wondering why she was sharing that embarrassing information with a strange young man.

Paul looked down at his salad. "Well, if I may say this, you have a long way to go before you should worry about extra pounds. I, on the other hand, had better keep eating my veggies."

Joy grinned at Paul's honest assessment of himself, but the topic of weight was too sensitive for her to continue the discussion any longer. "What did you do at your desk job?" she asked quickly, hoping to find a more comfortable subject.

To her surprise, Paul's smile and dimples disappeared, and he sighed heavily. "I was a copy editor and wrote a few small articles on a newspaper," he said.

"Oh, I see...I'm sorry if I upset you with my question," Joy said.

"No problem. I just don't like to talk about it," Paul said shortly. It was the first time since Joy had met him that he had appeared anything other than pleasant and friendly.

"That's fine. I didn't know," Joy said. "Uh – are you ready to show me how to split some wood now?"

"If you'd like," Paul answered quickly, seeming anxious to change the subject.

"Yes, let's go," Joy said, but she sort of wished she could go for a big, noisy power tool...a chainsaw maybe...instead. Actually, she wished she could press the power button on a thermostat instead, as she had in Pittsburgh...

Joy started to grab her new coat, but then she noticed Paul appeared to be dressed in layers – sweater over flannel shirt over t-shirt – so she chose a light jacket and a sweater instead.

An hour later, a respectable mound of chopped wood lay in front of Joy, a few logs of which she had split herself. She had removed her layers down to her flannel shirt (and Paul to his t-shirt) and felt slightly warm and extremely stiff. "Isn't this enough?" she sighed, kicking at one of her unevenly-cut pieces with the toe of her boot.

"I think so. Your stoves are pretty efficient. But now we've gotta stack this on your back porch or it'll be wet through by tomorrow."

"Do you have time for me to rest?" Joy said, desperately attempting to keep a whine at bay.

"Of course. Rest as long as you need. I'm going to keep going, though. I want to check out your jeep." Paul scooped up a huge load of wood and strode toward her porch. Joy sank unceremoniously to the ground and watched him.

The guy had the nerve to not even be tired, even though he'd chopped like four thousand hunks of wood. Joy groaned as she raised one of her arms to adjust her ponytail. She ached already, and Paul said she'd have to do this chore frequently – all winter long. And he was hauling that wood to the porch as though he were a stinkin' logging truck!

On his third trip back, he grinned at her and waved, not

condescendingly, but quite obviously just because he'd felt her eyes on him. Joy waved back. She had no good reason to feel so defensive around this man...really, she didn't. It was just that she needed so much help...she, elite businesswoman who'd moved half a million worth of property last month alone...and this unemployed country boy could do every aspect of life in Vermont so much more skillfully than she. Joy knew the Bible spoke highly of humility – but did God also expect her to exist in a perpetual state of humiliation?

Soon, Joy realized the longer she sat idly, the more inadequate she'd feel, so she dragged her sore bones and joints from the ground and began copying Paul, although her armfuls were tiny in comparison. The enormous pile of wood diminished rapidly with two people working, however, and before ten minutes had passed, they were finished. Paul gave her a high five and hurried up to the driveway to examine her jeep. Another flicker of resentment ignited in Joy as she chewed on a nail she'd broken. Paul assumed she knew nothing about snow tires and chains simply because she didn't have any yet. And "Helpless Maiden" was not her chosen role.

"Whew! You'll certainly need all four tires replaced!" Paul exclaimed as Joy approached the vehicle.

"I know," she said, trying not to sound obnoxious.

"You're also out of antifreeze. Guess you've got a leak."

Joy bit her lip and considered allowing him to remain deceived. "Actually, I haven't put any in yet," she said finally. "I had a different car in Pittsburgh, and my mechanic always adjusted the fluid levels when he serviced it."

"Well, you definitely need to get your fluids in order immediately," Paul said firmly. Joy snickered in spite of herself. Paul caught on quickly to the awkward nature of his statement and actually snorted. Joy laughed even harder.

He laughed so much he leaned against her jeep to keep from losing his balance. Joy realized she'd never really heard him laugh until now. He had a nice laugh – loud but contagious.

"Oh!" he gasped at last, removing his glasses and wiping his eyes. "Let's try this conversation again. Hello, Joy. Your car needs tires, and antifreeze as soon as possible. I can install them for you myself for a cheaper price than you'd pay at Walmart or something, but it will be too dark for me to do it until tomorrow."

"Hello, Paul. Thank you for your suggestions, but I'd like to go to Walmart so I can be ready by tonight. I have money, and I know how to use it!" Joy returned with a grin.

"Good decision, my friend! Will you be making this epic journey alone or would you like my expert company free of charge?"

"Oh, come along if you'd like," said Joy. "You seem to get such pleasure out of winterizing."

Paul's ears turned fiery-red. "I'm sorry," he said. "But you remind me of my sisters – and they let me watch over the condition of the truck for them."

Joy smiled to show him all was forgiven, and as they climbed into the jeep, she said, "Sisters? How many do you have?"

"Four, all younger. Marie is the oldest – she's twenty-four, but Jennifer, the baby, is just seventeen."

Joy reversed out of her driveway. "Wait a minute. How old are you, then?"

"Twenty-six this past August." Paul grinned. "How old did you think I was?"

"I – I don't know. Somewhere around my age, I suppose. I'm twenty-four...and a half."

"Happens all the time," Paul said. "But hey, in a few years, I'll be glad to look young for my age. Right now, it's kinda unprofessional though."

"I guess," Joy said, glad she'd not told him just how young she'd guessed him to be originally.

For the first time in their acquaintance, Paul and Joy shared easy conversation on the thirty-minute drive to Walmart. Something during the last hour, perhaps the shared laughter, had finally broken through their layers of formality and discomfort. "We're communicating," Joy thought in relief.

By that evening, Joy was the proud owner of four snow tires, more than enough antifreeze for the entire winter, a new set of shocks and struts, a maw, and an orange-scented air freshener to mask the smoky odor left by the service department. She did not flinch as she used her debit card for the purchase – she was ashamed to admit to herself that the entire process had been cheaper than the dress she'd worn to last year's Barrett Christmas Party. Strange how your perspective on money could change so rapidly.

Joy could feel the difference in the jeep's ride as soon as they drove out of the parking lot. "Whoa!" she said. "Aunt Joann won't complain about being sore from riding with me now! This jeep practically floats!"

"Yeah, but she'll choke from smoke inhalation from the employees," Paul said, coughing and rolling down his window. Joy did the same, and after a couple of minutes, only a faint odor of smoke mixed with citrus remained.

"You hungry?" Paul asked a moment later.

"Starved. Do you know any place in town where you can get something decently healthy?"

"Not in my price range, unless you count Subway or a McDonald's Grilled Chicken."

"Ugh. Boring. And the chicken's always dry."

"There's always *chez moi*, though."

"Is that some sort of French place?"

"Yes, but it's quite small and not very well-known. And it's got a limited menu."

"Where is it?"

"Oh, you've been there before. Three times, in fact – Sunday morning, Sunday evening, and Wednesday evening."

Joy slowed to a stop at a stop sign and stared at him. "Your house."

"Yep. I can make a mean chicken taco, and I've got all the ingredients on hand. Come on – I owe you. You fed me lunch."

"And you chopped up eight tons of wood for me!"

"It was no big deal...but if you'd rather be left to your own cooking..."

"Okay, okay. I accept," Joy said, pleased with his invitation. She turned toward the house where the church met.

"So...are you French?" she added after a pause.

"Half. My father came to America from Strasbourg, France, in

1981."

"And you speak French?"

"Of course. Otherwise, how could I understand my dad when he's upset?"

"You don't have a French accent."

"My mom is totally American. She doesn't know a word of the language. And she's an English teacher. I had to become perfect in both languages to keep both parents off my back."

"But wait – how do you have a last name like 'Graham'? Or is it really pronounced "Grrrahm" or something French?"

"My dad was adopted by Scottish missionaries to France," he said. "So yes, he is Jean Claude Graham."

Joy shook her head. "I feel suddenly like I've stumbled on a French colony," she said. "In the last week, I've met or 're-met' so many people who are French-speaking. I mean, even Aunt Joann, who I thought was a normal American, has turned out to be Quebecois! I feel like I should have studied French instead of Spanish in school!"

"Just don't let my dad hear you say Joann is French. French people don't claim French Canadians."

"Oh, yeah. Sure. Have you ever spoken French with my aunt?"

Paul grinned. "Yeah. It was ridiculous. She used so many Quebecois terms I could barely understand her, and she told me I sounded like French IV on tape!"

It felt very odd to be in the "church building" alone with Paul on a Monday evening, although the folding chairs had been stacked neatly along one wall with the pulpit and Lord's Supper table so the living room appeared almost ordinary otherwise. "Make yourself at home," he said, tossing his coat on a chair. "The tacos won't take half an hour."

"Can I help you?"

"No, I'll just wow you with my awe-inspiring culinary skills. Thanks anyway. Feel free to give yourself a tour."

Joy felt even more uncomfortable wandering around the house while a man made dinner for her, but she complied, and sauntered down the hallway full of photos of Paul and his family. His sisters were lovely, all of them with dark hair and blue eyes, although only one of them was pale and freckly like Paul. His mother also shared Paul's complexion, but she was very petite, unlike her husband, who appeared large and muscular like Paul.

Joy took a quick peek in the guest bedroom, which was nearly empty except for a desk and computer, the bathroom, which was pristine, and Paul's bedroom, which was littered with papers and covered in nearly floor-to-ceiling bookshelves. Joy was impressed to see his laundry neatly in a hamper and his bed made, although hastily...a relatively tidy man...what an unusual find! Even Calvin, the epitome of tidiness in his dress and grooming, made a mess of his house in between visits from his maid!

True to his word, Paul had prepared their meal in under thirty minutes. Joy eyed the chicken-corn-black bean-fruit mixture suspiciously, much more accustomed to the traditional Tex-Mex style with cheese and lettuce and tomatoes, but the flavor was so wonderfully different she didn't even miss the usual ingredients. "Paul, this is amazing!" she said. "Have you thought about getting a job as a chef or something?"

Paul only smiled in his shy way and ate his own taco. "Hope you don't mind that this French restaurant – well, actually, this French – Irish – Swiss restaurant – serves Mexican food."

"Are you kidding? This is exactly right. I need to collect recipes from you too."

"Lots of it comes out of a can, actually."

"Good! Maybe there's hope I can become a decent cook in time."

"Oh, I almost forgot," Paul said. "I intended to ask you in the car. What's your family ancestry?"

"I have no idea."

"But you're French Canadian on Joann's side, right?"

"No, we aren't related by blood. Her husband was my father's brother. I mean, I really have no idea. We didn't discuss that kind of thing at the dinner table or anything growing up."

"What did you discuss? We always talked about everything,

100

especially gross things so my second sister, Fiona, would get sick."

Joy sighed. "Money. Prominent families and their lives. How to maintain our position in Philadelphia. That is, when we actually ate dinner as a family."

"You aren't a Carnegie as in *Carnegie* Carnegie, are you? I mean, as in Carnegie the famous steel tycoon Carnegie, from history books?"

"Yep. That's my great-great-great uncle or something. I can't keep track. He's been dead forever, but his money isn't," Joy said gruffly.

Paul sat back in his chair and grinned. "So you're rich, to be brutally honest."

"At the moment, but that may not last long. My parents and I are barely speaking right now, and my father may cut the purse strings soon."

"That's tough. Well, for whatever it's worth, you don't act like you're kin to one of the most famous wealthy people in American history."

"Thank goodness," muttered Joy.

It was after nine when Joy returned to her house, and Paul picked up his truck and went home. Joy took a long, hot bath soon after he left because her joints were still complaining and then curled up in bed with the same novel she'd begun at the beginning of her time in Vermont. Her aunt called before ten and scheduled a cooking lesson for the following evening. Joy didn't tell Joann how she'd spent her evening – but she knew she'd have to the next night. And she dreaded the mischievous gleam she'd see in Joann's eyes.

CHAPTER 12

The air felt different when Joy stepped out on the porch the next morning. Instead of just cold, the air felt wintry, as though it held the promise of frozen precipitation. The sky was overcast, but the clouds were white instead of dark gray. The temperature on the porch railing thermometer hovered around freezing. Joy had initially considered a walk to Woodfield to check out its half dozen businesses, but she shivered and changed her mind. Instead, she poured another cup of Venezuelan coffee and curled up on the couch with her super-soft afghan and tried to write.

First, Joy read over the last few chapters of the extra-long novella she'd been crafting slowly since college. The female protagonist, Shelby, was a wealthy young woman who had rejected her parents' lifestyle and was serving as a war correspondent in World War II-era Belgium.

Joy skimmed the pages with growing disgust. Her current masterpiece no longer appealed to her. She'd known from the beginning she should have researched the history of the time period as well as the culture of the setting before she began, but that was no longer her main complaint with her work. Now, Shelby seemed stilted and stupid. She had an overly-romanticized concept of what she was doing. She'd been in Europe for a month but had the same fairy tale expectations of it she'd held in America. Joy tossed the pages away from her in disdain. Suddenly, she felt like Shelby – throwing her life in Pittsburgh away for an idealistic adventure in Vermont. And suddenly, she realized her writing was unrealistic at best. Just as Joy's time in the magic land of Vermont had been filled so far with intense grief, fear, sickness, and confusion, as well as some positive things, so also should Shelby feel about her time in Belgium. Her story was junk.

Joy lay back against the couch and closed her eyes. She had risked so many things on her ability to write worthwhile fiction, but *Shelby's Quest* would definitely not cut it. Maybe her father's prediction of her failure and misery was accurate.

She'd not had a chance to think much about Sunday's revelations of her father's conduct, thanks to her unexpected hours with Paul. But now, in the solitude of her toasty living room, the enormity of his secrets overwhelmed her with revulsion once more. She wanted to confront him about it, but she was too afraid of his anger. It also occurred to her that perhaps her mother, despite her equally annoying attitudes, did not deserve to be dragged through the humiliation of a prolonged discussion of George's deception. The worst part of the whole situation was that she really couldn't do anything to improve it. No matter what, Angelique had still been hurt as a young, scared woman. And no matter what, Joann had still been left alone to grieve when her husband died because Joy's father hated her. And...Joy had still missed out on ten years of love and care and Christian examples. That made her quite selfishly angrier than anything else.

Joy groaned and turned back to her typed pages. Perhaps the story could be revised...perhaps Shelby's personality could be totally overhauled...and then she read Shelby's words on page forty-nine, "This blend of tea is simply awful. Would you be so good as to bring me another?" and realized her heroine was terrible. She could not continue *Shelby's Quest* because she now hated it. She'd be forced to start again from scratch with new characters and a new plot.

Joy wracked her brain for one of the other story inspirations she'd had in the past, but nothing surfaced. It didn't help that real-life events continued to intrude on her thoughts. Finally, she tossed the papers aside and reached for her journal. She did not read over the old entries in it, for they reached back intermittently for several years and would annoy her also, but began scribbling down her thoughts and feelings of her first several days in Vermont. An hour and five pages later, Joy hadn't penned a word of fiction, but she felt a bit better.

The snow started around noon, big, wet flakes that clumped together easily. Joy bundled up in her new coat and boots and sat on the porch swing to watch it. Early October – and snow already, even while the leaves on the trees were still mostly attached at the lower and middle elevations!

Joy left mid-afternoon to go into Montpelier for her cooking lesson, her passenger seat stacked with the ingredients to cook several meals. She set out at a snail's pace, for the road was nearly covered already, but she was not afraid about being able to return later. Surely the snowplows would come through if it kept snowing. Joy drove cautiously the entire way. Pittsburgh city streets were sometimes this slick, but when they were, she'd typically used public transportation.

The fifteen-minute trip lasted more than thirty minutes, so Joy arrived at Joann's house only moments before her aunt. Joy knew where the spare key was located, but she dropped to the porch steps instead of going inside. The falling snow was still so beautiful against the backdrop of autumn leaves and small historic houses that Joy felt no desire to do anything else.

Before four o'clock, Joann came into view, walking briskly, a scarf pulled up over her mouth. "Aren't you freezing?" Joy called out.

Joann shook her head and unwound her scarf. "No, I'm used to walking in far colder weather, but the cold air still makes me cough sometimes. How are things out in the country today?"

"Slippery!"

"Did you have any trouble getting here? I was realizing while I was at work that we might should have rescheduled."

"No, it was all right. I – uh – actually, I got new tires and stuff last night."

"Really?"

"Yeah, uh...Paul came over and taught me how to chop wood and then checked out my car, but we went to Walmart to get it taken care of."

"Ah...how nice," Joann said, carefully hiding an impish grin. "That must have been...exciting...to get ready for the winter."

"Yeah...and then...we went to the church building and he cooked supper for us. Chicken tacos. They were amazing." Joy busied herself with unloading her sacks of groceries.

Joann set down the package of pasta she was holding a bit harder than necessary. "*Did* you now?" she exclaimed, eyes twinkling.

"Umhmmm. He's been very helpful."

"I'm glad to hear that," Joann said...and deliberately refrained from pumping Joy for any more information. She'd never had a daughter, but she knew Joy would not respond well to too much teasing at this point. And, in Joann's secret heart, she wished very much for Joy and Paul to become special to each other.

Joy waited in the living room as Joann changed into an old pair of jeans and a t-shirt, and then they began cooking. Their plan was to focus on hearty, warm meals this evening, eat one of them for supper, and prepare the others for Joy's freezer. By seven, they had completed a healthier version of meatloaf, with oats and tomato sauce instead of bread crumbs and ketchup; a thick vegetable chili; and a large quantity of "sick soup."

Joy sank into a dining chair, exhausted, as Joann dished up two bowls of chili and sprinkled them with cheese. "I have so much respect for women who cook for their families regularly," she said. "How do you ever have energy for anything else?"

"It does get easier," she promised. "Soon, you'll be so efficient that-" A crashing noise outside halted her reassurances and sent both women scurrying out to the backyard. There they discovered in a hurry that the afternoon's snow had at some point changed over to freezing rain, and Joann's biggest maple had lost an enormous limb.

"Whoa! This is ridiculous!" Joy said, sliding across the stoop. There was a thin layer of ice glazed on top of the snow now, and they had to grasp the porch railings to maintain their footing.

"The roads are going to be bad," Joann said as they sat down to their supper at last. "This is a little unusual for us – getting freezing rain on top of snow."

"I'll leave as soon as I eat. I can come back for the rest of the chili if you can bag the freezer portions for me until another day."

"I wish you'd just stay the night," Joann said. "The temperature is supposed to rise after midnight, so you could get home safely by daylight if necessary."

"Are you sure? I've already taken so much of your time tonight. I'd hate to take your privacy too."

"Joy. I want you to be safe. And I've had seven years of privacy."

Joy was embarrassed. "Of course. Okay, I'll stay."

"Good." Joann patted her hand. "And don't worry, I have an extra toothbrush somewhere."

"Oh, thank you! I was *so* scared about that!"

Although Joann was scheduled to open the library the next morning, she wasn't tired, so she and Joy ended up having a slumber party of sorts. Joy had spilled tomato sauce down her t-shirt and had no desire to walk around with a wet splotch on her front all night, so she accepted her aunt's offer of a nightshirt and changed immediately. The plaid flannel garment hung loosely on Joy's small-boned frame, for although her aunt was tall and thin, her frame size was much larger. They both snickered as Joy twirled around to model it.

Soon, Joann changed into a similar gown and removed her hair from its braid. Together, they popped popcorn with enough butter to negate the positive effects of their healthy supper and proceeded to the living room for a rousing game of Scrabble. Midway through the game, Joy caught sight of them in the mirror on the opposite wall.

They looked nothing alike, really – Joy's hair was completely straight and nut-brown, while Joann's deep waves were still mostly almost black. Joy's eyes were brown and her tanned features were dainty and even, while Joann's eyes were blue and her features, while also tanned, were larger and plainer. But somehow, Joy got the sensation that this was what it felt like to have a mom – not a mother, like Amelia, but a mom, who would play games with you in her pajamas. She smiled happily – then scowled. Her aunt had just laid down "zither" on a triple word score. This was no time for sentiment!

It was after eleven when Joann went out, incredibly, on pterodactyl. "No way!" Joy yelled. "That – that's impossible. It isn't even spelled right!"

"Are you challenging me?" Joann said, grinning.

"Yes!"

"I'll get the dictionary." Joann hurried up the stairs. Joy groaned. She hated to lose, ever, but it felt just plain wrong to lose to someone who'd quit school at seventeen. Surely her degree should give her a boost here!

Joann returned after a few minutes carrying a giant old

dictionary and her glasses. "Sorry for the wait. I wanted to enjoy my victory with comfortable eyeballs, and I never wear my contacts so late."

"Your victory, huh?" Joy said, in what she hoped was a threatening tone.

"Yep." Joann put on her rimless glasses and opened the volume, paging through expertly to her winning word. Joy watched her, noticing with a sudden pang that her aunt looked almost – old – with glasses.

"Aha! Pterodactyl! Here!" Joann thrust the heavy book into Joy's hands. Joy heaved an enormous sigh. Defeated. An embarrassing fate indeed.

Joy and Joann finally headed to bed around midnight. "There's an extra quilt in the hall closet if you get cold," Joann told her as they climbed the stairs. "The spare toothbrushes and shampoo and such are in the medicine cabinet in the bathroom, in case you didn't notice them when you stayed here before."

"Thanks," Joy said. "I saw them last week."

"And if you're still asleep in the morning when I leave for work, just make yourself at home as long as you'd like. Or – if you want to get up and gone early, help yourself to anything in the kitchen, of course. I may be a bit lazy and sleep in until the last moment tomorrow."

"Oh, I'll try to be up to tell you 'bye," Joy said.

"All right. Well, good night, dear. I'm so glad we were able to be snowed in together." Joann dropped a good night kiss onto Joy's forehead, as if her niece were no more than eight years old.

Joy impulsively flung her arms around her aunt and hugged her tight. She could not remember the last time someone had kissed her good night simply because they cared about her.

107

CHAPTER 13

Joy did manage to wake up before Joann's departure the following morning and shared a few bites of breakfast with her, although Joy could not keep from yawning frequently in her decaffeinated stupor. Joann eyed her sympathetically as Joy yawned so widely her jaw popped, but she refrained from any remarks about caffeine dependency. Besides, any such lecture would have been unnecessary; Joy was feeling quite critical of herself that her breakfast companion of twice her age was far more alert than she this morning – without the aid of coffee!

The roads were indeed much safer this morning, for the bright sunshine had melted the ice and some of the snow by the time Joy set out at ten. She even drove around Woodfield at last, taking in the lone gas station/convenience store, the post office, and the old-fashioned homes. Then, Joy took a deep breath and followed the unobtrusive green signs to Coburn College. She drove slowly around the small, wooded campus, avoiding eye contact with any people she passed. Joy tried to forget she had hoped to make this campus her home this year – and to avoid too much bitterness at the irony of living in Woodfield but not at Coburn.

Joy snacked for lunch, washed her dishes, tidied the living room and her bedroom, stared hopelessly at her novella again for several moments, wrote a discouraged page or two in her journal, and then sighed. Three o'clock, and she'd exhausted her day's to-do list already, except Bible study, which wasn't until seven.

Suddenly, her phone buzzed. Joy checked her text message. "Going on a date after Bible study, so I can't offer you a ride," it read. Joy snickered. Her aunt could text! "No problem. Enjoy! See you there," Joy answered.

Joann replied at lightning speed. "See you! We'll be studying the book of Ruth if you want to prepare."

Joy shook her head, in awe that her aunt, who resisted carrying a cell phone, could actually use one so effectively. She had just slipped the phone into her jeans pocket when it buzzed once more. Paul! "Want to take a walk after Bible study? Northern lights out tonight," he said.

Joy groaned. If she spent more time with the guy – she might actually be forced to decide how she felt about him, a task she did not relish. On the other hand, any sort of pleasant outing sounded nice in her current state of boredom. "Okay, sounds good," she replied. "See you tonight." She padded up to her room and grabbed her Bible from the table by her bed, marveling that it had collected dust just since Sunday. She flipped to the list of the books of the Bible, found Ruth, and began to read, scowling slightly at the ancient English. She certainly hoped Joann would remember to loan her that other Bible soon!

Joy had begun reading Ruth for only two reasons – to appear less ignorant and heathenish at Bible study and because the idea of an entire book of the Bible being named after a woman intrigued her; she did not have high expectations she would enjoy reading it. The nobility of Ruth and the kindness of Boaz snagged her attention, however, and she read the entire book, wondering how she had never read any of it before, or heard any of it except the "whither thou goest" wedding verse. Joy was astounded at the faith and courage of Ruth, and doubted any modern woman could possibly place such trust in another person – or in God, for that matter. It simply didn't seem human.

After a quick supper of her chili, Joy changed out of her old sweater into a nicer green one that set off her hair. Then, she headed off to Bible study with a sense of anticipation.

Paul led a song at the beginning of the Bible class, and then Wilson Roberts began the study on Ruth. Joy smiled gratefully as Joann handed her a worn navy volume. "Sorry," Joann whispered. "I kept forgetting to bring this."

Joy nearly forgot to listen to the preacher's first few remarks as she glanced through the Bible, which was in larger print, normal English, and chock full of notes in the margins. "But this is yours," she whispered back.

"I use this one now," Joann said, indicating the larger Bible with her married name engraved on the cover. "Keep it as long as you'd like."

Joy was finally able to turn her attention to the class after that, and she listened with interest as Mr. Roberts introduced the characters. "We have to remember where Ruth was coming from," he said. "She was widowed, apparently at a fairly young age. She embraced an unfamiliar religion. She left everything familiar to her – her home, her culture, her fellow Moabites, and followed someone she loved to an entirely new life, and yet she stayed strong. Some of you in this church have faced one or more of these situations, so you know her choices weren't easy..."

Joy felt Joann shift her position next to her and realized all those characteristics could very well be applied to her aunt. Perhaps this story was relevant to today after all.

Just before the preacher closed the class with a prayer, Joy turned to the front of the Bible to see how old it was, for Mr. Roberts had gone on a tangent and she'd grown distracted. She located the 1970's copyright date but also glanced at the dedication page. "To Joanna Joy Carnegie, on your baptism, June 27, 1986, from the Windsor church of Christ," it read.

Joy could barely contain her gasp. Joanna *Joy*? Joann's middle name was Joy? She poked her aunt and pointed to the name. Joann gave her a wink and then focused on the preacher's words again, but Joy's concentration was shot. As soon as the prayer was finished, Joy began peppering her aunt with questions.

"I wasn't named after you, was I? And do my parents even know your middle name now? Or when they named me? And-" Joann placed her hand on Joy's arm.

"I'm going to forget all your questions before you give me a chance to answer them," Joann said, laughing at her. "But the answer is no, you weren't named after me, and no, I'm sure your parents didn't know my full name or they would have never given it to you. I think your father knows it now, though."

"That's so cool!" Joy exclaimed, not caring she sounded like a teenager.

"I agree."

110

Ten minutes later, Joy was in the passenger seat of Paul's pickup, bumping up a winding mountain road. "So...tell me again...where exactly are we going?" she asked, peering out into the darkness.

"Hunter's Hill. There's been a lot of logging done of the top of the hill, so it's a great view of both the sky and the city lights. Unfortunately, it's also an eyesore in the daytime, but it will be a perfect place to see the aurora."

Joy shivered. At least Paul didn't seem to be a creeper...because this stretch of road was isolated!

Finally, Paul pulled off into an area of gravel and dirt. "The open part's half a mile or so up ahead," he said. "But this is the only good place to park."

Joy got down from the truck, tucked her wallet into her pants pocket, and gazed up at the sky. "I don't see anything yet," she said, a bit skeptically.

"They're pretty low. You'll see – wait until there aren't all those spruces blocking your view."

Neither Paul nor Joy said much as they walked up the rough pavement toward the top of the hill. Paul walked quickly, but Joy had little trouble keeping up with him since they were the same height. The temperature was dropping steadily, so Joy was grateful once more for her good coat. She wondered if Paul in his sweater and jacket was warm enough.

Soon, they passed the dark trees obstructing their view and an expanse of clear-cut land opened up ahead of them. Joy gasped as the greenish and pink streaks of the northern lights appeared on the horizon. They continued until they crested the hill and paused at last, Joy slightly out of breath, as all of Montpelier and Barre lay spread out below them. "Oh," Joy panted. "There's the capitol building. Whew!"

"Yeah...you okay there?" Paul asked.

"Fine...just not really used to hiking. I'm ashamed to admit I'm not in the best shape," Joy said sheepishly.

"That was definitely me after college," Paul said. "And then I had a desk job for three years."

"Thank you for bringing me up here. I've always wanted to see the northern lights. They are totally worth the climb."

"It's my pleasure. And – I'm pretty busy – but if you've got the money for gas, I could probably find the time to show you around the state too...that is, if Joann doesn't mind giving up the time with you."

"Somehow I doubt it. She's suddenly acquired this niece who's sticking closer than a leech, all in the course of three weeks."

"Suddenly? You mean, since you arrived? But I'm sure she's been looking forward to you coming!"

"Not exactly..."

"Oh, did you come to give her a hand since she's been sick?"

"Hardly. I didn't know she'd been sick until I arrived. She didn't expect me. And also, there isn't much I can do to help her anyway."

Paul stared at her in confusion. Joy sighed. "It's a long story, but part of why I came to Vermont was to find my aunt. I'd lost touch with her because of – uh – family problems, and I wanted to re-connect with her."

"That's funny – I mean, it's weird, because you two seem so close."

"We are, I think, but we've got ten years of lost time to make up for. I...um...I also came to attend Coburn College for creative writing, but only for the December Fiction Workshop. The regular courses filled up before I could join them."

"So you moved here to go to a one-week fiction workshop and to see your long-lost aunt? You're pretty brave," Paul said.

"Well, it's a little more complicated than that, but yes."

"I guess you'll have a lot of free time, then, especially since Joann seems to be back to her old self again. Are you going to get a job? Or do church work?"

"No...I'm trying to do some writing, but it's not going too well...and I'm learning how to cook...and I'm enjoying spending time in such a beautiful place...and I'm avoiding my parents, who are being very infuriating right now..."

Paul started to speak, then stopped and took a few steps toward the edge of the hill.

"What is it?" Joy said.

"What – what is your area of service, Joy?"

"What – what are you talking about?"

"What do you plan to do to help others? How do you plan to use your abilities and time to benefit people directly?"

"Ummm...I'm not sure...I hadn't thought..." Joy stammered at the intense tone in Paul's voice.

"Well, if you think of something you're willing to do, let me know, and I can probably give you a list of people who'll appreciate it. There are so many needs in our church and our community," Paul said tightly.

"Oh, I'm not handy at all, like you are," Joy said. "And I came to Vermont to sort of – find myself – I guess, so I'm not really wanting to take on – responsibilities – right now."

Paul ran his fingers forcefully through his hair. "And what of your responsibilities as a Christian? Since God has blessed you with this – privilege – this – this – freedom of independent wealth – shouldn't you be devoting time to service of some sort?"

"I am not like you, Mr. Fix-It!" she snapped. "I'm not satisfied with doing odd jobs all day long. I have big goals and dreams and-" Joy stopped short at the pain crossing Paul's face. Her anger faded a little as she heard her own furious words. "I apologize, Paul. Maybe you'd better just take me back now."

"Yeah, I would say so!" Paul began walking down the hill without so much as a backward glance at the lights. Joy had no choice but to follow, inwardly criticizing her inability to control her temper, but seething at the way Paul had spoken to her.

They didn't speak to each other until they reached the church building again more than thirty minutes later. "Thank you for showing me the lights," Joy said crisply as she climbed down from the pickup.

Paul nodded. "I'm sorry for my rudeness," he said. Joy nodded in return, sighed, and got into her jeep, regretting even through her anger that the evening had been spoiled.

Joy's jeep clock read just nine-thirty, and she reached for her cell phone to call her aunt and relay the evening's insults. Suddenly, she remembered Joann's date. Maybe just a text, then, that Joann could ignore if she preferred – if she was even carrying her phone. Then, a phrase entered her mind, causing her to drop her phone back into her purse. It wasn't a comment by Paul, although those were practically burned on her brain; it was something she'd said herself...that "there isn't much I can do to help her anyway." Joy groaned as she pulled out onto the small highway to Woodfield. She wanted sympathy and soothing so much, for Paul's words had hurt as well as infuriated her, but surely the least she could do was to leave Joann alone for the entire evening. Joy could remember from dating Cal that it wasn't very nice to have a problem dumped on you right after a pleasant date, either.

Joy stayed up miserably late that night, pushing the argument deliberately from her mind and devouring an entire Agatha Christie mystery. When she finally fell asleep at 2:00, her dreams were full of murders and criminals, all of whom looked strangely like Paul.

Joy had expected to sleep until noon on Thursday, but her sleep had been so fitful she got up before eight, grateful she'd survived the night with her life and all her body parts intact. She should have known better than to read a novel like that at night, alone in a huge, old house, especially when she was already upset. The most terrifying dream of them all had been the last one, that a purple gorilla with Paul's face had murdered her in the church building...and no one had missed her because she'd never made the communion bread before.

"Of course, Paul wouldn't miss me and my lack of *service*," Joy muttered. Her frustration at him had faded only slightly overnight, although picturing him as a purple gorilla helped a bit. She poured herself a cup of coffee and rubbed her aching head. Maybe she was just sleep-deprived, but her final nightmare did still haunt her a bit...not that Paul would murder her or that anyone was keeping tabs on her unleavened bread baking skills...but that no one would miss her too much if something happened.

"What use am I to anyone?" she thought. "Joann has Alex to keep her from being lonely. My college friends are all married. I have no siblings. My parents have never really had time for me. My one friend my age up here hates me now. And yeah, I have God, but according to Paul, I'm not living up to my responsibility to Him, so He's probably not too thrilled with me either."

Joy pushed her coffee aside and looked for her Bible, or better yet, her aunt's Bible, hoping she could open it up randomly to combat the tide of hopelessness rising in her mind. Realizing she'd left both in the car last night, she dashed outside in her pajamas to get them. She was also barefoot, and as she raced back indoors, she stubbed her toe on the threshold, tripped, and dropped the Bibles. She danced around on one foot, thankful she usually kept control of her language, and hollered gibberish. When the pain finally subsided, she picked up her small Bible, which was amazingly still closed, and hobbled to her aunt's, which had flopped open haphazardly. Joy fleetingly wished for a sign from God – for the Bible verse to make her become the best woman ever to be sitting there miraculously in the crumpled page opening.

Joy smoothed the rumpled pages and found – a dictionary. No, that wasn't right. It had to be a concordance. She vaguely remembered reading one during boring sermons in Windsor, although her old Bible did not have one. Maybe this meant God thought she needed to know everything and knew she had no idea where to find any of it!

Joy grinned at her superstition and sat down to investigate the concordance, completely forgetting about her coffee, although its blend was nearly as famous as her ancestors. She was delighted to discover it wasn't just a typical concordance – it also had topical listings of verses...and one of those listings was for "Christian Responsibility."

The first verse on the list was James 1:27. Joy located it from flipping through the New Testament. She read it rapidly, and with a perverse excitement, hoping to see something to prove wrong Paul's accusations. "What?" she shouted. "There has to be more to it than *that!*" Of course, she was aware being a Christian was primarily about her relationship with God, but how could religion be about taking care of children and old ladies? What about going to church? What about not drinking and cursing and committing fornication and stuff? And what about doing something big and noble to change the world?

Joy closed her Bible in disgust. Apparently, Paul could understand Scripture perfectly too. No one had bothered to clue her in that old widow ladies were a direct link to going to Heaven!

Joy's phone rang as she was washing dishes with a grumbling heart. She dried her hand hurriedly and noticed in surprise that it was Joann – who'd only been off work for three minutes. She hoped nothing was wrong. "Hi," she said anxiously. "Is everything all right?"

"Oh, well, yes, yes, I guess so," Joann said, sounding uncertain. "That is, yes, I'm fine, but I'm going to be out of touch for a couple of days, and I wanted you to know so you wouldn't worry."

"What? Why?" Joy said in alarm.

"I'm going to New Hampshire for the weekend – as a – well, a sort of – retreat, I suppose, because I need some privacy."

"Um...are you sure you're all right?" Joy persisted.

"Yes," Joann's voice was almost shy for the first time in Joy's memory. "You see, Alex – ah – proposed last night, and I have some – some things to work out in my mind...before I can – answer him."

"He *proposed*?" Joy said. "That's wonderful!"

"Yes – but very unexpectedly...so please humor me, Joy, and don't ask me questions about it at this moment."

"Oh...of course...uh...is there a number I can use to contact you if I need to for emergency reasons?" Joy stammered.

"I'll be at the Spruce Inn in Bethlehem if you need to contact me, and I'll have my cell phone with me in case I need to contact anyone, but I'll keep it turned off most of the time, I'm sure. I'll be back for work on Monday."

"Okay...do you need any help...like...packing or anything?"

"No, dear heart, I'm already packed. Thank you, though. Now say a prayer for me while I'm gone, and don't worry. I just need some space away from routine to think things through."

"I will pray for you. Have a good trip, and be careful," Joy said, her mind whirling.

"Thank you. I will. Love you!" Joann hung up before Joy could respond.

Joy sank down on the couch in the living room, still grasping her phone. There was little doubt in her mind that Joann would accept Alex's proposal; she figured that, as a widow, Joann just needed a little more time to process such a drastic step...to be sure she was really ready to remarry and such. That meant after only three weeks of quality time with her aunt, Joann would be swept away in a tide of wedding plans, honeymoon, and newlywed bliss. It was ridiculous – twenty-four hours ago, she had a new-found family relationship and a growing friendship to cultivate, and today, she was left alone with her stupid stories in this giant, cold house in the middle of nowhere. It was shamefully hard for her to be happy for Joann.

She absentmindedly picked up the newspaper she'd bought yesterday in Montpelier in hopes of finding a used microwave in the classifieds. She thumbed through it without focusing on the words or pictures until a photograph of Alex Martin caught her attention on the personals page. "Local pediatrician retiring in December," the headline beside him read. She read the entire little article, noticing Alex had only moved back to the area to care for his aging parents before their recent deaths. Joy gasped as a thought hit her – once Alex retired and married Joann, there would be nothing keeping them in Vermont! Joy felt sick at the thought of losing contact with Joann again so quickly. It was a good thing she was just renting this place for the winter – because there would be no sense in putting down roots if Joann was leaving.

CHAPTER 14

The weekend dragged terribly for Joy. She read another novel, made another good salad, chopped some wood, cleaned her bathroom, did laundry in the old but reliable machines that came with the house, watched a DVD on her laptop, made an appointment with a communications company to get internet installed the following week, and worried...a lot...about herself as well as Joann. By Saturday night, Joy was exhausted, bored stiff, and lonely.

Joy pulled the afghan from the couch, wrapped it around herself, and went out onto the porch. The air was still quite chilly, but the temperatures had moderated slightly, so in her jeans, heavy socks and sweater, and the big afghan, she was comfortable. She sat down sideways in the porch swing and began to rock.

Joy knew Christians were supposed to trust in God instead of worrying, but she made an effort to ignore that knowledge on this moonless night and worried to her heart's content. First, she was worried about her aunt, and with good reason, she said defensively to her conscience. Despite Joann's assurances she was healed from her pneumonia and its complications, Joy knew Joann's coughing still lingered a bit. She also knew Joann would be out hiking this weekend; it had been her favorite way to combat stress even a decade ago. Joy was nervous about the idea of Joann being alone in some mountain wilderness just weeks after almost dying.

Secondly, Joy worried about her own life. The past day's events had proven two things to her – she might be quite alone in the world once again before many months passed, and she *did* need something more purposeful to "do." Joy honestly had no idea of how she could serve other than by cooking or cleaning for sick or elderly people, and she had a sneaking suspicion she would make them sicker or ready for a retirement home if she attempted that before she knew more about housekeeping. She also didn't know if such service was indeed necessary or if she was even understanding that verse in James correctly. She certainly didn't know anyone else who considered those things as necessary as Paul did, anyway. Joy decided her best strategy would be to speak with Joann about it, without revealing the conversation with Paul, of course. The loneliness, on the other hand, was not something she intended to broach with a single soul. Wasn't she Joy Carnegie, businesswoman, who had been independent for two whole years since college and could take the world by the tail? Who needed a man...or a family?

On Sunday, Joy sat through two impossibly awkward worship services and a Bible class beside Alex, who looked as though he were dying to pump Joy for information about her aunt but did not open his mouth on the subject at all. Joy felt a pang of sympathy for him, imagining how much suspense he must feel when he obviously loved Joann so much. She knew he must be concerned for her aunt's safety as well.

Joy took pity on him at last after Sunday evening service and pulled him aside. "I'm sure she's fine," she whispered. "She's too tough for anything to happen she can't handle."

Alex smiled weakly. "I know. But it's still twenty-four hours until she's going to contact me."

"If I hear she's home safely before that, I'll let you know," Joy said. "And Alex, I'm confident that, no matter what she decides this weekend, she does love you very much."

"Yes," he said, patting her shoulder. "Thanks for the encouragement." Joy smiled and escaped without making eye contact with Paul, who was near the door.

Joy was soaking in her claw foot tub and reading her last novel after eleven that night when her phone notified her of a text message. She dried her hands hastily on a towel and grabbed it from the bathmat where she'd laid it. It was Joann! "Home safe and sound. Call you tomorrow night," it read. Joy breathed a sigh of relief and wondered momentarily if she should bother Alex so late. She knew if she were in his shoes, she'd be up all night, but he was kinda old...she finally decided to text him, hoping he could receive messages.

"Aunt J. home safe," she said. He replied almost immediately. "She texted me to say so. Thanks Joy."

Joy settled back into the warm water. Her aunt had known he'd be worried and contacted him early. This could be a good sign.

On Monday, Joy set out for the public library as soon as she knew her aunt was off work. She was so anxious to speak with her, but she knew Joann needed to see Alex first no matter what. Joy needed to find some new reading material, however, and she also planned to check the bulletin boards to see if any community service opportunities had been posted.

Joy drove up at four-thirty, thirty minutes after Joann's hours ended and an hour before the library closed. As she parked, she reminisced about how nervous she'd been almost a month previously when she'd last been in this parking lot and had re-connected with Joann. So much had changed since then, but Joy still felt uncertain when she considered her future.

Joy was impressed with the size and modernity of the library, although it was housed in a historic building. The main circulation area was large and spacious, with high ceilings and plenty of open space. She smiled as she passed the empty desk in the children's area; Joann occupied that desk in the mornings when preschoolers visited the library.

After thirty minutes of browsing, Joy had located five appealing fiction books, read every flyer and advertisement in the place, met Bonnie Johnston's mother, Pearl, and was no closer to her "Christian responsibility" than when she had left home, especially since she didn't have a backhoe or want an Australian Shepherd puppy, as the ads had mentioned. As she filled out the simple form to acquire a library card, she questioned Pearl about any community service options Montpelier might have.

"Well," the older lady said. "That depends on what you wanna do. We got some adult education courses here in the evenings you could help with if you're smart."

"Oh, I'm not a teacher," Joy said quickly.

"Neither is Joann, but she's scheduled to teach a class in November if she's up to the extra work. Besides, they're not all school work. She's teaching sewing or something crafty, I b'lieve."

"Well, I could teach a little about computers...or writing, maybe...or something like that..." Joy said.

"Let me get the schedule and look for our openings. Okay...we need a canning instructor, an art teacher, and...a career-building teacher."

"What does the last one involve?"

"Some computer skills, using the internet and such like, writin' up resumes, and job interview tips and things. This economy's been so tough we've got a lotta housewives and older people tryin' to find jobs with no idea how to be professional."

"I think I could handle that. Do I need to apply?"

"It's just a volunteer job, 'though the library provides snacks and drinks for free. Do you have experience job searching?"

"Um...not really, but I held a good job in Pittsburgh, as a realtor, and I have a degree in business."

"Oh, I 'spect you'll do, then. Not many people are willin' to take time to teach for free. Just ask your aunt. I'm pretty certain she taught a class on fire safety one time because no one else'd take it."

Joy agreed to begin teaching when the winter classes started in mid-November. As she returned to her jeep, she wondered yet again what on earth she'd gotten herself into.

Joy hadn't even turned the ignition key when she received a text. She read it anxiously; it was from her aunt. "Dessert at my place at 6?" she'd written. Joy responded in the affirmative and checked her watch. Good. Just enough time to inhale a mediocre salad from McDonald's beforehand. She was desperate to talk over the last few days with someone but was thankful some sense of selflessness prompted her she'd have to hear her aunt's whole story first.

The supper hour rush at McDonald's, one of the few fast food restaurants in town, delayed Joy, so it was definitely after six when she arrived at Joann's cottage. Her anxiety to hear Joann's news had increased exponentially as she'd eaten, so as soon as Joy parked, she dashed onto the porch and rapped seven times on the door.

"Hi!" she exclaimed when she saw her aunt. "You're back!"

"You know you don't have to knock," Joann said, smiling and hugging her. "And yes, I'm back! It's good to be home."

"Well?" Joy said, trying to inspect Joann's left hand, but all she could see was a very obvious white line where her wedding ring had been recently removed.

"I said yes," Joann said, her face aglow with happiness. "My engagement ring is too large. We're getting it fitted Thursday. Would you like to see it?"

"What a silly question! Show me!"

"Follow me." Joann led Joy upstairs to her bedroom and to her bedside table, where a black fuzzy box was displayed prominently. She opened it with her back to Joy, slipped on the ring, and turned around with her hand outstretched. "What do you think?"

Wrapped precariously around Joann's finger was a narrow silver band, intricately carved, with a single pearl in the middle. It was simultaneously old-fashioned and non-traditional...and totally...Joann. "It's beautiful," she said. "And so unique!"

"It's not a diamond, but that was my doing. I'd mentioned to Alex in the past I didn't have an engagement ring at all before I married your uncle, and I didn't care for the idea of wearing something priceless on my hand all the time. So he got me something very meaningful – that didn't cost a fortune. You know, pearls are supposed to represent tears – which both Alex and I understand can be tears of joy."

"It suits you perfectly," Joy said. "I must admit I've never seen anything like it, but it works. Totally."

"I agree. I can't wait to start wearing it, but it's just far too loose."

"I'm so glad you worked everything out," Joy said. "I'm very happy for both of you."

"Thank you. And thank you for your patience last week. I'm sorry I had to disappear like that." Joann replaced the ring and headed out of her bedroom. "I made maple fudge just a few minutes ago. Would you like some?"

"Sure...but how did you find time to even get engaged? You worked all day and made dessert!"

"It was a fast process. Alex picked me up from work, drove to the park, proposed, ate a hamburger with me, and raced off to his evening appointments. I think I was home by five, and fudge is easy to make."

"I'm glad you shared your news with me so soon. I was about to perish from suspense!"

Joann sighed quietly but did not reply at that time. Joy sat down on the living room couch as Joann retrieved the dessert from the kitchen. She placed the plate on the coffee table and sat in a chair perpendicular to Joy.

"I'm afraid my decision to escape was rather selfish," Joann began.

"Oh, I don't think so..." Joy protested, but Joann continued.

"But I had to be certain I wouldn't do something even more selfish by accepting right away."

"Why did you have to go, Aunt Joann?"

Joann sat back and crossed her ankles. "I went because Alex deserves to have me 100%, and I had to make sure I could give him that. You know I've been very lonely, of course, and you also know I'm an independent old goat, but I still have many memories of your uncle...daily...even hourly. Alex has never been married, so he doesn't have that frequent reminder of another spouse from the past. I had to be sure I could love Alex enough to be his just as completely as I was John's."

"How do you avoid comparing them?" Joy said, hoping she was not intruding too much on Joann's privacy.

"I can't help comparing them in some ways. They're very different people; John was tall and dark, as you know, for example, and loved working with his hands outside. Alex has a smaller build and has no experience with animals or farm work. John could hardly sit through a movie; Alex enjoys almost all kinds of movies. But my love for Alex is different than my love for John was. I'm at a completely different stage of life than I was at seventeen. I just had to spend a lot of time in prayer and in the Word and searching myself to see if my love for Alex is fair to him."

"Did you hike too?"

"Of course," Joann bit into a piece of fudge. "You know that's the best way to jump-start my brain!"

Joy was silent for a moment, then said, "Do you mind if I ask you one more question?"

123

"Go ahead."

"How did you know? I mean, how did you decide you loved Alex enough to become his wife?"

Joann deliberated before answering. "I believe I really made my decision when I opened an inside pocket of my purse to look for a tissue, and instead I found the note Alex put on the flowers he gave me in the hospital. He said, among other, um...kind words...that he was thankful I was recovering because he couldn't imagine his life without me...so...I tried up in Bethlehem to imagine my life without him...and the prospect was awfully bleak."

"That is a pretty good test, I guess," Joy said. "And it's very romantic."

The teasing gleam entered Joann's eyes at that point. "Oh, not so very romantic," she said. "Because then my nose started to drip onto the paper...since, although it was very sweet, it was not a tissue!"

Joy had been eating some fudge at last, but at Joann's remark she laughed so hard crumbs became lodged in her throat and she coughed and gagged for several seconds. Joann hurried to the kitchen for some water for her niece, who downed it appreciatively and finally took a deep, full breath.

"It was almost as romantic as those noises you were making just now," Joann added. "Perhaps you should make them when your boyfriend proposes someday."

Joy rolled her eyes and grinned. She really was happy for her aunt, and being with her even for the time being hid the ache of impending loneliness a bit.

"And so," Joann said. "What have you been doing with yourself the past several days? It seems a lifetime ago that we last talked."

"Nothing interesting, that's for sure!"

"How was your – ah – walk Wednesday night? Did you have a good view of the lights?"

Joy chose her words cautiously. She had already determined she would not drag her aunt through all the specific details of her argument with Paul. Especially on such a happy day for Joann. Instead, she would gloss over the disagreement and ask advice of her on the topic of the conflict. "Yes, the view was perfect. The walk, however, wasn't. We argued, and I've been waiting anxiously to ask your advice on some – um – questions – that have been bothering me since then – that is, if you don't mind, of course."

"I'd be glad to try to help out."

"Okay, first of all, what is your service, Aunt Joann?"

"My service?"

"Yeah, like your Christian service. What do you do to help people?"

"Why – whatever I can, I suppose," Joann said.

"What are some of the specific ways you help out?"

"Well, sometimes I cook or bake for people who are sick or grieving or had a baby recently...and I visit the little ladies at the nursing home...and I send cards...and...I don't know, Joy...just whatever people need that I can handle. It's not like I have a real specialty or anything."

"Then what would you say is a Christian's responsibility?"

"Hmmm...well, the first responsibility of any Christian is to help as many people get to Heaven with you as possible. Beyond that – it's living as much like Christ as you can and bringing glory to God in all you do. It also means you do assist your brothers and sisters in the church as well as the people in your community, whether it's physically or spiritually."

"What about going to church?"

"Worshiping God is more than a responsibility, although it is important to be faithful in your attendance to encourage and strengthen others and yourself. But...you know...your worship should be a privilege...it should be your way of attempting to show God how...how wonderful and worthy of praise you feel He is. It's possible to sit in a pew every week, even three times a week, but never worship."

"What about the old ladies and children?" Joy said.

Joann laughed. "Are you talking about 'caring for widows and orphans in their distress,' by any chance?"

Joy blushed, realizing she had just called the widow sitting in front of her an old lady. "Ummm...yeah...that's it."

Joann was still smiling at her niece's discomfort. "It is certainly necessary to help people who need it when you can," she said. "But that's not the only method of serving. Everyone has different gifts or talents. Some people teach Bible classes or lead youth events. Some people write books or create websites about the Bible and values. There's an outlet for so many abilities in the church. You don't have to bake pies for old widow ladies like me specifically."

Joy dropped her head. "I'm sorry...I..."

"Joy! I'm teasing you!" Joann said. "I didn't take any offense. Besides, compared to you, I am old. Relax."

Joy half-smiled. "Whatever," she muttered.

"Did you have any other questions?"

"Just...just how can I find a way to serve as a Christian? I don't exactly know how I'm supposed to act...and I can't cook like you or the widows and orphans would shrivel up and *perish*, and I'm not an expert in winterizing like Paul..."

Joann sobered quickly. "I think you should think about what makes you happy...not happy as in "oh, look at my new shoes" or "this is delicious ice cream" happy, but satisfied happy, deep down inside yourself. Then you should figure out how to use that action or ability for God."

Joann's suggestion made more sense to Joy than any other idea in her five days of frustrated pondering. "Thank you so much," she said. "I've never heard anything like this before...growing up, you know. We never paid much attention to needs outside our family, and Christianity was never a subject of interest in my conversations with my parents. And I didn't hear much about Christian life at church the few times I went in Pittsburgh, either."

"I know. You've got a difficult transition to make, dear heart. It's hard to imitate Christ when you haven't been raised with that mentality. But God doesn't expect you to know everything yet as a baby Christian; He expects you to continue growing in knowledge – and never stop."

"Everything is just so confusing sometimes. And embarrassing when certain people expect me to understand things I don't." Joy

126

reached for her third piece of fudge, not caring she'd actually outgrown her tightest pants, and chomped down on it ferociously.

"Joy, I've never told anyone except Alex about your family difficulties or your background," Joann said. "And I've definitely never discussed your religious background. Paul doesn't realize living as a Christian is still a new and frightening experience for you. He may assume you grew up attending a congregation of the church as he did."

"Oh." Joy chewed more quietly.

"That doesn't mean he should judge you, nor does it excuse you from your responsibilities as a Christian that you were raised without much emphasis on spiritual life...but he might not have hurt your feelings if he had known."

Joy didn't say a word for a full minute. "Paul's a good man, isn't he?" she said finally.

"Yes, he is. He really is."

CHAPTER 15

Joy spent the next two days thinking long and hard about what made her happy. She already knew a lot of things that did *not*, including washing dishes by hand, which she was compelled to do quite frequently since she'd bought so few dishes. She also did not think sending cards would be a good way to serve since she hardly knew a soul's name yet. And teaching a women's or children's Bible class was out of the question until she knew more about the Bible herself. Joy actually considered asking Paul to make her that list of what people needed, but her pride kept her from it. "Any benevolence I manage will be totally without his help!" she said aloud as she changed her shirt for Bible study Wednesday evening. It occurred to her as she drove to the church building that she could ask the preacher if he knew of anything. She hoped he would be discreet if he mentioned her to anyone. No good deeds announced on the streets for her!

The announcements caught Joy's attention that night – and not only because Paul made them. He explained to the congregation about the upcoming Children's Day that would take place at the building. The event was scheduled for Saturday, November 3rd, less than three weeks away, and Paul would be in charge of coordinating it. The children would come over in the morning and have Bible lessons before lunch, eat something kid-friendly, and play games all afternoon. It would be open to all children in the area from five to twelve years of age. Joy smiled. Maybe she'd hold off asking for opportunities to serve. Children's Day would be a perfect starting point, for although she'd had little experience in working with children, Joy knew the little church would need to rally quickly together to pull off such a potentially large event. She wondered how she could avoid working directly with Paul; then she realized he was still speaking.

"We wanted to have Children's Day earlier in the year, but it wasn't financially possible," Paul continued. "But, when we had the men's meeting Sunday night, we agreed we would still try to have it after all before winter arrives. If some of our ladies can divide up the responsibilities of the meal and we adapt our own Bible lessons, we can even afford to advertise. If you can possibly assist us in any way – preparation, teaching, cleanup, etc., please see me afterward."

Joy did not join the ten or twelve members gathered around Paul after the devotional, but she listened quite shamelessly from a distance to his conversation with Joann.

"Where do you need me most?" Joann asked. "I can do anything except setting up the day before, but I'm off work all day Saturday."

Paul consulted his sign-up sheet. "Let's see...is there an age group you'd feel comfortable teaching? We're going to have three classes, one for ages five – seven, one for eight – ten, and one for 11-12."

"Any age is fine...I've taught them all."

"Okay...in that case, can I call you in a day or two and give you the age no one else wants?"

"Sure. What else?"

"Well, I hate to ask you to double up, but will you provide the dessert? Your desserts are to die for."

"I can do that."

"Thanks," Paul said, relieved. "I'm...uh...sort of doing all the Bible class curriculum...and maybe teaching too, if no one else signs up...but I don't want to overburden you."

"I'll be fine, and if things get too hectic, I'm sure Joy would be glad to step in and help me," Joann said.

Joy winced inwardly. Cooking and teaching children. Yikes. She hurried to catch her aunt as soon as Joann had moved away from Paul.

"Hey," she whispered. "Are you and Alex waiting to announce your engagement until you're wearing your ring or something?"

"Actually, I want to tell Angelique first, and I hope to see her Friday. She's invited me and you down to spend Friday night and Saturday with her and the boys so we can celebrate Canadian Thanksgiving a few days late. Alex will drive down for lunch on Saturday. Can you come?"

"Oh, yes! How fun!" Joy said. "I will be there."

"Can you meet me at my house at four on Friday?" Joann said.

"Yeah, sure. I definitely can. Do you want to take my car or yours?"

"Let's take yours. I want to try out your new, cushy, *winterized* ride," Joann said. "Plus, I'm exhausted. I'm going to take my life into my hands and let you do the driving this time."

"Sounds good. I'll call you if I think of anything else I need to know before then."

"Good – just don't call before late tomorrow night. I will be occupied!"

"Ah...ring adjustment?"

"And dinner...and a movie..." Joann's smile stretched clear across her face.

"I'll remember that."

Joy had almost made it to her vehicle when she heard running footsteps on the ground behind her. She whirled to see Paul jogging toward her, puffs of steam rising from his breath in the cold air. "Joy," he called. "Wait a second, please!"

Joy steeled her nerves and emotions and wiped her face clean of any expression. "Hello," she said.

"Joy, I wanted to apologize," he said, not out of breath in the slightest from his sudden run.

"You already did," she said, knowing her tone was not much warmer than the outside temperature.

"Well, I want to apologize *sincerely*," he said, grinning slightly. "I'm sorry I was rude last Wednesday. It wasn't my place to judge you or to lecture you. I hope you can forgive me."

"Thank you. You were right, you know."

"I was very wrong in my behavior," Paul said.

Joy smiled. "So was I. I'm sorry too. Really, this time."

"So are we good?" Paul asked. Joy searched his eyes, saw friendliness, and nodded, but she still sensed she had fallen in his estimation this week...and no matter how ready he was to forgive, she *had* hurt his feelings too.

Suddenly, Paul sneezed, politely, of course, into his elbow. A look of weariness crossed his face for just a moment. Joy frowned. "Are you sick?" she said, surprised by how strange it seemed to think of Paul as anything but totally healthy.

"Oh, I think I'm picking up a cold. It's nothing," he said quickly.

"Go home and get some rest," Joy said. "At least you don't have far to go."

"No kidding," he said. "See you Sunday!" Joy watched his retreating figure in concern. It had never occurred to her what would happen if the local jack-of-all-trades got sick...there were a lot of people counting on him. She also searched herself for a feeling of relief that they had established communication again – and couldn't find it. Somewhere along the way, mere civility with Paul had become insufficient...she wanted the camaraderie back but feared it would never return.

Joy spent most of Thursday surfing the internet using her new service she'd installed first thing that morning. It wasn't as fast, certainly, as her service had been in the middle of Pittsburgh, but it was better than staring at the tiny screen on her i-phone and dealing with its patchy service areas. Joy defiantly ignored the six emails from her father, as well as one from Cal Barrett, but she read a few business ones, including her bank statement, which was still looking rather lush.

Then, Joy spent almost an hour on Facebook. She grinned when she noticed Joann had requested her as a friend – imagine, her aunt surfing Facebook more frequently than she – as had Alex Martin and Paul Graham. Joy added all three of them and then studied their profiles.

Alex's profile was quite basic, with minimal personal information and just a few photos, mostly of himself, in which others had tagged him. He included his birthday, religious and political beliefs, and profession, as well as a few Bible verses.

Paul's profile surprised Joy; it was very detailed and had been carefully maintained. Hundreds of photos of scenery as well as of Paul and his family were posted in meticulously-organized albums. Joy scanned his music and movie interests and was ashamed to admit they were "cleaner" than hers. He also had included an extensive list of books he enjoyed, something Joy rarely recalled having seen on other young men's pages. His page concluded with dozens of profound quotes and Scriptures, including several Joy wished she dared copy and paste to her own page.

Joy sat back on the couch to think. Suddenly, it seemed she and Paul had many shared interests – Five for Fighting and Coldplay music, photography, writing, animals, traveling, black and white movies, tennis. She wondered why she'd assumed that because Paul was obviously a country boy who was handy with tools and odd jobs, he was also an uneducated hillbilly who had nothing in common with her. Joy scrolled to the education portion of Paul's page and gasped. The man had a bachelor's degree *and* a master's degree – and had apparently completed both degrees in under five years!

Joy was ashamed of her stereotypical thoughts as she began absently clicking through Paul's photo albums. How could she have been so judgmental – to assume that just because Paul was burly and a bit scruffy and wore flannel shirts and liked to chop wood, he was less intelligent or civilized than her?

Suddenly, Joy paused at a photo of Paul at his undergraduate graduation. He'd obviously removed his voluminous gown already, but his cap was still on and he was smiling from ear-to-ear, embracing one parent with each arm. Two things struck Joy abruptly when she focused on the photo – one, that Paul's current lifestyle was certainly better for his health – he looked a good twenty pounds lighter now, and two, that his father, who was decidedly overweight, only had one leg below the knee and was balancing on a pair of crutches. "Everyone has their struggles," Joy thought as she continued to "stalk" through the album.

Joann's profile wasn't very detailed or surprising for Joy, who already knew many of her aunt's interests and had already seen examples of her stunning photography from years past. Her profile also was quite impersonal – the only photos of people included were a few from a summertime church picnic, tagged by Paul. Joy smiled as she came across a candid shot of Alex and Joann holding hands and smiling into each other's eyes...and she laughed aloud at a shot of

Joann, a healthier, ferocious-looking Joann, preparing to throw a basketball. But there were no more personal photos – and very few identifying facts. Joy sighed; she was fairly sure Joann had George Carnegie-proofed her Facebook.

Time dragged on Friday, especially since Joy was packed by noon, but at last it was time to leave. She tossed her duffel bag ($5.95 at the Montpelier Goodwill) and coat into the back of the jeep, threw away half a dozen empty coffee cups, and drove into town as fast as the law allowed. Of course, she arrived early, but true to her word, Joann walked up at ten after four. "Want to come in?" she called out as she approached.

"No, thanks! I'm all ready. I even went to the bathroom before I left like a good little girl!"

"Be back in five minutes!" Joann said with a grin. She was back in four, with her clothes changed and overnight bag in hand.

"What did you do, change in the entry hall?" Joy teased as she reversed out of the driveway.

"No. I'm just low-maintenance." Joann tossed her braid in an effort to portray someone who was just the opposite.

"Huh! I'm sure Alex is grateful for that!"

Five minutes later, Joy pulled out onto the interstate. "So...I see you're wearing your ring. Congratulations again!"

Joann beamed. "Yes, I finally am...and thank you."

"Do you have a date set yet?"

"Probably around New Year's," Joann said. "We want to have time to plan things, and Alex retires December 22nd."

"*This* New Year's? But how -" Joy's voice trailed off as she pictured the flurry of preparations ahead.

"We aren't having a big fairy tale wedding," Joann broke in. "It will be very informal – just the church and Angelique and her boys and a few old friends of mine as well as a few of Alex's. I doubt there will be forty people there."

"Where will you honeymoon?"

"Canada – probably Quebec and Nova Scotia."

"Oooo...how exciting," Joy said.

"Yes, we are really looking forward to traveling since Alex

will be retired."

"And...so...you'll be returning to Boston, right?" Joy asked calmly, although the thought of her aunt leaving so soon made her physically hurt.

"What? Boston?" Joann exclaimed. "What are you talking about?"

"I read the article in the newspaper about Alex's retirement. It made it clear his parents and then you were the only reasons he'd stayed here so long."

"We aren't moving! I mean, I'm not. He's going to move in with me...um...after the wedding, of course."

"Really?" Joy said, swerving onto the shoulder as she gave Joann a one-armed hug.

"Yes, that is, if we don't slide off the interstate," Joann said.

Joy corrected her driving and heaved an immense sigh of relief. Joann was silent for a full minute.

"My life is here, Joy, and so is Alex's," she said at last. "We want to travel, but our lives are here."

"Well, that's good news," Joy said, making a huge effort to keep her voice from wobbling from relief.

"Did you really think I'd want to move away after finally finding you again?" Joann said, placing her hand on Joy's shoulder.

Joy's tears did fall then, and she pulled safely off the road, crying too hard to see. "Why not?" she said. "You have every right to do whatever you want...I'm – I'm not your – your responsibility! And it's not – not your f-fault I'm alone!"

Joann pulled a tissue from her pocket and handed it to Joy. Joy thanked her, blew her nose, and kept talking. Joann made no comment but listened patiently as Joy vented her emotions.

"My parents don't – don't love me," Joy continued. "I'm just in their w-way. I always have been. That's why I – I was sent up here in the first place. You – you and Uncle John showed me more – more affection than the – than I had in the rest of my childhood. And I – I thought...I thought my father destroyed it...and then I found you...but I thought you were leaving...and I just – just found you – and..." Joy broke off into sobs, surprising herself that she possessed so much suppressed pain.

Joann spoke at last, her voice husky with pain as well. "Joy, dear heart, you are not alone. You are welcome wherever I am – and Alex feels the same way. You are *very* important to me, and I thank God every day that you came back, Joy. Every day." Joann coughed a bit. "And Joy, I'll be here for you – no matter where we go or where you go – for the rest of my life. I won't lose you again."

"But I don't want to intrude on your life. I don't want to be selfish...because I – I love to spend time with you...but you have your own life..." Joy protested.

"I don't consider family and friends to be intrusions! Have I ever given you the impression I consider you an intrusion?" Joann's voice rose in frustration.

"No – no – but I don't want to – to become one."

"I am so happy to have this opportunity to get close to you," Joann said, beginning to cry herself. "I cherished that summer with you more than you know, and when you left, it broke my heart. You see, I'd basically had a daughter for the summer, and I didn't want to let you go. I was so jealous of your parents that summer, Joy, and so angry at them for making you feel like garbage, cast to the curb while they vacationed. And when your father came to Vermont after John died – and threatened me – all I could think about was that I really would never see you again...that it was too late. So you see," Joann said, stroking Joy's head as though Joy were twenty years younger, "Any time I spend with you is a blessing to me. *You* are a blessing to me."

"Okay," Joy said, sniffing in a very small voice. "I'm – I'm glad...and I'm sorry for – for doubting you, I guess. It's just that – that I've always been in the way...and I don't want to be again, especially since you're getting married."

"Well, Alex and I will not be taking calls or visits from anyone on the honeymoon...but..." Joann said. Joy smiled shakily.

"I would hope not!" she said, blowing her nose again.

"Now, switch places with me," said Joann. "You're in no condition to drive, and Angelique is expecting us. She's likely to call the police on us, sure we've wrecked or something, if we aren't there

135

by six-thirty."

"But you're so tired you didn't want to drive this time," Joy said in concern.

"I'm fine...and besides, you drive like an old lady on these mountains. Move it!"

Joy gasped, giggled weakly, and obeyed. Seconds later, they were on their way once more. "Ugh..." Joy groaned, examining her red face and streaming nose in the visor mirror. "What a mess! Would you believe I hardly cried before I came to Vermont?"

"It's much healthier to let your feelings out," Joann said. "Emotional pain and stress are bad for your body. Let yourself cry, or you'll end up on blood pressure medication before you're forty."

"You didn't let yourself cry?" Joy guessed.

"Not for many, many years."

"Wow." Joy sniffed loudly and groaned again at the pressure in her ears and head.

"There should be more tissues in my purse if you need them."

"Thank you!"

CHAPTER 16

By the time Joy and Joann reached the farm, Joy had recovered from her ordeal, and aside from red eyes, had concealed the effects with facial powder. "Angelique won't press me if she can tell I've been crying, will she?" Joy asked anxiously as they turned onto Singing Star Lane.

"No, but she won't afford me that luxury. How do I look?" Joann faced Joy briefly before returning her full attention to the little road.

"Just a bit tired. I wouldn't know you'd been crying if I hadn't seen you."

"Good!"

It was 6:42 when they stopped in front of the farmhouse. Angelique dashed out to greet them as she had the last time, chattering in French and gesturing enthusiastically. She hugged Joann, smearing flour accidentally on Joann's cheek, and then coated Joy's sweatshirt as well. "Doing some baking?" Joy said, indicating the white powder all over Angelique's full apron.

"No, I am rolling in snow!" the French Canadian lady retorted, throwing her hands into the air. "Now come on, get your things and come inside. The temperature, it is dropping fast!"

Ten minutes later, the three women sat on the couch in front of the roaring fireplace, drinking hot tea and eating the richest roast beef sandwiches Joy had ever tasted. "I am sorry for the poor dinner," Angelique said. "But my kitchen is exploding with preparation for the feast tomorrow."

"This is great," Joy said. "Do you need any help with the food for tomorrow?"

"Not until tomorrow. I am finished tonight, and I have also sent the boys to a friend's house overnight. This means we can have a girls' night – I think you say it."

Joy hid a grin by drinking a sip of tea. She'd had more "girls' nights" in the last month than since college, and truthfully, perhaps more than in college, where she'd had the reputation as a nerd.

Suddenly, Angelique shrieked and grabbed Joann's left hand. "Ah! Quelle – ah – what is *this*?"

"Thought you'd never notice."

"Alex – he finally popped out the question?"

"Yes, finally."

"Ah, Joann! Such wonderful news! I was worrying he would never be a man and ask you...so slow he was!"

Joy couldn't hide her smile by then, nearly lost it entirely, in fact, at "popped out the question." She listened in amusement as Angelique and Joann changed to French and began discussing Joann's engagement at top speed. Joy watched, still amazed her aunt could adopt a completely different persona like this, as Joann gestured as expressively as Angelique. After a moment, the women realized they were excluding Joy, stopped abruptly, and stared down at their laps in embarrassment. "Sorry," Joann said. "We forget sometimes we've switched languages."

"It's okay," Joy said. "I don't know how you both can do that – you're so bilingual!"

"Ah, Joann is bilingual, truly. I never bothered myself to be perfect in English. Pierre and I spoke only French together," Angelique answered. "As usual, your aunt has much more intelligence than me."

Joann rolled her eyes. "You are crazy as usual."

Joy enjoyed her evening with the two older women. They had so many years of experiences and inside jokes between them that she did occasionally feel like a third wheel, but both Joann and Angelique were good about pulling her back into the conversation if they noticed they'd left her out for long. For the most part, Joy was content to watch and listen. She had plenty of opportunities to do so as they played two rousing games of dominoes and then reminisced for another hour in front of the fire.

Joy noticed that despite Angelique's years of heartbreak, she still seemed young, strong, and confident. Based on her stories from their last visit, Joy had calculated Angelique had to be about forty-six, around two years younger than Joann, but her hair was still black and her figure was still slender and erect. Angelique's eyes were dark too, and full of fire, and the only obvious lines on her face were at the corners of her mouth, as though she'd spent too much time clenching it in an effort to control her emotions. Angelique was also tiny, actually under five feet, and Joy imagined her own tall, large-framed father had probably seemed like a good protector to his first wife in the early days of their relationship. Joy realized Angelique must have been very, very attractive at fifteen, as her father had been before his wealthy lifestyle had softened his body and hardened his eyes. It was strange to think that if George had kept his marriage vows, Joy would have grown up with Angelique as her mother, speaking French and living half a mile from John and Joann.

During a lull in the conversation, Joy spoke up. "I – I'm sorry to bring up an unpleasant topic," she said. "But – I've been wondering for so long. How did my father turn out so differently than Uncle John? Weren't they raised by the same parents, with the same values?"

"You must answer this question, Joann. George had scorn for John in his heart even before we married," said Angelique.

Joann sighed. "Do you know anything about your grandparents, about John's parents?"

"No, except that they died when my father was a teenager or a young adult. He never speaks of them."

"George was your grandfather's name too – anyway, he and Julia died in a car accident when John was twenty-one...so George was – hmmm...about twenty-five? That was just a few weeks after I came to the farm. It was very difficult for the brothers. But you see, George and John were already choosing different lifestyles before their parents' deaths. Your grandfather George was an extremely religious man, but he showed no mercy. Your father rebelled against his father and embraced everything contrary to what his father stood for. He also resented John because George, Sr. left John the farm in his will. John paid more attention to his mother's more compassionate attitude – and managed to stay both righteous and kind."

"That's interesting," Joy said. "It really proves people have a choice how they turn out no matter their environment, doesn't it?"

"Yes," Joann said, smiling at a sudden memory. "John used to say he was a liberal psychologist's worst nightmare."

"Oh, because of the nature versus nurture argument?"

"I think so," Joann said.

"Okay, stop talking on top of my head, Smart One!" Angelique said.

"Start *using* your head, Pretty One!" Joann returned.

"On top of her head? Smart One?" Joy said. "What on earth are you talking about?"

Joann laughed. "Angelique meant we were talking *over* her head; you know, about things too hard for her to understand, but she is just pretending to be ignorant. And Smart One and Pretty One were the nicknames some of the people in the community gave us when we were still new in the area. We were both thin and tanned and awkward and foreign, never mind I was nearly a foot taller, and rather than use our names, they'd call me Smart One because my English was better and I was more serious, and Angelique was Pretty One, for obvious reasons."

"That was awfully rude and stereotypical," Joy commented with a frown. "And like – restrictive – you know, as though you could only be smart *or* pretty."

"It's okay. We didn't take them too seriously," Joann said. "We even adopted the nicknames and used them ourselves. And people did eventually take the time to get to know us enough to use our real names."

Angelique made a dismissive gesture and pulled something thin and crumpled from her pants pocket. "And now, Joann, because you in reality are a Smart One, will you please explain to me the meaning of this word...propitiation?"

Joy was startled, for the word sounded like a "Bible word," and the small booklet looked suspiciously like a tract. She heard her aunt gasp and looked at her. Sure enough, Joann had turned slightly pale.

"Where – where did you get that?" Joann said.

"From you, oh, maybe twenty-five years past, when you talked to me without stopping about your new faith and church,"

Angelique replied.

Joann held out her hand for the tract and turned it back to the cover, which read, "Understanding the Lord's Church." Joy wasn't sure exactly what was happening, but Joann still looked like she'd seen a ghost.

"Why now, Angelique?" Joann whispered. "Why are you studying now?"

"Are you not happy?" Angelique said, placing your hands on her hips. "You spent a decade being a pest about my heathen ways...and now I am listening."

"Of course I'm happy," Joann said, tears flowing abruptly down her cheeks. "I'm just – shocked...please excuse me...now, show me the word you're talking about, please...I'm sorry I..."

"Joann," Angelique said in a gentler tone than Joy had ever heard from her. "It is okay. I know you are surprised." She sighed, and when she spoke again, her voice was hesitant. "I am studying because I am afraid of death. No – no, I am not dying soon, Joann! Your face was so terrible just then. I am well, but there are many diseases in my family history, and for many years, I have lived in fear I will die young as my mother did. Last month, when you told to me the story of your illness, you did not share you were near death, but you are my dearest friend, and I know certainly you would not enter an ambulance unless you were. I realized after your last visit that you aren't afraid now. You were near death, but you are happy and calm. I want your peace."

"Then let's study," Joann said, wiping her eyes. "Joy, would you get my Bible from my bag upstairs, please? Oh, and my glasses?"

Five minutes later, the three women had gathered around the battered table. Joy was growing extremely sleepy, but she listened as closely as possible as her aunt and Angelique discussed the tract and then many Bible verses. Many of the verses sounded familiar to Joy, but she did not know their locations, and she found herself jotting them down on a paper napkin in case she ever needed them, although it was difficult for Joy to imagine ever playing Joann's role in a situation of this sort. Joy watched Joann hastily remove her contacts, apologizing and explaining that the lenses were nearly cemented to her eyeballs, and then plunge back into the animated discussion of salvation. She wondered how, at midnight, Joann was still going strong. And secretly, deep in her heart, Joy prayed she would one day have such wisdom.

Joy awoke at nine the next morning to the sound of the springs creaking in the big bed she and her aunt had shared for a few short hours. Joy's eyes flew open in alarm, but she shut them again quickly when she noticed the sound was just Joann trying to climb out of bed. "Sorry!" Joann whispered, putting on her glasses and padding to the door.

Joy grunted and rolled over to block the daylight peeping in around the curtains, but she couldn't get comfortable again. The double bed belonged to Pierre, Jr., Angelique's oldest son, and the mattress had a pit in the middle where he had slept for at least a decade. All six hours Joy had lain in the bed, she'd clung to her side to keep from rolling down into the pit and squashing against Joann. Awkward...especially since Joy couldn't recall having *ever* shared a bed with *anyone*.

Joy was lying in the pit, which wasn't any more comfortable than the edge, staring grumpily at the ceiling, when Joann tiptoed back inside the room. "Oh, you're awake. I'm sorry I wasn't quiet enough," Joann said.

"It's okay," Joy said, restraining her morning crankiness as much as possible. "This bed is ridiculous."

"Yeah. I think the top bunk would have been better," her aunt said, changing discreetly in the corner.

Joy averted her eyes politely and smiled as she thought about the previous night. The three women had studied until two, at which time Angelique said she needed to "sleep over" what they had discussed. She showed Joy and Joann to the boys' room, which contained the big bed and a bunk bed. "One of you can use the bottom bunk, and one of you can sleep in the big bed," she'd said, and then left them to their bedtime preparations.

Joy had been quite willing to take the narrow bunk until she saw the set mouse trap, surrounded by black pellets, just beyond the head of the bed. "Uhhh...what is this?" she said, pointing to it in disgust.

"Oh, nasty! Mouse pellets!" Joann said.

"Is that, like, their *poop*?" Joy said in disbelief.

Joann stared at her. "Yes," she said finally. "You've never seen it?"

"*No*. And I'm *not* sleeping there with *that* a foot from my face!"

"As much as I'd like to help you out, I've got to say I'm not either. There are few things I hate as much as mice," Joann said.

"Have you ever slept on a top bunk?"

"No – can't say I have. I'm afraid I'd roll off and hit the floor...of course, I'd probably give the mouse a heart attack...but I don't particularly want to break myself."

"Me neither."

"Well, the double bed's big enough for both of us sissies," Joann had said with a chuckle of resignation.

Now, Joy sighed in relief. The long night was over at last. She heaved herself out of the pit and retrieved her clothes from the duffel bag as her aunt headed downstairs to begin helping Angelique.

Joy had barely finished dressing when she heard excited cries from downstairs, followed by pounding on the wooden staircase. She walked to the bedroom door, puzzled, as Joann knocked once and flung it open.

"What is it?" Joy cried.

"Angelique – wants – Alex to – to baptize her when he comes for – dinner!" Joann gasped. "I'm so – excited – I'm about to hyperventilate!"

Joy threw her arms around Joann in a tight hug and then clattered downstairs herself to celebrate with their hostess, exhaustion and caffeine deprivation forgotten.

CHAPTER 17

At approximately four p.m., after Alex, Joann, Joy, Angelique, and her sons had stuffed themselves with an immense dinner of traditional Thanksgiving food, they traipsed down to the very pond where Pierre and John had perished so long ago. There, Alex immersed Angelique according to Biblical command, for the remission of her sins. All the women cried – a lot – especially when Angelique remarked that now the pond was a place of new life instead of death.

"And so," Angelique said briskly as they hurried back to the farmhouse, she and Alex shivering in their sopping clothes. "I will attend the church in Windsor tomorrow. Will you stay tonight also and go with me and the boys?" She indicated her three guests.

"I'd love to stay, but I'm leading singing tomorrow," Alex said. "Paul called me yesterday and has caught a bad cold. He could hardly speak for coughing," he explained to Joann and Joy.

"Oh, poor man," Joann said. "We'll have to take him a meal...but yes, Angelique, I can stay another night. What do you think, Joy? Do you want to stay or ride back with Alex today?"

"I want to stay," Joy said, pushing back murderous thoughts toward the big old bed with the pit.

The other three adults continued talking and making plans, but Joy couldn't keep her mind off Paul. She remembered the kindness he had shown her recently when she felt so miserable, and she wondered if anyone was taking care of him. She also remembered how exhausted he had seemed on Wednesday night; he *had* said he was already getting sick then. Joy envisioned the big man with the powerful muscles and the baby face, coughing and sneezing and helpless on his couch. Suddenly, she forgave him for his harsh words the week before. She had deserved a lecture after all – her plans had been awfully self-centered. And Paul really was a good person...so good, in fact, that people like her probably drove him crazy. She resolved to check on him as soon as they returned tomorrow afternoon.

The evening at the farm was a joyous time, filled with lively games, leftovers from the enormous midday meal, and constant banter. Even Pierre, Jr., Hugo, and Jean Marie warmed up to an extent and seemed to enjoy Alex's company more than the women's. Alex teased his fianceé about her tendency to start chattering in French at any moment until Joann actually slugged him in the shoulder, shocking him and creating a flood of laughter from everyone.

Finally, at nine, Alex pulled himself away and headed back north. He kissed Joann squarely on the mouth in front of them all, provoking cheers and whistles from the three teenagers. "We'll probably hit town just in time for evening service," Joann told him, her ears fiery-red. "I hope your song-leading goes smoothly."

"Thanks, but we'll miss your voice," Alex said, shrugging into his wool coat. "And yours, Joy," he added, ever the gentleman.

Joy grinned. She wasn't tone deaf, but her timid voice would never be missed either. How like Alex to include her, though!

No one felt like staying up until all hours that night; even the boys were tired after their time at their friends' house, where they'd done very little sleeping. By ten, the teens were bedded down and snoring in front of the living room fireplace, and Joann and Joy were closed in the boys' bedroom once again.

Joann had requested the first turn in the upstairs shower, pleading exhaustion. "Do you even have any idea how many decades it's been since I voluntarily stayed up until three?" she said, laughing, as she gathered her pajamas and shower supplies from her suitcase. "I'm fairly certain the dark circles under my eyes are growing more dark circles of their own!"

Joy had intended to wait her turn by reading the novel she'd brought, but she found herself studying the large bedroom instead. It was difficult to recognize because of seven years of male occupation and decoration, but it was the same bedroom in which she'd spent her fourteenth summer. Joy lost herself in memories for several minutes. In this room, she'd poured out her frustrations in her diary...she'd cried thousands of tears for her missed trip to the Bahamas...she'd ground her teeth in anger at her uncle and aunt's strict rules...and she'd lamented the fact they did not have cable or satellite TV, so she'd miss all her favorite programs for an entire summer. Later, after she'd come to love John and Joann, she'd spent less time in here, expect when she was writing and sleeping, because she'd been with her uncle or aunt or outside at almost every waking moment. Joy grinned as she recalled one particular day about a week after she'd arrived. It was the same day she'd casually donned her new purple bikini, wrapped a towel around her shoulders, and walked downstairs to swim in the pond. She had been sent back upstairs in ten seconds flat by her aunt, and she'd had a sour attitude the rest of the day. That afternoon, Joy had been helping wash the dishes under protest, and she'd splattered dish water across her clothes and muttered a word she knew she shouldn't say. Joann had calmly slapped her on the rear end with a wooden spoon and informed her that if she said it again, she'd wash dishes every day...and after every meal. Joy shook her head. It amazed her sometimes she'd had the sense to learn not only to love her aunt, but also to crave most aspects of her lifestyle.

Joann re-entered the bedroom again after just fifteen minutes, her long hair wrapped in a towel. "Okay, dear heart, I'm going to bed this minute," she said. "I'm way too old to stay awake any longer. And I'm sleeping up here," she continued, climbing deftly onto the top bunk.

"So you're too old to stay awake, but not too old to climb like a monkey?" Joy teased her.

"Something like that. Love you, kiddo."

Joy bit her lip. How long had it been since someone had said that to her so casually? She couldn't remember. "Love you too," she said quietly. "Hope you sleep better up there." She felt just a bit – healed – as she hurried to the bathroom for her shower.

The next morning began with a flurry of activity. Getting six people ready for church services is always hectic in a small house, but since four of them had literally never been, the chaos tripled. As Joann and Joy ate the meager remains of the breakfast Angelique had cooked for the boys before daylight, Angelique sat at the table with them and applied her makeup. Suddenly, she paused. "This isn't sinful to the church, is it?" she said, indicating her basic cosmetics.

"Of course not," Joann said.

"Well, you never wear it," Angelique retorted. "So how would I know? Ahhh...what am I doing? I will be so very odd to the others."

"It's just a little country church full of ordinary people," Joann assured her. "You must remember that from John's funeral. And if you dress nicely, no one is going to give your appearance a second thought."

"Yes, but I will *never* wear pantyhoses!" Angelique declared. "They were invented by a man. He was also a very evil man!"

Joy was trying to swallow a bite of toast at that moment and choked as she started laughing. Angelique continued. "And for what purpose do the women wear this – the pantyhoses? To hide the hair they are too lazy to remove? We should give the pantyhoses to the men. They have more hairs to hide!"

The service at Windsor was as slow-paced as Joy recalled from their previous visit, but she was the only adult who seemed to mind. Angelique listened to everything with rapt attention and even attempted to join in on the dragging hymns. Joann sat and participated peacefully as usual, and Joy knew her aunt was so thankful to be attending worship services with Angelique that anything would seem exciting. The boys fidgeted but were otherwise well-behaved, but Joy could tell they couldn't care less for this new lifestyle their mother was suddenly promoting. Joy tried to adjust her own attitude and said a quick, silent prayer for Pierre, Hugo, and Jean Marie, that they would somehow become interested as well. After all, one summer of church attendance, even in such a sluggish place, had been enough to stick in Joy's mind when she was fourteen...

Angelique talked happily in her ancient minivan all the way back to the farm. She praised the friendliness of the people and the sincerity of the acts of worship. She especially liked that the singing was congregational and without musical instruments. "And it was all English!" Angelique said. "The people did not have a – how do you say it? - competition to see who speaks more Latin. I could participate, not only listen and try to translate!" Joy raised her eyebrows. She supposed that was an interesting perspective. It's probably just me, Joy reflected. I'm probably just a calloused person. Isn't worship what *I* make it? I know it's not entertainment.

147

After another fast meal of leftovers, Joy and Joann packed up and left the farm to return to Montpelier. This time, Joann and Angelique parted easily, with many instructions to call and plans for Angelique to come up and visit for a few days before the wedding that winter.

"It's not so hard to say goodbye now I know we're sisters in Christ," Joann said, hugging Angelique tightly.

"Yes," Angelique said. "And my fears are so small now. I am very happy." She looked at Joann carefully. "And you are well at last," she said. "I will thank God for this."

Joy drove all the way back to Montpelier, and Joann, after discussing the wonderful events of the weekend for a few minutes, actually dropped off to sleep before they'd driven through White River Junction. Joy did not wake her; sleep had not been one of the primary events of their weekend.

Joy swung into the church house parking lot at 4:59. She and Joann grabbed their Bibles and scurried inside, taking their seats just as the announcements began. Alex, sitting in the front row, smiled and winked as they tried to settle in without disturbing everyone. Joy scanned the room for Paul, having realized he would be attending services no matter how he felt since he lived there. She spotted him in the very back corner, as far away from the other members as possible. He looked terrible but offered Joy a weak smile when they made eye contact. She suspected he felt awfully sick – his face was actually gray.

The service, and particularly the singing, which Alex led quite well, seemed very energetic and encouraging to Joy after being in Windsor, but once again, Paul was on her mind, and it was difficult to concentrate. She was especially concerned when she saw him leave three times during the service and could hear him coughing in the kitchen.

After the closing prayer, Paul disappeared immediately into the kitchen once again. Joy followed him and discovered him leaning on the counter as he coughed. "Paul!" she said in alarm. "You need to go to a doctor!"

"I know," he gasped. "I have an appointment tomorrow."

148

"Do you – need some help?" Joy said. "You – you look awful!" She stepped closer to him, but he held up a hand in caution.

"You'd better stay back," he said. "I'm burning up. I – I don't want you or Joann to catch this."

"Will you be able to get to the doctor? You shouldn't drive like this. Should we take you to the ER?" Joann exclaimed.

"No...no...I'm going to take...a bunch...of Tylenol and Ibuprofen...and go to bed...I get high fevers pretty easily when I'm sick."

"Are you sure?"

"Yeah," Paul said, starting to cough almost uncontrollably once more. "I'm sure."

Joy left him then, but throughout the evening and into the next day, she worried about him. She finally called her aunt as soon as she finished work and asked her what she thought she should do. "It's not that I'm scared of catching his cold," Joy said. "But it is true I'd need to stay away from you if I see him. A cough like that would not be good for you to be exposed to so soon after your pneumonia. And who knows – he may even have pneumonia!"

"Why don't you call him and see what he needs?" Joann said. "In the meantime, I'll make some more chicken soup and drop it by in a little while. Between the two of us, we've almost depleted my freezer supply."

Paul answered his cell phone on the sixth ring, his voice barely above a whisper.

"How are you?" Joy said.

"Sick," he croaked. "My temp was 104 degrees at the doctor today."

"Oh, my goodness!" Joy said. "What is *wrong* with you?"

"The flu and bronchitis," Paul said. "Oh, and a cold...that was why I have bronchitis. It – it..." he coughed loudly. "It lowered my immunity and settled in my chest."

"How did you catch all that?"

Paul coughed some more. "I drove Mrs. Tucker to the doctor on Thursday. She – she has the flu. She was admitted to the hospital, actually."

149

"Paul!" Joy said. "Do you need to go there too?"

He tried to laugh, but coughed instead. "No, I'm not eighty-seven."

"Well, my aunt is going to leave some chicken soup on the doorstep tonight. It's fantastic, and it will make you feel better."

"Yeah, I've had it once," he said. "But right now, I'm not keeping much down."

Joy cringed. "Isn't there anything I can do for you?"

"Uh...I really hate to ask...but could you write the class curriculum for Children's Day? Mr. Roberts...has...the – uh-" he sneezed violently, eight times. "Oh, where – where was I?"

"Mr. Roberts has -" Joy prompted.

"Oh, uh, yeah...he has the topics and stuff. I – I am really sorry...but you write...and the doctor thinks I'll keep running fever...for a couple more days...and I'm not worth much when I have fever."

"Of course I'll do it," Joy said. "Don't worry about anything. Just get well. And don't forget to go to the door for your soup. You don't want to get dehydrated."

"Thanks, Joy. You're – cough, cough, cough – great."

Joy hung up soon afterward and immediately called Joann to report on Paul's condition. "You certainly need to stay away from him," she cautioned. "He has the flu *and* bronchitis. I just hope he knows how to take care of himself properly."

"Don't worry. I'm stubborn but not stupid, and I have no desire to catch either of those. As for Paul, I'm sure he can take care of himself. Strapping young men get over the flu on their own every day," Joann teased her.

"I know..."

"But I'm also sure Paul appreciates your – ah – extreme concern for him," she added.

Joy sighed. "I *do* care about him, okay? Just not the way you're thinking."

Joann merely chuckled and changed the subject.

When Joy woke at eight Tuesday morning, she rolled over onto her back and contemplated her day. She couldn't remember for several seconds why she felt such purpose and determination about this particular day, but then the events of the previous day came back to her in a rush – Paul's illness, his request, and her lengthy discussion with Wilson Roberts about the Children's Day materials.

Joy threw the covers off and dressed rapidly in the frigid room, inwardly scolding herself for forgetting to replenish the wood supply before she'd gone to bed. She pulled on some thick socks and padded downstairs, fantasizing about her first cup of Venezuelan coffee. She had removed a mug from the cupboard and started toward the coffeepot when she realized she was already wide awake and thinking clearly pre-coffee! Was it the cold rooms with the dying fires? Was it the excitement of feeling useful at last, after almost two weeks of fretting? No matter. She didn't need caffeine today. Joy downed less than half a mug, poured the rest in a plastic container, and stuck it in the freezer. She'd save it for coffee-flavored desserts or something in the future if her culinary pursuits ever extended to those heights. Then, she scarfed a piece of whole grain bread with cream cheese (fat free, of course) and headed to the living room to write.

Joy had sat back sideways on the couch, feet up, to try to write the past few times she'd attempted it, but today, she dusted off the heavy oak desk in front of the window and placed her laptop, notepad, pens and pencils, and Bible there. The official-looking work station energized her; after all, this was what she'd come to Vermont to do with her life, albeit for a different purpose!

The members of the congregation had decided to use the subject of Bible heroes and heroines as their theme for Children's Day, so Joy's task was to create five short lessons each for the two younger age groups, with one lesson per selected Biblical person. Paul had almost completed the five lessons for the oldest group before he became ill, and Joy found herself wishing she could look at his work as an example.

The assigned people were Abraham, Joseph, David, Esther, and Mary, the mother of Jesus. Joy opened her aunt's old Bible to the New Testament first, thinking that creating lessons from Mary's life would be easy since her story was so familiar. She re-read the account of Jesus' birth in Luke 2 and sighed. Easy, huh? Now how was she going to explain the concept of divine conception so kindergarteners would understand it?

Joy wrote and wrote – pausing frequently to check her facts with her aunt's Bible as well as a simplified version she'd located on the internet. She also changed her mind about the wording of her sentences so many times that she soon transferred all her work to the computer so she could make alterations more easily. It was two p.m. before she had two satisfactory lessons on Mary. She stood to stretch, feeling extremely grateful someone else was in charge of the activities accompanying the lessons. She was also feeling rather overwhelmed since Mr. Roberts expected eight more lessons by Bible study time the following evening. She rubbed her eyes, which had grown tired from staring at the computer screen for so many hours. Why did Paul have to get so sick right now anyway? He was such a genius, apparently, that these lessons would have only taken him a few minutes to write when he was well!

Suddenly, Joy's phone vibrated. "Eat lunch," her aunt had written her. Joy frowned and glanced at her watch. As if on cue, her stomach growled. Joy sighed in frustration, not wanting to stop work but realizing she did need to eat. And it was also infuriating that Joann knew she'd be working so hard she'd forget to eat!

Joy felt so much better after her quick chicken salad that she lost all animosity toward both Paul for getting sick and Joann for predicting she wouldn't take care of herself. She sat down at the desk again and read over her lessons. They were actually – good. Really good. Joy smiled and began to read the account of Esther.

Joy took one more short break for supper but otherwise continued writing until almost nine, creating sentences with more satisfaction than she had experienced since high school. At last, she sat back, saved her work once more, and smiled. Every lesson was finished except the two on Abraham, and she could easily complete those in the morning. Joy stood and stretched,, slowly working out the kinks in her body. Air. Fresh air. That's what she needed now.

Joy flung open the door and stepped out onto the wide front porch, not bothering with a coat or shoes. The air was cold and crisp, but there was no wind, so she was nearly comfortable in her jeans and heavy sweater. She sent a brief text to Paul, inquiring about his health tonight and telling him how much writing progress she'd made. She leaned back on the porch railing and stared up at the stars. Peaceful. She felt peaceful, for the first time since her argument with Paul. She felt her phone.

"Good for you! I knew you could do it. Fever broke last night but came back tonight. Yuck, yuck," Paul wrote. Joy sighed. She wondered if Paul would even be able to attend Bible study in his own home.

As if on cue, her phone rang. It was Joann, who was informing Joy that the church would be meeting at Wilson Robert's house the following evening instead of at the church building. "Paul is too contagious," she explained. "And so many of our members are elderly and they can't risk the flu and bronchitis. If you want to come to my house for supper tomorrow, you can ride with me to his house afterward. It's pretty difficult to find."

Joy agreed to her aunt's plan, cringing at the thought that Paul was still so ill.

The following morning, Joy rose at eight and forced herself to eat breakfast again. Instead of even brewing coffee, she drank hot tea, convinced she was going insane, but the anticipation of the work ahead of her was keeping her as awake as a jolt of caffeine. The scary thing was she was choosing to drink that nasty old tea when she still had the good stuff in the cupboard. Vermont was doing strange things to this city girl!

Joy had Abraham out of the way by eleven, and after she glanced over all the lessons and made a few edits, she connected her printer for the first time and printed out two copies, one for herself and one for the preacher to look over and then photocopy to distribute to the Children's Day teachers. A sense of great accomplishment rose up in Joy as she stacked the pages together and put them in a manila folder, then set the folder near the door where she wouldn't miss it.

As Joy hastily assembled a small tuna salad from a simple recipe on the can of tuna, she texted Paul that she was finished, hoping to take a load off his mind. He replied immediately, "Thank you SO much! You really saved my skin. I'm eating by the way, and believe me, that is progress!" The only reason, the one and only reason, that Joy started humming happily as she mixed her lunch was because she was relieved to be finished with those lessons. Of course.

The Bible study at Wilson's house was informal and intimate, and Joy enjoyed the variety of the experience, but she was also frightened by the announcement that Paul had had a follow-up doctor's appointment that afternoon to see if he was improving sufficiently or needed to be hospitalized. She almost missed the conclusion of the announcement – Paul was indeed better – his fever broken for good and his bronchitis easing up – because of the sudden case of cold chills that passed through her at the thought of him being hospitalized. Her sigh of relief when the good news registered was loud enough that Joann heard it and stifled a laugh with a dainty cough.

As soon as the service concluded, Joann and Joy, who had carpooled to the isolated Roberts farmhouse, hurried back to town via the church building. Joy had texted Paul that she was leaving something in his mailbox after services. She had just stuffed a grocery bag of herbal tea and hot chocolate as well as a funny get well card into the box when the front door opened and Paul stepped cautiously onto the stoop.

"Hey!" he croaked. "Thanks for bringing me something."

"You're welcome," Joy said. "But you'd better come grab it quick!"

"What – I might catch my death of cold out here?" he said, trying to laugh.

"Ummm...something like that," Joy said, grinning.

"Paul, you listen to your doctor and do what he tells you!" Joann called from inside the car.

"Yes, ma'am," he said. "I will. But I'm getting better. No fever today, and Doc Haverty says I'll probably stop being contagious by tomorrow."

"That's wonderful. In the meantime," Joy said, removing the package and extending it toward him. "Drink lots of this and eat right. You look like you're losing weight."

Paul stepped down uncertainly, as though his legs were shaky,

154

and took the bag from her without touching her hand. "Thanks again," he said. "And hey – no worries. You know I've got enough meat on my bones to last me a long time. See you-" He began coughing deeply, turning his head completely away from her and grasping the railing of the house. Joy stepped back and waited until he could catch his breath. It really bothered her to see him so ill.

"Saturday," he whispered finally, grinning weakly.

"Okay," said Joy, wondering if he'd really be recovered by then. "I'm glad you feel better. Good night."

Paul bid her and Joann good night and wobbled back into the house, coughing again. Joy jogged around the car to the passenger's seat. "He looked awful, didn't he?" she said as Joann pulled back into the street.

"Pretty rough," Joann agreed. "But his sense of humor's just fine. He'll be all right soon."

Joy said very little on the dark drive back to her aunt's house. She was too busy thinking about the young man in the church building. He'd been in his pajamas and a hoodie tonight, with – oh, no! Bare feet! What a nut – it had to be below forty degrees outside! Joy smiled in spite of herself at the memory of his unshaven face and wild, wavy hair. Yes, he'd looked awful, but also quite endearing somehow...almost...cute...

Suddenly, Joy shook her head. What in the world was she thinking? She was really losing it if a pair of sad puppy dog eyes, complete with dark circles, could seem attractive. At least she didn't, like, *say* anything so dumb to Joann...that would have been humiliating. Joy glanced discreetly at her aunt's profile in the dark Jeep, then felt her face flush. Something about the set of Joann's mouth as she focused innocently on the city streets hinted Joy's secret was not so safe after all.

155

CHAPTER 18

Children's Day, despite its haphazard planning, was a huge success, primarily thanks to the endurance of about ten faithful workers of the East Montpelier congregation, including Joy, Joann, Alex, and Paul. They had arrived early to finish setting up, participated throughout the event, and stayed late to clean up. Joann, Alex, and Paul had taught the classes, and Joy had supervised the distribution of hot dogs and side dishes and dessert and drinks to ninety-two active children. Joann had also taken over the leadership of the outdoor games with surprising energy when Paul discovered he suddenly needed to sit down.

Joy watched Paul throughout the day, looking for signs he was overdoing it, but other than a nagging cough and a bit of pallor, he appeared normal except when he abruptly exhausted himself during kickball. Joy glanced at him once during lunch and noticed him wolfing down one of Joann's peanut butter cookies.

He caught her staring. "Hey, don't judge!" he said, only a bit hoarsely. "I dropped eight pounds this week and I'm *starved*! And this cookie is *awesome*!" Joy only grinned.

Joy and Joann were sanitizing the kitchen counters just after four-thirty when the last parent arrived to pick up her children. Paul sent the final three children on their way with their art projects and then bounded back inside.

"Guess what?" he exclaimed, dashing into the kitchen. "That lady, Mrs. Jenkins, who had the three kids here, she wants to come to worship tomorrow! She says her kids had such a good time she's going to 'give us a try.' Isn't that amazing?" He strode to Joy, threw his arms around her and hugged her tightly before hurrying away to find the other remaining members. At the doorway, he paused, swayed a bit, and continued at a slower pace, mumbling, "Whoa, I've been sick," on his way through the living room.

"Amazing," Joy repeated absently. Joann snickered, and Joy looked down and saw the faucet was running – she'd turned it on –

and couldn't remember why! She busied herself in wiping down the area around the sink, trying to figure out exactly why her heart was pounding. She was grateful Joann had the tact to keep quiet.

The two women continued to clean in an awkward silence for a few minutes. Although Joy and Joann could typically enjoy each other's company whether they were conversing or not, Joy felt now as though she needed to start talking about something – anything – but she could not keep her mind off how nice...and protected...she'd felt for the second and a half she'd been in Paul's arms. He'd smelled good too – like a cross between Irish Spring soap and mint, possibly from his cough drops.

Ten minutes later, Alex and Paul gathered in the kitchen with the women. "Well, that's it," Alex said, brushing his hands on his jeans. "We've survived with minimal catastrophe, I think."

"Except for the unfortunate orange soda experience," Paul reminded him with a chuckle.

"What's that?" said Joann.

"Oh, one of the boys had a bit of a cold and ran around outside in your games, got overheated, drank four cups of orange drink, began coughing, and promptly lost it all on the living room carpet," Alex said.

Joy gasped and made a horrified face, but Joann just laughed. "Poor child," she said. "Did the stain come up?"

"Oh, yeah," Paul said. "I took care of it – even disinfected the area. Fortunately, he hadn't eaten much lunch." Joy shuddered.

"Good job, gang," Alex said. "And now, I'd kind of like to sweep my fianceé off to dinner. Any objections, Jo-Jo? Please don't have any."

Joy and Paul shouted with laughter as Joann blushed. "I'd love to," she said. "But I gave Joy a ride today, so we'd need to take her home first."

"Oh, don't worry about that," Paul said. "I can take her home."

"Are you sure?" Joy said, a strange feeling of excitement rising inside her. "You're probably exhausted."

"Sure," he said, winking at her. "You aren't too big of a burden."

Joy nodded her agreement, told Alex and Joann goodbye, and hurried to Paul's bedroom to grab her purse from the bed, where every church member had placed their belongings for safekeeping. She re-entered the living room and stood uncomfortably as Paul stepped into his bathroom and blew his nose.

"Oh..." he groaned as he washed his hands. "I still sound disgusting."

"I'm just glad you're better," Joy said. "You always seem so – well, healthy and strong, you know, that it was a little...weird to see you so sick."

Paul smiled. "I don't seem to be able to do things in moderation," he said. "If I get sick or hurt, I do a really thorough job of it and worry as many people as possible."

Joy returned his smile uncertainly. "Well," she said. "I hope you haven't overworked today."

"I hope not too...but if a certain lady were to make sure I didn't have to...oh, say, cook a meal for myself tonight...I'd be less concerned." Paul dimpled and batted his eyes.

Joy raised her eyebrows. If she wasn't mistaken, Paul was flirting with her. And she was sure he was practically begging to spend more time in her company, despite the fact he knew she didn't know how to cook.

"That's quite a request..." she said coyly.

"I know, but I've been *very* sick," he said, looking for all the world like an overgrown child.

"Such a man! Milking your sickness for all it's worth! Okay, yes. Come over for supper. But don't expect anything fancy. I'm not a French Swedish Pomeranian Mexican chef like you are!"

Paul laughed all the way out the door and to his pickup until a coughing fit forced him to become calm again. "Joy," he gasped. "Just where do you think my relatives are from?"

"Uh, what did I say? Let's see...France, Sweden, err...Pomerania...and...uh...Mexico? No – Spain?"

Paul began laughing again. "Why don't you start driving and stop laughing at me?" Joy snapped, mostly in jest. "Isn't that the crazy list of nationalities you told me a few weeks ago?"

"I'm French, Irish, and Swiss," Paul said, starting the car at last. "I'm not Mexican – I just like Mexican food."

"Close enough."

"And I'm *certainly* not a Pomeranian!"

"Don't sound so defensive...are you prejudiced against them or something?"

"A Pomeranian isn't a nationality, you goofball. It's a white, fluffy breed of *dog*!"

"Oh." Joy felt her face growing hot again. "Sorry."

"Joy," Paul said. "You're funny. Thanks for the laugh. I needed that."

"Glad to be of service," she said with a sigh. It was going to be a long evening. Joy recalled how quickly they had begun arguing on their last outing together, and realized she might have let a pair of handsome blue eyes and a couple of strong and manly arms sway her into a situation she'd regret. After all, she'd already made a fool out of herself once, and they'd not even reached the Montpelier city limits!

But Joy was wrong. She and Paul did not argue. In fact – she wasn't even sure they had disagreed on anything the entire three hours they spent together. Joy went about her bedtime preparations in a haze that night, reliving the hours between five and eight in great detail. She'd served him a good nutritious meal, the last of the meatloaf she'd made during her cooking lessons with Joann, peas, and a respectable salad. Paul ate gratefully – and much – apologizing that he was getting his appetite back and was hungry continuously. Joy felt so nervous in light of his earlier flirtatious attitude she could hardly eat a bite.

After the meal, they'd bundled up again and migrated to the porch, Paul to stand at the railing to look at the stars, and Joy to the porch swing. Paul was talking excitedly about the success of Children's Day again, and although Joy was listening and adding all the appropriate affirming noises, she was also watching his profile in the moonlight. She'd noticed tonight for the first time how wide and powerful his shoulders were – probably from chopping and stacking wood for half the geriatric population of Montpelier.

Suddenly, Paul whirled and came to sit beside Joy in the

swing, sending her heartbeat up a few dozen notches.

"You know, Joy," he'd said intensely. "Children's Day would have totally failed without all that writing you did at the last minute. You completely saved the day, and I want you to know how much I appreciate it. It really meant a lot to me that we were still able to hold it, and I promise you I was in no condition to write a paragraph, much less eight lessons!"

"Well, I'm glad it worked out, and I'm glad you recovered quickly enough to go today," she'd replied. "I – I was really concerned about you."

Paul had just smiled at her and changed the subject, and for the remainder of their time together, they'd discussed lighter things, but somehow, Joy sensed Paul approved of her a little more than before.

Joy had settled herself under the covers when her cell phone rang. She grabbed it quickly, always fearful of late night calls, but breathed a little easier when she saw it was Paul.

"Hey, you weren't asleep yet, were you?" he asked.

"No, you caught me in time."

"Well, I just got off the phone with my mom, and she really wants me to visit this coming weekend. I realized you've never seen Stowe, so I was wondering if you'd like to come too? We'd leave Friday evening and come back Saturday evening. I'm scheduled to lead singing Sunday morning if I can stop coughing before then."

Joy's mouth was hanging open for light years before she remembered to close it. "Um," she said profoundly.

"I'm sure Jennifer would let you sleep in her room," Paul added, sensing Joy's discomfort. "She has an extra bed in there since Celeste got married this past spring."

"Uh...yeah, okay," Joy said finally. "I don't think I have anything else going on."

"Joy," said Paul. "It's all right if you want to say no. I won't be offended. If it makes you feel any better, though, I'll just show you around and then you can stay in a hotel. There are plenty in Stowe, and my family can be a bit overwhelming."

"No, no, it's not that," Joy said. "I was just surprised – and –

well, yeah. Surprised. But I want to go, really! And I'd like to meet your family."

"Great! We can discuss details later. I'll let you get some rest." Paul held the phone away from his mouth and coughed. Joy winced as she heard him trying to catch his breath. "And thanks again for supper. I enjoyed it," he continued at last.

As soon as they'd said their goodbyes, Joy ended the call and let out a shriek that was part excitement and part frantic female. What was going on? Was she *really* going to go stay with a strange family so she could sight-see and spend time with Paul? Joy glanced at her phone again. 10:30...not really that late. Could she risk a call to her aunt? Joy pondered for a moment longer, remembered Joann had had a date that night, and called.

"Are you awake?" she said eagerly when Joann answered.

"No, dear, I'm dead asleep, having a wonderful dream about dolphins," Joann cracked, laughing at her niece.

"Oh, okay," Joy said, pausing only briefly at her aunt's off-the-wall humor. "Well, anyway, do you have a minute?"

"Yes, of course. What's going on?"

"You aren't still out with Alex, are you?"

"No, Joy! Now spill it before you burst!"

"Paul invited himself to dinner at my house tonight. Then, just a minute ago, he called and asked me to go with him to Stowe next weekend to sight-see and meet his parents! I said yes! Am I out of my *mind*?"

Joann laughed until Joy grew impatient with her. "You don't have to laugh *that* much," Joy said irritably. "I wanted some advice!"

"I'm sorry," Joann said, a smile still in her voice. "You just sounded like you'd said yes to a marriage proposal from him or something. And no, you're not out of your mind. Stowe is a beautiful place, and I'm sure the Grahams are good people."

"But – won't it be rather weird that I'm staying with his *family* as though I were his – his *fianceé* or something?"

"I doubt Paul would have invited you if it weren't a common thing for him to bring friends to their house. And he has a big bunch of sisters, doesn't he?"

"Yes, four, but at least one is married."

"They'll help break the ice. You'll probably become friends with them, and then everything will seem more natural."

"You're probably right. You usually are. Thanks for listening to my wild rambling."

"I'm happy to. Oh, and Joy?"

"Hmmm...?"

"May I give you one more piece of advice?"

"Sure."

"Don't fight your feelings for Paul. He's a good man, and I think he's really growing to care for you."

"Aunt Joann!" Joy said. "You – I – I mean, oh, good night!"

"Good night, dear heart."

Joy hardly thought of anything other than her upcoming weekend until Tuesday night, when she was briefly distracted by the realization that her first class to teach at the library was in just two days. She spent several hours preparing an introductory session, complete with icebreaker games and prizes, as well as a short speech about professional attire, and almost immediately went back to thinking about the trip to Stowe. Normally, the prospect of teaching, especially teaching adults mostly older than her, would have been enough to tie her stomach in knots, but the upcoming time with Paul and his family took precedence on her mental list of stomach-knotting activities.

Wednesday night Bible study did little to ease her nerves, for Paul was there, of course, looking much healthier, and wearing a bright blue shirt nearly the color of his eyes. Joy spoke to him briefly, only long enough to inquire after his health and to confirm their Friday departure time, but long enough to increase her heart rate once more. "Joy Carnegie," she lectured herself as she drove home briskly. "You are acting like a fifteen-year-old with raging hormones. So Paul is a nice man who just so happens to be strong, intelligent, and inexplicably attractive to you. You thought those things about Calvin too. Get over it!" She refused to consider Joann's advice.

On Thursday, Joy conducted her first career class at the library. She felt quite intimidated at first by her students – two young men near her age, three middle-aged women, and one man who could have easily been seventy. Before many minutes had passed, however, she began to relax. All six of them were polite and engaged in the material, as well as the games afterward, and Joy was enjoying herself thoroughly when someone knocked on the door. Joy jumped as Joann poked her head in and said, "I hate to break up the fun, but it's 7:08, and the library is technically supposed to be closed now."

Joy stared at the clock and was amazed at the passage of time. "Sorry," she said, ears burning. "We were having a good time, and now I've kept you late. I hope you'll forgive me and still come back next week!" Her students all promised good-naturedly, and Joy had collected her belongings and left within two minutes.

Outside the classroom, in the main portion of the library, Joann was turning off lights. "I didn't know you ever closed," Joy said, straightening chairs in the children's section.

"I don't, but Pearl – you know, Bonnie Johnston's mother? - started feeling sick this afternoon, so I took her hours."

"That was nice of you."

"She's certainly covered for me plenty of times, especially when I was in the hospital."

The women were headed to their respective jeeps when Joann stopped short. "Hey," she said. "Alex and I are going to play Scrabble in a few minutes. Do you want to join us? It's not as much fun with just two people."

"I believe it is time for a rematch," Joy said. "I think that sounds like an excellent idea. And I hope both Alex and I beat you to a pulp!"

"My, my, how violent," said Joann. "And how sad that your evil plans will be thwarted. Oh, by the way, why don't you leave your car here. I'll drop you back by later. The driveway can't hold three vehicles, and the city really frowns upon cars parked in my street."

Joy climbed into her aunt's jeep and was immediately hit by a sense of deja vu. She thought back over the last several weeks as Joann drove through the dark streets. How thankful she was for so many things, but primarily she was thankful to be on such comfortable terms with Joann. She was also so relieved that her aunt seemed to have regained much of her old stamina at last.

"Why did you drive to work today?" she asked suddenly.

"Oh, I was just running late this morning, and sprinting is a bit difficult for me these days," Joann said. "I seem to get tired if I try to run seven blocks in one minute. That is, I did yesterday."

Joy laughed. Sprinting, indeed. Joann was certainly back to her healthy self.

The Scrabble game was an entertaining but ultimately humiliating experience for Joy. She'd never been one to play Scrabble – or any board game, because her parents never took the time to do anything so simple, but she considered herself to have a good vocabulary. However, Alex and Joann both put her to shame. Also, Joy had previously considered herself competitive, but the level of competition between Alex and Joann was unreal.

"That's spelled wrong," Joann said instantly as Alex laid down the letters for "abscess."

"No, Jo-Jo. It couldn't be. See – ab – cess. And besides, I'm a doctor. I ought to know how to spell words like this!"

"Joy, can't you see it's wrong?" Joann persisted.

"I – I'm ashamed to say I don't know," Joy said, sighing.

"Well, I'm challenging you, sweetie," Joann said to Alex, hefting the huge dictionary. "You aren't going to go out with a misspelled word!"

Alex rolled his eyes at Joy and shrugged helplessly. "Jo-Jo," he said. "You've met your match. I'm sorry. I know it's hard to admit."

"Abscess!" Joann said loudly, pushing the dictionary into her fiance's hands. "See?"

Alex squinted at the small print and covered his face in embarrassment.

"Where? Where?" Joy asked, scrambling out of her chair to read over his shoulder. When she read the word and saw her aunt was, once again, correct, she giggled, then sighed, laid down the letters for "ran," and watched as Joann won the game.

"How do you do it?" Joy asked a few minutes later as she and Joann were preparing mugs of hot apple cider in the kitchen.

"Do what, dear heart?" Joann was digging in a cupboard for her nutmeg, which Alex liked sprinkled in his cider.

"Win at Scrabble against someone who went to medical school, for crying out loud?"

Joann located the spice at last and emerged from her cupboard. "I don't know," she said. "I've just always been good at it. I read all the time, and I like expanding my vocabulary, and I've always spelled well. Oh – also I'm bilingual, of course. Perhaps that's why."

"Well, for whatever reasons, you're crazy good at it. And it's good Alex loves you, because you stomped him tonight."

"Alex is secure enough as a person and as a man that he can handle being defeated at Scrabble," Joann replied. "I think it's a very important characteristic in a man – that his male ego isn't too large to stand being beaten by a woman at a game."

"He probably loves you for your brain," Joy said matter-of-factly.

"Oh, dear. I hope that's not all. What happens when I lose my mind?"

Both women were still howling with laughter when they brought the mugs of cider into the dining room to the very patient man waiting there.

165

CHAPTER 19

Friday morning dawned overcast and bitterly cold, so Joy packed her heaviest clothing for the trip. She also chose her sturdiest clothes, sensing that sight-seeing with Paul, just like hiking with Joann, would most likely involve intense physical exertion. Joy was packed by noon, although Paul wasn't picking her up until three, so she forced down a bowl of soup and settled in on the couch to do some journaling.

Suddenly, Joy's cell phone sounded. Pachelbel's "Canon in D." A ring tone she hadn't heard in more than a month. All the negative emotions she'd experienced toward her father in the past two months came racing back to the surface. Joy thought about ignoring the call, but she predicted George would not back down until she answered. She looked at her watch. Still thirty minutes until Paul would arrive. She accepted the call and said "Hello" as calmly as she knew how.

"Hello, Sophia. Are you prepared to return to Pennsylvania within twenty-four hours?" George said without even a trace of warmth in his voice.

"Of course not! I told you weeks ago I wasn't coming back. Why are you calling and asking me such a ridiculous question?"

"You obviously haven't read my emails or you would understand. This is unfortunate. I wrote to you that I would officially disown you if you did not return by November 10th, which, if you have access to a calendar, you know is tomorrow."

Joy gasped, not sure she could breathe from sudden pain. As long as she could put off thinking about the situation with her parents, it didn't hurt much, but now the sensations returned with a vengeance. "What exactly does this mean?" she said, hating she couldn't quite keep her voice from faltering. "You aren't supporting me financially, and you've been furious with me for weeks now."

"It means that unless you return to your place in life, you won't be hearing from us or receiving gifts from us. We won't be talking to you or even about you, and we won't welcome visits or accept phone calls from you. And I'll see to it the realtors in Vermont know just how irresponsible and incapable you are, so don't expect to get a job easily. Trust me, I *can* make that happen."

"So let me get this straight. You're going to try to set me up to fail so I'll do what you want?" Joy said, beginning to shake.

"I prefer to see it as disciplining you for your stupidity and rebellion."

The urge to scream at George Carnegie rose up instantly inside Joy. She longed to throw his adultery in his face, to call him all the unprintable names she could call to mind, to threaten to turn him in to the police for blackmail. Two months ago, she would have given in to the temptation, but today, something kept her from it. Joann's voice saying, "Well, just because something might be true does not mean I have the right to say it, and God, not I, will judge George Carnegie," crossed Joy's mind like a fresh breeze.

"In that case, our conversation is finished," Joy said, as calmly as though she were transacting a real estate closing. "I will pray for you, and please give Mother my love." She gently tapped "End" on her phone and collapsed on the couch in despair.

Paul found her there twenty minutes later when he knocked on the door and she called for him to enter but did not move. "Joy!" he said, rushing to the couch, where she lay face down. "What in the world is wrong?"

"I don't know if I can go this weekend," she said without lifting her head. "I won't be a good guest at all."

"Forget the trip! What happened?" Paul spotted a huge antique ottoman, dragged it to the edge of the couch, and flopped onto it.

"Nobody has died," she mumbled. "Don't worry – just go on and have your weekend. I'll – I'll survive."

Paul was no expert in counseling, nor could he claim experience dealing with reserved females since his mother and sisters let him know quite readily what they were feeling, so he might have followed her directions if he hadn't heard the tears in her voice and guessed someone had hurt her terribly. Paul leaned closer to her and began rubbing the shoulder nearest him with his big fingers. "I want to know who hurt you," he said. "I want to help."

"There's nothing you can do. Thanks." She still wouldn't look at him or raise her head.

"I can listen. My ears are pretty big, you know."

"You've got to go to Stowe, and the story is long, pathetic, and dumb."

"I have plenty of time. And nothing about your pain is dumb."

Joy rolled over, shrugging off his comforting hand, and squinted at him through red eyes. The pattern of the old sofa had become imprinted on her cheeks, and she looked about twelve, Paul decided. "Are you serious you'll listen?" she asked, pulling at her sweater self-consciously.

"Of course."

She closed her eyes, still lying down, and drew a ragged breath. "Okay," she said. "I guess your perspective on this might be helpful. But – we've got to talk while you drive. I refuse for you to keep your family waiting on my account!"

"That's fine," Paul said. "So – you're all packed and ready?"

"Yeah. Just let me slip into the bathroom and wash my face. I look like a lobster, I'm sure."

By the time Joy had refreshed her stinging eyes and rinsed the salt from her cheeks, Paul had loaded her little pile of belongings into his pickup and was waiting for her patiently. She slipped into the passenger seat with her backpack.

Paul started the ignition and reached for the gearshift, then paused. "Oh, wait," he said. "Two things. Here," he said, handing her a pair of gloves and a box of off-brand tissues. "I forgot to mention that the heater has been acting up, but the part's back-ordered. You'll need to keep your hands warm."

"And my nose will probably run too?"

Paul grinned. "Well, that generally does happen when people cry – and I figure you'd rather not use the gloves on your nose, at least in front of me."

Joy nodded gratefully as Paul pulled out onto the road. Naturally, although she'd blown her nose in the bathroom, the life or death necessity for further tissues hadn't occurred to her!

"So," Paul said after he'd driven a mile. "I hear this story is long, and we've only got an hour to drive. Who has done what to you?"

Joy clutched her waist instinctively as the physical pain hit her once more. My – my father," she choked out. "He disowned me – just now...well, about half an hour ago."

"Oh...that's awful! Why right now?"

Joy launched into the entire story, sparing no details of her father's treachery, past and present. She also gave him a brief character sketch of her shallow and incompetent mother. Joy even told Paul about the guilt and grief she'd experienced over the death of her uncle after she'd lost touch with him, as well as the sense of desertion when her father had tried to convince her Joann cared nothing for her. She'd just completed her spiel when Paul's pickup lurched, sputtered, and died.

Joy looked around her for the first time in at least thirty minutes and discovered they had left the highway and were on a much smaller paved road. Paul made a noise of frustration and fell back against his seat. "I'm a dummy," he groaned.

"What's wrong? What happened to the pickup?"

"We've run out of gas! I was going to stop on the edge of Montpelier and get some at the cheapest station in the county, but I – uh – got engrossed in your story, and I forgot! I can't believe it!"

"Oh – I'm sorry-"

"It's not your fault! I should have remembered. I was too busy cherishing evil thoughts toward your father."

"He seems to provoke those in a lot of people," Joy said, sniffing. "What were yours in particular?"

"Using my black belt on him, primarily."

"You have a *black belt*?"

"Just first degree. Now, I've got to get this truck off the road."

"Do you want help? Not that you need it, apparently..."

"No, just get out and help me watch for cars. Then we can call my folks. Unfortunately, we're still quite a hike away."

"How far?" asked Joy, obeying him.

"Eleven miles or so."

In five minutes, they were inside the truck again, safely off the road, and Paul had contacted his mother, who promised one of them would be on their way as soon as they could get a gas can filled. "And now," Paul said. "Let's talk about you again. I'm sorry we got sidetracked for a while there, but now we have the perfect opportunity to finish our conversation, thanks to my brainless performance."

"So we're going to sit here calmly and freeze and chat until we're rescued?"

"Well," Paul said. "I suppose it's not going to be necessary to freeze. I'm not going to let you get hypothermia. But we should only be here half an hour or so...so you can stay squashed against the door as far away from me as possible without being in any danger of freezing."

Joy slumped in her seat self-consciously and looked at Paul. "So...what do you think I should do about my fiasco?"

"I don't think there's anything you can do, Joy, except grit your teeth and go on. And pray for your parents' souls."

"Am I right in refusing to go back? I mean, I don't approve of how my parents live their lives, but I hate to think I just, like, lost my family," Joy said, rubbing her aching forehead.

"They made the decision, not you. You're not doing anything wrong or unnatural. In fact, it sounds like you've just been escaping from a very unhealthy situation. And it also seems you have a pretty special lady who is willing to be your family."

"I don't know what I'd be doing without her. I mean, honestly, Paul, I don't know what kind of miserable excuse for a human I'd be if it weren't for her example, and my uncle John's, that summer, and her continued encouragement now."

Paul patted her arm as she started to cry again. "I mean, Paul, I didn't even go to church much in Pittsburgh. I didn't read my Bible except once in a while. I was baptized into the church in college, but I never became part of a congregation after I graduated. I was working too many hours, and there was no one to hold me accountable. I was dying inside, and I didn't even know how much until I came here." She reached under her seat for the box of tissues and blew her nose. She waited for words of criticism – or at least admonition – from the man beside her. She should have made time for church. Had she repented? Didn't she know that being a Christian required commitment? It was certainly good she'd seen the error of her ways...

"I'm sorry," Paul said at last, his voice deep and rough. "I spoke so completely wrong and judgmentally to you last month."

"What?"

"You know. When we were seeing the aurora and I bashed you for not doing enough. I hope you can forgive me."

"You had no way of knowing-" Joy began, protesting.

"That's just the point. I didn't know you well – and I had no place judging you, scolding you as though I were some sort of authority on service. It was hypocritical and, well, sinful, and I really feel awful about it. And even if I had known your situation, I shouldn't have attacked you like that." Paul began coughing after his speech, so Joy waited until he finished before she spoke.

"I forgive you, Paul. I forgave you weeks ago. And, although I know it's wrong to judge people, I should thank you. You woke me up to how selfish I've been. I've been very self-centered all my life, and if I'm going to change my life, I've got to change that too."

"You've hardly been selfish lately. There's no way you could have been – with looking out for me and totally saving Children's Day. Oh, and your community service at the library."

"How did you hear about the library?"

Paul pressed his lips together as if debating whether or not to disclose his source. "Oh, I believe a certain French Canadian among us might have let it slip that you were busy preparing for it."

Joy rolled her eyes. "It's not exactly a thing to brag about...you know, all hail Joy Carnegie, who's finally doing something useful once a week!"

Paul chuckled. "I think you're really finding your talents up here," he said.

Joy smiled slightly. "I hope so. And I also need to apologize. I've misjudged you too. I thought just because you're unemployed and living in the church house, and you seem, you know, satisfied, you didn't have much ambition in life. I've since realized what you do is very important, much more important than high-paying jobs or degrees, although I know now you *do* have degrees too. I said some terrible things to you that night, and I don't know how to say how sorry I am."

"I forgive you too. I know it probably does seem like I'm sort of a bum. There are reasons I live like I do – reasons I'll tell you sometime, but not now – but I have hopes and dreams...and I am still pursuing goals. I'm just not there yet, and I'm thankful to be doing something useful in the meantime."

"Can you tell me about your future goals? I really respect you, but I feel that I don't – um – understand you, I guess."

"I don't talk enough about myself, Joy. I – I can't – can't explain it all, but I don't share much, you're right. It's easier somehow. But yes, I'll tell you some of my goals. First of all, I want to marry and raise a big Christian family. I want to be as good of a husband and father as my dad has always been. Secondly, I want to be as healthy as possible. You'll see tonight that good health doesn't exactly run in my family, but I'm determined to do my best to stay in good shape for the people who need and love me. And third, I want to teach high school. I'm almost done with my teaching credential, so I can start applying for positions very soon. I'll hopefully be qualified to teach English and/or journalism and/or P.E. And that's entirely too much about me for the moment."

Joy stared at him in silence, surprised, but not shocked.

"What? Why are you looking at me like that?"

"I'm thinking Aunt Joann was right about you."

"Should I be scared?"

"No, goofball. You know she thinks the world of you. I'm just remembering she said you were a good man."

"And you're a good woman," he said. "Don't let your father make you question that." He put his arm around her shoulders and gave her a squeeze, then didn't move his arm. And Joy was not nervous. Only glad.

"Look!" Paul said after a moment, hurrying to open his truck door. "It's my mom!"

CHAPTER 20

The pickup driven by Paul's mother was even more battered than his, Joy realized as the older woman pulled off the road and killed the engine. Joy stepped cautiously from the vehicle, shivering slightly in the darkening air. She waited as Paul and his mother met between the two vehicles and hugged as though they'd been apart for years. The awkwardness of the situation hit Joy once again...she was just an intrusion on this visit, after all...

"Joy!" Paul called to her then. "Come on over! My mom is dying to meet you." Joy was startled, but she approached them immediately.

"Hello, Joy," Katie Graham said, her voice sweet and low-pitched. "I'm so glad to meet you. I've been so looking forward to meeting our little tourist."

Joy murmured the correct greetings self-consciously, but all she could think about was the phrase "our little tourist." Not – Paul's friend – "friend" pronounced with painful significance. Not - "your guest" - as though that were all Joy would ever be to her. No, Katie – was that what she was to call this motherly woman? - had already made her feel welcome after opening her mouth just once.

"And you're to call me Katie, all right? Mrs. Graham sounds like a housekeeper in a Scottish mystery novel, and I won't answer to it. Now – let's see to the car. Paul, come on, hurry up now. Joy's practically turned blue." Joy blinked several times, astonished.

Paul obeyed his mother, transferring the gasoline from the huge gas can into his pickup. "Mom, I don't need all this gas," he laughed. "How many gallons did Dad put in here anyway?"

"Oh, I just filled it full," Katie answered. "I know you don't need it all. The can needed refilling before any more snow comes anyway."

Paul stopped pouring and set the can on the ground. "You're filling the gas cans these days?" he said tightly.

"Usually," said Katie. "Paul, you haven't been home in six

months. He's – he's getting weaker."

"My dad," Paul said to Joy, in a tone that told her now was not the time for questions.

"Well, we can get caught up at home," Katie said quickly. "I'll see you there," she hugged Paul, then turned to Joy and held her close for a second as well. "Now, turn on the heater for Joy, son," she added. "She's shivering."

Paul grinned sheepishly. "It's broken, Mom – won't be fixed until next week."

"In that case, come along with me, Joy. There's no sense in freezing with that boy of mine. Just because he's built like a polar bear doesn't mean we all are." Katie took Joy by the arm and began leading her gently away from Paul. Joy gave one nervous glance back at him over her shoulder – he was laughing – and allowed herself to be led as if she were in a trance.

The miles to the Graham farmhouse seemed to pass in an instant, to Joy's surprise. Katie kept up a steady stream of comforting small talk until she turned into the long driveway. Then, she braked and placed her hand on Joy's shoulder. "Joy, I want to mention a couple of things before we go in, not to scare you, but to make you a bit more comfortable meeting the family. First of all, Paul's sisters are in an uproar that he's bringing a young lady to visit. No – it's okay. I realize you're not in a courtship – you're here as a friend. And the girls know that too, but this *is* the first time in the eight years since he went to college that he's brought home a female of any variety, so they may be a little – nosy – although they've been warned, all right?"

"Of course," Joy said, smiling. She could stand any amount of scrutiny from Paul's sisters as long as his parents understood the situation...and her comfort level with Katie had just rocketed higher thanks to the woman's discretion and compassion for her.

"And also," Katie continued, the cheerful light in her blue eyes dimming for a moment. "Paul's father is quite sick, nearly an invalid, actually. He's had diabetes and heart disease for many years, and although he's just sixty, he's wearing down fast these days. Paul's taking it pretty hard."

"I'm very sorry."

174

"Thank you. We're coping, and counting our blessings, but I thought you'd rather be warned we're a bit – unusual – in some ways."

"I appreciate your thoughtfulness," Joy said. "And I hope having a visitor won't be too much extra work for you..."

"Oh, gracious, no. You won't be any trouble. We have people in and out all the time, and Jean doesn't permit anyone to baby him just because he's sick. The girls have had friends over all the time, and neighbors drop in, and – you know – we've basically an open door policy around here."

Because of Katie's short stop in the driveway, the two vehicles arrived at the cozy-looking two-story house almost simultaneously. Katie parked, hefted the gas can out of the truck bed, and called out, "Jennifer! Come take this to the barn!"

A short, solidly-built teenager in overalls appeared, said, "Hi, Joy!" with great enthusiasm, and took off with the heavy can at a dead run. Joy watched her go in some amazement. If Paul were a girl with pigtails and a deep tan...

"My youngest, Jennifer," Katie said with a laugh. "She never walks anywhere – she runs. Come on in and get warm and meet the rest of the gang – well, except Celeste. She's married a southern boy and is way down in South Carolina now."

Paul jogged up to Joy at that moment. "I'll be your moral support," he said.

"Good," Joy said, but in reality, the Graham family wasn't too intimidating. And Katie just made Joy want to sit down and tell her everything about herself.

The ample front porch reminded Joy of hers, as did the wide old staircase as soon as she entered. She breathed in deeply – this house was a home – warm and smelling of cinnamon and baking – and was immediately greeted by Marie, Fiona, Jennifer, who had returned via the kitchen door, and Jean.

They hugged her. They all hugged her exuberantly, except Jean, who shook her hand enthusiastically as he balanced on his crutches. And Joy, who frequently went weeks without a hug in her pre-Vermont days, felt like a tennis ball bounced from person to person – and loved every minute of it.

The introductions were made rapidly, in 75% English and 25% French – for it was evidently common for Jean to speak both in the same sentences to his children. But soon, Marie gasped, shouted, "My pie!", and dashed back into the kitchen, and Jean hobbled to the recliner to sit down, so they all ended up gathered in the comfortably old-fashioned living room to chat.

A fireplace kept the large room so toasty that Joy soon shed her coat, Paul's gloves, and her sweater. Paul had already stripped down to his t-shirt and jeans. He was busy telling his family about Children's Day when he had a sudden fit of coughing.

"Paul, you don't sound well," Fiona said softly. Joy had already pegged her as the quiet one.

"And you're thin! Seriously, Paul! You haven't been skinny since I was, like, a baby!" Jennifer exclaimed. "Are you sure you're okay?" Joy bit back a laugh. There was nothing quiet about Jennifer!

"Thank you, Brat," Paul said sarcastically. "And yes, I'm fine! You know how long it takes me to shake a cough."

"He was pretty sick," Joy put in. "We were concerned."

"Traitor!" he hissed at her, and they all laughed then.

By the time supper, a thick stew loaded with vegetables, was served, Joy felt as though she had known Katie and Paul's sisters for years. She was a bit more shy around Jean, who said little but smiled often, but only because of her sympathy for his obviously poor health. The family crowded around the large, scarred kitchen table and consumed most of the pot of stew and half a pan of cornbread, although Joy noticed neither Paul nor his father ate any of the bread. Conversation during the meal was lively, and mostly consisted of Marie, Fiona, and Jennifer telling embarrassing childhood stories about Paul. Joy laughed until the ache in her heart almost disappeared.

"Let's play Scrabble," Fiona suggested as they were finishing the meal. "Do you feel like playing, Dad?"

"Yes, but we have only one game. Only four people can play," said Jean in his unique French-Scottish accent.

"Oh, I have homework," Jennifer said. "Plus, I'll lose. It's inescapable."

"And I'll do the dishes..." Marie began, but Katie interrupted her.

"No, sweetie. You love Scrabble, and you made most of supper. Go ahead – I'll get the dishes."

"I'll help you, and that will leave four people to play," Joy said.

"Oh, are you sure?" protested Katie.

"Quite sure. My aunt slaughtered me in a Scrabble game this week, and I can't stand the thought of another one so soon," Joy said, laughing.

"Ah...yes, your aunt is known for her insane Scrabble game," Paul said, overhearing. "I'm glad she's not here tonight!"

In five minutes, Joy was closed in the kitchen with Katie and an enormous mound of dirty dishes. "Wash or dry?" Katie asked, tossing Joy a faded blue gingham apron.

"Probably I'd better wash," said Joy, cringing inwardly. "You know where to put things when they're dry."

Without further ado, they began, with Joy scrubbing feverishly to keep ahead of the older woman, who, after five children, was a dish-drying machine.

"And so I imagine there are a dozen questions bouncing around in your head about us," said Katie without preamble. "The girls don't generally leave much opportunity for anyone else to talk at supper. Don't be shy – ask if you'd like."

Joy was again shocked – and a bit appalled – by Katie's perceptiveness, but she hid her surprise and spoke cautiously. "Well, I was wondering how Paul's dad lost his leg."

"He lost it because of his diabetes – oh, about five years ago, I'd say. Yes – five years ago, during Fiona's senior year of high school. We still had a small working farm then – several acres of crops, an orchard, and a few animals, and Jean hurt his leg on the tractor. It became infected and never healed properly. Diabetics can have terrible difficulty healing from infections, especially when they're as brittle as he is. Jean's been diabetic for twenty-five years, you see."

"That's awful."

"Yes, it was a hard time. It was when Jean had to stop working, and I began teaching again. I'm an English teacher at the high school, but I'd quit when Paul was born. Paul helped us out for a while once he started his newspaper job, but when he lost that, things were scary until I was hired."

Joy stopped short. "Um – Katie," she said, looking into Paul's mother's eyes, which were a brilliant blue like his - "There *is* something helpful you might be able to tell me. What happened to Paul at that newspaper? When the subject comes up, he just shuts down and gets – almost – well, angry. Can you explain without breaking his confidence?"

"Of course," Katie said, patting Joy with a damp hand. "And, Joy, it's no secret. Up here, it's common knowledge. That's why Paul moved down to Montpelier. He just can't bear to share the story himself."

"Okay, if you're sure he won't mind your telling me..." Joy felt a sense of growing nervousness in her stomach. Maybe she would finally have some insight into Paul's occasional dark moods.

Katie shook her head. "He'll be relieved you know. Paul was fired from his position as copy editor because he unintentionally incriminated his boss in some unethical business dealings. The editor of the paper was also a state representative, and he had an interest in a large corporation pushing a ruling in favor of billboards."

"Billboards?"

"Ah, yes. You've not been in Vermont long. There's a perpetual struggle between big companies and the rest of the state about whether or not to allow big, ugly billboards on our highways. It came up for a vote in state congress recently, and was narrowly defeated. Anyway, this corporation was paying the editor/representative indirectly, through the newspaper treasury, to vote for legalizing billboards. That's obviously quite unethical."

"I would say so!"

"Paul didn't write many articles, but one he wrote regularly was the newspaper's financial report, which the citizens of Stowe demand because village funds help keep the paper afloat. The editor told Paul not to record some large, mysterious sums that appeared in

178

the treasury, but Paul investigated and found he would be dishonest to the village if he did not, so he included them in his report as well.

"Needless to say, the village investigated the funds, and found out what the editor had been doing. Paul had been amazed – he'd trusted his boss and just assumed the man was being a little lazy and did not want to bother including the mystery money in his records. The editor took advantage of Paul's confusion and implied Paul had been helping him cover up the funds for months but had decided suddenly to expose him because he was upset about not writing more articles."

"Are you serious? That's so wrong!"

"Yes. The police were called in, and although they could not determine any wrongdoing on Paul's part, the village didn't believe them. The editor had fired Paul on the spot, but because there also wasn't any proof that Paul *had* been honest, the village told the replacement editor *not* to re-hire Paul. Naturally, Paul was angry and embarrassed that he'd been a bit too trusting, but that was only the beginning. When Paul began applying to other papers, he discovered that his ex-boss had contacted all the other papers in the state and had fed them lies, so Paul was basically blacklisted wherever he went. And he won't move far away because Jean is so sick."

"But – but – that's so – so wrong!" Joy sputtered, scrubbing the cornbread pan ferociously.

"It's really changed Paul. It hurt his pride terribly, that I had to go back to work, and that he couldn't support himself even with two degrees. But he looks happier this visit than I've seen him in years, and I think all the physical activity in his current work has been his lifesaver. He has his daddy's build, and heart disease on both sides of the family, so he's working hard to stay healthy. That's been the the one big blessing throughout the entire mess – he's had time to get fit again."

"He told me today about his plans to teach," Joy said quietly.

"Yes, and I hope he can find a teaching job soon. It will really be good for his – well, I suppose you'd say his self-esteem."

"Whew," Joy said. She rinsed her hands and the sink. "I – I think I understand him a bit more now. I can't believe he had to go

179

through all that – that injustice. It makes me want to go slug some people."

"I've wanted to do that for two years, although I continue praying for forgiveness," said Katie, her eyes dancing with mischief. "And if Jean hadn't been recovering from heart surgery when it happened, he'd have probably gone to jail for murder. He's an old French hothead. But then, I'm an old Irish hothead, so it makes for exciting times around here sometimes."

"And that's my last question," said Joy, laughing. "How in the world did the two of you end up together? You're different nationalities, ages, obviously – where did you meet?"

Katie grinned at her. "Oh, so you don't think I'm sixty, dear? Thank you so much. As a matter of fact, Jean is only six years older than me."

"No way." Joy's jaw dropped. She'd been trying to figure out if Katie had even been an adult when she'd given birth to Paul.

"Yes way. But yes, we have different backgrounds. Our story isn't very strange. Jean saw an ad in a British paper about land for sale in Vermont, and, since his adopted parents had just passed away, he was desperate to leave Scotland. He bought this house and thirty acres, sight unseen, and moved here in 1981. I was living with my parents and teaching right here in Stowe, wondering if I'd die an old maid, when this muscular guy with an insane accent showed up at church service one day. And the rest is history..."

"That's incredible he just decided to move to America and ended up here."

"I was very thankful," Katie said. "We've been married twenty-nine years now."

Suddenly, a frustrated shout rose from the living room. "Maybe we'd better check on them," Katie said. "Jean and Paul get terribly competitive."

Sure enough, Jean and his son were in the middle of a heated discussion – in French – when the women entered, with Marie and Fiona adding frequent contributions. Katie marched into the fray and calmed them, reminding Jean he couldn't afford to get over-excited, and reminding Paul it was just a game – in English.

180

The men calmed down, grinning sheepishly, but Joy could hear Jean's labored breathing from across the room. "What were they arguing about?" Joy asked in a whisper as the game resumed. "I don't know – maybe Paul's scoring?"

"You don't speak French?"

"Not really. I'm stupid at languages except, thankfully, English."

"I don't know how they can do that – be so perfectly bilingual. I mean, Paul and his sisters don't even have a trace of an accent when they speak English."

"I *am* an English teacher," Katie answered, winking. "And I homeschooled them until they reached high school, so we had plenty of time for pronunciation practice!"

In ten minutes, the game was finished, with Fiona claiming a narrow victory, and Jean said good night right away, although it was only eight o'clock. Joy watched Paul, stony-faced, watching his father, barely able to get himself across the room.

Katie was watching Paul too. She rose quickly from the couch and approached her son. "I'm sorry," she said after Jean was out of earshot. She held her son close for a moment.

"Is there nothing all those expensive doctors can do for him?" Paul said.

"Not really. They – they said at his appointment last week that there are definite signs of congestive heart failure now."

Paul closed his eyes and sighed. "I was afraid of that. And – and you, Mom? How are you holding up?"

"Healthy as a horse except my pesky asthma. Yes, yes, son, I'm watching myself. I know." Joy stared at the floor as the little woman comforted her grieving firstborn.

Everyone else in the old farmhouse was ready for bed by ten o'clock, a fact that amazed Joy since there were just two small bathrooms in the house. She had realized mornings came quite early for them, so she'd claimed last dibs to the bathroom once shared by all five children.

Now, Joy told Jennifer, who was in the other twin bed reading, good night, and headed to the bathroom for her turn at last. "Don't hurry," Jennifer said just before Joy shut the door. "I can sleep through anything."

The tiny bathroom felt homey and welcoming, with its old-fashioned wall radiator on low and the damp, thick towels draped carefully in every available location. Joy had been informed she could use any number of lavender towels or washcloths she desired; that was Celeste's color. Joy brushed her teeth, carefully avoiding three females' neat stashes of lotions and cosmetics as well as a pair of glasses she suspected were Paul's. Then she grabbed a fluffy towel and stepped into the shower – and discovered why they kept the bathroom so warm. The water never got hot, just tepid, and after the first five minutes, it began growing colder. Joy was out and dressed and shivering as soon as she could possibly pronounce herself clean. Was Paul's family too poor to keep the hot water heater turned up, or just too poor to improve the plumbing in this bathroom? Or just too tough to care? Probably the latter, Joy thought in frustration as she dashed down the frigid upstairs hallway back to Jennifer's room. Everything about Vermont so far had been an exercise in "toughness" of one type or another!

Jennifer was still awake when Joy returned. She grinned as Joy grabbed a book and dove under the covers like a drowning woman grasping a life preserver. "Kinda cold?" Jennifer asked, not unkindly.

"Yes," Joy said. "How do you stand those cool showers when it's *really* cold outside? Are you all as tough as *Marines*?"

Jennifer laughed until she actually cried. "Marie must have – have forgotten!"

"What?"

"The person who gets the last bath turns off the water heater so it doesn't go on heating all night. Then, Mom or Dad turns it back on in the morning. I guess Marie forgot you were here and needing a shower tonight. I bet you were miserable in there!"

"Well, let's just say I didn't do any unnecessary exfoliating!" Joy said, relieved that her teeth had stopped chattering at last.

"Yeah, you need all those dead skin cells to keep you warm!"

Both girls found that so funny that they began giggling

uncontrollably. "I must be tired!" Joy said. "It wasn't that funny. No offense."

Jennifer grinned again. "Oh, I'm terribly offended." She yawned. "Why don't you just go to sleep?"

"Because Paul tossed this book at me downstairs and told me to figure out where I wanted to go," said Joy, holding up a dog-eared guide to northern Vermont's attractions.

"Oh, yeah. You've got to pick out a really great place. That will be hard. There are so many cool things to do in this area."

"But not so many in November, fortunately," said Joy, reading about Mount Mansfield's alpine slide, which had closed a month previously.

Jennifer watched Joy reading for a moment. "You're good for Paul," she said suddenly.

"What – I mean, we're not-" Joy said.

"Oh, I know you aren't his girlfriend yet. That's not what I meant, although I think you'd be perfect for each other. I mean that it's good for him to have a friend again. I was so glad to hear that a young person had started to go to church down there. Paul looks a lot happier than he did last time he visited; well, except when he's thinking about Dad's health, that is."

Joy, remembering Katie had said the same thing about her son, only smiled, but Jennifer kept speaking.

"Paul's a lot older than me, you know. Almost nine years. I was just a little kid when he left home, but he's always been my – hero, I guess. He used to take such good care of me for Mom when she was still trying to run the farm after Dad lost his leg. And he was never too busy to make time for me. I've been so worried about him, Joy. He works so hard, and he's been so alone since the mess at the newspaper. I worry that no one is taking care of him – he just runs around taking care of everyone else. All those old people. He's always pushed himself to the breaking point if he thinks others need him."

Joy interrupted Jennifer's reverie cautiously. "It is true that Paul works hard helping people," she said. "But I think it really makes him happy. And also," she said, choosing her words with careful deliberation. "I believe he is doing a decent job of taking care of himself. He's – he's told me he wants to be sure he stays healthy for – for all of you. I certainly had no idea until recently that he was concerned about inheriting health problems, but he eats well – better than me, even, and I try very hard to keep my weight down." Jennifer looked relieved. "Also," Joy continued. "He really was very sick last week. He was quite – uh – strong and fit-looking before that."

Jennifer nodded and stared more closely at the older woman. "Joy," Jennifer said. "You're blushing! You think my brother is cute, don't you? You do!"

Joy's face was on fire. "I wouldn't say cute, exactly, but yes, of course, he looks – nice-"

"Whatever," said Jennifer. "You're crazy about him. I'm not blind. And I think it's awesome!"

Joy glared at her. She simply couldn't help herself. The determined, blunt, dog-worrying-a-bone attitude Paul had sometimes infuriated her just as much in his youngest sister.

"I think I'll go to sleep now," said Jennifer, her dark eyes dancing. "I can see you're mad, and I understand why. And if Paul finds out I pumped you, he'll kill me. But it doesn't matter because you'll be my sister soon and you'll *have* to put up with me!" She rolled over and pulled the covers over most of her head.

"I just want to know if Paul was as *obnoxious* as you when *he* was a child," muttered Joy, not really caring if Jennifer heard.

"Oh, much worse!"

Joy heard the muffled laughter in Jennifer's voice, and after some reflection, decided the teenager had been teasing her, probably the same way she teased her sisters and Paul. Joy lay sleepless for almost an hour, analyzing all she had learned so far on her visit. Paul was – Paul was just an interesting man. She wished she could have known him before he had been hurt so badly. It was ironic he'd been blacklisted, just as her father was threatening to do to her. Paul was really rather wonderful, and although he made her furious sometimes – didn't people say that was a good thing in love - "Whoa!" Joy actually said aloud, sitting upright in bed. She glanced in alarm in Jennifer's direction, but the lump under the covers didn't move at all.

Joy sat there for several minutes. Where had that word even

come from? Love? She'd never even been sure she loved Cal, after dating him for three years, and she'd never even dated Paul. He'd never held her hand, never touched her in anything but a friendly way. And – she did appreciate his dimples and blue eyes and obvious strength, but he wasn't even handsome, exactly. Not her type. Not even more than an inch taller than her.

Joy lay down once more and sighed. This same man was also expecting her to leave at eight o'clock and go sight-seeing. She'd have to let him choose the location. Joy fell asleep quickly then, but she dreamed of Paul – that she was living with him – as his wife – on top of Mount Washington in Pittsburgh – in a church building with no electricity or indoor plumbing.

CHAPTER 21

The aromas of bacon and coffee woke Joy at six, and despite her difficulty falling asleep, she was ready to rise – if for no other reason than she didn't want to have any more frightening dreams about Paul! She slid into the bathroom, shocked it was available. As she splashed water on her eyes, she was happy to note that someone had turned the water heater back on already!

Joy was headed back to Jennifer's room when a door flew open and Paul emerged, sleepy and tousled and in a ragged sweatshirt and pajama pants. Joy greeted him, self conscious about her own sweats and un-brushed hair, and he replied hoarsely and gave her a friendly hug, before stumbling into the bathroom himself.

Joy dressed rapidly in the bedroom, keeping an eye on Jennifer so she could dive into a corner if the younger girl awoke. She wore jeans and one of her favorite plaid flannel shirts, two pairs of socks, and her boots. She was sitting on the bed with her back to Jennifer's, braiding her hair, when she heard the girl's voice, scratchy with sleep.

"Your hair is pretty. I like the color."

Joy turned quickly. "Oh, you're awake. Thanks. I hope I didn't wake you."

"Nope," Jennifer said, so good-naturedly that Joy, who still didn't care for early mornings, was impressed. Jennifer stretched like a lazy kitten and scrubbed her eyes with her fists, looking terribly young. Joy felt a pang of guilt over her grouchy words the night before.

"Uh, listen, Jennifer," Joy began. "About last night. I – I shouldn't have-"

"No, don't apologize," Jennifer said cheerfully. "I was being a brat. I know I was. Sometimes I just say whatever comes to my mind. My dad says – in incredibly annoyed French, of course – that my tongue wags like a psychotic poodle's tail."

Joy had been prepared to be quite repentant, but she shouted with laughter instead, picturing the opinionated Frenchman delivering such an insult to his daughter. "Well, I need to work on my sense of humor," Joy said. "I was an only child, and my parents were much too – sophisticated – to banter back and forth like that. And by sophisticated, I mean totally *stiff*."

"No one can accuse us of that," Jennifer said, throwing off the covers and standing up. She crossed the room to stand next to Joy, and Joy noticed Jennifer barely hit her chin in height. She gave Joy a big hug. "Friends?"

"Sure," said Joy as Jennifer scampered toward the door.

"That's good – 'cause I meant every word!" Jennifer slipped out the door and was running to the bathroom before Joy could do more than gasp.

"Brat!' she hollered after her.

Joy headed down the hall to the staircase a minute later, and once again met Paul leaving his room. They headed down the stairs together. "I hear you're bonding quite well with Jennifer," he teased.

"You heard me?"

"Yeah. My door was open. It means she really likes you, you know. If she didn't, she'd be as sweet as sugar."

"Huh." Joy looked at Paul again more closely. "Hey – what's different about you this morning? Oh – no glasses! Are you wearing contacts?"

"No, I'm not blind enough to need 'em all the time. I just stuck them in my pocket for driving today. I think I need a new prescription because they've been hurting my head a little lately."

"Your eyes are *really* blue." Joy covered her mouth as soon as she spoke.

Paul winked at her and headed into the kitchen. Joy followed more slowly, cringing. She'd sounded like a lovesick teenager!

There was good coffee in the kitchen – strong, too – Joy could tell from the aroma, but she didn't drink any. She'd only had a half cup twice in the past ten days, and already she felt calmer in the mornings. Paul didn't drink it either, opting instead for skim milk, but Marie and Fiona downed a mug each before hurrying out the door to their jobs as CNAs at Stowe's small medical center.

Joy lingered at the table with Paul and his parents, because it was still early and Katie wanted to give him a haircut before they left to sight-see. Jennifer was already outside, where she preferred to spend every possible waking moment.

"Okay, so Marie and Fiona are working at the hospital, and Celeste is married, and Jennifer is – a – senior? - in high school...does she want to do medical care too – or go to college?" Joy asked.

"Jennifer couldn't care less about college," Katie said. "She wants to do something adventurous, like be a tour guide or a rafting guide or something. We've tried to convince her to find some other career goal as a backup plan, but she just doesn't want a normal job."

Jean leaned toward Joy. "Paul is my academic child," he said conspiratorially. "He is a genius, like his mother."

"Oh, be quiet," Katie said, whipping an old sheet around Paul's shoulders. She began snipping the dark waves so quickly Joy feared he'd end up bald.

"Yeah, I'm the only nerd of the bunch," Paul said between falling wads of hair. "And stop giggling, Joy. I'm very sensitive about my nerdiness."

"Uh huh. Right. Now – I haven't been able to choose a place for us to go today," she said. "You'll just have to pick. There's too much to see."

"I guess we'll just go to Moss Glen Falls and Mount Mansfield then, unless you want to see all the shops and stuff instead," Paul said.

"I'll have pity on you and choose the waterfall if you'll have pity on my lack of hiking skills," Joy said.

"Fair enough. Just bring layers – you'll need them all until we get up a good walking pace."

Joy nodded, but she felt like sighing. It was going to be another embarrassing day out in the wilderness!

It was eight-thirty when Paul and Joy set out in his truck. "Do you mind if we drive around a bit first?" Paul said. "I'd like to show you the town a little, and we also need to grab some sandwiches or something for lunch. Oh, and get gas."

"Of course not. I know you're just being a tour guide for my benefit, so just lead the way. I hate you're taking away time from your parents to do this."

Paul punched her arm gently. "Stop worrying and enjoy yourself. I am. Now, let me show you my favorite place to write when I was growing up."

Paul drove them to Emily's Bridge, a covered bridge on the edge of Stowe. They drove across it and also stopped briefly so Joy could snap a few pictures. "I'd sit on that big rock down there," Paul said, pointing at the tranquil stream below. "And I'd write for hours. I'd have a seat like a block of ice afterward, and icicles for fingers and toes, but I didn't care." Joy banished her laugh at the mental images his words evoked.

Paul then drove past the tiny community center where the church of Christ met on Sundays, his sisters' high school, and the local newspaper office. "Mom told you more about my days here at the paper, didn't she?" Paul said, slowing to a stop in front of the small building.

"Yes – but – how did you know?" Joy said, staring at him.

"She said this morning you'd had a heart-to-heart discussion in the kitchen last night and she'd answered some questions for you."

"I hope you don't mind. I didn't want to pry-"

"Definitely not. I've been trying for days – no, weeks, actually – to think of how to tell you, but it's a bit – degrading – no matter how you word the story." He accelerated past the office.

Their last item of interest on the tour was the old downtown, the center of tourism for the area. Paul drove slowly through the streets as Joy took in the dozens of gift shops and cafes, still decorated for fall. "Welcome to Shopping Row," Paul said. "If you want anything from Vermont, this is certainly the most expensive place to find it."

"I knew it was better to go to the waterfall and the mountain," Joy said. "Thanks for the warning!"

Joy waited in the car, rubbing her hands to warm them, as Paul stopped at an older-looking gas station to purchase fuel and lunch. He filled the tank first, then went inside. He returned in a few minutes with a bag full of food.

"Best deli sandwiches around!" he said as he dropped the bag into Joy's arms.

"This is a ton of food," Joy said skeptically.

"We'll work off every last extra calorie. No fears."

Joy pulled three twenties from her pocket. "This is for the gas and lunch," she said, shoving them at Paul. "I don't know the exact cost of the trip, but that should cover it."

Paul hesitated and then took two of them. "That will do it," he said. "And Joy? If things were different, it would all be my treat, okay?"

"There's no reason you should pay for me," Joy said. "I certainly expected to pay for all the extra gas for sight-seeing, and the extra food. I'd be glad to pay for the gas to and from Montpelier too, but-"

"No," Paul said. "I can handle *that.*"

Their first official stop was at Moss Glen Falls. Joy immediately pulled on all her extra layers as soon as she stepped out of the vehicle. She was going to look like a waddling penguin, but she'd be good and warm. It had be below thirty still, at nine-fifteen. She'd make herself as comfortable as possible in the body temperature department since she knew her muscles would be dying soon.

Paul set a moderate pace as they entered the narrow path, for which Joy was tempted to thank him profusely. Joy soon found herself appreciating the crisp air and the dense forest. Maybe this hiking thing wouldn't kill her after all.

After fifteen minutes, Joy no longer noticed anything other than her screaming calves. The problem was that although Paul's pace had remained constant, the incline of the path had increased sharply. Joy struggled to keep up with him but soon found herself panting – and warm – far too warm.

Paul noticed her discomfort at last, and he stopped short. "Getting overheated?" he asked.

"You might say that. I think I've broken a *sweat* somehow under here," Joy gasped.

"You want me to fold up your coat and put it in my backpack? I think it'll fit."

"Oh, would you? That would help a lot. I – I am ashamed to say this is a rough walk for me..."

Paul smiled and began rolling her coat carefully. "It's pretty steep for a while, but we're almost there."

"Oh, good! I'd really hate to wimp out on you – but my legs are *so* sore!"

"We haven't even gone to Mount Mansfield yet!" Paul teased her. "If you think *this* is difficult..."

Joy wrinkled her nose in disgust. "Are you trying to murder me?"

"Just kidding! Man! If looks could kill...Anyway, we'll ride a ski lift up the mountain, all right? It's way over 4,000 feet high. We're not going to attempt that today."

Joy could not restrain a huge sigh of relief.

After ten minutes more of hiking, made much easier for Joy without her heavy coat, they finally reached the waterfall. It was beautiful, and over one hundred feet tall, although not in a continuous drop. "Ohhhh..." Joy breathed. Her waterfall education had been sadly neglected – she'd only seen five or six in her life, and even fewer up close like this one.

"Worth the climb?"

"Oh, yes!" Joy said. "Good choice, Paul. I'm so glad you brought me up here."

They sat on a rock on the edge of the falls and drank from the thermoses of still-warm apple cider Katie had sent with them. "I like coming here during off-season," Paul said, contentedly. "There aren't many other people around, although there probably will be later in the day when it warms up a little more."

"It is peaceful," Joy said. "I haven't actually done much hiking – but this is nice."

"Now I can tell you haven't spent many years around your aunt," Paul said. "If you'd grown up around her, you'd probably be the most experienced hiker in Vermont. From what she's told me, this fall is the first one in her life she hasn't hiked every chance she got."

Joy rubbed her chin. "I guess I should try to learn to enjoy it more. I suspect she's done less of it the last few weeks to spend time with me, and she knows I'm pathetic at it."

"It might be a good goal," Paul said. "And the exercise will keep you calm and feeling healthy."

"And maybe counteract all this comfort food," Joy laughed.

The pair headed down the trail again after Joy took some more photos, including one of Paul when he wasn't paying attention. She secretly vowed to print it at Walmart – just so she'd have a picture of him. After all, he was turning into a great friend...never mind the freakish dream from last night!

Joy led the way down the trail for a short distance, rejoicing in the easier walking. Suddenly, Paul jerked her braid and pretended to whip her with it. "Giddyup, slow poke!" he said, pushing in front of her at top speed.

Joy grabbed a long pine needle cluster from the ground and dashed to catch up with him. She chased him, brandishing the small branch like a whip, as he broke into an actual run. Joy was not in shape, but she could run a decent sprint back in high school P.E., and was much lighter on her feet than Paul, so she got near enough a time or two to switch his shoulders.

The race finally ended when they saw another hiker approaching. They stepped off the trail, gasping, to let him by. "Okay, okay, I give up!" Paul said, starting to cough. "You win. Whip me if you wish. I can't – breathe – properly yet."

"Excuses, excuses!" Joy said, but she did not attempt to re-start their contest. Paul was wheezing, and she could tell running was still a bit beyond his strength. He'd had fever just a little over a week ago, after all.

They reached the pickup five minutes later. Joy collapsed into her seat, exhausted. "Okay. That's enough sight-seeing," she said. "Let's go back to Montpelier now. I want a nap."

"Wimp," Paul said, tossing his backpack at her and starting the engine.

"Um...excuse me...I chased you *down* on the trail! Who are you calling a wimp?"

Paul just laughed and headed toward Mount Mansfield. It was almost eleven when they arrived at the base of the peak where visitors could board the ski lift to the summit. Joy eyed the gondola cars, suspended in mid air except for a thin connection to the cable. "Why don't we just drive to the top?" she said.

"The road's closed...has been for two weeks or longer. Besides, the gondolas are fun. Haven't you ever ridden one?

"Yeah," Joy replied. "Heights aren't my thing."

"It's safe. Come on! We can eat lunch on top of the mountain."

As Joy climbed inside one of the shaky little cars with Paul, she decided she was finally certifiably insane. The only things between her and instant death were a few thin wires, and she was risking her life with a crazy man just to see the top of what appeared to be a very foggy little mountain.

She sat down gingerly on the padded bench with Paul. "If I plunge to a certain and painful death in one of these things, I'm totally blaming you," Joy said.

"If you plunge to your death, chances are I won't be around either...and do you believe in blaming people for things when you're already dead?" Paul said.

"Oh, stop being philosophical-" Joy began, but the car started moving then, and she froze, staying silent the rest of the way up the mountain. Paul could see she really was quite nervous, and he placed his arm protectively around her shoulders as they swung higher and higher.

After what seemed like a century to Joy, they finally got out at the summit. Joy had taken three steps away from the gondola when she exclaimed, "It's snowing!"

"I wondered when you'd notice," said Paul. "It started about halfway up the mountain."

"Ohhh...and look at the view!" said Joy, hurrying nearer the edge of the mountain. The clouds and fog mostly covered the distance between the mountain and the ground, but a small window had opened up for several seconds, and Joy could see distant mountains as well as the Von Trapp family lodge. Up close, the trees were becoming coated with the dense, wet snowflakes.

"This snow won't all melt until spring," said Paul.

Joy shivered. "I guess not! It's ridiculously cold up here!"

After finding a sheltered spot to eat their sandwiches, as well as the pretzels and some of the fruit Paul had selected, they took a few pictures, even posing for one together, and headed back down the mountain, for the snow was growing harder, and the iciness of the wind was uncomfortably sharp. This time, Joy did not mind the ride so much, partly because she was so grateful for the relative warmth of the gondola's interior.

"Are you too cold?" Paul asked her, realizing she was still shivering.

"I'm p – pp – pretty cold."

"How many pairs of pants do you have on?"

Joy stared at him until he blushed. "Sorry," he said. "It's just we'd better keep moving as much as we can if you only have one layer."

"My legs aren't cold," Joy said. "It's my face...and my feet."

Paul rummaged in his backpack and pulled out a pair of thermal socks as well as a thick, crocheted scarf. "Maybe these will help a little until we start hiking again. I know the socks will be huge on your feet, but you need the insulation."

Joy thanked him and added the extra socks to her wool ones. She then tied the scarf around her head and ears.

"Awww...how cute," said Paul. "You look like my Pomeranian grandmother!" Joy rolled her eyes. She was glad Paul seemed so relaxed with her this weekend, but he was really an insufferable clown!

Ten minutes later, they were back in Paul's truck. "What next?" said Joy.

"Well," Paul said. "If you're up for some more hiking, we'll go through Smugglers' Notch. It will have to be on foot because they close it in October for the duration of the winter."

"Oh, yeah! I think I read about that in the guidebook you let me borrow last night. It sounds very interesting."

"It's a longer climb than the waterfall, but we have four hours until dark," Paul said.

"Sure...why not?" Joy said, resigned. "Bring on the mountains!"

Paul parked on a small gravel pullout in front of a sign warning of the road's closed condition. He vaulted neatly over the sign; Joy climbed over it more cautiously. "Is this safe?" she asked.

"Yeah, as long as there's not too much ice. We'll sort of play it by ear. I don't think this pass has received as much snow as the top of Mount Mansfield. And see – it's not even snowing now."

When Joy collapsed into the pickup four hours later, she knew all her previous brushes with physical exertion in Vermont were mere practice for this particular afternoon. She wasn't actually sure if she still possessed calves; the sensation had gone out of them entirely at least half a mile back up the pass. And there was a blister on her heel at least the size of Pittsburgh. And she was hungry enough to eat a horse...and a camel.

The trek had been fascinating – the incredibly winding highway that had eventually narrowed to one lane, with huge mirrors posted on trees and poles to increase visibility around the hairpin turns, the boulders behind which smugglers had lurked in previous centuries. But Joy had temporarily lost her appreciation of Smugglers' Notch in favor of a hot bath and a hot meal – as soon as possible! She lay back against her seat without moving.

"Ahhh..." Paul said as he started the engine. "That was so much fun! You're a good sport, Joy"

"Thank you for taking me," she mumbled.

"Are you hungry? There are apples left."

"Yes, but it's too much effort," Joy said.

Paul laughed and passed her the remaining thermos of cider instead. They rode most of the fifteen miles back to the Graham farm in silence, but Joy could sense Paul was feeling peaceful and satisfied – with her.

CHAPTER 22

After a hot, nourishing supper of chicken pot pie, Joy thought she might survive, even if she had to wait until late that night for a long bath. She embarrassed herself just a little by scarfing down two large servings, more than anyone else except Paul, but no one seemed to notice her hearty appetite. Finally, Joy sat back. 'That was sooo good," she said. "But now I'm sleepy."

"You could just stay another night," said Jennifer.

"I'd like to, but my driver seems to be anxious to get back."

"I'd be glad to stay," Paul said. "But I'm supposed to lead singing. Alex has been leading for weeks now, and he would probably like a break. I hope my cough is enough better I can get through it."

"Why don't you try and see?" said Marie. "We haven't sung with you in ages."

Before Joy knew what was happening, Paul broke out into "Home of the Soul," and his family followed his lead in perfect four-part harmony, with Paul switching to bass in the chorus and returning to lead at the beginning of each verse. Joy had heard the song, but she did not know it well, so she just muttered a few words of the alto with Katie and Jennifer during the chorus. She could certainly tell where Paul had gotten his tenor – Jean's was pure gold. She marveled that this family – this quirky, vibrant, awesome family – could just jump into song and make such beautiful and heartfelt music...without accompaniment or even notes printed on a page. And just sitting around the dining table, at that.

"Wow," said Joy after the last verse ended.

"Ah, that was very nice," said Jean. "But Joy, why do you hide with the altos? Your voice is soprano."

"Oh...I – um...didn't really know the song...and I haven't done much singing," she stammered.

"What's a song you like, dear?" said Katie.

"I know "Amazing Grace" and "Just As I Am" and...uh...a lot of newer songs," Joy said. "But not too many by memory..." She could feel herself blushing. Such a heathen!

Paul immediately started "Amazing Grace," and Joy relaxed in the familiar words, relieved she could at least participate a little. After that, they sang a mixture of lively "Stamps Baxter" style hymns and newer "devotional" songs, and Joy knew several well enough to join in. As the minutes passed, she grew less and less self-conscious about singing in such a small group, and more able to focus on praising God and enjoying the fellowship of Paul and his family.

Thirty minutes later, Paul had begun coughing a little, and Jean could no longer muster the breath necessary for the fast-paced choruses, so they concluded with a prayer, led by Jean, for Paul and Joy's safety.

Then, Katie rose and casually began clearing away the supper dishes, as if there hadn't just been a thirty-minute concert over them. Joy tried to assist her, but she was shoved back down in her seat by Jennifer. "It's my turn," Jennifer said, jumping up so quickly she almost took the woven tablecloth with her. "And you're leaving soon. Fiona and I will do them."

The younger women shooed their mother out of the kitchen as well, so the rest of the group migrated to the living room, except for Jean, who dragged himself to bed instead. Before he left the room, however, he paused beside Joy, who was seated on the couch, and laid his hand heavily on her shoulder.

"It has made my heart happy to get to know you," he said quietly. "Thank you for the friendship you have given my son. Please think of us as family, and welcome yourself into our home any time."

Joy thanked him self-consciously and promised to return again sometime. The room was silent after Jean's solemn words; it was almost as though he had pronounced some sort of French blessing upon her. To Joy's shock, when she glanced over at Paul, there were tears in his eyes.

Joy and Paul said their goodbyes soon afterward. Once again, Joy was bounced back and forth between hugs, which she returned quite willingly. Katie was the last to reach her, and she kissed her warmly on the cheek as well. "Don't be a stranger," she said.

Katie held onto Paul for a long time. "Don't wait long to come back," Joy heard her whisper. "I don't know how long he has." Paul nodded.

"Take care of yourself," Paul said. "Don't try to do everything, Mom. Let the girls help you as much as possible." Katie nodded, looking every bit of her age for the first time since Joy had been visiting.

Suddenly, the sad moment dissipated, and everyone was smiling and hugging – and Katie was looking young once more. When Paul and Joy finally climbed into the frigid cab of the pickup, the silence was almost deafening in comparison to the frenzy of goodbyes in the farmhouse.

Paul had driven a mile before Joy spoke. "Your family is awesome," she said.

"Well, I think so, but I was hoping they didn't scare you too badly." Paul pulled his glasses from his shirt pocket and replaced them over his ears. "Not allowed to leave 'em off at night," he murmured.

"Oh, I wasn't scared – well, maybe I was just a bit overwhelmed by Jennifer last night, but not anymore. I really like them all. I'm so glad you brought me!"

"I'm so glad you came."

Joy was quiet for a few more minutes. Finally, she said, "Paul?"

"Hmmm?"

"Is it always bad to be envious?"

"What kind of question is that?"

"I just wondered...because I totally envy you for your family. I mean, they are so – fun, and interesting, and – and good – and *happy,* even though their lives aren't easy. And it's obvious they love each other."

Paul didn't say anything, so Joy continued. "I've hardly even thought about my father's phone call this weekend because I was so busy enjoying your family. And it's terrible – but I don't even miss my parents. I just miss the – the idea of our being a family. I miss the hopes I used to have that my parents and I would someday be more like your family."

198

"I am very thankful for my family," Paul said. "I know I've been so blessed. And I'm sorry you – you haven't been blessed in that particular way. But I think sometimes – sometimes our families aren't just our parents and siblings. You know, we have the church as a family, and also close friends, and of course more extended family members...so Joy, you've been able to choose your family in a way." Paul rubbed his forehead. "Am I making any sense?"

"Yeah...yes, you are. I – I forget sometimes that as a Christian – even a wimpy one – I do have a family in the church. And I have Aunt Joann...and Alex...and while I'm at it, I think I'll claim you and your family."

"Ah...and now...what role do I serve in your big clan? If you say 'brother,' though, I will bop you on the head with a 2 x 4."

Joy giggled. "I was thinking more along the lines of 'favorite uncle.'"

Paul growled and whacked her on the shoulder.

The following week was somewhat uneventful except for the heavy knowledge Joy carried in her heart that her father really had cut her off. She had proven it beyond doubt on Sunday when she tried to access the online bank account into which her father deposited funds for family emergencies – just to see if she could – and found that both the user name and password had been changed. It was official; she'd been disowned.

Joy ate supper with Joann on Sunday night after evening services and told her in full detail about Friday's phone call...and cried, again. Joann put her arms around her and held her as she sobbed. "The awful thing, Aunt Joann, is this doesn't even change anything. I haven't been in my parents' good graces since September anyway...but it just feels so – so real now. I mean, Thanksgiving is next week, and my parents are pretending I don't exist!" Joy said, burying her face into her aunt's bony shoulder.

Joann's own temper was flaring and her blood pressure rising, but she managed to control her tongue and to concentrate on comforting her niece instead of raging aloud at her brother-in-law and his wife. She also vowed to celebrate Thanksgiving – American Thanksgiving – this year, for the first time since John's death. Alex

199

had already been hinting he wanted a homemade pumpkin pie, and although Joann had always felt more attached to the Canadian holiday in October, Joy deserved to be fussed over and fed a beautiful meal of American comfort food. But beyond basic comforting phrases, Joann had no words of wisdom or advice to offer Joy. There were no words to remedy it.

Joy spent the earlier part of the week preparing for her second library class, which would include actual learning for her students this time. She felt a bit nervous, but she remembered her success from last week and kept her fears under control. She also welcomed the opportunity to have a useful task to occupy her mind and keep her from sitting around and feeling sorry for herself. Her efforts paid off too, for her second class proved to be just as popular as her first.

When Joy woke up on Saturday morning, she felt different somehow. She couldn't exactly put her finger on how – or why – for quite some time. She pondered on it as she sipped the skim milk flavored with two tablespoons of expensive coffee – a compromise she'd discovered that week. She just felt – lighter – somehow, strange since it was only eight a.m., much earlier than she'd risen any other day this week. Suddenly, as she was basking in the warmth of a shower, it occurred to her. She felt at peace. With herself. With her life choices. With the person she was becoming. Joy really could not recall another time in her adult life – except perhaps immediately after her baptism – she'd ever felt such peace. She smiled and sent up a prayer of gratitude, feeling very satisfied and confident – then yelped as her phone rang and she smeared a huge glob of shampoo directly into her left eyeball.

Joy managed to answer the call on speaker phone while scrubbing her eye and splattering water throughout the bathroom. So much for peace – how about pain!

"Joy, whatever is the matter?" asked Joann calmly. Because of course she was always calm. Even at 8:30 a.m. And undoubtedly even with shampoo in her eyeball.

"Shampoo in my eye!" howled Joy. "Hold on a minute!" She flushed her eye with water from the sink for nearly a full minute, then said, "Uhhh! I think – I'm back."

"Do you want to call me back, dear? You seem very busy!"

"No, no, it's okay. What is it?" Joy tried to sound as patient as possible while dripping midway between tub and sink.

"It's such a beautiful day, Joy! Did you know it's supposed to be 55 degrees and sunny today?"

"And..." said Joy, hearing "hiking" in Joann's voice.

"And I'm going hiking in your general direction – well, up into the edge of the Northeast Kingdom, actually. Do you want to come? We won't go too far, because we won't have many hours before dark."

"Okay, I'll come," said Joy, making every effort to be enthusiastic, although her muscles had barely recovered from Smugglers' Notch. "But wouldn't you rather go with Alex?"

"He's going to be busy every waking moment until December, wrapping up his practice," Joann said.

"Well, yes, then. What time will you be ready to leave?"

"I'm sitting by the door with my boots on," said Joann. "If you'd said no, I'd have gone alone. It's too nice of a day to waste, and I have more energy than I have in weeks."

"I'll be ready in fifteen minutes," Joy promised, hoping she could find her own hiking boots. She'd thrown them off somewhere last weekend – she wasn't entirely sure where – in her haste to get a hot bath.

Joy's cell rang once more as she was hurrying downstairs to wait for Joann on the porch. She answered without checking the screen, certain it was her aunt announcing her arrival, but to her surprise, it was Paul. Joy answered while she locked the door.

She waved at her aunt, who was indeed waiting in the driveway, and climbed into the Jeep while exchanging pleasantries with Paul. Joann gave her a knowing grin, a side hug, and the gift of silence as she drove on without trying to ask questions.

Joy talked for five minutes and then said goodbye. She couldn't suppress a happy sigh before turning to greet her aunt at last.

"Well...good morning!"

"Good morning!"

Joy snorted as she watched Joann trying to hide her curiosity. "Yes, yes, that was Paul. He asked me if I wanted to eat supper with him tonight. Someone from church gave him a huge casserole, and he doesn't know what to do with it all."

"Aha."

"We will be back by seven, won't we? Paul said that would give us until dark to hike if we wanted."

"Oh, yes. We'll be back by then easily. That was – thoughtful – of him."

"Um-hm."

"Oh, come on, Joy. I don't want to pry, but I can't help but see it. You like him, don't you?"

Joy sighed and stared out the window without seeing a single tree or hill. "Yes," she muttered finally. "Yes, I like him very much."

The drive to the Lyndon area, where they planned to hike, was long, over an hour and a half, but Joy thoroughly enjoyed it. The scenery shifted from a "New England" feeling of farmland mixed with forests of both deciduous and evergreen trees to a more northern landscape of miles and miles of almost exclusively pines, spruces, and firs. They bought the ingredients for sandwiches in a small grocery store in Lyndon before setting out on a portion of the trails spanning Brighton State Park.

To Joy's relief, the temperature was indeed moderate, and after the last weekend's climbs, the trail didn't seem terribly steep. Also, Joann's pace, while steady, was significantly slower than Paul's, although Joy did secretly suspect Joann was deliberately setting a speed Joy could maintain.

Nevertheless, Joy was thankful when Joann called a halt for lunch. They assembled their simple turkey sandwiches on a large, flat rock face overlooking lower, spruce-covered hills. Joy sank down gingerly onto the rock with a soft groan. "Nothing like moving to Vermont to show you just how badly out of shape you are. I know I'm a healthy size," she said. "But I think my arms and legs are made of limp spaghetti. Is it possible to have 0% muscle mass?"

"Keeping the pounds off by hiking is really a lot more fun than eating like a bird," Joann said. "It's good for building some strength too."

"I know, I know," Joy said. "But what could you possibly

know about struggling with your weight? You're thinner than you were a decade ago!"

"Okay, okay. Touché. This is the thinnest I've been since high school," Joann admitted. "But that's what ten days in the hospital will do to you, and I haven't picked it all back up yet."

"After almost two months? Is that normal?" Joy said, stopping her chewing in concern.

"It takes a long time to regain twenty pounds healthily. No worries, kiddo."

"*Twenty* pounds? Really?"

"Twenty-two, actually, I believe. And since I have such a large frame, I've looked scrawny indeed this fall. I'm surprised you didn't run away from me in fright the first time you saw me!"

Joy just rolled her eyes, but she felt no humor. Joann had been so ill. What if – Joy couldn't let herself finish the thought.

"We've chosen a tentative wedding date," Joann said, brushing bread crumbs from her jeans. "Tentative upon your ability to attend, that is. It's Saturday, January 12th. Do you think you'll be available?"

"Of course! There's no way I'd miss it!"

"But the date is acceptable? You don't have anything scheduled that weekend?"

Joy laughed. "The only event I have scheduled for the rest of my *life* is the Fiction Workshop that begins in a couple of weeks. The new year is just totally – blank – for me."

"Well, put January 12th on your calendar, then. And also...would you mind too much being my maid of honor?"

"Your maid of honor?" Joy squeaked.

"Yes. It may seem a bit silly for me to have an attendant at a simple, small wedding – and a second one, at that, but Alex has a younger brother he wants to serve as best man, and I want you to have a part in the wedding."

"I'd love to," Joy said, trying to hold back the sudden rush of tears threatening to fall.

"Oh, good!" Joann grasped Joy's hand and squeezed it. "Thank you!"

"No, thank you!" Joy said.

CHAPTER 23

That evening, an exhausted Joy knocked on the front door of the church building right on time.

"Hey! The weary hiker arrives!" said Paul as he opened the door. "Come on in. The casserole has five minutes left in the oven."

Joy hurried inside and removed her jacket. "Mmm...smells good," she said.

"I think it will be. It has mounds of cheese on top. I'm going to be repenting in sackcloth and celery sticks for days after this."

The casserole did prove to be a success, and Joy enjoyed her portion thoroughly after her five-mile walk. She helped Paul wash the few dishes afterward, amazed an activity she had always detested had now become such a convenient bonding time. They migrated to the living room couch afterward, and ended up curled up at opposite ends, facing each other, for the best talking angle.

Paul sighed deeply. "I've been thinking," he said.

"Sounds like it's been quite a strain," Joy said.

"You're as big of a brat as Jennifer!"

"I'm sorry...I guess...please continue."

"Do you remember when I told you last weekend I don't talk much about myself?"

"Yes, I remember."

"Well, I think I need to tell you some more about myself. I – I want you to know."

Joy nodded encouragingly, but she was wondering why Paul had to sound so foreboding. Was he about to confess he'd once robbed a bank or had wives in twelve states?

"I'm going to receive my teaching license in a month unless I contract yellow fever or galloping impetigo or something and can't complete my final three courses. I got a letter yesterday saying I passed my comprehensive exams, which I took a month or so ago, so I'm almost finished."

"Wow, Paul! That's wonderful! But – don't you have to do

student teaching or something?"

"I did it last year, early. This licensure program is pretty flexible. It's all online except the student teaching."

"How exciting for you! So...you can start teaching in January?"

"Well, technically, but I doubt anything will open up until later...probably for September. But...that's not why I'm telling you this...I'm not wanting to brag. I wanted to tell you about my plans after that. I'm going to start building a house once I have a teaching job, Joy. It will hopefully be near here...maybe between here and Barre. It's going to be for my family, so they can sell the farmhouse. They'll probably move as soon as possible, especially since Jennifer is almost done with school. Also, you may or may not have heard this past weekend, but Fiona is engaged, so she'll be married by then. And I'll still live on my own. But...I wanted you to know that I feel that I have to stay in this area, even though I could most likely find a teaching job almost anywhere."

"I thought you would be around for a while – to be near your dad," said Joy.

Paul nodded. "I – I just wanted you to know...not that I expect it to influence your – your decisions or anything..." He cleared his throat. Joy could see the beginnings of a blush starting under his freckles.

"It might – influence them," Joy dared to say. "Your – your friendship has been a significant part of my time in Vermont, and although I don't have plans to stick around after the winter, I also don't exactly have plans to leave either."

"I'm not really – free, Joy," Paul said, forming his sentences with great effort. "My dad might have two years...if he doesn't contract pneumonia or anything, and I don't want my mom to have to teach until she just drops. I really don't want her to have to work at all, but it's necessary right now. But – if I were free...I'd do things differently. I'd be – I'd be treating you to something a lot fancier than a casserole from Matilda Mathis at my house, for one thing."

Joy had listened to Paul's extended speech with alternating emotions of fear, sadness, confusion, and excitement. "There's

205

nowhere else I'd rather be at this moment," Joy said slowly. "I've had a lifetime of expensive restaurants."

Paul nodded once more. "I'm glad," he said. "And thank you for – for getting to know me on my terms. I know I'm not the easiest person to befriend...at least, unless you're eighty-five and need a ride!"

"I haven't exactly been Pollyanna myself," Joy said ruefully. "I embarrass myself when I think about how prickly I've been at times."

"I was always fascinated by cacti," said Paul, his eyes twinkling.

That night, as Joy analyzed her evening as usual, she was still somewhat puzzled by the reason for Paul's confidences. She could almost believe he was implying he'd be interested in dating her if his future weren't so uncertain and full of difficulties...but it seemed ludicrous that he would like her romantically. It also seemed ludicrous to Joy that her current "best friend" was a big country boy from Vermont. Just the same...*something* had caused him to speak more about himself tonight than in the previous six weeks combined. Joy only hoped she hadn't betrayed her interest in him. It certainly wouldn't do for him to figure it out before she even understood it herself!

There were not any library classes the following week because of Thanksgiving, so instead of preparing to teach on Thursday, Joy spent the day in quiet celebration with Joann and Alex. They had invited Paul to join them, but he had been assigned an unexpected final project in his most difficult class, so he had to decline. The day was filled with family time, excellent food, and for Joy, deep concern, for Joann was sick.

Joann was not too sick to cook, or to enjoy herself, although she did make every effort to stay out of the others' faces so she would not breathe on them. However, she was sneezing almost incessantly, and had a congested cough, and her eyes were watering so much she had opted to wear her glasses all day long instead of her contacts. And Joy was terrified.

She watched Joann closely for any signs she might be growing worse, or becoming weak, or experiencing shortness of breath. She even asked Alex, in a hushed tone of voice when Joann was in the kitchen, if he thought this illness was going to cause her to have a relapse. Alex smiled at her kindly.

"I don't think so, Joy. Your aunt is a lot tougher than she may seem. And she's not even running a fever. You shouldn't be worried."

After the delicious meal of turkey, dressing, vegetables, and pumpkin pie, the three of them decorated Joann's small Christmas tree. Joann dropped to her knees to plug in the lights behind the tree but began sneezing violently and had to stop to blow her nose. When she stood up at last, she looked so weary Joy stared at her, wondering if Alex could possibly be wrong in his diagnosis.

Joann caught her staring, took one look at the expression on her face, and announced that she and Joy needed some fresh air. Before Joy could protest, Joann had pulled her by the arm out the back door. Joy shot one nervous backward glance at Alex, who was grinning, of all things. Why did she have the feeling she was being taken out back for a sound spanking?

Joy waited uncomfortably as the two of them stood on the deck, facing each other, but Joann did not open her mouth for at least thirty seconds.

At last, Joann spoke, but it was not in the angry or impatient tone Joy had expected. "You're such a worrywart, dear heart," she said. Her voice was gentle. "It concerns me that you always expect the worst." She coughed, then continued. "You've been moping around all day, convinced I've got one foot in the grave just because I have a cold."

"I'm sorry," said Joy. "I didn't intend for you to notice. I know you hate for people to worry about you." She stared intently at a clump of brown grass at her feet.

"No, Joy, you don't understand. You don't need to worry about me in secret. You need to stop worrying! You're going to give yourself an ulcer or something." She sneezed several times into a tissue, removed her glasses, and wiped her streaming eyes.

"But coughing is bad for your heart, isn't it?"

Joann rubbed the bridge of her nose. "Joy, have you ever had pneumonia?"

"No...I don't think so..."

"Well, let me tell you, it is nothing like a cold, or even a sinus infection. When I was sick in September, I couldn't have cooked Thanksgiving dinner to have saved my life. I'm serious. I had double pneumonia, Joy. That means both of my lungs were affected. I was coughing so hard I was blacking out. I was coughing up blood. For days. And also, this wasn't my first bout with pneumonia. I'm prone to it, possibly because of all the secondhand smoke I experienced as a child and a teenager. I've had it four – no, five other times, just not severely enough to be hospitalized. And I'm still here. Just fine. So you don't need to panic when I sneeze. Please."

Joy drew her hand across her eyes. "Okay," she whispered. "I'm just scared to – to lose you," she said. "It's been such a blessing...and a relief...not only to find you, but also to become close to you. And – and I don't know what I'd do without you – right now." She stepped nearer her aunt and hugged her tightly.

"You'd survive – and be the beautiful woman you are," said Joann, hugging her back. "But for now, let's rejoice in the fact we do have each other. I don't anticipate kicking off from a head cold anytime soon."

Joy giggled through her tears. "Neither do I."

"That's good, because I expect you have one now. I think I just breathed 7,000 germs on you."

"I don't care. I can handle-" Joy began, and realized her double standard before she'd completed her sentence. She stopped short, humiliated.

"Come on, worrywart. Alex probably thinks we're drowning in estrogen out here by now."

"No," Joy retorted feebly. "Just mucus!"

Joann laughed until she started coughing, but Joy refused to be afraid this time.

By Sunday morning, Joy did indeed have Joann's cold, so she stayed home from services to avoid infecting anyone whose immune system might be compromised. She didn't run a fever, or even have the croupy cough that characterized her aunt's illness, but she did of course feel tired, sluggish, and annoyed by constant sneezing. Something that was missing from when she had been sick in October, however, was her sense of panic.

Joy padded into the living room with a cup of hot chocolate, a sandwich, and her box of tissues. She sank down onto the couch with a sigh. Yes, she felt gross, but she wouldn't have missed out on the time with Joann and Alex for anything. And yes, it was frustrating to have succumbed to the cold germs, but Joy didn't have the same desperate need for independence as previously, so she didn't feel angry or attempt to deny she was sick.

By noon, Joy was pleasantly surprised to realize she missed church. Not just the social aspect of fellowshipping with the other members, but the actual process of worshiping God. This was, in fact, the first service she'd missed in Vermont, so it was also her first absence in two solid months. The old Joy, the hard-boiled Pittsburgh Joy, would have felt entitled to miss; after all, she'd "put in" an awful lot of time lately. But the new Joy read three psalms and said a long prayer – and wished her sore throat would allow her to sing.

Joy had just finished praying when she heard tires on the driveway. She threw the afghan around her shoulders and stepped out onto the porch to investigate. To her surprise, she saw her aunt and Alex climbing out of Alex's vehicle.

"Hi!" Joy said. "This is a nice surprise!"

"We brought communion and thought you might want to have a little service together," Alex said.

"Oh, yes, thank you!"

"How are you feeling, Joy?" asked Joann, hugging her niece.

"Just kind of yucky. Not as bad as you were on Thanksgiving. Come on in. It's cold out here, and you still have a cough, Aunt Joann!"

"I hate I had to be so generous and share my germs," Joann said.

"It's no big deal," said Joy. "But – you're much better?"

"I'm fine. Finally finished sneezing, I think! Have you run a fever?"

"Not so far. Did you?"

"No, never. It's just been a cold."

"How have you managed to escape?" Joy asked Alex. "Do you have an immune system of steel?"

"Yes," he said. "I am a pediatrician. I was exposed to every cold virus known to mankind ninety times before you were born."

They settled in the living room around the wood stove and had a simple, brief time of worship. Alex led two songs, although neither woman could sing much yet, a prayer, and served Joy the unleavened bread and grape juice of the Lord's Supper. He also read a chapter from the book of John and made a few comments on it. After another prayer, they were finished.

"Thank you," said Joy again. "I wished so much I could be with you all this morning, and I felt plenty well enough to go, but I think I'm disgustingly contagious, so I decided I should stay here."

"Good decision," Joann said. "So many people are still getting over the flu, and many of the older people really struggle with bronchitis in the winter. Now, we're going to leave and let you get some rest. Do you need anything?"

"You've already given me everything I need," said Joy, hugging her aunt.

Joann smiled, then gasped. "Oh, how could I have almost forgotten? Paul wanted to come with us, but I told him to stay away because of his school demands. I hope you don't mind too much."

"Definitely not! He doesn't need any more sickness to deal with this month."

"He did want to see you, though. I believe his exact words were, 'Please send her my – uh – my concern.'"

Joy raised her eyebrows. *"That's* what he said?"

Joann's expression was pure mischief. "Yes, but you cannot tell me he was not intending to say another word instead of 'concern.'"

"Oh, I don't know-"

"Hush, Joy. You can't convince me." Joann squeezed Joy's shoulder. "Now, get some rest."

Joy told them goodbye and sat back down on the couch, but she didn't try to sleep. Instead, she began writing, frantically, in her journal. She really hadn't written in it enough to call it a journal –

scarcely five times since she'd lived in Vermont, but it was high time she worked through some of her feelings about Paul on paper. Three pages later, she was finally willing to admit a solid attraction to him, both inside and out, but she was no closer to knowing what to do about it – if anything.

Joy felt almost completely better by Wednesday, and by Thursday was able to teach her library class without even sneezing. It was not a moment too soon, because she wanted to feel perfectly well for Saturday. Saturday, December 1st. The beginning of the long-awaited Fiction Workshop at Coburn College. The workshop would last from Saturday until Saturday, and, except for the two sessions that coincided with Sunday worship services, Joy intended to savor every last moment and every possible detail of the event. After all, the workshop had been her first motivation for moving to Vermont, and although Joy now recognized it had not ended up being her primary motivation, she was quite excited to be able to participate in it at last.

Joy had originally intended to spend her fall crafting dozens of witty short stories and completing *Shelby's Quest* in preparation for the workshop so she could consult with the teachers, all published authors themselves, about the quality of her work. However, after re-reading the few attempts she'd made in the past two months, she decided to start completely fresh. She'd absorb everything she learned, write feverishly at night, and ask for advice during and after the classes and seminars. Surely the instruction she received would drag her from her literary slump!

Joy woke earlier than necessary on Saturday morning and stood in front of her small wardrobe – the farmhouse had no bedroom closets – in confusion. What to wear? She sensed the other workshop participants would be dressed up – most likely in fashionable but unusual styles, but nothing in her limited wardrobe exactly shouted fashionable or unusual. More like serviceable. Or plain. Suddenly, Joy laughed aloud at herself and pulled her favorite sweater and most comfortable dress pants from their hangers and tossed them on the bed. She'd gone two months without giving a thought to fashion – and had enjoyed herself thoroughly in a wide range of situations. There was no need to regress now. And after all – who exactly was she

211

planning to impress with her clothing anyway? Right – no one. She determined to dress appropriately, but without pretension. Bohemian scarves and leggings and swaying, colorful jewelry weren't her even if she had access to them today.

It was 8:56 when Joy drove into the parking lot of the auditorium building at Coburn. She had found herself ready long before registration was scheduled to begin at 9:00, but she had killed time by driving around the small campus five times. She hurried nervously toward the door, which was marked with a large sign reading "16th Annual December Fiction Workshop." Two other women, clad in pinstriped suits, reached the doorway at a similar time as Joy, but she stepped aside to let them pass, feeling suddenly a bit intimidated by her casual attire and unpublished status.

Joy stepped up to one of several registration tables at precisely nine a.m. An elderly man was seated there, and he took her name, located her professionally-printed name tag, and handed it to her with a program of events and a schedule of classes. "You'll need to select a schedule," he said. Joy skimmed the schedule and discovered she could choose either the red, green, blue, or yellow track. Red was a program for already published novelists; green was for published authors of short fiction. Blue was intended for unpublished writers who planned to remain with short fiction, and yellow contained sessions for unpublished writers who had not yet found their precise genre. There was also a silver category, but it cost extra and was by invitation only; it was designed for established fantasy/science fiction authors. Joy quickly signed up for the yellow division. "Thank you," the man said. "I hope you enjoy the workshop. The opening ceremony begins at 9:30 in the auditorium."

Joy walked slowly into the large room, noticing there were only about fifty other participants scattered throughout the three portions of the auditorium. She sat down at the end of a row near the back of the center section, hoping no one would introduce themselves to her until she was certain her voice would not shake when she spoke. It was appalling that a successful realtor like herself would be so terrified about attending a writing conference, but she had only begun working in real estate because of her father's wishes and

212

influence, so she felt quite alone and amateurish. Who did she think she was, paying nearly a thousand dollars to spend a week writing alongside people who actually made a living with fiction? Except for the few poems and stories she'd submitted in Brown's student literary magazine, no one had ever even read what she'd written. Who was she to call herself an author?

Joy had regained much of her enthusiasm by the end of the opening session, however. The speaker, a renowned writer of historical fiction, had spoken about the power of fiction so eloquently Joy was inspired, and she practically skipped to her first class, a one-hour course with other unpublished authors. The topic was "Using Setting Effectively," and Joy could hardly wait.

The classroom was quite crowded with tables, chairs, a desk, an old television on a prehistoric TV cart, and stuffed bookshelves along almost every wall. Only nine people were seated in the chairs, and one rail-thin woman with frizzy black hair was writing on the whiteboard with her back to the class. Joy quickly found a seat and opened the special notebook she had purchased for this very occasion. The participants had been advised to bring both a notebook and a laptop, but Joy had always secretly preferred creative writing by hand.

"Good morning!" the woman with the mane whirled abruptly to face the ten of them. "I am Ms. Fellows...Ms. Vivian Fellows, but please call me Viv or Vivie. And now I want to know who you are, but please don't ramble on. This is a writing workshop, not Facebook."

The class chuckled and began introducing themselves rapidly. Some members mentioned their professions, some their home cities, and even one her age – eighty-three. But none of them talked long, for Viv cut an imposing figure despite her slender size. Joy gave her first name and mentioned she was living in Woodfield for the time being – but nothing else. This course was the last time and place she wanted to enter a discussion about her ancestry or her career. She estimated she was the youngest attendee by at least twenty years.

"All right. Let's write," said Viv once they had finished. "I've written a simple, unadorned sentence on the board. You each have five minutes to write a setting for this scenario. Remember, setting includes *all* the tactile elements of the scene – not just visual. Now – write!"

Two or three people began scribbling immediately, but most of them sat, like Joy, staring at the sentence on the board: "The man entered the garden." Joy had finally forced herself to write one pitiful sentence - "It was springtime, and he could smell the roses blooming" - when Viv clapped her hands and stopped them.

"You're too inhibited!" she said, waving her arms in a manner anything but. "You're all sitting around like rush hour traffic. Find you a space in this room where you feel comfortable. Go on – grab your notebooks or computers and move! Hide under the furniture. Sit *on* a table. Turn your chairs to the wall. I don't care!"

Most of the students looked at Viv sheepishly and shifted the positions of their chairs a few inches and began writing immediately, as if afraid she would ask them to do something even more strange. But Ethel, the woman who had bragged about being eight-three, stood painfully and dragged her chair to a corner flanked by two bookshelves. She sat again, facing the bookshelves, and began to write. One of the youngest students other than Joy, a forty-something man with a blue streak in his hair, obediently crawled under the table. And Joy, wondering just exactly what lay ahead of her, scooped up her notebook and pen, crossed the room to the TV cart, pushed it out from the wall a few inches, and wedged herself on the floor behind it. She sneezed suddenly from the dust, but otherwise, she felt a sudden odd sense of enjoyment in her writing environment.

Viv was speaking in a soft voice. "Once you've found the place where you can comfortably write, your querencia, start again. I'll give you ten minutes this time. And I'm going to turn out one of the lights and play a little music."

The ten minutes passed too quickly, but Joy did feel good about the page she wrote during that time. She crawled out from behind the TV and returned to her chair, brushing the gray dust from her black pants.

"I hope you'll use your querencias again in future sessions," Viv said. "And that those of you too shy to find yours will do so in the future. You'll have me an hour each morning and afternoon – this is your techniques class, so you'll have ample opportunity to become comfortable in this space. And now – who will share your setting first? We'll share and discuss until we run out of time."

By the end of the hour, Joy had learned two main facts – she wrote well behind fifteen-year-old TVs, and everyone in the class was quite talented. Some of them had practically written masterpieces for their assignments today. Joy paused by the door as she was leaving and spoke to Viv. "I was wanting to do a little more research about a word you mentioned," she said. "It wasn't English...something like care – quar..."

"Oh, yes. Querencia. It's Spanish."

"That's it. Could you spell it for me, please?"

Viv complied, and Joy hastily scrawled the letters on her hand, thanked her, and raced to her next session, a course on publishing novels.

By six, when the final class for the day had ended, Joy was exhausted. And overwhelmed. And starved. Her sandwich at twelve-thirty had evaporated long ago. She drove slowly the two miles to her farmhouse, wondering if her brain could possibly hold an entire week of eight-hour days of information. She had also decided authors weren't an awfully friendly crowd; only three people had spoken to her, one of which had been the blue-haired man. And he'd asked for her phone number!

Joy pushed open her front door and was assailed by the aroma of – soup? She quickly dropped her notebook and laptop bag on the entry way rug and dashed to the kitchen, hoping in passing she wasn't being robbed by a foodie robber or something. In the kitchen, she spied a dish drainer full of still-wet cups and bowls and a half-sheet of notebook paper on the sparkling-clean counter.

Joy read the note quickly. "I thought you might be too tired to feel like cooking," it read. "There's vegetable soup with ground turkey in the fridge. Hope you don't mind I used a bit of your margarine. Love, Aunt Jo-Jo." Joy smiled at the signature and felt her entire body sag in relief. There was enough soup in the stockpot to last her most of the week – and Joann had done the dishes too. And scrubbed the counter – and she'd even discovered how to remove the

215

red food coloring stains that had been there when she moved in!

Joy ladled out a bowl of soup and placed it in the microwave – which had also been cleaned – noting it was still slightly warm. In five minutes, she sat down to a delicious, healthy meal and ate gratefully. Then she called her aunt.

"How did you know?" she demanded before she said hello.

Joann laughed. "I assume you found your supper."

"Yes! It was great! I really needed a good, hot meal tonight, and I was so tired I probably wouldn't have made one myself. How did you know?"

"I know my niece."

"Well, anyway, you're a lifesaver, as usual. But you *really* didn't have to do all that cleaning!"

"Oh, it wasn't much. I needed something to do while the meat browned."

"I don't think I should stay in Vermont too long," Joy said, mostly but not entirely joking. "You're going to spoil me so I'm completely incapable of independence!"

"Everyone needs a little spoiling every now and then," Joann said. "And now, I have to run. My oven timer is due to go off any time."

"You haven't eaten?"

"I'm about to eat right now. I'll see you tomorrow, though, and I want to hear all about your adventure then, okay?"

"Okay." Joy sat back in her chair and rubbed her eyes. Independence. What was it really? Could it include being given meals and having your house cleaned randomly by a sneaky aunt? Was she jeopardizing her survival skills by settling in somewhere where there were these unnaturally good people who insisted on doing things for her that she should handle on her own? Had she broken free from the bonds of her Pittsburgh life just so she could become enslaved by a different kind here? Was there something – perhaps – in the Bible about this?

Joy retrieved her Bible full of her Joann's notes from her bedroom. She recalled seeing a topical index of verses in the back. Her study soon led her to Scriptures about the early church, who had

216

shared everything they owned with each other. It certainly hadn't bothered them to depend on each other, but wasn't that a different culture...a different context?

Joy suddenly spotted a comment running sideways along one page, written in her aunt's neat script. "Give it to God. You are not an island," Joann had written.

Joy could not discern which verse the comment was supposed to reference, but it directed her mind into another train of thought entirely. Did it also scare her to depend on God? After all, He was supposed to be the only One on whom she could depend fully. But how could she learn to put all her trust in Him if she couldn't even accept the kindness of those around her?

Joy felt goosebumps pop out onto her arms, and she rubbed them briskly. She'd needed breaking. She'd been Sophia Joy Carnegie, wealthy, charming, poised. Arrogant. Self-sufficient to a fault. Faithless. And who was she now? Just Joy. Unemployed. Single. Uncertain about her future. Weepy and emotional. Always resisting the urge to cling to anyone who seemed to care whether she lived or died. Disowned. But surviving – and even, often, happy. Growing as a Christian. Making friends. Closer to Joann than she'd ever been to another person, at least that she could remember. Learning how to live simply and selflessly. Forgiven. Joy shivered, but not from the temperature of the room.

She had come to Vermont to break free from the shallowness and materialism and emptiness that had plagued her in Pittsburgh, but she'd come with the attitude that she could control her life. But she couldn't. Not really. And if she didn't learn to depend on her family and friends, she'd certainly never learn to depend on God, who was in control.

Joy put her head in her arms right there on the kitchen table and stayed like that for a long time. And she did not write fiction that night.

CHAPTER 24

Except Sunday, when Joy traveled back and forth between Coburn College and Montpelier so she could worship as well as attend as many writing sessions as possible, the first few days of the workshop seemed fairly similar to each other. All the participants would meet together in the auditorium for a group session first thing each morning. Morning technique classes, and for Joy, a class about publishing or marketing one's writing would follow. After an hour's break for lunch, classes would resume with another technique course and a production class, in which she was actually expected to write significant chunks of text. Joy also had "homework" in the evenings, including journaling, creating a short story, and drafting the first five chapters of a novel.

On Friday, the format changed. Each writer was assigned a "mentor" author who met with him or her for an hour to discuss his or her works one-on-one. They spent the rest of the day in production class, preparing a short-short story to be submitted to a panel of judges at the end of the day. The judges would read the stories, select the top three from each division, and read them on Saturday as part of the closing ceremony.

The list of writing mentors was distributed first thing Monday morning. Each mentor on the list was an established author of some sort, but some were obviously more famous than others. Joy's author, a suspense author, was one of the best known, and although Joy had never read her books, she'd definitely been familiar with the woman's name for many years. Her time slot lasted from 5:00 to 6:00, the last session of the day.

Joy wrote anxiously all morning and afternoon, wanting to be as close to finishing her short-short story as she could be before her session with Ms. Dexter. She finally finished at ten minutes until 5:00 and dashed into the ladies' room to check her hair, face, and teeth for any unpleasant surprises. She was prone to rubbing her face frequently when she wrote, and she'd been using blue pen. Sure enough, a faint blue smear adorned her cheek, like eye shadow applied by a toddler. Joy hastily rubbed it off with a wet paper towel and tried to swallow her nervousness. She still found herself dismayed that her veneer of self-confidence and urbane polish had so thoroughly deserted her when it came to this writing workshop.

Ms. Dexter proved to be about fifty, with spiky gray hair, piercing dark eyes, and a professional, almost masculine style of dress. She held a folder marked with Joy's name that included three poems, two short stories, and the five novel chapters Joy had completed in her production class. Joy also handed her the story she'd just completed.

"Thank you," Ms. Dexter said. "If you'd like to sit down, I'll read this now." She indicated the chair opposite hers. Joy complied, wondering if she could stand the suspense of a well-known author actually perusing her hastily-written work on the spot like this. She tried to focus on her surroundings – her *setting* – instead. There were five other mentor/student pairs here in the college library, which was small but well-stocked, especially with poetry, fiction, and creative non-fiction volumes. The other mentors murmured to their "mentees," but Ms. Dexter just sat. And read. And did not permit an expression to cross her face. What a stoic, Joy thought.

Finally, Ms. Dexter sat back in the chair. "I'm Mary Dexter," she said. "But you must know that already. Please, call me Mary, and don't be nervous because you've seen my face plastered around bookstores."

Joy blinked at her bluntness, but managed a quiet greeting.

"So, tell me about yourself, Joy."

"Well...I...um...am living in Woodfield right now. I'm originally from Philadelphia, but I went to Brown and then lived in Pittsburgh until recently. I'm twenty-four. And I've never had anything published except on campus at Brown."

"Why do you write?"

Joy froze. "I – I enjoy it. It's fun, and I was good at English in school. And I like making up characters. And it's...well, soothing."

"Would you say writing is an escape – or perhaps, a safe place, for you?"

Who was this Mary person, a shrink? "I guess so. Yes."

"Joy, I've read all your submissions, and I've formed an opinion of them. But first, I want to ask you *your* opinion of them."

Joy attempted to mask her frustration. No matter how she sliced it, this experience was going to prove humiliating. "I don't know," she said. "I've been in a writing slump the last couple of months. I do know it has felt great to be writing again this week. But I don't know if I'm really much of a writer compared to the other people here."

"Two things, Joy. First, you are a writer. You write because of a need inside you, so you are a writer. Secondly, don't compare yourself to anyone else. As a writer, you must write for yourself first and foremost. If you satisfy yourself, you are successful even if you never sell a word."

Joy nodded. Thank you for reminding me."

"That being said, you're sitting here ready to kill me because I won't hurry and give you my opinion." Mary cracked a smile for the first time as Joy blushed miserably. "It's all right. But I'll give it to you in good time. I have a few more questions first." She turned to the pages of poems, flowery, formally-rhymed verses about seasons in Vermont. "Did you feel these words spilling from your brain, or did you sit down and determine to write poems about 'crimson maples' and 'frost-kissed chrysanthemums'?"

"I – I sat down and decided. Nothing poetic spills from my brain these days."

"Ahhh. And – let me see – these novel chapters – they're about a backpacker in Europe...Have you actually traveled to Europe yourself?"

"No, but I've always wanted to go."

"It's a good plot idea. I would enjoy reading a book about it. And now, one more question, Joy. You said nothing poetic flows from your mind right now. I won't ask you why, or if poetry used to flow from your mind, but I must ask – what *does* come easily to you at this time?"

"Nothing very creative...emotional, incoherent rambling in my journal at random times. It's...it's embarrassing."

"Don't be embarrassed by a need to process feelings. I recommend you write about them as much as possible.

"And finally, your submissions. None of them are very good, Joy. Yes, technically, they're excellent – your mechanics are almost flawless. And you have some good ideas. However, they aren't natural. Your characters aren't convincing, and their dialogue seems contrived. It's obvious you aren't familiar with your settings or the experiences the characters claim."

"So I can't write."

"I don't know if you can write well from the standpoint of appealing to readers. My impression is there's potential you *can*, but, for whatever reason, you aren't."

"Does nothing I've submitted seem publishable – or show *any* promise?" said Joy. She hated the whine she heard in her voice, but she considered herself lucky not to be crying.

"Not in your submissions. However, I did see this, on the back of your poetry page." Mary turned over the typed page and revealed several scribbled sentences.

"Oh, sorry. I thought I turned in my clean copy."

"I'm glad you didn't. Now – please tell me, what is this?"

Joy took the page from her and scanned the lines in humiliation. Stream-of-consciousness ranting about slavery and independence she'd done during free writing behind the TV. Ugh.

"Just some thoughts – some personal thoughts – from free writing time in my techniques class."

"There is more promise in that frenzied, honest scrawl of words than in the rest of your work put together."

"Really?"

"Yes, because it is *you*. For some reason, those feelings envelope you at this time. Write about them. Journal. Write spontaneous poetry. And if you must write fiction and create characters, allow them to search and suffer and grow with you. Until you understand yourself, it will be almost impossible for you to understand these characters you write about today. Your best writing will not be chosen by you; it will choose you."

Joy thanked Mary numbly when their session had ended, and

just as numbly drove home in the darkness. She wasn't any good as a writer. Someone famous had told her so. Her writing was garbage. She was too naïve and unpracticed and inhibited by her identity crisis to write something even halfway decent.

To her dismay, Paul's truck was sitting in her driveway when she arrived at the farmhouse. She'd forgotten – completely forgotten – he'd invited her to eat at Subway with him. So much water had gone under the bridge since Wednesday, when he'd invited her – and her plans for a career as an author had been swept under it as well. She gritted her teeth, grabbed her notebook and laptop, and strode to his truck.

"Hi," she said, much friendlier than she felt.

"Hi...uh...bad day?"

"You might say that. Why don't you come on inside? I'd like to change clothes and get my heavy coat before we leave."

"Are you still up to it? We can wait until another time if you'd like. My coupons don't expire until the end of the month."

"No, it's fine. I've got to get used to this. I mean, I'm still young, and I can't just lie around and mope because I stink at life."

Paul flinched. "Whoa. Really bad day. Why don't you change and then sit down and relax for a few minutes. You sound really tired."

"Whatever." Joy galloped up to her bedroom, realizing fully how rude she'd sounded.

When she stomped back down in five minutes, Paul was in the kitchen, brewing her a cup of tea.

"And what *is* it with you Vermonters and your *tea*? Tea is *not* the cure for everything!"

"Oh, this isn't tea," Paul said, perfectly solemn. "It's a sedative."

Joy's jaw dropped. Anger and laughter fought for dominance, but at last, she just laughed. "Okay, okay. I'll drink the tea. And I'll be calm. And nice."

"Then it isn't a sedative. It's ecstasy." Paul paused. "What happened today, Joy? I haven't seen you this – this cynical in weeks."

Joy made the mistake of watching Paul as he spoke, and the

kindness and concern in his eyes was so transparent that something broke in her defense and she started sobbing. Again.

At first, she couldn't even tell Paul what was wrong. She was vaguely aware of the kitchen chair scraping as he stood, and of his big footsteps as he walked behind her. Suddenly, she felt his strong fingers kneading her shoulders, finding and uncoiling the knots from the day's tension. It felt so good that she cried some more.

Finally, Joy began talking. She told him about her plans to come to Vermont and be a writer, of her writer's block since she'd arrived, of her current scorn for her past novels and stories, and of her hard work that week during the workshop. And then she told him what Mary Dexter had said about her writing.

Paul said nothing beyond a few affirming sounds; he just continued massaging her shoulders. When Joy's spiel ran down at last, she waited for him to respond, but he was still silent. "Well," she sniffed. "What do you think? Isn't that pathetic?"

Paul cleared his throat. "I think you should take Ms. Dexter's advice before you declare yourself a failure. You've gone through so much lately, and you're changing so quickly, I can't honestly imagine how you'd find the mental energy to create good fiction. But I hate you got disappointed. That always hurts."

"But what if she's wrong, and I *never* learn to write well? I mean, I staked my whole life on this, Paul!"

"I know. And I understand that. But if you don't end up having that talent, you'll find something else. You're a wonderful woman. And you've had a crazy fall season. Cut yourself some slack, work through your emotions, and try again in a little while. I believe in you."

Joy sighed, wiped her face with a paper towel, and stood up. She looked at Paul – not up, really, just across at him. And she hugged him as though she never wanted to let go.

CHAPTER 25

Joy didn't see Paul again after their trip to Subway, except briefly at worship services, for several days, for he was completely absorbed in final exams and papers. He had confided in her as they ate that night that he wasn't afraid of scoring badly – but of not being able to finish the enormous amount of work remaining in his courses. Joy understood the overwhelming stress he was experiencing and did not so much as send him a text message to distract him.

Instead, she focused on three things – journaling, whether she felt like it or not; preparing for her library classes for the month; and assisting Joann, who had begun her wedding planning at last, a month before the event. Alex's retirement date was scheduled for December 22nd, so he was essentially absent from much of the planning, and although neither he nor Joann were terribly particular about most of the details, there was still a great deal of preparation to make.

On Saturday morning, one week after the conclusion of Joy's workshop, she and her aunt drove to Burlington to go dress shopping. As Joann zipped up the interstate, she explained the type of dress for which she would be searching. "I want to find a very simple dress," she said. "But it must be a traditional wedding style. Alex has insisted."

"Really?" Joy grinned at the thought of her no-nonsense aunt swathed in layers of lace and beads and tulle.

"Yes, that was really his only strong preference about the wedding...well, except that he wants his brother to be best man. And although I'll feel awfully silly trying on wedding gowns at my age, I'm not going to deny him the privilege of seeing his bride in a fluffy white dress if that's his desire."

"At least you shouldn't have trouble finding a dress at this time of year."

"Oh, I always have trouble finding dresses," she said. "Why do you think I so rarely wear them? It isn't easy to locate a dress to fit someone with shoulders like a football player."

Joy covered her mouth to keep from giggling. "Well," she said, but found herself unable to say more. She couldn't deny her aunt's assessment of herself.

"Don't try to be polite," Joann said. "You know I'm right. Just be thankful you're such a standard size. Finding your dress will be easy."

"My dress? I don't have to have one. This day is about you!"

"Are you planning to wear your peasant skirt? Or your blue jeans?" Joann said gently.

Joy sighed. "I guess you're right. But let's concentrate on your dress today. And I'm not a standard size anything anymore. I think I've gained at least five pounds since I came to Vermont."

The wedding dress shopping did prove quite a long ordeal. Both women were disappointed by the selections at all three bridal shops they visited that morning. Joann was appalled by both the excessive frilliness of the choices and the immodesty of the styles.

"I guess I'm officially a frumpy old woman," she said, sinking into a booth at Friendly's, where they had finally stopped for lunch. "I haven't seen a single dress I could even imagine putting on in public."

"Most of them *are* rather – um – revealing," Joy said. The shopping trip had been an embarrassment for her, because although she had avoided exposing so much skin on a daily basis, she'd sort of assumed it was inevitable on formal occasions. Seeing Joann squirming at the idea of showing so much of herself in public reminded Joy of this inconsistency, and she was ashamed when she remembered several outfits she had donned for official events over the years.

"Oh, I wasn't talking about the necklines just then," said Joann. "I wouldn't ever feel appropriate in those, even if I were twenty and a size two. I meant they're all just so fancy and – and conspicuous!"

Joy nodded, but her mind was whirling. Surely there was a way Joann could find something modest and simple. "Have we gone to all the stores in Burlington?"

"Not quite. There's one more in the older part of town, near the lake. I suppose we'll try that after lunch, unless you're too sick of watching me shop."

"Of course I'm not. I just hope you can find a dress! Could you make one if you don't?"

"I could – but I really don't want to. I made my first one, and it was a ridiculous amount of work."

The last bridal shop was located in the historic downtown, an area Joy had never seen. It was located inside an old brick building, and although the dresses hanging inside were no different than in the other stores they'd tried, the atmosphere was much more comfortable and personal. The woman who greeted them was elderly and kind.

"And which one of you is the bride?" she asked.

Joy smiled, liking her already, for in all the other stores, the clerks had just assumed Joy was the bride and had appeared visibly disappointed she was not.

"I am," said Joann.

"What style of dress are you looking for, dearie?" said the woman.

Joann, who was beginning to get a tension headache, sighed. "Something very simple, without a train, and with a neckline instead of a belly button line. Oh, and sleeves, or at the very least, very wide straps." She smiled at the saleswoman apologetically.

The old woman laughed. "You aren't looking to exhibit everything, eh? Good for you. Let's consult a catalog. There are plenty of choices you'll like better."

"I'm afraid I don't have time to order anything. The wedding is on January 12th."

"Oh, my. Let's see...surely there's something..." She scratched her head and looked at Joann carefully.

"About a size twelve, aren't you?" she asked.

"In some places," Joann said, blushing. "But my shoulders are very wide, and..."

"And you have the waist of a girl. Yes, I see that. However – I have an idea. Just a minute." She disappeared through a door in the back and re-emerged shortly afterward with a dress inside a huge plastic bag.

"This is a dress we special-ordered for a Mormon girl. As you

226

can see, it's much less revealing than most. She had to cancel her order because her fiancé dumped her a month before the wedding, but the dress had already been shipped. She was larger than you, but I believe I could alter this dress to fit you if you like it."

Joann examined the dress through the plastic and smiled. "I'll certainly try it on."

"Take it on back to the fitting room. You'll need help getting into it, though. There are fifty buttons down the back."

"My niece can help me. Thank you."

Joy followed Joann into the tiny dressing room. After a lengthy struggle of shifting positions and embarrassing moments as Joy assisted her aunt in dressing when she'd never even seen her unclothed for more than a second, Joann was buttoned into the dress, and looked beautiful.

The back was still lower than she preferred, and it still seemed excessively lacy and elaborate, and she had exactly four inches of extra space throughout the dress' bust and waist, but it was acceptable. "Nothing a little alteration can't fix," said Joann. "What do you think?"

"I think you look stunning. Let's get out where you can actually see yourself in the mirrors."

Joann was pleasantly surprised by her appearance in the dress, and she agreed to purchase it. The store owner agreed to take in the seams and add some rows of lace to the back of the dress for a total purchase price of just three hundred dollars. Also, one of the bridesmaids' dresses from that wedding party happened to fit Joy perfectly, so within an hour, they had arranged all the details, including pickup of the altered gown the next Saturday, and were driving back toward Montpelier, shocked but incredibly relieved.

"I can't believe we got that out of the way so quickly," Joann said.

"And so cheaply! Seriously – an exquisite wedding dress and a bridesmaids' dress for $350!"

"And the hassle is finished. That's the best part. The rest of the planning will be a breeze in comparison."

"So what's your next step? Invitations?"

"I've already ordered them online. We got a promotional sample of twenty-five, so they were free except shipping."

"Only twenty-five?"

Joann smiled. "Yes. I told you it would be a small wedding, remember? Except for the church here and the one in Windsor, Angelique and the boys, a few co-workers from the library, Alex's family, and my father-"

"Your *father*?"

"Yes, didn't I tell you he's still alive?"

"Maybe – but I forgot. Where is he?"

"Prince Edward Island. He won't come to the wedding, but of course I want to send him an invitation."

"Why won't he come?"

"He's very anti-social...almost a hermit. After living in Quebec for so many years, and then being forced to live for three years in the States to find work, he's determined to stay put from now on. He's also quite opposed to my faith."

"Does he keep in touch?"

"Once a year, at Christmas time, he writes me a letter 'whether he has anything to say or not,' as he phrased it once a long time ago. I write to him fairly often, though."

"Wow. When was the last time you saw him?"

"It's been many years. John was still alive. He and my father didn't get along because John tried to convince him to study the Bible with him."

"So...you basically lost your family when you were even younger than me, right?"

"Sort of. But I don't miss my father very much, I'm sorry to say. He's a hard man."

"Yeah," said Joy, heaving a sigh.

They were almost back to Montpelier when Joy's phone vibrated. She grabbed it from her purse and checked it eagerly, hoping it was Paul...and it was.

"Done! Just woke up!" he'd written.

"Paul's done with his school work!" Joy said. "He must be so relieved!"

"And probably ready to celebrate," Joann said.

As if she were a prophet, the phone buzzed again. "Are you busy tonight? I feel like a bird let out of a cage!" Paul wrote.

Joy bit her lip and began to reply. "You'd better not be saying no to that man!" Joann said. "We can eat supper together any time."

"Are you sure you don't mind?"

"Joy, dear, really! You know me better than that! Go celebrate with Paul."

Joy grinned and sent him an immediate answer.

CHAPTER 26

Paul could not afford to celebrate as elaborately as he preferred, and although Joy could, she didn't dream of mentioning that fact, but they managed to have an enjoyable evening anyway. After chicken salad wraps at Joy's house, Paul drove them to nearby Barre, where they strolled the streets of the historic district for hours, talking nearly nonstop.

"I finished my course work at four a.m.," said Paul as they roamed the dark, quiet streets. "It was due at eight, so I cut it pretty close, but it's done, and I feel confident I did a good job on it. Then, I chose one job – just one teaching job – it's up the road less than an hour from here in Cabot, and applied for it because I could."

"That sounds like something I would do! Do you think you'll get it?"

"No," Paul said. "They prefer someone with at least five years' experience! But I'll start applying for more tomorrow. Next year's job postings have already begun popping up." He yawned. "Unh...and although I got a good eight hours once I finally went to sleep, I'm exhausted."

"You've been working like a dog for days," said Joy. "You probably have skimped on sleep."

"Yeah, probably," he said, rubbing his unshaven chin absently. Joy noticed the whiskers made him look at least five years older.

"I think life is going to get a lot easier for you now," said Joy. "You certainly deserve it."

Paul smiled slightly. "Well..." he paused for several seconds. "I'm not going to say I wouldn't mind it."

They walked in silence for a while. "Oh," Paul said suddenly. "I almost forgot. My mom called yesterday and invited you for the weekend before Christmas. I'm headed up to Stowe that Friday evening, and we're celebrating early, because the girls and I all have to work on Christmas Eve and Christmas Day. Would you like to come? We'd be back for Sunday evening service."

"Yes, please!" Joy exclaimed. "I don't think I have any plans except on Christmas Day, with my aunt and Alex, so that sounds great. I can't wait to see your family again!"

"Good. And I'm sure they can't wait to see you. I think Jennifer in particular misses you!"

Joy rolled her eyes. "I'm sure she's planning some sort of ambush on me. But – I just realized – is your other sister coming? Won't she need her bed?"

"Actually, she and her husband are traveling up from South Carolina, but they'll stay in my room, and I'll take the couch downstairs. That way, you can still share with Jennifer."

Suddenly, Paul stopped short. "The weekend before Christmas – that's *next weekend*, isn't it?"

Joy laughed loudly at his expression. "Yes, Paul."

Paul removed his glasses and scrubbed his eyes with his fist. "Where has my life gone? It's like I went to sleep the day we got back from Stowe the last time, and I'm just now waking up."

"I'm glad you have a chance to rest. Maybe you can take a nap tomorrow afternoon or something."

"No, we have the holiday party with people from church, remember?"

"Oh, I totally forgot about that!" Joy exclaimed. "It's a white elephant party, isn't it?"

"Yeah, a cross between white elephant and dirty Santa. Some of the weird gifts have been circulating among the members for years, apparently. I think Alex said there's a rubber chicken that has appeared seven years in a row!"

"I don't have a clue what to bring," said Joy. "When I moved to Vermont, I pretty much sold or trashed everything I owned, except what fit easily in my jeep. I have a few things in storage, but they're in Pittsburgh."

"Well, I've got something, but of course it's a secret. You should ask your aunt if she has something."

"Yeah...what time is it? Eight-thirty? I'm going to give her a quick call."

Sure enough, Joann had several ideas of unique or strange presents Joy could bring, but she said Joy really needed to choose one herself from the attic.

"What time is the party? Right after morning service?"

"Yes. There's a potluck and then the party. You won't have time to come over beforehand tomorrow." Joann paused. "Are you with Paul?"

"Yeah, but he's standing here about to split his jaws from yawning, so I'll probably be finished soon."

"Come on over then. Hey, you could even spend the night if you'd like. Then you could rummage to your heart's content."

"I'll do that. I'll drop by my house and grab my clothes for tomorrow and then head over there. I really appreciate it, Aunt Joann!"

"It's no trouble. I've always got things to throw out. See you soon!"

"Bye." Joy turned to Paul. "You don't mind, do you? You're looking tired enough to fall over, and I'd like to be able to participate."

"Of course not! Let's head back to the truck. I know some back roads to get us back to Woodfield more quickly than if we drive back through Montpelier."

"Are you awake enough to drive?"

"I will be if you're very, very entertaining. Or maybe you could sing?"

"Sing? As in, a solo? Not on your life, mister!"

"What a shame."

"Well, I can drive if you want," said Joy.

"Can you drive a stick-shift?"

"Uh...no...guess I'll just have to be entertaining!"

"You're always entertaining, actually."

"Is that supposed to be a compliment or an insult?"

"You choose!" Paul said. Joy pulled off her scarf and started whipping him with it, so he ran the last block to the truck, staying well ahead of her this time.

An hour and ten minutes later, Joy pulled into Joann's

driveway. She looked up at the eaves of the house as she waited for her aunt to open the door and wondered how there could be both a slanted-ceiling upstairs *and* an attic.

Her question was answered as soon as Joann led her into the upstairs hallway. "Oh! It's just storage under the eaves, isn't it?" said Joy.

"Yes. There's some here and some accessed from my bedroom. I'm going to just give you a few directions on where to look, and then I'll go back downstairs and finish the Christmas cookies for tomorrow." Joann crossed the plywood flooring into the darkness and pulled a string from the ceiling, and a light bulb illuminated the room.

"Okay, here's a pile of things you'll recognize from the farm. Obviously, there are many things I don't want you to give away, but you can use your best judgment. Basically, if it's totally tacky, you can take it."

Joy opened the loose flaps of a small box and discovered a mound of cards and papers. She glanced at Joann quizzically.

"Those are mostly cards and letters your uncle received. There may also be a few he wrote to your father in case lines of communication opened again."

"Wow." Joy brushed the papers with her fingertips.

"Feel free to look through them. There aren't any romantic ones in there; I stored anything remotely scandalous somewhere completely different."

"Are you sure?"

"Yes. John didn't have any dark secrets you'll stumble upon." Joann sniffed. "Oh, and here." She handed Joy a package of tissues. "You may need these. There's quite the layer of dust in here."

Joy took the tissues, murmured her thanks, and sank to her knees. The white elephant gift could wait a bit...she couldn't resist snooping through Uncle John's cards first. The first one was a birthday card of an old man with a wheelchair posed at the top of a steep hill. She grinned and opened it. "Happy 40th Birthday," she read. "Do not drive too fast. The mountain is so steep. And you are definitly [*sic*] over the hill now! Love, Pierre and Angelique." Joy

233

gasped. So much had changed in the past twelve years, and it was hard to believe both John and Pierre had already been gone for seven years.

Joy chose a folded sheet of notebook paper next. Inside, she found half a page of neatly-slanted script that seemed vaguely familiar. It was a letter for her father, dated in early 2000, but it was not signed. Joy began reading and was in tears within seconds.

"Dear George," John had written. "I'm afraid I'm the bearer of bad news once again. We've had a terrible month at the farm. My Joann lost another baby about three weeks ago. She was four months along this time, so we'd been so hopeful. She began having blood pressure difficulties almost immediately, so the doctor put her on bed rest for the entire pregnancy, even for the holidays, but it wasn't enough, and she miscarried again. She also experienced such bad hemorrhaging the doctors warned us there could never be any more pregnancies. They may perform a hysterectomy after she recovers a bit more.

"I know we don't talk anymore, George, but I wanted to let you know what we've been dealing with. Joann is so strong; I think she's handling it better than I am. I'm really struggling with the fact I will probably never be a father." The letter stopped abruptly there, and Joy assumed John had never gotten up the nerve to send it, or else had re-written it in a less vulnerable way. She wiped her cheeks, not caring she was also smearing dust on them. It amazed her that John and Joann had experienced such tragedy only two and a half years before she met them.

Joy let out a shuddering sigh and lifted another sheet of paper, dreading what she'd find in this letter. It was another letter to George – similar length but actually concluded and signed.

"Dear George," she read. "I wish you would reconsider your decision not to allow us to visit for Christmas," Joy gasped and checked the date – 1989! "I know you and Joann exchanged angry words in the past, but she and I are so anxious to meet your little girl – our niece! Just because we don't share the same beliefs doesn't mean we aren't still family – and that I don't still love you, brother. Please write immediately or call – even collect, if you'd like, if you change

234

your mind. Love, John."

Joy sighed. So not only had John and Joann learned to love her after her visit, they had tried to be a part of her life from the beginning, even though they must have still been struggling to forgive George for his scandalous behavior toward Angelique. She checked her phone – 10:30. She'd better stop this reminiscing and choose a gift or she'd be in the attic forever – and Joann would catch her *emoting* all over the boxes.

Suddenly, another paper from the box caught her eye. It was on actual stationery instead of plain notebook paper. "Okay, one more. Only one more," Joy muttered, and opened it up.

She cried out and fell on her backside with a thud. The letter was written to her! Her arms erupted in goosebumps when she noticed the date – September 2, 2005 – three days before her uncle's death!

She'd only read the greeting line when she heard Joann's footsteps on the stairs, but she couldn't make herself stop reading.

"I'm about to head to bed, but take as long as-" Joann's voice trailed off as she saw Joy still engrossed in the same box, sitting on the floor, her face wet. Joann stepped quickly around the heaps of boxes to Joy's side.

"What is it, dear heart?"

Joy handed the sheet of stationery to Joann. It read, "Dear Joy, I remembered, see? I'm calling you by your middle name, just like you told me to so many times three years ago.

"Joy, I don't know if you will ever see this letter, but I wanted to tell you again, as I have in my other letters, just how much your aunt and I miss you and love you. We think about you and pray for you every day. We pray you are happy and safe, and, most importantly, that you have become a Christian. We aren't allowed to contact you right now, as I hope you know, so you aren't wondering what happened to us, but we will find you as soon as you turn eighteen. We don't want you to enter adulthood without being sure of our love and support. Joann walked by as I was writing this and said to tell you she wants to hug you and make you some of your favorite cookies! Love, Uncle John and Aunt Joann."

Joann bit her lip, and Joy could see the tears standing in her eyes. "At least you get to see this one," she said. "I guess he forgot to mail it."

"You noticed the date?"

"Yes, I did." She sniffed and wiped her eyes. "I never imagined you'd run across something like this."

"I read several other letters too...and some of them were also...intense."

"Maybe I should go through this box again. There may be some things I don't necessarily want to pass down to future generations – or to future owners of this house."

"Maybe so." Joy stood up, stiff from nearly an hour on the chilly floor. She offered her hands to Joann and pulled her back to her feet as well. The women hugged tightly.

"Well, it doesn't it appear you have a gift for the party yet," said Joann.

"No. I got completely distracted by those cards and letters." Joy sensed her aunt's need to change the subject, so she cautiously re-folded the letter from her uncle, replaced it in the envelope, and put it in her pocket.

"Maybe something old isn't the answer," said Joann. "Maybe something ordinary and slightly embarrassing would be better."

"You mean – like wrapping up a roll of toilet paper or something?"

"Yes. That wouldn't be a bad idea, actually."

"But it would be too obvious what it was. What else could I bring? I like this train of thought..."

"I've got it!" Joann said. "Follow me." She led the way back out of the storage area and into her bedroom and then her bathroom. She squatted on her heels, knees cracking, and began searching in the cabinet under her sink.

"Aha! This!" she said, presenting Joy triumphantly with the largest bottle of Pepto-Bismol Joy had ever seen.

"Where on earth did you get *this*?" Joy said, hefting it like a dumbbell.

"It was a free promotional gift that came with one of my

prescriptions several months ago. Our local pharmacy sometimes gives out funny rewards to regular customers. Once I also got a huge package of adult diapers."

Joy snickered. "This is perfect, Aunt Joann. It must weigh five pounds."

"At least."

Joy struck a pose with the bottle turned up to her lips, pretending to chug the entire thing.

Joann gave her shoulder a shove. "Oh, go on and get out of here, you little nut. I need to go to sleep, and I don't allow Pepto addicts in my bathroom after eleven."

Joy gave Joann a quick hug and obligingly disappeared into the guest room.

CHAPTER 27

The following day proved to be one of the most entertaining days Joy had experienced in a long time. After the usual worship service and Bible study, the men of the congregation hastily cleared away the folding chairs, brought long folding tables out from the bedroom Paul didn't use, and assembled them in the living room, re-arranging the chairs around them.

Then, Joann and two other women rushed around decorating the tables. Joy sidled over to examine Joann's table – red plastic tablecloth, real sprigs of holly, and silver confetti with bells and holly designs. Another table was decorated with pale blue, white, and silver, with snowflakes cut from white felt.

Instead of a traditional Christmas dinner, the potluck was "finger foods" - pizza, tacos, chips, vegetables and fruit and dips, desserts, and other simple foods, most of which were holiday-themed. Joy examined the large table of food and determined to take a long walk after the party. She bit into an old-fashioned popcorn ball and banished her diet guilt for the day.

The next event was a surprise to everyone except Wilson Roberts. He had downloaded a Christmas karaoke program on his computer and announced to the rest of the room that he would be passing out prizes to the winners in four categories – best children's song, best slow song, best fast song, and best duet. "And," he said. "I want you all to participate!"

Twenty-seven pairs of eyes stared blankly at him. "Come on!" He looked as excited as a child at the prospect of everyone performing Christmas songs together. "Just because you don't sing well is no excuse, either. Come on! Look, I'll put on an easy one. "Rudolph the Red-Nosed Reindeer. You all know that. Who'll come sing it with me?"

Joy sat, covering her smile with her hand lest Wilson assume she wanted to join him, and surveyed furtively the other members. They all were smiling, some genuinely, and some in barely-masked horror. Apparently, karaoke was not a customary event for an East Montpelier party.

Finally, Paul sighed loudly and got up from the table. "Okay, okay," he said. "You don't have to stare holes through my skull, Wilson!"

The duet that followed was positively hilarious, for Wilson and Paul "hammed it up" and added bits to the song at random times. Paul, upon noticing Wilson was totally and unashamedly off-key, managed somehow to pitch himself so the song sounded as terrible as possible. By the end of the song, Paul was singing in falsetto.

Everyone cheered and applauded, and Paul reclaimed his seat, his red cheeks nearly obscuring his freckles. The silly performance broke the ice, and many of the members also took a turn singing after that. Menthol Lady, who Joy now knew by her name, Matilda Mathis, even wobbled to the front of the room and belted out a song with more volume than Joy would have thought possible. Joy giggled when she realized her selection - "Grandma Got Run Over by a Reindeer, the G-rated version."

Not surprisingly, Alex and Paul were in high demand, and they both sang several times, alone and in small groups. Paul even convinced Joy to join him in "We Wish You a Merry Christmas," although she purposefully hid behind his strong voice to hide her shaking. To Joy's amazement, Joann even allowed herself to be persuaded to sing frequently as well, although she typically hated to perform. She and Alex sang "Merry Christmas, Darling" so smoothly Joy felt sure the couple would win the duet prize.

After an hour, everyone had had at least one chance to sing except a toddler and Margaret Tucker, who was still troubled with coughing since her bout with the flu in November. When Wilson stood up again, Joy assumed he would begin announcing the winners of the different categories, but instead he said, "We're not done yet, folks." David, the thirty-something father of the toddler, who had been forced by his wife to sing "All I Want for Christmas Is My Two Front Teeth," groaned pitifully, and they all laughed. "We can't be finished yet," Wilson continued. "Nobody has sung my favorite song of all time...'White Christmas.'"

Everyone began murmuring among themselves, suggesting various members who would do well with that song. Suddenly, Matilda called out, "Joann! Joann hasn't sung a solo yet!"

Joy snapped her head in her aunt's direction. Joann was shaking her head emphatically.

"Come on, Joann!" Wilson said, his booming voice assuring every person could hear his pleading. She continued to refuse, a faint blush beginning under her tan. "Please?" said Wilson. "You're our strongest female singer!"

Joann glanced helplessly at Joy, who waved her on, and then Alex, who just grinned at her.

Finally, she gave in and crossed the room to the computer. Wilson handed her the microphone. Joy had never seen her looking so uncomfortable. "Just remember you all forced me into this," she said, and began singing – and completely nailed it. Joy applauded until her hands hurt. Who knew? Joann had an excellent range, perfect pitch, even singing solo, and good volume, but was content to sit quietly and sing during worship – and not much of anywhere else.

"*Where* did you learn to sing like that?" Joy said under her breath as Joann returned to the chair beside her.

"Everyone knows that song," said Joann.

The prizes, big bags of assorted chocolate candy, went to David for best children's song, Paul and Alex for best duet, Matilda for best fast song, and Joann for best slow song. "Miss Joann is our new star," Wilson teased her as he gave her the candy. "We're booking her to provide all the musical entertainment at next year's party. We have to listen to Paul all the time, so we definitely need her. What do you folks think?" Everyone agreed with enthusiasm, including Joy.

"Traitor," said Joann to Joy as she sat down once again.

The gift exchange game occurred after karaoke. The congregation had created their own rules for the games, the most important one that any gift swapped more than twice would become a permanent fixture at future parties.

Joann was the current holder of the famed rubber chicken gift, so her contribution automatically brought plenty of laughs. Paul's gift of – imagine! - a roll of toilet paper – shocked Joy. Her own gift created a commotion as well...it was opened by Mrs. Tucker, who immediately drank a swallow of it and croaked, "Oh, *thank* you, sweetheart!" Joy was actually pleased with the gift she opened – a giant container of instant oats. She turned around to check to see what Joann had ended up with – and snorted. Joann was sporting her gift – a pair of 1960's cat-style sunglasses!

By the time the party was cleaned up and the living room set up for evening services, there was no time remaining for Joy's long walk. Instead, she rode along as Joann drove Mrs. Tucker home a half a mile away – the elderly lady had started nodding off after the apparent relief the Pepto Bismol had provided her!

Joy sighed happily as Joann hurried back to the church building. "That was such a fun party!" she said. "I don't think I've ever been to anything exactly like it."

"Wilson   plans   it   every   year," said   Joann. "We never know what to expect, but it's always fun...just sometimes more embarrassing than others!"

"Well, you shouldn't be embarrassed. You were incredible!"

"Nonsense. I was on-key, thankfully, but hardly incredible."

"Is there anything you can't do?"

"Drive and give you the swat you deserve simultaneously!"

After a typical evening service, Joann invited Alex and Joy to her house for salad and sandwiches. Alex's face fell. "I can't, sweetie," he said. "I'm cutting out an ingrown toenail at eight. I have to leave in just a few minutes."

"Yuck," said Joy. "What an – odd – evening activity!"

"Yeah, I suppose, but you have to understand the situation. This patient is a very stubborn man who has been living with a bad toenail for months. I've advised him many times to get it cut out and let me do a minor surgical procedure to keep it from happening again, but he's always refused. When he heard I was retiring, though, he decided he'd rather I took care of it after all, instead of another doctor he didn't know."

"I thought you were a pediatrician!" said Joy.

"I am – but this person is an exception to my typical patients."

241

"Alex has made many exceptions for people he knows," said Joann, patting his shoulder. "I can't keep track of all your responsibilities these days."

"But that's all over on Saturday," Alex said, kissing her cheek and slinging his coat over his arm. They said goodbye to him, and he left immediately.

"Well...kiddo...guess it's you and me again," said Joann.

"If you'd rather I didn't come since Alex can't..." began Joy.

"No, of course not. I'll just be relieved when he finally gets to rest. He's been pulling seventy-hour weeks this month."

"Wow...I'm glad he's almost done. I'm sure retirement will be nice for him." Joy stopped in her tracks as a significant thought hit her. "Wait a minute! We've been so caught up in talking about Alex retiring, but what about you? Are you staying at the library?"

Joann smiled. "No," she said. "Actually, Alex and I just discussed it yesterday. I'm giving my two weeks' notice tomorrow, and several of those days we'll be closed anyway for the holidays."

"You look pretty happy about your decision."

"I'm very happy. I've enjoyed my job, but since I won't be in financial need anymore, I'd much rather focus on being a Christian and a wife."

"Then I'm excited for you," said Joy, hugging her. "I only wish I had your problem – being so useful I had to choose among several things to do."

"No worries, dear heart. If you look for opportunities to serve, they'll come along."

Joy spent the next two days Christmas shopping, Monday in Montpelier, and Tuesday in Burlington. The first day, she felt extremely unsuccessful, which made her determine to strike out for Burlington on her own for the first time. She made a list of all the presents she needed to buy, plus a few things she wanted to purchase for herself, and was still appalled by how short it was. She hesitated, and slowly added her parents to the list as well. Yes, they'd disowned her, and her father had demanded she cut off all contact with them, but what could it hurt? There was nothing more he could do to her.

By the end of Monday, Joy had only crossed off two items

from her list, a cookie sheet for herself and a Christmas tree ornament shaped like a stethoscope for Alex. She left Woodfield early Tuesday morning and first drove to Walmart in Burlington. She already knew the Walmart near Montpelier was out of trees.

She chose tinsel, colored lights, ornaments, and a tree topper for herself, having decided that although she would not celebrate Christmas in customary ways from her past, it would be disappointing not to have her own personal tree. When Joy reached the aisle of Christmas trees, she discovered they were almost sold out. Joy walked up and down several times to be sure she hadn't missed anything, but all she saw were two three-foot green trees, a black tree, and one that was bright lavender, of all things! Joy sighed in frustration. So she hadn't exactly been brimming with Christmas spirit just after Halloween when the stores had started stocking trees. So sue her. She wanted a tree! And not some overgrown toilet brush either!

Joy sauntered through the rest of the Christmas section, wondering what other stores sold trees. In Pittsburgh, she'd never bothered with a tree of her own since she'd spent most of the holiday working both years and the rest of it at her parents' mansion in Philly. And their eighteen-foot real Douglas firs appeared in the foyer each December 1st as if dropped by elves from a helicopter. Suddenly, she realized the two women standing behind her were discussing trees as well.

"We always get a live tree from Lowe's," one of them said.

"Oh, I wish we could," the other one said. "But we're restricted to artificial ones."

"Your son's asthma?"

"Yeah."

Joy moved on with her cart, hoping the women didn't notice she'd been eavesdropping. She hadn't spent any time in Lowe's – didn't think she'd ever stepped in the door, in fact – but she was going to get there as fast as possible, before they sold out of live trees. She didn't really mind they were messy and uneconomical; as soon as she'd realized she could actually purchase a live tree nearby, her mind had been made up.

Twenty minutes later, Joy was the proud owner of a seven-foot Douglas fir...and a tangle of expensive rope she'd surrendered to an employee right away so he could strap the tree to the top of her Jeep. "That should get you home if you take it easy on the curves a bit," the young man said, slapping her window with his palm.

"Um...what about the interstate?" Joy said. "I'm – uh – I'm from Woodfield."

"Where?"

"Woodfield – east of Montpelier."

The employee stared at her for a moment. "You'd better take it slow," he said at last. "It will shift around if you drive too fast." He paused once more. "Any particular reason why you drove this far for a tree?"

"I'm going shopping downtown-" Joy began. Both she and the young man started laughing at the same time, and Joy's ears and cheeks were on fire. "Don't ask why I came here first," she said.

He smiled at her. "I have some extra rope in the storage closet," he said. "I'll get it and reinforce things a bit, free of charge. Stay here."

"I'm not exactly planning a wild escape at this point," Joy muttered as he sprinted back to the lawn and garden area.

Joy drove more slowly than any other vehicle on the highway and, later, the surface streets of Burlington. She noticed about three dozen drivers stare at her vehicle as they passed her, and a carload of teenagers even pointed and laughed and honked as they whizzed by. "Man, people, get a life!" said Joy. "This is Vermont. It's not like you haven't ever seen people transporting Christmas trees before!"

Joy parked in a free lot several blocks from downtown, calculating she could eat lunch and walk to all the shops so she could avoid another Christmas parade until she headed home. It was only when she'd locked her car and started across the lot that she looked back at her tree – and gasped. Her super-helpful Lowe's employee had added some rope to the tree, all right. He'd also added caution tape and a small red and white sign reading "I brake for Santa!" No wonder she'd been the spectacle of the town! Joy wasn't sure if she should be angry he'd pranked her when she was vulnerable, appreciative of his wit, or grateful that she would certainly stand out too much to crash into by mistake!

Fortunately, Joy's lunch at the cafe she selected was fast and delicious, and her shopping went quite well. Within two hours, she'd chosen a gardenia-scented candle for her mother, a strawberries and cream one for her father, who loved that dessert, a poinsettia for the Graham family, a book of French cuisine recipes for Paul, and a brightly colorful cashmere scarf for Joann. She'd also grabbed a few interesting-looking novels for herself. She plodded back to her jeep, arms laden with bags, dreading the long, slow drive back. It'd probably take her two hours, she reflected. It took three.

CHAPTER 28

When Paul arrived Friday afternoon to pick Joy up for the weekend, he had to unload half a cord of wood for her. She was already packed and ready when he knocked on her door, so she helped him carry the already-split logs and pile them in the corner of the back porch she'd designated for her wood. To Paul's embarrassment, he slipped on a small patch of ice and grazed his finger on a corner of the porch railing as he grabbed it to keep from falling. Joy convinced him to come inside and wash it, although he hated to take the time.

Paul praised Joy's Christmas decorations as he followed her up to her bathroom for a Band Aid, cradling his finger to avoid bleeding on the floor. The situation in the bathroom felt oddly private, somehow – with Paul washing his hands cautiously so he wouldn't splash Joy's toothbrush, and Joy digging in the medicine cabinet for the correct size of Band Aid. She found one at last, and after Paul dabbed the scrape dry with a tissue, he tried to bandage it.

Joy was washing her own hands, which were grubby after carrying the logs, when she noticed Paul still struggling with the Band Aid – it was his right hand he'd hurt, so he was only using his left hand and wasn't making much progress. "Here. I'll do it," she said. She took his big, warm hand in hers, deftly bandaged his finger, and hoped with all her heart he couldn't tell the touch of his hand had accelerated her heartbeat instantly.

"Thanks," Paul said, squeezing her hand and quickly releasing it. "It feels better already. You must have a magic touch."

"Nope. I'm clumsy, so I've put on a ton of Band Aids! You should have seen me when I was a kid trying to learn how to sew on a button! I stabbed myself so many times!" Joy realized she was chattering nervously and made a conscious effort to close her mouth. It wouldn't do at all for Paul to figure out how he affected her. It just wouldn't do at all.

The trip to Stowe went much more quickly than Joy remembered, probably because she didn't spend the entire way venting and crying this time. During most of the hour-long ride in the barely-heated pickup, conversation was light, but they did have one awkward discussion as they neared the Graham farmhouse.

Joy was so excited by the prospect of a weekend with Paul's big, crazy family that she let slip a remark about her past life she'd never mentioned to Paul. "I'm so thankful to be spending the weekend like this instead of at the Barrett Christmas party," she murmured.

"At the what?"

"Oh, I guess I should explain," Joy said, faltering. "That's the huge party my – uh – my ex-boyfriend's family hosted each Christmas. It was one of the most important social events of the holiday season in Pittsburgh. It's tonight."

Paul chuckled a little. "I'm not sure why," he said. "But it's hard for me to picture you with a boyfriend."

Joy bristled. "What?"

Paul ran his hand through his hair in frustration, feeling inept. "I don't mean you're not – um – able to have one...I mean, that no one would want to be with you...I just...don't think of you as being – as having a boyfriend because I've never known you with one..."

"It's okay." Joy laid her hand on his flannel-covered arm. "I think I understand what you're saying." She took a deep breath. "I dated Calvin Barrett for about three years. He – he broke up with me in September, when I was planning to come to Vermont." She sneaked a glance at Paul, whose face was expressionless, then returned to staring down at her hands. "He thought I was insane to quit a high-paying job to go pursue my writing in "the wilderness," as he called it, so he pretty much gave me an ultimatum between him and my wild adventure...so I came here."

"Do you miss him?"

Joy wrinkled her nose. "No...but I miss the attention sometimes. Does that make sense?"

"Of course. I'm glad he didn't completely break your heart, though."

Joy nodded, and wondered if she dared to ask him the question bouncing in her head. Before she made up her mind, Paul spoke up.

"I've never had a steady girlfriend," he said.

"Never?"

"Never. I've been on a few dates, but not that many. And I've never been a "couple" with anyone or anything like that."

"But – why? You – you're so nice – and you're not, like, freaky, or anything..." Joy stammered.

"I don't really approve of the concept of dating. I believe in courting."

"So...sitting on the porch beside your girl drinking lemonade and talking with her parents?"

"No, silly. I mean I don't believe in dating someone I wouldn't seriously consider marrying. It's an old-fashioned concept, but I think it's much safer and healthier for both the man and the woman."

"Wow...that's...interesting. I don't think I've ever heard that philosophy, at least outside of historical fiction anyway. And – there weren't any women in Stowe willing to court too? Or at your university?"

"Not too many. I think it may be a little intimidating, and a bigger commitment than most are willing to consider. Plus, I'm not looking for just anyone. I'm looking for a woman who loves God and tries her best to follow His Word."

Joy didn't say anything for almost a minute. "I don't think I've ever met anyone like you," she said at last. "But you're beginning to make sense to me. I like the way you think...it's just very, very strange." Paul laughed again, but Joy only smiled and lost herself in thought.

No girlfriend, ever. Did that mean Paul had never even – kissed – a woman? Was he really that – that pure? Joy couldn't think of a single one of her other friends or acquaintances who were half so cautious in their relationships. She shuddered suddenly at the memory of some of the lingering kisses she'd shared with Calvin, and at the times she'd come so close to sharing even more. Calvin had no qualms, but Joy had managed to hold on by her fingernails to that one conviction at least.

"Afraid to be with such a social outcast?" Paul teased her as he swung onto his parents' road.

"No! I'm just – just thinking about how differently my life

would have gone if I'd been raised with your morals," Joy said. "My parents basically just told me to stay on the right side of the law, date people in my social stratum, and avoid doing anything to embarrass them."

Paul grinned and turned into the driveway. Joy heaved a sigh of relief and put their highly uncomfortable conversation out of her mind. Here came Jennifer – at a dead run, as usual!

They exchanged hugs right away with Jennifer. "You look a lot better this time," she told Paul, after scrutinizing him for several seconds.

"Glad I meet your approval," he said, pulling on her braids.

Soon, the rest of the family except Jean had gathered around the pickup and were exchanging their typical hugs. Joy moved through, hugging them almost assembly-line style, until she realized she'd never met the last woman in line. "Oh, you must be Celeste!" she said, hugging her anyway.

"And you're Joy," Celeste said, smiling. "I'm so glad to meet you at last. My whole family has been talking about you for weeks!"

"You and Paul could be twins!" Joy exclaimed. Celeste was Paul's "pale and freckly" sister, unlike the others who were tanned, and although she was far slenderer than her brother, their faces and hair color were almost identical.

Celeste laughed. "I can assure you he's older...*much* older!" she said, cutting her eyes up at him impishly.

Joy was also introduced to Scott, Celeste's husband, who, despite his Southern accent, seemed to fit in perfectly with the Graham family. He was obviously older than Celeste's twenty years, friendly, and as blond as she was brunette. "It's great to meet you," he said. "I'll have an ally now when they all gang up on me!"

"Do you think I'd defend you against Jennifer?" returned Joy. "Last time I crossed her, I lost seven fingers!" Jennifer grinned and threw her arms around Joy a second time.

"I've missed you," she said.

Jean had struggled to the porch by the time they all squeezed up the narrow porch stairs. He hugged Joy too this time and pronounced her "a sight for sore eyes." Joy stared in awe at the simple living room, which had been transformed into a place of beauty with Christmas decorations. A huge tree, too uneven to be from a store, guarded one entire corner of the room, and garland, bows, and homemade décor covered nearly every surface. The fireplace mantle contained an arrangement of pine cones, candles, and lights.

"You're artists!" said Joy.

"We can't claim any credit," said Marie. "That's all Mom. We like to tell her she must have been an interior decorator at the North Pole in a former life."

"You have such a talent," Joy said, turning to Katie. Katie laughed and squeezed Joy's hand.

It wasn't long until they had all crowded around the kitchen table for supper, homemade pizza complete with every topping known to mankind. "This is a Christmas Eve tradition, and we're pretending it's Christmas Eve," Fiona explained, handing Joy a chipped blue plate.

"It looks amazing," Joy said, staring at the imposing slice she'd been served. It was piled with three types of meat, two cheeses, and a mound of veggies.

"Just pick off what you don't like!" Katie called out. "We all do." Sure enough, Joy noticed a mound of olives growing on Katie's plate, a pile of sausage on Fiona's, and a heap of all the veggies on Paul's.

"Paul!" Joy gasped.

"I know, I know," he said. "You can't believe I'm being so bad when I'm usually so good. But pizza, good Mom-made pizza, is one thing I refuse to clutter up with vegetables." Joy shook her head, remembering all the healthy meals Paul had created in her presence. She was secretly a bit relieved he didn't have perfect self-control all the time; it made him a little more approachable, somehow.

Another Graham Christmas Eve tradition was to sit around the brilliantly-lit tree and share blessings from the past year. As soon as they were finished eating, they hurried to the living room and turned out all the lights except the rainbow-colored bulbs on the tree. "What about the dishes, Mom?" asked Jennifer. "It's my turn to wash and Marie's to dry."

"Forget the dishes for now," said Katie. "They won't go anywhere in the next hour." She kissed her youngest on the head and then dropped gracefully to the hardwood floor under the tree. Joy settled in beside Katie, and Paul plopped down directly beside her.

"You'll enjoy this," he promised.

"First, I want to explain our tradition to Joy," said Jean. He was the only one sitting in a chair, so he seemed almost like a king looking down over the rest of them. "Scott shared last Christmas Eve with us, but this is Joy's first Christmas with us, so I will tell her about our process. We take turns sharing, in this order, something God has blessed us with since last Christmas, something that has been difficult for us, something another person has done for us, and something we hope to accomplish by next Christmas. These events may be obvious things, but usually they are more personal, smaller things we may not typically discuss so much." He coughed, deeply and with excessive congestion. "Do you understand, Joy?" She nodded, feeling suddenly shy. "You can go last," Jean continued, sensing her discomfort. "And if you aren't able to share your heart, you can say something minor. One year, Fiona's boyfriend, who is now her fiancé, shared that he hoped to kiss her more often by next Christmas. He received a slap for that statement."

Joy giggled. "You slapped him?" she said to Fiona.

"No, Dad did!" she said, and Joy laughed even harder, her nervousness forgotten.

The time of sharing was another new experience for Joy, who had never participated in such an equal sharing of hopes and dreams and pain. Some of their contributions made her smile, such as when Jennifer said she hoped to be somewhere more dangerous by next Christmas, and when Paul shared a few specifics of how Joy had helped him when he was sick that fall. Some of their words made her sad, though – Jean saying it had been difficult for him to give up driving, and Marie sharing that she hoped she would finally meet someone with whom she could fall in love. Joy herself shared the blessing of a renewed relationship with her aunt; the difficulty of adjusting to an entirely new life in Vermont; that Paul had assisted her with her house and winterizing when she was completely helpless and ignorant; and that by next Christmas, she hoped to be a published author.

A short silence followed her last words, and then Katie spoke up once more. "I know I've already taken my turn," she said. "But I need to add another blessing. Just one, I promise, although you know me...I could go on yakking about them all night. I want to share how Joy has been a blessing to me. Even though I only met her a few weeks ago, she has been keeping an eye on my oldest baby for me. No, Joy, don't shake your head at me. I know you've done a lot for him...and yes, Paul, I know you've been taking care of yourself for a long time now! I just feel better knowing Joy is around to notice if you're doing all right or not."

"I agree," said Jean. "Is everyone finished now? Okay. Let us pray." As Jean prayed in his richly-accented voice, Joy blinked back sudden tears. It felt strange to be so – appreciated – with no strings attached. If she were going to write an autobiography of her first twenty-four years, that's what she'd call it – *Strings Attached*, because her entire life prior to moving to Vermont seemed to be made up of "stringy" situations. But here – the people loved her for herself, not how she could benefit them.

Katie and Joy ended up doing the dishes together again, because all the girls had procrastinated on wrapping their gifts. Paul offered to wash instead of either Joy or his mother, but Katie protested and sent him into the living room to spend time with his dad instead. Joy couldn't believe her total feeling of deja vu as she scrubbed the stubborn mozzarella on one of the plates. Evidently, Katie felt it too. "Any more awkward questions you want to ask?" Katie said.

"Oh, dozens," Joy joked. She wiped a stray strand of steamy hair out of her eyes. "But actually, I was wondering how you do it – how you handle a full-time job, being a wife and mother and a Christian, and taking care of Paul's dad. I can't even imagine."

Katie smiled slightly, looking almost shy. "I take it a day at a time," she said. "And I rely on God, of course, most of all, but also on my children. They're all very mature, and they help out all the time. And although I can't lean on Jean for financial support or physical

252

protection anymore, he is still my rock on this earth. You can see for yourself how strong of a person he is."

"Yes. He's amazing to have such a good attitude when he's so sick. You're both amazing."

Katie only smiled again and continued to rinse the plates expertly.

"You must be glad you're healthy so you can take care of him," Joy said. Katie didn't answer. "You *are* healthy, aren't you?"

"I am reasonably healthy. I just didn't expect your question, and the timing is ironic. You see, I had a checkup this week, and the doctor told me he was starting me on blood pressure medication in a month unless it goes down. But yes, I'm fine. Just stressed, and not quite the spring chicken I think I am."

Joy stopped washing abruptly at her words. "Does Paul know about this?"

"No, but I'm going to tell him after our celebration. I'd rather not, but he needs to know or he'll be very upset at me."

"I wish there was something I could do to help," Joy said, biting her lip.

"There is. Keep an eye on my boy, just the way you have been. I'm not worried about him knowing that you're around."

"I don't do much," Joy said. "I can hardly cook, and he seems so self-sufficient that he's always helping me."

"You do more than you realize." A roar of laughter from the living room made both women smile.

"Paul seems close to his dad," Joy said.

"He is, although they've also had some major disagreements over the years. They both have quick tempers, as do I. We all have to work to control our tongues...well, except Fiona. She's the peacemaker, and the one who shushes us in public."

"I wish I had a good relationship with my parents," Joy said, surprising herself by sharing even this small bit of information.

"Paul told me your relationship with them was very strained."

"Yeah. I just can't believe they actually disowned me, you know? If I have children someday, I can't imagine ever being that angry at them."

253

Katie gasped. "I – I didn't know that, Joy. Paul didn't tell me any details. Oh, my. I'm so sorry you're having to deal with that!"

Joy stared at the sponge she was holding. "I haven't felt close to them since I was a child, but I miss the idea of it – of having a good relationship with them. Does that make sense?"

"Of course."

"And our holidays," Joy continued. "They – they were always very...lavish...and elaborate, but they were never warm and meaningful like yours...that is, after I realized presents didn't equal happiness."

"Well, presents don't make up a large part of our holidays," said Katie. "We've never had much financially, so we've had to focus on more important things."

"That's better, I think," Joy said. She rinsed the sponge and washed and dried her hands.

"At any rate, we'll adopt you," Katie said. "Consider yourself a part of the Graham family from now on. We can't replace your family, but you just run up here and visit us when you need loving, okay?"

Joy's smile lit up her entire face as she threw her arms around the little woman.

CHAPTER 29

To Joy's surprise, a tiny, brilliantly-wrapped gift lay on her stomach when she awakened the next morning. She blinked several times, wondering if the heavy, spicy pizza from the previous evening was giving her another wild dream, but the bright red box was still there. She sat up reluctantly and rubbed her eyes. Jennifer was nowhere to be seen, but Joy knew the present had to be from her.

She tore into the paper, opened the box, which was actually a breath mint container, and pulled out a pair of heavy duty earplugs. She laughed aloud despite her drowsiness. Just then, Jennifer dashed back into the room, her long, wet hair streaming behind her. "Ah, found 'em," she said.

"Yes. Thank you. I look forward to drowning you out by no later than eleven tonight."

Jennifer snickered. "Oops...forgot something," she muttered, exiting the room again at a dead run.

Joy grinned at her retreating form, then yawned. She had fallen asleep last night to the sound of Jennifer's voice. Jennifer had been telling her about the time she'd camped on Mount Snow, but somewhere around the second raid by raccoons, Joy had dozed off. She wondered if Jennifer had put her to sleep on purpose so her gift would seem funnier.

Jennifer was back almost immediately with her hairbrush. Joy stood, stretched, and pulled an envelope out of her Bible. "Hey, Jennifer," she said. "I've got something for you too, but no one else except Paul is getting an individual gift, so keep it on the DL, okay?"

Jennifer snorted. "The DL! Wow, you're old!" She opened the envelope and removed the two skydiving tickets Joy had purchased online on a whim at the last minute. "Aaagh! How did you know?" Jennifer shrieked, launching herself at Joy and knocking her back onto the bed with her hug. "This is the best present *ever*! I've been wanting to go *forever*!"

"I hope your parents don't kill me for giving them to you. Paul thought they'd be all right with it since you'll be diving with a professional...and it's safer than some of the other adventures you're planning."

"Oh, they'll be fine with it. Thank you sooo much!"

"You're welcome. Now who'll you ask to go with you?"

"How about you? You gave me this super present, and we'd have a ton of fun going."

"I appreciate the offer, but I like my feet to stay on the ground, thank you. The ski lift at Mount Mansfield just about did me in."

"Maybe I'll ask Paul...I would ask Mom...she'd go with me if I could...but her doctor would have kittens if she did. Yeah, I'll ask Paul..." She looked at the tickets again. "There's no date on them."

"No, they're open-ended...anytime until a year from yesterday."

"Thanks again, Joy!" Jennifer said, giving her another bone-cracking bear hug. "I've gotta go tell Mom!" She was halfway down the stairs before Joy regained feeling in her upper arms.

After a breakfast of multi-grain pancakes with genuine maple syrup, the family gathered around the tree to exchange gifts. Paul stood by the tree and handed them out one at a time, a job he had assumed after his father's amputation. To Joy's dismay, she received presents not only from Paul, but also from his parents, Scott and Celeste, and his other three sisters as a group.

"But I just bought you a *plant*!" Joy said. "I mean, except Paul and-"

"Just open them. They aren't much," Katie interrupted gently.

Joy exclaimed over the handmade purple socks, the package of notepads, the fountain pen, and the lotion Paul's family had given her and wondered how Katie could have possibly found time to knit socks for her. Paul's present was heavy, solid, and thick – a book, Joy could tell. She tore off the wrapping paper and saw an enormous, obviously secondhand cookbook entitled "The Way to a Man's Heart." She blushed instantly as everyone howled with laughter. "Maybe you'd better open yours from me," she managed to say.

Paul eagerly unwrapped his own thick cookbook of French cuisine. "No way!" he said. "You are a mind reader!" He crossed the room to hug her.

"Great minds think alike..." she muttered.

"I do not think their minds are great, only hungry," Jean announced. "And now, they will fight a duel to decide who will cook for whom."

"Her," said Paul, pointing to Joy at the same time as she pointed to him and said, "Him."

They all laughed again. "Paul, you're assuming a lot, aren't you?" Jennifer said. 'I mean, by the time your stomach is satisfied, she'd be too tired to try to find your heart!"

Paul began hollering at her French. Joy fanned her flaming face with a discarded piece of cardboard...and wondered if Paul had intentionally chosen a book with such a significant title.

After a traditional Christmas dinner, everyone except Jean and Katie went outside to the long hill of pasture land on the north side of the farmhouse. Although the temperature was a practically balmy 37 degrees, a good three inches of snow remained on the ground. It was soft today and perfect for sledding. There were seven sledders and only six sleds, but Fiona solved that problem by loaning her sled to Joy and using a recently-cracked plastic laundry basket. Joy had not sat on a sled since she was about twelve, but after the first terrifying trip down, she was hooked and slid and climbed and shrieked with the rest of them.

Before Joy could believe it, an hour had passed, and Scott remarked that he could only feel the upper ten inches of his body.

"Because you're cold or because you're getting decrepit from sledding?" said Jennifer.

Joy gasped, sure the thirty-year-old Scott would be offended, but he just laughed and groaned, "Both!"

"Let's go back in," Paul said. "We have one gift left for Dad and Mom, and we want to be sure we have time to enjoy it."

The present proved to be a second set of Scrabble that each Graham sibling had contributed to buy so eight people could play at one time. "I'll sit out," Joy said quickly. "I'll have fun watching."

"No, no, please don't. I'm going to go up and get a nice hot shower," Scott said. "I'm just not used to this Northern climate. I don't know how ya'll think this is a warm day!"

So Joy found herself playing her third game of Scrabble in under two months. They were divided into two groups, of course, with Marie, Jean, and Katie in her group. Joy couldn't forget the total beating she'd had from her aunt, so she tried to be as ruthless as possible to see if she could win this time. Sure enough, she beat the other members of her group, although Katie was the first to go out and only lost by one point.

The championship round was abbreviated, for darkness was approaching, and the girls had a few chores to accomplish around the farm. Paul had won in his group, so they went nose-to-nose in a lightning match, with the first person to reach 100 points declared the winner.

"This is it," Joy said firmly as she took her seat across from him.

"This is what?"

"My winning streak is going to continue on and on indefinitely," Joy said, feeling too competitive to mind the seven pairs of eyes staring at them.

"Oh, yeah? Think again, Miss Carnegie! You won't know what hit you...as soon as I finally draw a consonant!"

"Hmmm...Scrabble trash talk," said Scott, who'd finally warmed up and returned to watch the final match. "Not sure I've heard much of that before."

"You have to put yourself in Paul's shoes," Celeste whispered to her husband. "He used to be a proofreader, and in fifth grade, he won the Scripps-Howard Spelling Bee for the state of Vermont. He has a reputation to defend!"

"I heard that," said Paul, his eyes not leaving the Scrabble board.

"So did I," said Joy. "Did you go to that national competition, then? The one on the sports channel on TV that takes forever?"

"No," Paul said. "I chose that week to get hospitalized with strep throat and scarlet fever. It was probably the biggest disappointment of my childhood...but I know all those obscure words in the study booklet they gave us, so I can still beat you!"

Joy laid down all her tiles to spell "xylitol," thus earning almost all the required points in one turn because of the 50-point bonus for using all seven tiles. "I don't think so! Beat that, buddy!"

Everyone cheered except Paul. "No way!" he said. "That's just dumb luck!"

"Not that dumb...she knew how to spell it, unlike me," said Jennifer. "Face it, bro! You're getting whipped!"

"No, I'm not. She has ten points to go. And why are all of you rooting for *Joy*?"

"She's much sweeter," said Katie. Paul gaped at her too.

"My own mother has turned against me!"

Poor Paul had lost by his second turn, having drawn just one consonant, a 'v.' Joy finished her triumphant game with 'lower' on a triple word score, gaining her significantly more than ten points. Paul dropped his forehead to the table.

"Okay, okay," he said. "I concede in the face of your crazy luck."

"And..." Joy prompted.

"And...skill...I guess," Paul muttered, still melodramatically sprawled over the table.

It was as they were eating leftovers for supper that night that Jean began coughing uncontrollably. At first, they all assumed he'd just inhaled a bit of food instead of chewing it properly, but he continued coughing for so long it soon became obvious he was struggling for breath.

"Did you choke on food, Dad?" Paul asked quickly. "Do you need the Heimlech?"

Jean managed to shake his head.

"I think it's the congestion from his heart," said Katie, hurrying to get her cell phone. "I'm going to call 9-1-1. Marie, get my inhaler. It's probably on our bathroom counter. Fiona, get some honey and squeeze him out a spoonful. Jennifer, get his insulin from the fridge."

Joy stepped aside with an equally bewildered Scott as everyone completed their jobs. She watched helplessly as Fiona fed him the honey and then administered the appropriate amount of insulin to counteract it, but Jean didn't stop coughing at all.

"It's like he's literally strangling on the congestion!" Celeste said.

By the time the ambulance arrived, Jean's face was pale with a faintly bluish tinge from lack of oxygen, but his coughing was beginning to subside after two doses from Katie's inhaler. "We're going to transport him to the local medical center," the EMT said. "His oxygen level is way too low. That was quick thinking with the inhaler, Mrs. Graham."

"It's definitely the first time I've been thankful to have asthma," Katie said, trying to laugh, but it came out as a sob. She sniffed, wiped her eyes, and added, "Paul? Can you ride with him, please? I have a feeling they'll admit him for a while, and I'm going to gather up a few things and then drive over."

"Sure," Paul said. "And, Joy? You want to ride over with Mom and the others? I'd hate you to stay here alone."

"Of course." She would have hiked 100 miles for him if he'd asked at this moment. He was being so strong and calm – they all were so calm...but Joy knew he had to be terrified.

Scott and Celeste left with Marie, Fiona, and Jennifer in the back of their car, and Joy stayed with Katie as she threw a few items into a duffel bag...a bag already nearly packed. Katie noticed Joy staring. "My emergency room bag," she said. "It's had frequent use over the years."

"Do you need me to drive?" Joy asked as they hurried out the door. She took the bag as Katie locked the door and headed to the pickup.

"No, thank you," Katie said. "It will give me something to keep my mind occupied." Joy tossed the bag in the tiny backseat/storage area of the cab and climbed in, realizing in frustration that the truck was a stick shift anyway...she *had* to learn how to drive one!

They reached the hospital, a very small building, after a bumpy fifteen-minute drive Katie had made in almost complete silence. Katie parked and strode into the emergency room like a woman on a mission, and Joy was right on her heels, surprised such a

260

short woman could cover the ground so quickly without actually running.

The entire family was in the emergency room waiting area when they arrived – except Paul. "I'm going on back," Katie said breathlessly, and she disappeared through the examining area doors. Joy took a seat beside Jennifer.

"How're you holding out?" she murmured to the girl.

"I hate this," said Jennifer. "I hate not knowing, and I hate the fact that no one can explain exactly what's wrong or give Dad any relief."

Joy nodded. "It does seem strange."

They all sat there without saying much for about half an hour until Paul came out, looking exhausted.

"What is wrong this time?" Marie asked quickly, not realizing that she'd spoken in French.

Paul replied in English. "His lungs are filled with tons of fluid because of his heart failure. They aren't functioning properly and will have to be drained, and the doctors are concerned they may have to do it every week or two because they filled up so fast."

"What does that mean for him?" asked Celeste.

"It means his lungs are working way too hard, and any sort of respiratory infection could be disastrous. It's what we've been expecting – but hoping would still be far away in the future. They..." Paul's voice faltered a bit. "They are just going to put a shunt in to try to drain off the fluid. He'll be home by tomorrow if there aren't any complications."

Joy could read between the lines that Jean had made a major step in the wrong direction – that the basic goal now would be keeping him comfortable rather than curing him. She stood up and hugged Paul, who hugged her back eagerly.

"They'll let two of us back at a time if one of you wants to join Mom now," he added. "He's conscious and would be talking if they let him."

"Go on, Jennifer," said Marie. Jennifer looked around at the others for approval, but they also waved her on, so she pushed through the double doors into the examination rooms.

261

By one, Jean's breathing had stabilized enough to be moved to ICU to await his shunt, which the doctors planned to insert first thing in the morning. Katie accompanied him to his new room and then headed to the waiting room.

"I'm going to spend the night," she announced. "But I wish the rest of you would go on back to the house and get some sleep before worship in the morning." They all protested, but Katie was very firm. "Your dad would not want you missing church because of this," she said. "And I'll be fine. There's a big, soft reclining chair in his room." Finally, they relented, and after Scott led a quick prayer, they headed back to the farm, not saying goodbye to Jean because he was sleeping at last.

Throughout the crowded ride home, the interminable wait for a turn in the shower, and the hour Joy lay in bed, awake and listening to Jennifer crying into her pillow, one thought remained in Joy's mind – that this represented the "beginning of the end" with Paul's father. She prayed over and over – whenever she could – that she was wrong.

Despite the sadness and fear floating in the air the next morning, Joy couldn't help but feel a twinge of curiosity at the prospect of being able to visit Paul's home congregation. She wondered if it would be tiny and vibrant like the one in Montpelier – or tiny and *dead* like the one in Windsor. And she wondered if she would feel as comfortable there as she was with Paul's family.

Joy rode with Paul to worship service, and the others followed ten minutes behind; Paul was leading singing and wanted to arrive early. "Joy, what would you say about giving your aunt a call to see if she can take you home this afternoon?" Paul asked as they bumped across the frost heaves. "I'm thinking I should take off Monday and Tuesday after all. I'll be surprised if they release Dad today."

"Sure, I can do that," Joy said. "But – are you sure I don't need to stay here and help out somehow?"

"No, I think we'll be fine. Celeste and Scott can stay another week, so there'll still be a houseful of people helping out. But thank you...I really hate to bring you and then abandon you like this..."

"No, you need to be here!" Joy answered, so decisively Paul was startled. "In fact...I'll call her now so she won't make any plans at church or anything."

Five minutes later, Joy ended her call with a confirmation of a ride back as soon as Joann and Alex ate lunch. "Aunt Joann said she'd make sure it was announced at church too," Joy told Paul. He only nodded.

The church that met in Stowe's community center was even smaller than either the one in Montpelier or the one in Windsor, with fewer than twenty-five members present, including the Grahams, Scott and Celeste, and Joy.

"Not troubled with overcrowding, are they?" Joy said in an undertone as Paul flipped through the tattered songbook, selecting his songs to lead.

"Not anymore. We used to be much larger...we even had a building, but we lost it when I was a teenager, right after we lost our preacher."

"Who preaches, then?" Joy couldn't imagine how a congregation of that size could survive without a preacher. Actually, come to think of it, she'd never known a church not to have one of some sort.

"The men of the congregation – all five of them – take turns. My dad is the alternate because of his health problems. He takes fifth Sundays, when they exist, and fills in when someone else is sick or out of town. So I guess you could say we're basically an ME church."

"A what? A Maine church?"

"A mutual edification church. You know, when the men just share the jobs among themselves?"

"Paul, I didn't grow up in this, remember? I have no idea what you're talking about. I was sitting here wondering if Maine churches were different than Vermont ones somehow."

Paul grinned. "Right...I did forget." He started to tease her then, but was almost immediately interrupted by the majority of the other members, who had been greeting Celeste and finding out what was going on with Jean. A whole horde of ladies had suddenly swarmed around them, hugging on Paul and commenting on how strong and handsome he'd gotten in the months since they'd seen him.

Paul introduced Joy, and they also made a fuss over her. The

263

oldest-looking of the group, who had introduced herself as Jewel Collins, stared at Joy for a long moment. "How in the world did you snag yourself such a beautiful, sophisticated gal, Paul?" she said brusquely.

Joy gasped, both at the woman's assumptions and at her insulting words toward Paul. But Paul only laughed.

"Oh, I didn't, Jewel," he said calmly. "She's not mine. I'm only borrowing her. She's fallen in love with my family. I'm fairly sure she just came up here to see my mother."

"That makes more sense," Jewel said, nodding emphatically. "Well...whyever you're here, girlie, keep this character in line, you hear me? He's a mess!" Jewel reached up, gave Paul a resounding kiss on the cheek, and headed across the big room to her seat.

The other five women laughed as Joy stood, trying not to gape as she stared after Jewel. "Don't worry," a younger woman named Lisa said, patting Joy's shoulder. "That's just her way...you know, blunt...she and Paul give each other a hard time all the time. She loves him to death."

"Okay..." said Joy, still incredulous.

"It's true," said Paul. "I should have warned you...but she only does it because we're close. Don't let her scare you...she's all bark and no bite," he added after the other women had smilingly taken their seats.

"Well, for the record," Joy whispered, for the announcements were beginning. "I didn't *just* come up here to see your mother!"

Paul grinned and winked at her.

The singing was surprisingly tuneful, given the terrible acoustics of the room, but Joy was surrounded by the lovely voices of Paul's sisters, and Paul pitched each song perfectly, so she could follow quite well. The sermon was clearly organized and easy to understand, despite the fact the speaker had a slight speech impediment. Joy forced herself to focus and discovered she was learning from the stammering elderly man, who would have never been encouraged to preach in many gatherings. The service didn't drag; instead, Joy could hardly believe when it was over. She was amazed to realize she'd stayed completely alert, despite her concern for the Grahams and her five hours' sleep the night before. What had changed? Joy was pretty sure every church service hadn't suddenly become infused with oratorical and musical brilliance.

Joann arrived at the Graham farmhouse right on schedule. Joy was washing the plates and glasses from their lunch of leftovers when her aunt drove up. She paused subconsciously to listen as Joann greeted Jennifer, who opened the door – it was suddenly quite important to her that Joann wouldn't overwhelm the family with the same type of sticky sympathy they'd received from so many people already. "Jennifer?" Joann said after the door opened. A long silence ensued, during which Joy peeked quickly into the living room. Apparently, Joann, who had never met Jennifer, had held out her arms to hug her, and Jennifer had gone straight into them without a word exchanged. Joy smiled; she needn't have worried.

Joy finished up hurriedly in the kitchen and then dried her hands and headed to the living room, almost running headlong into her aunt.

"Oh, hi, kiddo," said Joann. She handed Joy a disposable foil pan. "These are some leftovers. Maybe you'll know where to put them." Joy opened the smallish refrigerator that could barely hold enough food for a family of five, much less their guests.

"I'll see what I can do," she said. "Oh, and hi, by the way. Thanks for taking up your day like this."

Joann made a dismissive noise. She slid her hand into her jeans pocket. "Oh, I almost forgot. I've a roll of quarters for the vending machines at the hospital. Should I give it to Paul?"

"Probably so. That's an awesome idea, Aunt Joann."

"Well, I'd much rather have brought them actual snacks, but at least they can buy water and juice and nuts with these, I hope."

Joy ran upstairs to grab her bag and purse, and when she came back down, Paul was just finishing a phone call. "That was Mom," he said to everyone within earshot. "The shunt seems to be functioning effectively, so they're releasing him first thing in the morning if there aren't any complications."

"That's great!" Joy said, heaving a sigh of relief. Celeste closed her eyes briefly and leaned against her husband, nearly overcome.

Paul noticed Joy's duffel bag for the first time. "Heading out now?" he asked.

"Yeah, unless you need me for anything," Joy said.

"No, you've been a big help – being here for us," said Paul, and Celeste echoed him. "I'll call you," he added quietly to Joy. "Have a safe trip back."

"Thank you for a good Christmas," she said. "I will – I will pray for you – for all of you."

Paul hugged her tightly, and after hugging the others as well, she and Joann left without further delay.

"Do you need me to read you your directions in reverse or anything?" asked Joy as Joann drove quickly down the long driveway.

"My directions? Oh, no, thanks. I don't have any. I looked them up online, and I remember how to get back."

To Joy, who was still convinced the network of roads between Stowe and Montpelier was a labyrinth, this seemed like a feat indeed. "Wow," she said, then immediately yawned.

"You must be feeling drained," said Joann.

"Yeah, you might say that," Joy said, sighing. "This weekend hasn't exactly turned out to be relaxing. I feel so badly for them all. It was so strange – one minute Paul's dad was okay...sick and weak as usual, of course, but – like, stable, you know – and the next minute he totally couldn't breathe...like his body was drowning him or something!"

"That must have been terrifying. Congestive heart failure can be very traumatic."

"I wish there was a way I could help...but they're very independent...anyway, until that happened, I was having a great time. It was the best Christmas celebration I've had yet."

"I'm glad you were able to make some happy memories first," said Joann. They rode in silence for several minutes. Joy noticed her aunt seemed unusually quiet – and – perhaps – worried? More than just about Jean Graham?

"Is everything else all right?" said Joy, fighting to curb the sensation of alarm that rose up within her so easily.

"I'm not sure how to answer that," Joann said. She pulled into a small parking lot and put the car into park. "I've been trying to decide how – and when – to tell you...that Amelia Carnegie is at my house – as I speak."

Joy gasped and tried to speak, but couldn't. The immense relief that nobody else was sick or dying was soon replaced by frustration and a frisson of fear. "What – why -" she sputtered.

"I have no idea, except she wants to speak with you quite urgently – so urgently, in fact, she left Pittsburgh without cash or credit cards and is going to have to spend her meals and the night with me."

Joy fell back against the seat with a thud. "Well, Merry Christmas to us," she said. "Why don't you just turn around and keep driving to...say...Nunavut...or somewhere where we can hide!"

"You have to talk to her, Joy. She chartered a plane to the local airport to see you."

Joy rolled her eyes. "Of course she has to be conspicuous about it," she snorted. "She couldn't just fly into Burlington first class like a normal rich person."

Joann's mouth twitched, but she didn't smile. "In her defense, she might have been afraid we'd refuse to come pick her up. She was terribly upset when she discovered she couldn't stay in a hotel."

"How's she treating you? 'Cause if she's rude to you, she's leaving before another word comes out of her mouth..." Joy could feel her blood pressure rising.

"Joy. Calm down. She's been civil...and even if she were being rude, I'm not going to be offended. She's not capable of hurting me."

"Can I apply for new parents? Isn't there an adoption agency for reasonably-sane adults?"

Joann just leaned over to hug her and then pulled back out onto the narrow road.

CHAPTER 30

By the time Joann pulled into her driveway, Joy was so nervous she'd chewed off her left thumbnail, a habit she'd given up a decade ago. "I don't know if I can do this," she said.

"You can...and I'll stay with you the entire time," Joann said. "You won't be alone." Joy nodded and walked slowly to the door.

Amelia was sitting on the couch with a magazine in front of her, but she rose immediately when Joy entered the room. She opened her mouth and then closed it again.

"Hi, Mom," Joy said. "This is quite a surprise."

Amelia frowned, and Joy remembered too late how much her mother had hated being called "Mom." Amelia's flawless face cleared almost right away, though. "I received your candles yesterday. Thank you for remembering us at Christmas," she said.

"You're welcome. I'm glad they got there on time." Joy rubbed her head, which had begun to ache with the definite indication of a tension headache. "Mother, why did you come to see me? I was under the impression I was dead to you now."

"To your father, maybe, but not to me!" Amelia burst out. "He – he doesn't know I'm here. He thinks I'm in Boston with Rosalie and Max Driscoll, at their son's wedding. I – I had to see you...to see how you're doing!"

"You didn't need to lie on my account. I'm fine."

"Yes, I did! George would divorce me like – like-" Amelia stopped short.

"Like Angelique?" questioned Joann softly, her only words since they'd returned from Stowe.

"Yes! If he knew I was associating with you, Sophia, after he disowned you, and that I was in this home..." Amelia had the grace to trail off apologetically.

"But you were furious at me when I left...and you despise the lifestyle I've chosen," said Joy. "Why did you come? If it's to convince me to change my ways, this conversation is over."

268

"I don't approve, no," said Amelia. "I can't imagine why you saw the need to – to *countrify* yourself like this...and to choose a life of poverty over the glamour of Pittsburgh and real estate. I also do not see how you could have let Cal Barrett slip through your fingers...or how you abide spending all your time and energy in *church*...but I *am* your mother, and I want you to be safe even when I'm convinced you've lost your mind."

"I'm quite safe, thanks mostly to Aunt Joann, who my father has tormented for years."

Amelia turned to Joann, who stood half a head taller than her. Joann met her gaze without accusation. "I don't know you, nor do I think we would socialize much in Pennsylvania, but my husband's behavior toward you was uncalled for and terribly rude...and frankly, I am glad you refused to give in to his demands. Also, thank you for putting up with my daughter's flight of fancy in coming up here."

"Your daughter has been a blessing to me," said Joann, staring steadily down at Amelia. Amelia averted her eyes and began chattering on another topic.

"I really don't think I should stay tonight," Amelia said. "It's obvious my presence is not welcomed here, and perhaps I can tell George I changed my mind about attending Brently's wedding..." She began to search the room visually, almost wild-eyed, as if seeking an escape route.

Joy could not bring herself to argue with her. She knew she should...after all, the woman was alone in a strange town without funds, but she simply could not open her mouth and articulate the sentences she should have spoken.

Joann waited only a few seconds for Joy to answer, realized she would not, and said, "No, Amelia. There's no need for further lies. Please, stay with me tonight. I have a guest bedroom you would find quite adequate."

"Yeah," Joy bleated, forcing the single syllable out with such difficulty her voice cracked.

"And Joy, would you like to stay here tonight as well?" Joann asked.

Joy managed to avoid making a face. "Yes, I think I'll do

that," she said. No matter that Amelia had been shockingly civil thus far...there was no way in the world she was going to allow her the power to sneak in her famous verbal digs at Joann.

After a few more minutes of stilted conversation, Amelia excused herself to the bedroom Joy typically used when she stayed with Joann. "If I am to be even the slightest bit hungry for this home-cooked meal you insist upon, I must rest for a while," Amelia said. "I was awake until four a.m. deciding how I could locate you, Sophia."

"Of course," said Joann. "Joy and I will be leaving soon for evening worship, but we'll be back in two hours or less. Please, make yourself comfortable."

Amelia nodded and glided toward the stairs. "And...uh...Mother..." Joy said. "I don't answer to the name Sophia anymore, remember?"

Amelia stared at her. "Sometimes, I really do not understand where my daughter has gone," she said.

"I've not *gone* anywhere. I've just found myself."

The congregation said a prayer specifically for Jean Graham that evening. Alex led it, and although he'd never met Paul's father, Joann and Joy had impressed upon him the frightening details of the situation, so he was able to pray quite eloquently. He also asked God to lift the Grahams' other physical burdens as much as possible, causing Joy's respect for Alex to climb another notch. She could have never managed to mention the Grahams' financial needs with such subtlety.

Amelia came downstairs moments after Joann and Joy walked in the door. "I trust you were sufficiently uplifted," she said. Joann opened her mouth to reply, then shut it again.

"Are you – are you hungry yet, Mother?" Joy said cautiously.

"I suppose I could tolerate a bite to eat now," Amelia replied. "Although, of course, I can't have much, I'm certain, without wrecking my diet. I hope you haven't completely abandoned yours, S – ah...daughter. Don't forget you have heavy genes on your father's side."

"I'm taking care of myself," Joy said through clenched teeth.

'The soup and salad will be ready in five minutes," Joann said.

270

"The soup is tomato with organic cheese and no added preservatives. The salad has grilled chicken, avocado slices, and slivered almonds. I don't have an exact calorie count for you, Amelia, but all the ingredients are fresh and unprocessed."

"Well," Amelia said. Joy hid a grin that her picky mother could not find a criticism of Joann's nutritious cooking.

The meal was understandably strained, but they got through it. Joann felt a definite sense of pride that Amelia ate a cup of soup and a moderate serving of salad without complaint. Joy noticed Amelia's appetite as well, having scarcely seen her mother consume a normal portion of food at one sitting, and surmised she must have been half-starved. Joy tried not to resent Amelia for her unwillingness to just say, "Hey, I'm starving," like most people.

Paul called Joy as she was spooning up the last of her soup. She jumped up and dashed from the dining room to take the call. "Hey, what's up?" she said. "How's your dad?"

"He's still stable, and the shunt is functioning well. He's set to go home after the doctor comes by in the morning, which should be around seven."

"Whew! How wonderful. I'm so glad everything has calmed down."

"Yeah."

"What's wrong? You sound – worried – about something else..."

"I had a talk with my mom this evening. She – she told me she's having health problems, too, from the stress, I guess."

"Ahhh," said Joy, sighing and perching on the arm of the living room couch. She was wondering if she should press him for details as though she didn't know them already.

"She also told me she'd already mentioned them to you."

"Yeah, I pulled it out of her without intending to, but she implied it wasn't anything too urgent or whatever."

"If it's serious enough for her to submit to the idea of medication next month, it's pretty serious," Paul said. "My mom doesn't *do* medication. She practically died having an asthma attack when she was younger before she would agree to keep an inhaler. I'm concerned about her having to keep up with everything in addition to dealing with the stress of my dad's poor health."

"I guess teaching high school isn't exactly the most relaxing job in the world either," said Joy.

"Hardly! And the state keeps piling on more and more regulations and paperwork all the time."

"I'm sorry, Paul. I wish there was something I could do."

"Just pray," he said, and they said their goodbyes. Paul's voice had grown very hoarse near the conclusion of their conversation. Paul had been crying.

Joy wandered back into the dining room where Amelia and Joann were now sharing tea. "I'm glad you joined us again," Amelia said. "I have something for you." She removed an envelope from her tailored jacket pocket and handed it to Joy.

Joy frowned as she took it and glanced inside – and gasped. One hundred dollar bills – dozens of them!

"What did you do, Mother? Rob a bank?" Joy exclaimed.

Amelia sniffed, offended. "Of course not. I just want you to have a few extra funds now your father has removed you from our financial protection."

"I thought you left home without funds!"

"I did – this money is for you alone."

"But this has to be-" Joy began, thumbing through the bills.

"It is six thousand dollars, all in hundreds, so it can be used even in small stores."

"Mother, no, I don't need it! I've been independent from you financially since right after college-"

"I insist," Amelia said. "You can't possibly exist much longer without an income, after all, no matter how much Joann is assisting you."

Joy began spluttering. The nerve! As if she'd thrown away a high-paying profession to come and sponge off Joann, who worked in a library! She opened her mouth to let fly her angry thoughts but Joann intervened so smoothly Amelia was none the wiser.

"Please don't be concerned for my financial situation, Amelia," said Joann. "Joy hasn't needed my support. She's quite self-sufficient."

Amelia stared at her daughter, who was taking deep breaths for self-control. "Fine – then go splurge on something – some nice jewelry, or a handbag or shoes. I can see you are determined not to need me or my money." Amelia rose, gracefully as always. "And now, I believe I'll go to bed. I would like to leave by eight tomorrow morning." She sailed out of the room and upstairs without another word.

Joy stood without moving in the middle of the dining room with the envelope in her hand. "I don't want this," she whispered. "Aunt Joann, I can't accept it."

Joann pursed her lips. "Could you accept it on behalf of someone else?"

"What do you mean?"

"Could you accept it if it meant you were able to bless someone else who was struggling financially?"

Katie Graham's face flashed across Joy's mind. "Why, yes," she said, a grin stretching her face. "Yes, I believe I could!"

Joann and Joy spent the rest of the evening quietly paging through photo albums together. Joann had even managed to unearth an album from John's teenage years. Joy studied photo after photo of her always-smiling uncle and the occasional shot of her father when he was home from college. It amazed Joy that although he had probably been considered much more attractive than John, the supercilious expression on George's face hid most of his good looks.

The next album spanned several years when John and Joann were obviously in their thirties. In one portion of the album, however, there were a dozen blank sleeves where photos had been at some time in the past. Joy looked questioningly at Joann.

"Those were photos of preparations we'd made...for...for my second pregnancy," Joann said, her voice barely audible. "I couldn't stand to see them afterward, so I hid them."

"Oh, yeah," Joy said. She stared at the photo just before the blank places, convinced she could see just a hint of a baby bump in her aunt's plumper profile. The photos just after the gap showed quite a contrast in both her aunt's and uncle's appearances; those short months had aged them significantly, and it was many pages before Joann looked quite well again.

Finally, at ten, Joy yawned, stretched, and turned to her aunt. "I can't believe I'm saying this," she said with a laugh. "But I'm ready to go to bed. We were up crazy late last night."

"Well...what'll it be? Bunking with me, or the couch? I'd just offer you my bed outright, but the last time I slept on the couch, I could hardly move the next morning."

"I'll just take the couch. It doesn't seem uncomfortable to me, and I'd never dream of kicking you out of yours, and um...no offense, but I'm really not fond of sharing!"

"Neither am I," said Joann. "I had to adjust the first time I got married, and I'm going to have to again." Joy smiled as she saw the faint flush staining Joann's cheeks. They both rose from the couch, and Joy carried the albums to the bookshelf and put them away.

"I'll run up and get you a good pillow and some quilts," said Joann. "And if you want a shower, you're welcome to use my bathroom."

"Really? That would be amazing. I – I...uh...somehow...wouldn't feel exactly comfortable running into my mother when I'm brushing my teeth. We didn't share bathrooms even when I was growing up."

"Sure...now, did you get everything from the jeep when we landed, or do you still need to unload your bags? I can't remember for some reason."

"I must have left everything in the car. I think I was rather preoccupied!"

Joann tossed her the keys and hit the stairs at a run to fetch the covers for the couch. Joy hurried out, shivering at the temperature of the air, and grabbed her overnight bag, backpack, and - wow, really? - her purse from the backseat.

Joann was already trotting down the stairs again by the time Joy came back inside. "Go ahead and shower if you'd like. I'll make up the couch for you."

"Oh, thanks! I appreciate it," said Joy. "It's just been a long day."

"Are you all right?"

"Yeah...well, I don't know," answered Joy. She ransacked her bag for her pajamas. "I don't really know what to think – or how I feel. Every time I think I have a grasp on how to handle my parents, they surprise me again. I would have never dreamed my mother would defy my father like this...but at the same time, I can't stand to be around her."

Joann nodded. "I'll pray for you tonight – that you'll know how to handle it."

"Would you – would you do that right now, if you don't mind? It might help me to hear the words, and I'm drawing a blank on what to pray myself at the moment."

"Of course."

Ten minutes later, as Joy stood under the hot spray of Joann's shower, the words of her aunt's prayer still remained in her mind.

"Please help Joy to discover the good in her mother's visit," Joann had prayed. "And please cause Amelia to be influenced by the increased peace and spirituality in Joy."

Joy selected a bottle of shampoo from the small array on the ledge and breathed in the light, floral scent. It was true that good could be found in any situation...she'd just have to search harder than most in this one. She forced herself to try to relax and prepare for a night of rest. And tomorrow – tomorrow was Christmas Eve!

Joy awoke the following morning to the scents of turkey bacon and pancakes – probably Joann's homemade whole-grain ones, in honor of the holiday. She stretched luxuriously and opened one eye – and saw Amelia sitting in the stuffed chair, staring at her.

"Mother!" she croaked, struggling to a sitting position – ouch, apparently, youth didn't protect her from the couch after all! "Why were you staring at me while I was sleeping?"

"I certainly haven't had much opportunity to look at you when you've been awake or asleep recently," Amelia said. "You're looking healthy – and, as much as I don't want to admit it, happy..."

"I – I am, thank you." Joy rubbed her eyes and threw the covers off her fuzzy pajama-clad legs.

"How long do you plan to stay up here?"

"I really don't know. Until I need or want to leave, I guess."

Amelia nodded. "Joann actually sent me in here five minutes ago to tell you that breakfast is ready," she said. "Perhaps we ought to go to the dining room."

"I'll be there as soon as I visit the restroom," Joy promised. "You go on. Aunt Joann's pancakes should be enjoyed hot and fresh."

"I never eat pancakes."

"You should." Joy stood, stretched again – man! - and hurried to Joann's bathroom.

Thirty minutes later, after Joy had consumed a mighty stack of pancakes and a serious heap of turkey bacon, and Amelia had begrudgingly accepted half a pancake, Amelia and her suitcase were standing by the front door, prepared to depart. Amelia had already called the taxi she had reserved the day before, although Joann had insisted she could drive her instead.

"I hope you have a smooth flight," Joy said finally, after they had all stood there in an awkward silence for a while.

"Thank you. I expect it will be unpleasantly bumpy, like the last trip, but I was willing to make the sacrifice."

Joy fought the urge to roll her eyes, and she was saved from the necessity of replying by the taxi's arrival.

"At last," Amelia huffed. "Such backward service, and in the capital city, at that!" She turned to her daughter, saw the disapproval Joy could not mask quickly enough, and sighed. "Soph – ah...Joy," she almost spit out the name. "If you need anything, call me. I know you're angry, and determined you can survive without me, but I am your mother, and I am available if you need me."

"Thank you," Joy said simply. "And...thank you...for coming to check on me."

Amelia pressed her arm lightly with one gloved hand, thanked Joann for her hospitality, and disappeared into the taxi without a backward glance. The driver loaded her suitcase into the trunk and sped away, driving far too fast for Joann's quiet street.

"Well." Joy could think, quite suddenly, of absolutely nothing else to say.

Joann stepped closer to her niece and put her arm around her shoulder. Joy collapsed against her, not crying, for a wonder, but so spent emotionally it no longer seemed possible to hold up her own weight. Joann remained, still and steady, until Joy regained control of herself and pulled away at last.

"And now," Joann said. "I think we're ready for a little holiday celebration, don't you?"

Joy smiled weakly. "Yeah. Do you have some Christmas CDs or something?"

CHAPTER 31

Joy ended up spending the next two nights at her aunt's house as well. Joann drove her home the next morning for just a few minutes so she could pick up more changes of clothes and another book to read, but Joy remained with Joann for the rest of that day and the next. She also managed to have a good time despite the lingering emotional confusion of Amelia's visit.

Alex arrived at Joann's house Christmas Eve afternoon. "Jo-Jo, I'm free!" he exclaimed, wrapping his arms around her as she stood at the counter and kissing so soundly and suddenly she dropped her wooden spoon. "I've cleaned out my office – the last box has been packed to ship down to Kevin." Alex's nephew was inheriting the majority of his equipment and furnishings for his own family practice. "I have several boxes of books and framed photographs I have to find a place to store, but that's it. And – I'm all yours!"

Joann, who had recovered her spoon as well as her composure, smiled widely at him. "I'm so glad, sweetheart," she said.

"So...what would you like me to do?" Alex asked, rubbing his hands together.

"Mercy, Alex, wouldn't you just like to rest?" Joann said.

"No! I've been forced to put life on the back burner for weeks now. Surely you can put me to work somehow. Is there – oh, maybe a light bulb you can't reach to change or something?"

Joann raised her eyebrows at him in an exaggerated fashion, walked three steps to his side, and just stood and looked at him steadily, not saying a word. Joy burst out laughing as Alex drew himself to his full height – a mere inch taller than his fianceé, and grinned sheepishly.

"Okay, okay," he conceded. "So I'm not exactly going to be of service in the height department. But – what about strength? Surely you have something enormously heavy I can move for you!"

Joann rapped her spoon on the rim of the bowl of homemade

frosting she'd been mixing. "I can't think of anything, unless of course you'd like to take the couch around the block for a run," she teased him. "But if you're that restless, you could help us decorate Christmas cookies. The frosting's ready now."

"All right! Can I use that – that color stuff to make them red and green?"

"Food coloring?" Joann asked.

"Yes, that's it."

"Yes, dear," she answered, sharing a look of amusement with Joy.

"Oh, good!"

Paul called Joy as they were decorating the cookies. She had been laughing hysterically at Alex, who had gotten reckless with his blue frosting and had accidentally flung some of it into Joann's braid, but she sobered quickly when she saw who was calling.

"He's home," Paul said. "We had a few delays this morning, but they finally released him about noon."

"Whew, what a relief for all of you, I'm sure."

"Yeah, it's been...an ordeal, I guess you'd say."

"When are you coming back?"

"Tomorrow evening, if he's doing okay. At least Mom and Jennifer have time off to stay with him. After school starts again, Fiona is going to quit her CNA job so she can stay with him while Mom works. She's getting married in June, but at least they'll have the summer to figure things out after that."

"Ahhh...so...that's going to be an income loss too, right?" Joy said, hoping he wouldn't be offended by her bluntness.

"Yeah. Please keep them in your prayers for that reason too," Paul said easily.

Alex and Joann had moved to the living room by the time Joy finished her call a few minutes later, so Joy headed in there to find out some information about an idea that had popped into her mind as she and Paul conversed.

"Alex," she said, running into the room. "How much do CNAs make?"

"Oh, not a lot...not much above minimum wage – maybe nine

an hour," said Alex.

"Wow. Well – I have a plan...can I run it by you so you can tell me if it's utterly insane?"

An hour later, a tentative plan for the money Amelia had forced upon Joy had been laid. Joy would make an anonymous grant to the rehabilitation center where Fiona worked to provide her with a six months' internship credit to care for her father – at double her previous wages. She'd receive a biweekly paycheck as usual, but she'd nurse Jean instead of reporting to work. Alex discovered that he knew Fiona's immediate supervisor, and he felt confident she would approve Joy's scheme. "I'll call her first thing on Wednesday morning," Alex promised.

"That's wonderful! Thank you so much for helping me out with this!" said Joy, giving Alex a big hug.

"I'm happy to help. You're doing a very good thing," he said, returning her hug in pleased surprise.

"It's not a sacrifice, seriously. You should meet Paul's family. They're so...*nice*, and brave, and well, awesome, and they're struggling so hard. I mean, they turn off the hot water at night to save money!"

Alex and Joann, who both remembered when their parents had done the same, exchanged smiles. Joy was still talking and gesturing wildly.

"And Katie, Paul's mom, was raising her kids like – organically, or something, you know, on a farm and eating homegrown vegetables and homeschooling and stuff, and then Jean lost his leg, and she had to stop and go back to work full-time and put the kids in public school. But they're all so – so *good*, even though they've gone through all that!"

"I guess Paul isn't half bad himself, eh?" Alex said.

Joy blushed wildly. "Is it – am I – am I that obvious?"

"I don't know, dear heart," said Joann. "We know you pretty well."

Joy sighed. "It's so weird. He's totally not my type at all! And he's so good at everything he makes me feel dumb...but I keep – thinking about him...and wanting to be with him. And I have so much respect for him, which is a nice change from my ex-boyfriend..."

"Your 'type,' as you say, may be changing quite a bit," Joann pointed out. "After all, you've changed yourself."

"Well, it has definitely occurred to me that there's something – you know – wrong about choosing a man for his appearance first...although it's difficult to stop thinking that way," Joy said. Joann nodded.

"I guess women are always on the lookout for us tall, dark, and handsome guys," said Alex, feigning a sigh and brushing his light, thinning hair with one hand.

"Oh, hush," Joann said. "Just be glad everyone our age is one type – shrinking, widening, and graying! It makes life much simpler." Joy snickered, but Alex shook his head and began playing with Joann's still nearly-black braid.

"No, you aren't that type, or any other, Jo-Jo," he said. "You're just beautiful, inside and out."

Christmas Day was uneventful – and wonderful. As a heavy snow pattered down outside, Alex, Joann, and Joy exchanged gifts under Joann's small tree. Alex was pleased with the ornament from Joy as well as the sweatshirt Joann had purchased for him from Jay Peak. Alex and Joann had gone together on one gift for Joy – her very own game of Scrabble. "What *is* it with you New Englanders and this game?" she shrieked. "Do you sit around in your *igloos* all winter and dream up how to win at Scrabble?"

"Yes," Joann said.

Joann loved her fancy scarf from Joy. "Such beautiful colors!" she said. "And it's so soft! I have to try this on properly. Give me a minute." She ran upstairs and was back in five. She'd changed out of her Long Trail sweatshirt and into a cranberry knit blouse and had draped the scarf artistically above the rounded collar. And – to Alex's delight, she'd un-braided her hair.

"Sorry for the delay," she said. "I had to brush that frosting out so it wouldn't ruin my lovely new scarf!"

Alex stared at his soon-to-be bride in mute admiration. "Man, Aunt Joann, you clean up well," Joy said.

Joann had a separate gift for Joy as well – a small album filled with photos. Joy gasped as she turned the pages...the first one was a baby picture of herself, and the majority of the others were of her on the farm at fourteen, including one excellent shot, presumably by Angelique, of her with her aunt and uncle. Then, the last five photos were from her weeks in Vermont this fall. The final one was from Children's Day and was of her with both Joann and Alex in the kitchen at the church building.

"How did you make this?" Joy exclaimed.

"Oh, old negatives, and a few conversations with our brethren."

"This is perfect! Thank you!" No other Christmas gift had ever meant so much...although a certain cookbook might have come close.

Paul called again on Wednesday as Joann was driving Joy home. He was talking so fast Joy couldn't even understand him at first. Finally, she could make out enough words to realize he was babbling about getting a teaching job.

"Paul – Paul...what – what did you say about a teaching job?" she said, having to interrupt him at last.

"That school in Cabot hired me, Joy! Without even an in-person interview! You know, the one I applied for in the middle of the night when I'd done all my school stuff? It's high school journalism and 7th grade English, which is awesome, because I can still use my background. I start May 1st, which is a strange start time, but the current teacher goes on maternity leave then, and then she's quitting, so I'll meet the kids and have them for six weeks, and then have totally new ones in the fall. It's not an ideal situation – but I don't care! I have a job, Joy! A good job!"

"Oh, Paul! That's amazing. I'm so proud of you and happy for you!"

"I'm going to tell my mom she can quit now, and they can move down here so we can pool resources. They may have to live in a rented cardboard box until I can build a house for them, but we'll manage! Oh, and I almost forgot, somehow the rehab center where Fiona works heard about Dad's situation, and has offered her an internship to take care of him for sixteen dollars an hour! I don't know *how* that worked out; it doesn't even make sense, but it will certainly be a blessing."

"That's – great," said Joy, as warmly as possible. Good grief! Things had come together so quickly she hadn't even figured out how to keep her cover yet.

"Anyway, I have to run, but I wanted you to be the first to know, Joy! I'll call you again after I'm done with my jobs for the day, all right?"

"Sure! I'm really excited," Joy said, feeling warm inside at his words.

"He got a job?" Joann said anxiously.

"Yes! He starts teaching in Cabot on May 1st, and then he'll return the next year. And he's going to move his family down here as soon as Katie finishes teaching this year! And – Alex already pulled strings to set things up for Fiona!"

"What a blessing," breathed Joann. "He has to be so relieved and thankful!"

"He is. He was so wound up I could hardly catch what he was saying at first. He must have quite a resume, to have been hired for the first job he applied for like that!"

"I would say so! So his family will hopefully be coming this summer...we'll have to keep our eye out for rental properties for them – something big, with a bedroom on the ground floor. That will be challenging."

"Yeah," Joy said. Her own huge rental house flashed to mind. It would be perfect for the Grahams. They'd have to look for a house like it. Surely they could find one within six months.

"There are so many reasonably-priced places for sale in this area," Joann continued. "If I had the finances and the business savvy, I'd buy and remodel some older homes and rent them out. Our area is very unfriendly for single-family home renters, but there are so many people these days who need to rent."

Joy didn't respond to her aunt's statement at first. She sat in complete silence until they reached her house three miles later. Then she turned to Joann. "I think you're a genius," she said.

Joann laughed at that. "Hardly!"

"No, I'm serious. I think you've just given me an idea – my first non-insane idea, of what I can do with my life."

"What – carving out rental properties?"

"Yes, and at rates good, low-income families can afford! And I could do some real estate on the side, so I could still make enough myself to get by!"

"And just think how you could show Christ to those people, dear heart," said Joann, turning her ignition key.

"Oh, Aunt Joann! That's it! You're right – this is going to be what I've been looking for! It's going to be my – my purpose – my service! I can't believe I never thought of it!" Joy stared out the window at the fluffy expanse of snow around her house. It seemed odd there weren't birds singing and a brass band playing, announcing Joy Carnegie had found the point of her life in Vermont!

Joann's voice penetrated her daydreams. "Are you sure you aren't burned out from real estate?" she asked. "I've the impression you were sick of your job in Pittsburgh..."

"But don't you see, Aunt Joann? The goal of my job in Pittsburgh was to earn money – as much of it as possible – and to hunt the wealthiest, most socially important clients. This – this – is going to be something else entirely! The goal of this job will be to *help* people!"

Joann smiled and focused on the view from her window.

"What are you thinking?" Joy demanded. "Are you thinking I'm an idealistic nut? 'Cause I know it's going to be tough, and very frustrating, and sometimes I'll have to evict people who are, like, fighting roosters in the kitchen or something!"

"No, Joy. I was thinking about how proud I am of my niece."

The next two weeks flew past unbelievably quickly to Joy. Her library class had ended, and she found herself with a huge amount of spare time on her hands, so she began accompanying Paul on many of his odd jobs, jotting down locations and phone numbers on real estate signs throughout the area. Paul approved heartily of her plans, especially after she shared her own rental search experiences with him.

"And then I saw the tenants had *eleven* guinea pigs," Joy said.

"And I started losing my brain through my nose!"

"That sounds pleasant," said Paul.

"It was terrible. And I was convinced I was so ignorant I was going to die up here. I was pathetic. It's hard to believe that was not even three months ago."

"Life can change pretty fast," Paul said, grinning from ear to ear.

"Thinking about your new job?"

"Of course!" They rode in silence for a while, and then Paul added, "Hey, I have to go up to Calais tomorrow. I'm delivering wood to Matilda's niece. There's nothing for sale up that way you'd be interested in, though. It's way out there in the country."

"Would that be woodchuck country?"

"You might say so," he laughed.

"Do you mind if I still come?" Joy said, a sense of shyness causing her to ask very quietly.

"No, I don't mind!" he said, pushing his hair, which was too long again, out of his eyes. "You're welcome to come with me whenever you want. It's just it wouldn't be a productive trip for you, real estate wise."

"I don't just come to look for houses for sale," Joy muttered.

Paul bit his lip. "I guess I knew that." He smiled again, showing all his dimples. "In that case, I'll pick you up at nine."

CHAPTER 32

Before Joy could believe it, it was the evening before Joann's wedding. Unlike most couples preparing to marry, Alex and Joann did not spend the evening racing around like maniacs to finish last-minute details, because everything was basically ready. The ladies of the congregation had decorated the living room of the church house with fresh sprigs of holly, sparkly tulle, and paper snowflakes dusted with silver glitter. The singers providing the music, all Alex's friends from Boston, had practiced a few times as the ceremony participants rehearsed their entrances and exits. The simple dinner at a diner downtown with Alex's family had been consumed. Angelique, her sons, and about ten members from Windsor were scheduled to arrive the next morning in plenty of time to help out before the three p.m. Ceremony.

That night, Alex had been banished from seeing the bride-to-be until the ceremony, and Joann and Joy were in their pajamas at Joann's house. They sat on the couch, munching on popcorn. Joann sighed deeply.

"Tired?" asked Joy.

"No, not really."

"Nervous?" Joy said.

"I'm not really nervous per se," said Joann, tucking her feet under her. "I just want to get the ceremony over with. I don't do ceremonies. And I don't care to have everyone staring at me. I'm very excited to be getting married, but I could have done that quietly, without a formal ceremony." Joann rubbed her eyes. "I sound quite pathetic and cranky, eh?"

"You sound like someone too humble to want to be the center of attention, even for a special occasion," Joy said. "And also like someone who understands the wedding is not the main part – it's the marriage."

"Mmmm...I just sound cranky," Joann said. "But I *do* dread putting on that huge, fluffy dress and parading around like an elderly cake topper!"

Joy covered her mouth to hide her smile. "What are you doing with your hair?" she said.

"Oh, I think Angelique is going to put it up for me somehow, maybe with a few flowers. Alex asked me if I minded not braiding it, but I don't intend to let it go completely wild like I'm twelve again."

"And – are you wearing makeup? Or having a manicure?" Joy asked, hesitating. It occurred to her she'd never seen Joann in makeup – or nail polish – or heels – or any other unnecessary frills except small earrings.

"No, dear heart. I don't own any cosmetics, and I'm not going to pay for a manicure. I did clean out the dirt from under my fingernails, though. Don't worry."

Joy shook her head and ended her cross-examination. Tomorrow's wedding was going to be the simplest one she'd ever attended...but, come to think of it, anything else would be totally out of character for her aunt.

"Well," said Joann, standing and brushing the salt from her hands into the empty popcorn bowl. "This bachelorette party seems a bit lame, don't you think?"

"Oh, is that what this is supposed to be? Well, I don't have any embarrassing gifts to give you, I'm afraid...and no, we're *not* going to play Scrabble! I have to smile at you all day tomorrow," Joy said.

"So, what can we do? Surely there's something legal, moral, and surprising – but not hostile – that we can do. I'm not sleepy at all."

Joy was completely taken aback; Joann was serious. "Ummm..." she said. "I – I have no idea. I'm not really aware of Montpelier's random Friday night attractions."

"Ice cream!" Joann said suddenly. "Let's go get McDonald's ice cream cones!"

"In our pajamas?"

"We'll be wearing our coats, and we can go through the drive thru. And after that, we can drive up to Hunter's Hill and eat them while we look at the city lights."

"In January? After holding our cones for thirty minutes

287

without eating them?"

"Oh, whatever! We can get McFlurries instead. Come on!"

"Aunt Joann, if I didn't know better, I'd say you were hyper!" Joy said, pulling on her boots over her fuzzy toe socks.

"I might be!"

"I assume you're thinking about the marriage now instead of the wedding?"

"Yep!"

Forty-five minutes later, Joann and Joy sat atop the hill in Joann's jeep, shivering and slurping down their McFlurries.

"So...working on your fourth month in Vermont..." said Joann. "How's it feel?"

"Cold! Of course!" She said. "But seriously? It feels wonderful. These have been the best months of my life. Yeah, the first few weeks were rough, and some difficult things have happened, but I just feel – settled – most of the time. I never miss Pittsburgh anymore. And I honestly feel I have found myself."

"I suppose Paul has an awful lot to do with that," Joann said.

Joy's face warmed immediately. "Yeah. And Aunt Joann...I'm beginning to think he cares too. He – he hasn't said so, partly because of his family responsibilities, but he's hinted a few times. And I'm willing to be patient."

"That makes me very happy to hear...and now, what about your spiritual health? When you came up here, you were pretty – ah – tormented, I think, but it certainly seems you're more peaceful now."

"I have a long way to go...but I'm making progress...and I'm learning I'm not going to progress without prayer – and reading my Bible – and church and fellowship. I need to stay involved in the church. I can't ever just – just fall away like I did before. I know that now. I'm glad I found out in time."

"You can't imagine how glad I am too," Joann whispered. "I was so afraid you were going to fall through the cracks, and you'd never find your way to the Lord, dear heart."

"I'm here – in the church – to stay," Joy said. "No matter what happens, I'm going to stick with it, Aunt Joann. And it's thanks to God, of course, but it's also thanks to you and Uncle John. You're

288

proof Christians can actually influence people by example."

Joann patted her arm but didn't respond.

Joy continued as though a dam inside her had broken loose. "I need to tell you, though, I was really hurt – and angry – during my teenage years. I'd left Vermont thinking you and Uncle John loved me, and then I heard absolutely nothing from you. It was only when Uncle John...um...passed away and my father forbade me to go to the funeral, and refused to go himself, that I ever doubted you'd forgotten me entirely."

"I'm not surprised, Joy. I'm sure it did seem like we'd forgotten you. But, well, kidnapping – even teenager-napping – is illegal, even in Vermont..."

Joy smiled slightly. "I know. But I – I also need to tell you I am really happy for you now. I wasn't – completely – back in October when you first told me Alex had proposed. I – I've been very selfish, I'm afraid, but I was upset because I didn't want to – to be alone again...and I was upset with you."

"I know, Joy."

"You *know*?"

"Yes, dear heart. But I appreciated you were supportive anyway, and I knew you did want me to be happy."

"Well...I feel dumb," Joy said. "But...I wanted you to know I don't feel that way anymore. I – I...oh, whatever. I had issues."

"Joy. You can stop with the true confessionals. I'm getting married, not dying. We'll have plenty of opportunities to talk in the future, if the Lord wills."

"Yeah." Joy sighed. "I – I just still feel like I'm having to make up for lost time."

"Okay. This is what we're going to do, all right? We're going to pretend those years don't exist, okay? We won't keep talking about how much we regret all that lost time, and we'll forgive the ones who caused it to happen. We'll enjoy our relationship *now*, in the here and now, and continue talking and laughing and having adventures and freaking Alex out, okay?"

Joy blinked. "Okay," she said. "I'll do that. It won't be easy, but I will."

"And I will too. Goodness knows it's time I forgave George again. I have to keep forgiving him periodically, you see, like clockwork...or a...an annual physical or something. And it's overdue...I need to do it again."

Joy laughed until her already-full eyes overflowed. "I love you, Aunt Joann," she said, realizing it was the first time she'd initiated that phrase to anyone since childhood. "So...I guess our agreement means I have to stop being mad you aren't my mom?"

A quick look of pain passed across Joann's face. "I guess it does," she said. "And it means I'll have to be thankful you are my special niece – and friend – and not be upset you aren't my daughter."

"Deal," Joy said, offering her hand to Joann to shake.

"And now, it's eleven-thirty, so we'd better get back and hit our beds or I'm going to have suitcase-sized bags under my eyes tomorrow. Imagine – a baggy-eyed bride! Would that mean I was bringing a lot of baggage to the marriage?"

"You're a nut," Joy said. "And by the way, since when have you used the term "freaking out" in conversation?"

"Since I started spending time – hanging out – with someone half my age. You've been a terrible influence!"

They descended back into the city in laughter once more.

CHAPTER 33

The next morning dawned sunny but quite cold. Joy woke up earlier than necessary and noticed the thermometer on her aunt's deck read -5 degrees. She shuddered as she began mixing the ingredients for oatmeal, the only hot breakfast she'd mastered – and her aunt's favorite. She rubbed her eyes tiredly. It had been almost one a.m. before they had finally settled down and headed to their beds, and it was just now seven. Joann had informed Joy she would be setting her alarm for seven-thirty, but Joy intended to have her aunt's oatmeal and tea on the table by then. Angelique and her sons were due at ten.

The oatmeal was ready when Joann padded downstairs in her long flannel nightgown. Joy was sitting at the table with a book, too excited to sit still without her mind absorbed, and did not hear her aunt approach.

"Oh, Joy, you're great!" Joann said, dropping a kiss on top of her head from behind. Joy jumped slightly.

"Oh, good morning!" she said. "I couldn't sleep any longer. I hope you don't mind something as ordinary as oatmeal and tea for breakfast."

"It's perfect. Thank you! May I get some right away?"

"Of course!" Joy said. "Maybe it'll be edible."

"Your meals generally are these days."

The two women ate in silence for a while, listening to the heater running. Joy sighed in contentment and inhaled the spicy scent of the kitchen. "Are you and Alex planning to stay in this house or buy a different one?" Joy asked suddenly.

"We'd like to sell it and buy something together," Joann said. "This place is comfortable, but we'd both prefer to be outside the city a bit...not far, but enough to have a little land and a view of something other than our neighbors."

"Yeah, I'm really enjoying being in the country," Joy said. "I do have to try not to think about how isolated I am compared to any other place I've ever lived, but the solitude is actually appealing now."

"Have you thought about where you'll live now you have some definite life plans?"

"Not much. I like my house...and I *really* like my landlord and my rent, but I don't need so much space. You and Alex don't want to live there instead, do you?"

"No, certainly not!" Joann said. "I can't imagine keeping up such a big, old house for just the two of us! I don't know how you clean it and have time for anything else!"

"I don't!" Joy said. "I close up most of the rooms and just clean the ones I do use."

"Aha! Your secret! But we seriously don't want anything large. We're not going to be housing a swarm of grandchildren or even a massive family reunion. And Alex would prefer something in good condition so we don't have to worry about it falling apart."

"Just make sure you get one with an extra bedroom or two. If and when I marry and have children, we'll descend on you like a plague of locusts."

"We'll squeeze you all in somehow," Joann promised.

Joy and Joann lingered at the table a few minutes longer than necessary, savoring the peace before the chaos of the wedding. It was only 8:15, however, when a loud knock, followed by three more, sounded at the door. "Who could that be?" Joy said. "We're not even leaving for the church building until eleven!"

"I wonder..." Joann murmured, grabbing a shawl from a peg by the back door and throwing it around herself. She hurried to the front door and opened it with Joy at her heels.

Angelique burst through it, talking a mile a minute, in French, naturally. She hugged Joann, then Joy, but she didn't stop talking. Joy just stood there. One would assume an explanation and/or translation was forthcoming. One could only hope...

At last, Joann turned to Joy and burst out laughing at the dazed expression on her face. "She couldn't sleep, so she got the boys up at five and came on up."

"Ahhh," Joy said understandingly, without understanding. She spoke not a word of French, but she somehow doubted it took 200 words to say that, even in French!

"So," Angelique finally switched to English. "Are you decent? Can the boys come inside?"

Joann grinned. "Well, I'm decent, but I'd rather be dressed. I'll go upstairs and change. They can come in as soon as I'm gone."

"Yes, go put on yogurt pants or something," said Angelique, removing her coat and scarf.

Joann shared a look of amusement with Joy and ran lightly up the stairs to put on jeans and a sweatshirt.

Pierre, Jr., Hugo, and Jean Marie traipsed in, silent and awkward as usual. Joy greeted them, and they answered monosyllabically and stood in the tidy living room, as out of place as cats in a pond.

"Would you all like to watch a movie or something?" Joy said. "I know you don't want to watch your mom styling Aunt Joann's hair."

"Yes, please," Jean Marie answered, his voice cracking on the second word.

"Sit down, then, and pick one out," Joy said. "The DVDs and VHS tapes are in that drawer of the TV table. I think there are some comedies and action movies in there."

"I will go to the car to get my hair supplies," Angelique said, exiting quickly.

Joann was downstairs again when Angelique returned. "Come on, friend. Let me give you the tour," she said. "You can't possibly intend to spend almost three hours on my hair."

"Of course! Give me the tour," Angelique said. "It is ridiculous that I see your house for the first time today!"

"I agree!"

They went upstairs first, so Joy dashed to the kitchen and washed their two bowls, spoons, and mugs hastily. She was brushing the crumbs from the counter into her hand when they reappeared in the kitchen. "Are you cleaning? For my visit?" demanded Angelique.

"Just a little."

"You can stop. I have seen the house of Joann Carnegie-almost-Martin much more messy than this!"

Joann slapped Angelique's shoulder. "Hush! You'll ruin my

reputation," she said.

"Ah, but it's true. Your aunt and I learned to clean our houses together."

"I'd been living in motels for several years before I married your uncle," Joann explained. "Anything beyond vacuuming and making beds was new to me."

"Did you grow up living in motels?" Joy asked.

"After about – oh, age ten, I suppose. My father lost his job then, and the bank took our home. He'd almost saved enough for another house when my mother died, but after that, he didn't care anymore."

"And my mother couldn't clean," Angelique said. "She was usually – ah...how shall I say? - smashed. So we, your aunt and I, learned house cleaning together."

"Wow." Joy could say no more. These women never ceased to amaze her.

The boys had settled on – laughably – *Anne of Green Gables*, Joy noticed as Joann and Angelique lapsed into French again. She tapped Joann's shoulder to get her attention and pointed to her ear to indicate they should listen to the boys' selection of films.

"It is because of Hugo," Angelique said, giggling. "He believes red-haired women are the most beautiful."

"Alex's youngest niece has red hair," Joann said, eyes twinkling. "She's here for the wedding."

"How old is she?" Joy asked.

"Sixteen, I think."

"Oh, dear!" Angelique cried. "Now I will have a lovesick son to control!"

The women eventually sat down at the same table Joann and Joy had just vacated. "So," Joann said. "Tell me about how things are going, Angelique. I haven't heard a word out of you since we last visited, except about the wedding."

"This is your special time, and we should focus on you," Angelique began, but Joann laid her hand firmly over her friend's smaller one and interrupted.

"I'm getting married, not being canonized for sainthood! All

294

this attention is making me crazy, anyway!"

"I'm having a struggle," Angelique admitted. She paused, considering her words more carefully than Joy had ever seen before. "I have required the boys to attend church with me, but..." She dropped her voice to a whisper. "Pierre, Jr. and Hugo fight me about this each week."

"Have they explained why?" asked Joann.

"Yes. It is because they realize that their father never obeyed. He was not baptized, not by immersion. And they are hearing now that baptism is necessary for salvation. They are angry and confused, and I cannot explain to them the 'why.'"

Joann and Joy both sighed, unintentionally in unison. Joy wondered what her aunt would say...and wondered what the answer was to the boys' theological questions, anyway. She'd been confused about that situation as well – and now Joann was speaking.

"I'm sorry all of you are experiencing these struggles. Have the boys talked to anyone else about it – another Christian?"

"No. They hardly speak three words on Sundays. You know they have such shyness."

"Maybe they would talk to Alex," Joann said.

"He has felt this? The pain of family who died without salvation?"

"Not with close family, but he is very wise..."

"I don't think they will share if he hasn't felt the same...but maybe they would share with you?"

"With *me*?"

"Yes!" said Angelique, and Joy had to smile at Joann's expression.

"I'm no counselor or theological scholar, Angelique," said Joann. "Nor do I claim to understand why some good, religious people decide to be baptized when others don't."

"Yes, but you lost your mother, and she was very faithful to her religion. And you will be kind but not...how do you say? Descend to them?"

"Condescend to them?" said Joy.

"That is right. Please, Joann. I know you have so much things to do, but I love my sons, and I want that they are baptized also."

"If you're sure you don't want to find someone else, I'd be happy to speak with them. I'll call you as soon as we've returned."

"Thank you. You are a wonderful friend."

"I..." Joann stopped, and just shook her head.

"Well. Enough difficult talking. Let's start creating your wedding hair!" Angelique said, jumping up from her chair.

"What are you creating it from?" Joy laughed.

"Yes, I didn't agree to a wig," said Joann.

Angelique made a dismissive noise and deftly began removing Joann's hair from its thick braid. "There is enough hair here to do anything you will want!"

By ten minutes until eleven, Joann was completely ready except for changing into her wedding dress, which she would do at the church building to avoid crushing the fragile fabric. Her long hair was piled loosely on top of her head except for a few wavy tendrils Angelique had arranged to dangle down and frame her face. Joy took several pictures of Joann and Angelique and realized they could both nearly pass for college girls in their flushed-faced excitement. True to her word, Joann had not used a single cosmetic product, nor had she put on expensive jewelry. She wore single pearls in her ears that matched her engagement ring. "Aunt Joann," said Joy. "You look so pretty...and just like yourself."

"That will change once I put on my cake topper dress," Joann said.

"No, it won't. The dress is simple for a wedding dress...really. I doesn't look strange on you at all."

"As long as Alex is happy..." Joann said.

Once the women and Angelique's sons arrived at the church house, everything seemed to speed up, so the minutes moved as fast as seconds. Joy found herself doing the strangest things – finding Alex's brother's reading glasses he'd misplaced the night before, re-stocking the bathroom with toilet paper and paper towels, zipping the back of Angelique's dress and buttoning up Joann's, and – most awkward or unusual of all – tying Paul's tie. "Explain to me again how you've gone twenty-six years without learning how to tie a tie," she teased him, hoping she wasn't blushing.

"I hate the things, that's how," said Paul. "I've probably spent less time in a necktie than you have in – in..."

"Hiking boots!" Joy said before he could make any guesses.

"Something like that."

"Well, I'm sorry you're experiencing neck torture, but I know Alex and my aunt are awfully glad you can be their usher."

Paul smiled, but Joy could see that it was a strain.

At that moment, Joann hurried through with the garment bag holding her wedding dress draped across her arm. She caught sight of Paul and Joy and stopped short. "What have you been saying to the poor man, Joy? He looks like he's got a wisdom tooth coming in!"

Joy grinned at Paul's further discomfort. "He wouldn't tell you this," she said. "But his tie is making him miserable."

"Really? Well, take it off, Paul."

"But – all the other men in the ceremony are wearing them. Won't it ruin the – you know, symmetry or something?" Paul said.

Joann rolled her eyes. "Take it off. I mean it. There's no reason for anyone to be uncomfortable today."

"If you're sure..." he said. Joy laughed at the hesitance in his voice since he was already untying it at top speed.

"Of course."

"Thank you!" Paul dashed off to put the offending tie as far away as possible.

Many onlookers would have described Alex and Joann's wedding as quite ordinary, except for its simplicity and the ages of the bride and groom, but Joy was captivated by the entire brief ceremony – from the traditional vows to the love songs from several different decades to the look of complete devotion and utter joy on Alex's face when he caught his first glimpse of Joann. Somehow, that look erased the final hint of pain Joy had been feeling about her aunt being with a man other than her uncle John.

The whole ceremony lasted less than half an hour, and soon, the reception was underway. Alex and Joann had chosen light fare – sandwiches, deviled eggs, and vegetable and fruit trays. Joy, who had skipped lunch, ate ravenously, succeeding to do so, to her total amazement, without smearing anything on her ice-blue bridesmaid's dress. Suddenly, she discovered she was on her twelfth chocolate-covered almond...and that she hadn't been conscious of eating any of them...she'd been daydreaming instead...about Paul! Joy glanced around her, feeling exposed, and then hurried to pitch the rest of the contents of her plate of food into the garbage can.

Alex and Joann made it through the rituals of giving cake and punch to each other without incident, but when the time came for Joann to toss her bouquet, the guests got a good laugh. The trouble began because of the bride's killer throwing arm. When Joann turned around and hurled the bouquet, she threw it so hard it slammed into the standard eight-foot ceiling and then rocketed into the nearby garbage can. "Noooo!" wailed Alex's youngest niece – Patty of the red hair – and she made a dive for it.

Unfortunately for Patty on several levels, she'd decided to wear a pair of borrowed spike heels to the wedding, which caused her to have far less than stellar balance...and she soon followed the bouquet headfirst into the industrial-sized garbage can.

Everyone reacted immediately, especially Joann, who was dying with embarrassment, but Hugo kept his cool and reached the struggling girl first. As if he rescued desperate damsels from trash cans every day, he calmly pulled her out of the container and offered her his napkin to wipe the icing off her face. All eyes were on poor Patty as she wiped her face and slung punch off her arms into the can. She stood stock-still for several seconds with her eyes squeezed shut, and then she reached into the can and retrieved the disgusting bouquet. "I got it!" she shouted, raising it into the air...and then...she smiled up at Hugo. They all cheered, and Hugo and Patty stood together for dozens of photos.

After a much less exciting garter toss, in which Hugo was sadly unsuccessful, Alex slipped from the room. Joann came up to Joy and whispered that she needed to be freed from the dozens of buttons again.

"Well, you did it," said Joy, working loose the delicate buttons. "How do you feel?"

"Happy," said Joann, sighing with relief. "Very, very happy."

Within seconds, Joann had slid into new charcoal wool pants and a soft turquoise sweater that highlighted her blue eyes. "Ahhh...much better!" she said.

"Yeah, you look more comfortable now," Joy said. "But you were also so beautiful for the ceremony."

"So it wasn't completely ridiculous? I did feel like we were making such a fuss."

"Are you kidding? Your *husband* was so excited when he saw you, he almost passed out!"

Joann smiled. "I guess that sounds promising." She paused. "Well, kiddo. I'd better tell you goodbye now. There will be so many people to say it to in a minute when we make our getaway."

"Yeah." Joy stood awkwardly in the middle of the floor, at a sudden loss to know what to say or do.

Joann had no such qualms and hugged Joy as hard as she had the first day they'd reunited. "Thank you for everything," Joann said.

"No, thank *you*," said Joy.

Five minutes later, Alex and Joann were gone, after a frantic run through their birdseed-tossing guests. They climbed into Joann's jeep – which the DuPont boys had decorated to an obnoxious degree – and headed to Quebec.

CHAPTER 34

It was long after dark by the time the church building had been cleaned and re-assembled for services the next morning. Joy, the DuPonts, Paul, and Wilson were the only ones left at that point, Alex's family having left promptly after the reception so they could reach Boston before late evening. The Windsor contingent had also departed soon after Alex and Joann left. Joy was re-arranging the leftover fruit and vegetables in the refrigerator so Paul would still have room for his own food when Angelique sauntered into the kitchen, yawning.

"Okay, Joy," she said. "We need to go home. I now remember I only closed the eyes for four hours last night."

"You look exhausted," Joy said. She hugged her tightly. "Thank you for all your help."

"I am so happy to help with this day," Angelique replied. "And you will see me more frequently. Joann is my dearest friend, and it is time for me to show that again."

"Good. Have a safe trip – don't get too sleepy."

"Oh, the older boys can drive if I grow sleepy. We will go home, give food to the animals, and go to bed!"

Wilson and Paul were visiting in the living room as Joy saw Angelique and the boys out the door.

"I hear you're hunting a rental for your family," Wilson said to Paul.

"Yes, they hope to move in June, as soon as Jennifer graduates."

"Will they be buying after their home sells?"

Joy knew she shouldn't eavesdrop, but she froze in place at Paul's response and listened shamelessly.

"No. They're – they're actually losing their house and farm," Paul said. "They'll need to rent until I'm established enough in my job to build something for them."

"I'll keep my ears open," Wilson promised. "See you

tomorrow, son." He raised his voice. "'Bye, Joy!"

Joy jumped. "'Bye!" she called out, then returned to her thoughts. Why couldn't Paul's family share *her* house? She didn't need a fourth of its spacious rooms, and with the low rent and moderate utilities chopped in half...

Paul stepped into the entry way and interrupted her plans. "Still here?" he said, putting a heavy arm across her shoulders.

"Just leaving," Joy said, beginning to hunt for her wallet and keys. She'd have to clear her idea with Alex next week before she shared it with Paul...

"Don't rush," Paul said. "I feel like I've hardly seen you the last few days. I kinda got used to having you around the last few weeks."

"Yeah. I can't believe the wedding is over. I'm really excited for them."

"Can we take a walk?" Paul asked. "I know it's cold, but I have an extra coat you can borrow if you need it."

"Sure – and I'll welcome the coat!"

They headed down the side road that ran perpendicular to the church house. Joy was toasty warm in her own winter clothes plus the coat Paul had loaned her. "This is nice," she said.

"Yeah. Really nice. I suppose we should go get some leftovers after a while, but I'm much too full at the moment to even think about eating another bite. I hope you aren't hungry."

"Not at all! I haven't eaten that much since...well, since the last major holiday!'

Paul laughed. "I've been wanting to talk to you, actually. Um...I was remembering something you said a while ago about not caring about going to expensive places. I was wondering if you were serious about that."

Joy raised her eyebrows. "Uh...yeah...of course. Why?"

"Because...oh, man. I'm going about this totally backward," Paul stammered. "What I really mean to say is I wondered if you'd be interested in...um...courting."

"*Courting*? You mean, courting *you*?" Joy said, stopping in the middle of the road.

301

"Yeah." Paul raked his hand through his hair. "You are very special to me, Joy, and I want to – to spend time with you whenever possible. You're my best friend, but...but beyond that, I would like to...I mean, do you think we could consider a – a future together?"

Joy had to force herself to keep breathing. "So – so this courting thing...it means you want to *marry* me or something?"

Paul laughed at her, but so kindly Joy took no offense. "It means I'd certainly be thinking about it...and seriously." He took Joy's hand between his, more gently than Joy would have believed possible with his strong fingers. "But I don't have much to offer except, well, except my love, and that I will be here for you just like you've been here for me. I can't take you on fancy dates...or any dates at all a lot of the time, for that matter."

"I don't care," said Joy. "Do you think we could actually make things work?"

"I believe we can, God willing." Paul squeezed her hand now, so Joy was reminded of why his gentleness had surprised her. "So...will you be my girlfriend, Joy? Can you find it in your heart to be with me?"

"I don't have to look very far," she said, turning to face him. "Of course I will."

Paul's grin stretched across his face, and without a spoken word, they turned around by mutual consent, and headed back hand in hand. Paul's cell phone rang when they had reached the parking lot.

"Sorry," he said, showing at least three of his dimples. He prepared to ignore the call, but Joy took hold of his arm.

"It's okay. It could be about your dad, and we have all the time in the world," she said.

Paul accepted the call but put it on speakerphone. It was his mother.

"Hi, sweetheart," she said. "What have you been doing today?"

Paul winked at his girlfriend. "Oh, I've been finding Joy!"

THE END

302

WHAT PEOPLE ARE SAYING ABOUT
FINDING JOY

"Thoroughly enjoyed."
– Brittany R.

"I absolutely LOVED your book!!!!! It was a wholesome, feel good, uplifting, and very well written book that did not lose me one time!"
– Donna P.

"Comforting...I have no qualms or hesitations. I can completely recommend *Finding Joy* to you."
 – Lisa S. (Rilla Z blog)

"I enjoyed this book from start to finish...I know a book is good when I finish the novel and immediately begin to miss the characters...seeing Joy grow throughout the story while seeking to put God first in her life is an experience that resonates with all Christians and with those trying to find Christ. Definitely a must-read!"
– Holly C.

"Well-written and one of those 'can't put it down' reads...refreshing..."
– Jackolyn W.

ABOUT THE AUTHOR

Sarah Floyd lives in the middle of nowhere in Vermont with her husband, sons ages almost 3 and 7 months, and Australian Shepherd dog. It took her more than fifteen years of dreaming to get to Vermont, but she finally made it. Sarah enjoys books, foreign languages, European travel, waterfalls, covered bridges, and colorful fabric. She is also the author of *Enough Joy* (2017), the second book in the Voice of Joy series. Sarah loves to hear from her readers; you can contact her at voiceofjoy123@yahoo.com.

Made in the USA
Middletown, DE
21 September 2022